CROW RIVER JUSTICE

C. STEWART

*Dedicated to Barb Dromgole for her
ready smile, big laugh, and
her love of cats.*

"The author constructs a remarkably complex animal world with its own moral code and laws, which William must navigate. It's not entirely unlike the human one, except for the fact that the "animal world is always at war," and so allowances must be made for the naturalness of predation. Such a fantastical tale can easily go off the rails into the absurdly contrived or the cloyingly saccharine—the protagonist is a kitten, after all—but Stewart manages to avoid both of these pitfalls. The result is a very funny and inventive novel that manages to achieve something rare: a glimmer of authentic originality. A deeply intelligent and humorous examination of an anthropomorphized animal kingdom." —*Kirkus Reviews*

"Crow River Justice" by Colleen Stewart offers a multidimensional exploration of both human lives and the animal world. The author blends the two in ways that feel natural and enlightening. This book shares insights on animals, diving deeply into their daily lives and covering everything from their feeding habits and social bonds to the complexities of predation while telling a captivating story. The concepts of survival, the idea of "justified predation," and even the gray areas around what we might call cruelty were very well explored. A standout aspect for me is how the author brings human life into focus from a fresh angle and reminds us of the surprising ways our worlds overlap with the animals'. This invites us to rethink our influence within the natural world and what it means to truly coexist. The story is fascinating and well-paced. There was nothing about the book that I didn't like." —*Online Book Club*

ONE FOR SORROW
(Lancashire nursery rhyme)

One for sorrow,
Two for joy,
Three for a girl,
Four for a boy,
Five for silver,
Six for gold,
Seven for a secret never to be told,
Eight for a wish,
Nine for a kiss,
Ten, a surprise you should be careful not to miss,
Eleven for health,
Twelve for wealth,
Thirteen, beware it's the devil himself.

PROLOGUE

On a bright early morning in mid-May, the field still held on to a fine mist when the three fox pups scrambled out of the den entrance. The two sisters wrestled as the male pup stood off to the side. He had never been out of the den. He saw a rusted white trailer in the middle of an empty field close to the den entrance. It was all new and exciting.

The fox mother and her mate had made it clear to the pups that they were to stay away from that place. It was dangerous housing a large clowder of nine feral cats all winter. They had entered through a rusted hole in the wheel well. None had emerged in the spring.

The pup's eyesight, hearing, and sense of smell were sharp. He could pick up a mouse squeak at 700 yards, but no sound emanated from the trailer. Only a horrid smell - an intense, choking chemical odour mixed with corruption. It was his first experience with the scent of lingering death, but also something else unnatural that made him gag. He would mind his mother.

A roar of a truck motor sent the three pups scurrying back into their den. A black-and-white car pulled in behind the truck. Doors slammed, and loud, deep voices sounded across the field. The pup peeped from the den entrance. Two humans and more unfamiliar scents. One was pungent and sickly sweet, coming from a liquid the truck man poured around the perimeter of the trailer. Moments later, fire flared from it, and the pup choked at the black smoke.

The fox parents returned abruptly. They hurried the male pup and his two sisters through the burrow and out of the den's second exit to emerge from the ditch farther away from the burning. The family skipped across the road and into the forest. They would move to a new den.

The pup would never forget the smell of feral death, the choking, unnatural chemical odour, or the scents of the two humans responsible for the bitter blaze that devoured it all.

Chapter 1

I had expected the boredom of rural life in retirement would be my death. I was wrong. It was a shovel and a feral cat named Karl.

At a loss without a case to prepare or a judge to sway, was I to spend my final years writing a memoir? I sat in my home office each day in my oversized, comfy cracked black leather chair that still bears a deep, precise depression where I had long placed my derriere. My daughter Jules had found me an antique rosewood desk that faintly smelled of linseed oil and old Cuban cigars (I don't smoke, but Cuba holds fond memories). A shiny new cell phone sat on that desk beside the latest upgraded desktop computer to allow consultations by Zoom should anyone still care for my opinion.

Born William Hawkins, they knew me at the criminal bench as the Hawk. After thirty-five years, my criminal law practice had sold. I had stayed honourable while serving those who ignored the warning of the thirteen crows and ended up dancing with the devil.

Grudgingly, I agreed with my wife to retire, initially begging for a pied-à-terre in the city to maintain my addiction to the law. Couldn't I just visit retirement on weekends when I was not otherwise engaged in another plea deal balancing the crime against the criminal? I expected my practice would continue until they took me out back in a body bag. But Clare would not have it.

Clare was my wife and my life. She organized our home, our finances, and the administration of my law office. She had stood by my shenanigans for all those years. A country house in retirement was all she wished for. I left my practice to give my beloved a semblance of peace while she was being ravaged by chemotherapy to defeat the cancer riddling her body.

Why did I have a home office? When I first retired, I delayed packing up the files and sat reading them like I was saying goodbye to old friends. The home office was empty of files, as blank as the pages of my new memoir notebook. It had been an afterthought, a small room tucked into the back of the new house beside the garage. That garage was to be my man cave, full of brand-new shiny saws, screwdrivers, grinders, and other strange tools I couldn't name. Jules bought them. What did I know about carpentry? I built legal defences, not birdhouses. I could fix a plea, but not a clogged toilet.

After having stared at the walls for over an hour, not writing a memoir, it became my habit to take a walk to visit Clare at the small, local cemetery.

Not that I liked to walk. Being outside was misery. I did not kayak, fish, or shoot like every man and woman in the area. I hated animals and bugs, of which there was an abundance.

Sandy lived alone across the road in the small blue house. She watched out for both of us but never shared my walks. Sandy was attractive but a recluse, seventy years young, distinguished by her single long white braid that trailed down her back to her knees. She, too, was suffering through treatment for another form of cancer. Often, she rode with Clare while I drove when her nephew couldn't bother to help.

The locals had cut an ATV trail through the forest to the cemetery. I heard many flipped their rigs on the hefty rocks that lifted out of the path. I trudged through the forest trail to the cemetery, dodging animal scat, cigarette butts, and empty liquor bottles.

Bugs thrived and fed voraciously on the trail. Black flies and mosquitoes riddled my arms with wounds, even though I had slapped hard enough to raise purple bruises. I could liberally paint on N, N-Diethyl-meta-tolumide (deet) and maybe die sooner myself from the chemical exposure.

Sandy had given me a bear whistle. Why the heck would I have wanted to whistle up a bear to eat me?

When I arrived at the grave, my breath caught in my chest. The blanket of blackflies, combined with my shock, sucked the oxygen from my body. My legs turned to rubber. I wobbled until my foot took over. The left shoe sought the field goal, connecting with a load of animal dung, booting it far from the top of Clare's resting place. That was too much.

"You're all monsters. Which one of you did this?" I screamed into the woods. "I'll burn this forest down with all of you in it," I yelled while swatting at the mosquitoes until I dropped to my knees and sobbed.

Sandy found me a short while later, walked me home, and we talked over a pot of coffee about how to live and die. Our house always impressed Sandy, and she whispered it was haunted. Balderdash. It was a large log home built by a renowned architect. The property sat on the market for years - empty after the death of its owner. Clare had tracked down the real estate agent and offered the small change left at the bottom of her purse. She got it. She was amazing.

A good 2 ½ hours from the city, the cabin sat in the middle of nowhere, back of beyond, surrounded by trees and wild things in a country community called the Crow River Estates. The lots were spacious and intended for privacy. Our property lay tucked into the woods, surrounded by empty lots on either side and nestled on the southern edge of the slow, wide, well-stocked Crow River.

I thought the house was nice if a bit empty, still a haven from biting mosquitoes. Echoes boasted sixteen-foot ceilings framed with large pine beams. A massive floor-to-ceiling stone fireplace commanded the living room. Four picture windows offered views - a stand of trees and a long driveway to the road were out front. A perfect view of the river with its glistening diamonds could be enjoyed out the back if you were so inclined.

We took our coffee at the dining room table. It was at the other end of the cabin by the kitchen. Red Italian brick surrounded the stove. Black marble mapped out a rectangular cooking zone, separating the kitchen from the dining area. The dining room invited dinner guests to the front of the house and sliding glass patio doors opened out to a flagstone terrace out front. Friends could wander after dinner for drinks on the terrace if we had any friends.

Sandy lent an ear and sipped my coffee. Retirement meant living in limbo, the first circle of hell. There was too much peace, too much tranquillity, and after Clare died, too much sadness. I knew Clare's demise had crushed Jules, as it had crushed me. Our move to this cabin was supposed to be a beginning, but it would end in too many deaths, proving again that there is no justice, whether at work or in life. Maybe the house was haunted.

How to live? I couldn't return to the city and leave my only daughter to continue in the cabin alone. I would never leave Clare to rest in her country cemetery without visiting daily. Jules had offered to take care of me in my old age. I heard "dotage". But Jules would eventually meet someone, marry, and move on. I didn't know how to move forward.

Sandy gave me a quick, light hug as she left to resume her own life. She walked with a slow, pained hunch down the driveway and across the road. She looked young but walked old. I watched out for her until she was home.

I saw between the house and the garage. Sandy had dragged three white plastic chairs from her patio to the firepit. She had planned a bonfire as her last hurrah on Friday night. Jules and I were on the invitation list, but Jules had to work the night shift and was too new to the job to get time off. I wasn't keen to go alone. It looked like Sandy had about three friends based on the number of chairs. I didn't plan to go, needing a break from humanity and all its ills. That break became more permanent than I had intended.

I had resolved to drop in on the afternoon before the bonfire to offer my personal farewell and for a cup of coffee. She usually had a pot on. As the sun dropped from its highest position, the feral cats began to arrive. There were two gnarly flea-bitten beggars, affectionately named Karl and Socks by Jules. One of us would lay food out in front of the dining room in old plastic Chinese food containers. Jules bought catnip like they needed an excuse to laze drug-addled on the front terrace. Lord, I hated them the most (maybe not as much as the blackflies).

MEEOOWWWW... OOOOOOWWWWWW!

The howl of the feral. Murderous and mangy, chasing and killing chipmunks and songbirds. Ticks and fleas covered these cats. They constantly scratched at their bodies. Their horrific stench simmered in the heat originating from the spray of males that showed up en masse, presumably to garner the attention of females. They were disgusting mongrels, all.

The steadying, sweet fragrance of love that had crowned Clare in life also held musky undertones from wisteria and jasmine. The feral stench had replaced this beauty.

MEEOOWWWW... OOOWWWWWW!

I watched with my coffee and listened to what Clare called the song of the feral cats.

Song my eye.

Each day after my walk, I usually pursued my only other activity - the garden. Yes, retirement found a top barrister standing outside in a swarm of bugs over three raised beds on the east side of the lot, holding a hose, and reviewing the night's damage. Something had a taste for everything I tried to grow. It could have been the two deer that I had seen around or the porcupine. I considered digging it all up this time, or perhaps I should stop watering everything and just let it die.

MEEOOWWWW... OOOWWWWWW!

My true nemeses had been those feral cats.

As the howl grew, I saw that the sound emanated from the lungs of the ugliest muscle-bound, prizefighting tom. Socks was the singer. He was usually first at the plate, and when I returned each morning from the garden, he darted back from his empty dish to give me space to enter the house.

Socks was a grey cat with elongated dirty white legs. Jules and Clare both took exceptional care of that particular godless feral when he first showed up touting an injured front paw. They fed him cat nip (the thinking was that it would act like CBD for his pain). Smart cat. The bad leg started the daily feeding. Once he ate, the leg miraculously healed. I knew he was faking it. Then he started bringing Karl along for a bite to eat.

I would test them daily, giving chase down the driveway. My song was, "Get off my property." I don't think they fully appreciated my musical performance.

MEEOOWWWW... OOOWWWWWW!

What now? Yes, it was Socks.

Sandy said unloving caregivers had dumped Socks. (Would that make them un-caregivers?) She said feral cats didn't meow, and Jules agreed. But he was still a male, and he or Karl sprayed an ungodly stink on my front stoop. Was it to irritate me? I could trap and transport, and someday I might even secure the courage to raise this with Jules.

MEEOOWWWW... OOOWWWWWW!

"What is it, cat?" I sang loudly in return while watching out the glass door of the dining room. He had turned his back to me as he continued to howl. I understood why they called it caterwauling.

MEEOOWWWW... OOOWWWWWW!

Out the front door, I gave chase to Socks for a bit of fun. I would never get away with the chase if Jules was home. Socks took off like a rocket across the drive to a tree trunk and hefted himself up a good twenty feet with those front socks of his.

MEEOOWWWW... OOOWWWWWW!

He was even louder twenty feet up a tree.

Sandy was a bit of a contradiction. She didn't mind that I watered a few cats like they were thirsty flowers or if I occasionally chased them.

I returned to the house to mull over Sandy's thoughts about living and dying. She leaned towards the latter. She didn't cherish every last second of life like Clare had.

After each treatment, Clare had rested out back of the cabin listening to the graceful dance of the wind, waving through the pines and cedars that lined the river's shore. She enjoyed the squawking of the jays, the constant cawing of the crows, and even the empty, soulless howls of coyotes. She would have loved to follow next year's winter swans gliding like ballerinas up the unfrozen sections of the river.

Sandy felt the pain was too much and wanted it done. She had consented to an assisted suicide - a legal option at the time. Sandy said her doctor approved. Cancer for her was terminal and her suffering would only worsen, or the drugs they threw at her would incapacitate her. So, the plan was to accept a morphine overdose. The deed was to occur on Saturday, to fit with the nephew's work schedule. Why he couldn't take a day off during the week for his dying aunt was beyond me.

A nurse practitioner planned to deliver the lethal drug. Not just anyone could help a person die (legally, that is). In Sandy's case, someone didn't get the memo.

MEEOOWW!

Socks climbed down the tree. The kibble bag sat in a lonely slump on the counter. Whoops. Heh, heh. That explained the noise. Socks had been calling for dinner service, and I was under strict instructions from the police (Jules) to put out kibble. I had to oblige before she got home from the detachment and discovered my failure.

I grabbed the bag and proceeded out to the feral dish, which Jules would retrieve and clean when she got home. She would then deliver the can of wet mush. I would not, for the life of me, come within one foot of the stink wafting out of those cans.

MEEOOWWWW...

Why had I fed them? One of them was probably responsible for the load of crap on my Clare's grave. I sat frowning, sipping cold coffee at the dining room table.

Socks ate a couple of bites of kibble and left.

It was not just the cemetery incident. Crow River Estates was full of criminals: thieves and murderers. Thieving deer and porcupines destroyed the garden, favouring the Swiss chard. There were murderous villains like the large fox often seen trotting across Sandy's front lawn, lurking and searching for lesser beings to eat. Coyotes howled in the distance over something dead. Other vandals destroyed personal property. Either the beaver or the porcupine would not leave the back deck posts alone. Repairing chewed chunks of wood would eventually put me at great expense.

CAW CAW CAW!

Oh, and let's not forget the squawking that preceded the theft of the kibble. The crows (the corvids, I mean) were usually many and loud. I watched as the largest black crow swooped down to sneak kibble as soon as feral backs were turned. Were we to feed the entire forest? The thieving crow finished it.

With no way to police these creatures, Sandy, always a contradiction, recommended poison on the deck wood or around the garden. Tempting. But I wouldn't want to alienate my daughter or the whole animal-loving rural community. I was not actually an animal killer. Odd though. Sandy, another who spoiled Karl with bits of expensive human food, would come up with poison as a solution to the other wild creatures. Really, I was just not suited to living with wild things. One of them had squatted on Clare's grave. I wouldn't forgive or forget.

Karl replaced Socks and chased the thieving crow back into the trees. I hated Karl most of all. Maybe someone had dumped the howling Socks on the side of the road, but Karl had been born mean, wild, and ugly.

Karl was as silent as the dead. Never a chirp, whistle, or meow out of that one. He held your gaze with the most intense stare, beady eyes on everything everywhere. He would stare, judging me and huffing cat snot all over the window. His face was smashed in and half the fur was gone from one cheek. That cat had seen one too many fights. Did he fight bears? What a mess. Karl's square head sat on a bulky build. His shoulder muscles were Herculean, made for tree climbing. Yet he was relatively skinny in his behind. This would have been for traction during his climb to freedom to avoid foxes and coyotes or to hunt.

Karl always tilted his head slightly, like he was trying to figure out why I left out food. What was I up to? Jules said true feral cats would never fully trust humans. Smart cat.

Karl would sniff at the kibble at each meal with disdain and glare at me, denouncing my cruelty at offering such garbage. Yes, my sin was that I carried dried-out, odourless, drab food instead of the malodorous canned mush. My larger sin was that I enjoyed making them wait for the food, proving I wouldn't jump to their tune. Clare had jumped and what did that get her? Scat on her grave.

When I cleaned his feral snot off the dining room glass door, spraying it down with the hose became more satisfying when Karl was standing right there, waiting for food. Heh, heh. Oops. Missed the feral snot and watered a furry flower.

Sandy didn't just like Karl. She also treated a large fox for his mange, hiding expensive drugs in locally sourced certified organic hamburger meat. Sandy explained it to me (like I would be interested). What's the point of treating a wild animal? Mange was contagious and harmful to other animals and humans. Why didn't she use her poison on the fox? Why not let the thing just die? Wasn't that how nature worked?

That big crow sat in his tree watching me. I remember there was an old poem about counting crows. The number you count was supposed to warn you about the future or it would describe and warn of the unseen. You're supposed to heed the warning of the crows. I say, balderdash. I see crows all over our property and they don't tell me a thing. One crow waited for the kibble. What was that rhyme? *One is for sorrow.* That was it.

I carried out more of the kibble for Karl. Across the road was Sandy's bright red Camaro. Would she be willing to sell it to Jules?

"Here's your dinner Karl. Don't let the crows steal any," I added as an afterthought.

But as I shook dribbles of kibble into the bowl, Karl walked cautiously right up to my feet. He never got that close. I stepped back quickly, afraid to pick up his parasites. Then he spun around and ran a few yards up our long gravel drive. He turned back and flashed his eyeball at me. He stopped, advanced cautiously and deliberately towards me, and started it all again. Did he want to be chased? He approached too close when he walked back. I could almost feel the itch of his fleas. Was that a tick on my pant leg? Then he repeated this crazy performance three more times. Something was up.

"OK, alright," I shouted. I obliged him, trailing that cat as if I were on a leash.

I followed him down the drive for a bit. Karl got excited. When I stopped to get my breath (I was that out of shape), he hopped up and down and repeated his "Follow me" routine. I stepped up my pace for a game of chase, and he ran forward faster. I stopped, and he stopped and started back towards me. With a human in tow, Karl strolled across the road, swaying and flicking his tail as he crossed into Sandy's yard.

I followed through the walkway that ran between Sandy's small blue-painted house and her smaller matching blue garage (the she-shed), just as Karl stopped dead on his paws, lifted his nose, and then shot off to the back forest, and disappeared past the stand of cedars and pines at the back of the lot. I picked up the odd stench that wafted through the air—a faint chemical odour reminiscent of ammonia from a morgue on a bad day. My head turned towards the stench that seemed to come from the she-shed/garage.

The screen door squeaked as Sandy suddenly appeared at her back door. I pivoted back towards the house. Her eyes focused on someone behind my left shoulder. She smiled broadly at the person but then suddenly frowned and screamed, "NO!"

CAW CAW CAW!

Thirteen crows rose from the trees lining the forest's edge, but only one crow remained to attest to the sorrow of my demise. I was dead before I hit the ground.

Chapter 2

The early-morning air was crisp and chill. Even with my lids closed, the sun dazzled brightly. One eye cracked open to an unnatural, frightening vision. I lay outdoors on the ground, resting under a fur blanket with no clue to my location. I stretched as the chill seeped into my fingers, which were also covered in fur. Fur gloves? Sharp little white objects, like needles, projected out from the mitts. They almost looked like claws. My eyes searched the length of my body as I rolled to examine the same teeny claws protruding from the ends of fur boots on my feet.

Claws! I gasped, pulling my front limbs up to my face. Both of my eyes flew wide open. What in Hades are these? I looked down at stubby little paws and claws!

The same brindle fur of my arms also covered my legs, like Russian Cossack pants. Turning my head for a better view of my hind end, I gasped. Was that a ruddy tail? It flicked back and forth like an irritated snake.

A mirror would have given me the full view. *Mirror, mirror on the wall* came to mind, but this was no fairy tale. It was a nightmare. The last time I stood before a mirror, I'd had a thick head of overgrown curls, more salt than pepper, framing my oversized black horn-rimmed glasses. My paws sought my face and patted as I shut my eyes tight. Nope. No glasses. I padded the ground around my head. Nope. Still no glasses. I tried to stand up on my hind legs but fell over. I needed to wake up. The last time I'd stood, I'd been looking at Sandy. A shock, pressure, and excruciating pain had walloped the top of my head. Then black. Nothing. Something had hit me. Was that it? Did I suffer a head injury? My head still throbbed.

A serious head injury would have had repercussions. Were these just hallucinations? A faint squeak emerged when I opened my mouth. Hah. Both visual and oral hallucinations. Was this some version of a schizophrenic meltdown?

I squeezed my eyes shut even tighter hoping for the return of real life, complete with dirt-encrusted nails and baggy blue jeans on a flat, tailless bum. Still no luck when pawing around one more time for my glasses. If I opened my eyes, would a lovely young blond, blue-eyed nurse be ready to offer more painkillers? Yes. A simple drug-addled state of semiconsciousness after an injury.

As I peeked through crusted eyes at my reality, my gaze lifted skyward to avoid the visual field containing paws and claws. Painfully bright sunlight blinded me.

The next fright was olfactory, though I wondered if the head injury caused me to suffer parosmia. The air was vibrant: rot and grime, sweet and sublime. Woodsy, moldy fallen brush, and ripe green and brown leaves. I had allergies to all of this, but suddenly, the scents were glorious and I didn't even sneeze. I had loved wood smoke rising from bonfires and fireplaces, but now it made my back twitch. Fire! The thought made my fur stand on end. Then, out of nowhere, the luscious aroma of bacon on a grill wafted past, causing drool to slide down my chin. Food. I was hungry. I needed food. Maybe a diabetic coma could explain it all? But I wasn't diabetic.

I tried to stand up on my hind legs again but fell forward onto all fours. I kept trying to stand and wouldn't stoop to crawling. It was humiliating to walk without standing tall.

When I dropped again onto a mound of leaves, the urge arose to rock back and forth, stepping and squeezing my tiny claws on the soft, fragrant bed. It was all wrong, but it felt right. A rich loam covered in rotting leaves offered an overwhelming sense of security. I gave in, stretched, and laid my head down to resume my sleep, hoping the world would normalize after a few more winks. I had to be dreaming. It was a nightmare, wasn't it?

When I opened my eyes again, humongous brown and black rotting leaves as long as the full length of my body surrounded me. Beyond my head rose a ginormous pile of firewood seemingly made of California redwood logs. It was something out of a fairy tale. Like Paul Bunyan. I knew Paul Bunyan wasn't real. Still, the sight of those logs and leaves was a wonder.

Nothing compared to the musty, pungent stench that wafted past my nose when I tilted my head backwards. It emanated from an old, hairy, gnarly fur monster strutting around the logs towards me. From human memory, I recognized the stench of the feral cats, that used to be vile, disgusting, horrendous! Now, it didn't smell all that bad. This monster had to be almost ten times my size. It was also covered in brindled fur, and the body resembled mine but was much larger and had more black streaks than the brown of my furry coat. The monster loomed over my head, an enormous black tiger-like being ready to pounce and likely eat me.

To avoid an inevitable confrontation, I flew forwards and tried to stand and run but twisted, landing on my back. My Cat! His head was almost the size of my whole torso.

Again, I shut my eyes fast, clenched my butt cheeks, and started praying for a swift end to this nightmare. Eat me fast, you great, hairy—

"I said, wake up, Kitten. Now!" it shouted down at me. "I need to get you out of here. I know it's not normal at this time of day, but there are coyotes out this morning, and I'm not going to be their breakfast, and I'm not wasting any more of my time saving your furry butt."

Did it speak? Was it going to eat me or maybe save me for later? I looked carefully at that face. Without thinking, I shouted back, "Karl?" Just as my small mental voice shook at his name, my little furry form quivered. The cat smelled of Karl, though actually a bit better. It was a giant Karl. A Paul Bunyan Karl. My nemesis.

He stared down at me and slowly blinked once as if it meant something. An instinct within me grew. The blink was a sign of trust. Was he prepared to trust me, or should I trust him? I honestly sensed the meaning of the blink, but that wouldn't cut it. I didn't know where that thought even came from, but after thirty-five years of trusting my human instincts in court, I went with the human rather than the cat instinct and concluded the monster was not trustworthy. I shut my eyes again.

"Kitten. Open your darned eyes." I did as he lifted his left hind leg. I flinched, but he merely brought the leg forwards to violently scratch the left side of his head with enormous hind claws. Fleas would be my guess. Or maybe ticks. Or something unknown but still disgusting!

Then it hit me: He talked to me!

"You can't talk, Karl. No, no. You can't talk. You're feral. They don't talk or meow or whatever. Jules said so!" I was stupidly nervous. I think I shouted, but I was only using my mind. "This is a nightmare, and you're the monster in it."

He glared, stopped scratching, huffed, and appeared to be considering a careful response.

"Whatever you want to call me is fine. Karl, it is." He bobbed his head up and down, offering a visual cue to acknowledge the name. His lips didn't move.

"And no, I do not meow. I am a fully grown male, for Cat's sake. I am not a kitten. You are a kitten and will meow at me or your mother if my mate ever shows up."

Karl turned his head back and forth scanning the area. "Where has my beautiful girl gotten herself? We've been moving the kitten nest around so much over the last 6 weeks that I can't keep up with where she is taking them next."

He turned back and announced, "It's time to go, Kitten, or this will become a real nightmare if those coyotes come back."

Karl stretched out his right paw and with one quick movement, flipped me onto my stomach. I lay there spread-eagled with that same monster paw bearing down on the centre of my back. I had shut my eyes tight again. (It was just too much to take, frankly.) Monster Karl's maw then clamped down on the back of my neck.

My mind shut down as I prepared for death. Instead, it felt like I had crawled into one of those cheap hotel beds and someone had turned on the shimmy and shake feature. Something had me by the neck. Except it didn't hurt. I lost no parts. No blood spilled. Karl had me in his mouth and didn't even break the skin. I slumped in his jaws as he bit down harder on my scruffy neck fur, leaving me paralyzed. He picked me up, and as I bounced away in Karl's jaws, the ginormous woodpile slowly grew smaller.

Everything recognizable was so much bigger. First, he carried me through the great redwoods (they were probably the trees that lined the side of Sandy's yard). He dodged across the expanse of rocky desert (the gravel of the road) onto the massive green grassland so dense I couldn't see where we were going (likely the lawn I had failed to mow yesterday). The half-acre lot in front of my log cabin was now at least ten times its original size.

"Home. You're taking me home?" I asked.

"Arrrammmararrrrr." An incomprehensible reply rose out of

the back of my neck. He couldn't walk and talk at the same time? That didn't instill confidence. With the weight of my stress, I closed my eyes again and didn't open them until the rich smell of green grass dissipated.

CHAPTER 3

Before me was the monumental oak front door of my cabin. He dropped me unceremoniously on the front stoop, which was still in need of repair from water damage last spring. I had not gotten around to fixing the stoop, but I didn't know how, anyway. I owned a garage full of tools that I didn't know how to use. Worse still, with these tiny paws, tool use and house repairs would not happen anytime soon.

I tried once more to stand on my hind legs, only to fall against my front door. What did Karl expect me to do? Neither of us could grip the door handle ten floors up. Even if we could get that high, we could not pull on the truck-sized handle with my teeny paws or even Karl's gnarly mitts. What was Karl thinking, bringing me here? I fell back onto four legs.

"Do you know me? Do you realize where you've brought me?" I probed careful not to acknowledge my true identity or that this was my own home.

"Just sit there and listen up, Kitten." Karl loomed over my head. "Yes, I know exactly who you are and where you live. I did not witness your death, but you likely deserved it. From the forest behind Sandy's place, your bright white soul lifted, flew, and settled in my mate's kitten. To see this and understand it is a natural gift given to feline fathers. You're now mine. You're six weeks old, and I recognize your soul even in that fur that is so like my own fur, though with too much brown for my liking. Black is more stately."

"Dead? If you didn't witness a death, maybe I'm just in a coma somewhere. How do I get back? And don't you want to be with your real kitten? I must have taken someone's place in this body. You must know how to put me back and get your own kitten back." I almost begged.

Karl sniffed hard. "There is no going back. The feral kitten you displaced has moved on to another incarnation by this time. And you are not in a coma. I didn't bring you here. I have no control over this. You are the one that came back, and if you don't know how it happened I can't help you."

The prodigious Karl had finally pulled a frown out of me. Ridiculous, I thought.

"Come back from where? Died? Souls! What in Hades are you even talking about?" My little tail started slashing back and forth, gaining speed as my ire rose.

Karl gazed deep into my eyes. "Ah. I understand. Humans would call it reincarnation. Buddhism. But you're not religious. Interesting. You came back and now live a new life in a new body because you have something to learn, or you just won't let go of something from your prior life. That's all I know. Beyond that, it's your mess to figure out and fix. I don't make the rules. Don't ask me why or how Kitten. Go with the flow. Instinct should eventually kick in and guide you. It will get easier as you get older."

My tail twitched and swung. He claimed paternity and some bizarre Eastern religious foundation for my state of fur-ness. Ridiculous. (Frankly, I preferred my brown over his black-based brindle). I needed to reassert myself. Paul Bunyan was not real. There had to be a way back to the real world.

I stood up on all fours this time and paced in front of Karl. Time to introduce myself and reclaim my identity.

"My name is William Hawkins, but you can call me Hawk for short. Don't call me Kitten. It's not my name. And you're not my father. My father was Lieutenant General James Hawkins, now deceased after a lengthy and successful career in the RCAF. I do not accept this nightmare. As Scrooge said to Marley, 'You may be an undigested bit of beef, a blot of mustard, a crumb of cheese, a fragment of underdone potato.' And I need to wake up."

Karl spun me back to face him with a swipe of that mighty paw. His ears lay flat against his head, and he bristled slightly. He spoke even more slowly but with an edge this time.

"You are Kitten. That is what I, your father, named you. Hawk is not a kitten's name. I am not calling my runt a hawk. Hawks are killers, and if one tracked anything your size, it would swoop down and eat it. And do you want the other animals to think we are both stupid?" He added, "Oh, and you can thank me later when you see the size of the coyotes out this way."

Karl knew I didn't want to let go of my humanity or my name. "Here's what I can offer. When the lady takes you in, if she gives you a new name, we'll go with that. But until then you will be known out here as Kitten."

A bit stunned, my absurd response was to offer a further introduction. "That kind lady you refer to is my daughter. Her name is Jules. She got a job as a cop at the local OPP detachment." As if he would care or even know what I referred to in my rambling. It was an odd position to be in for a respected, confident barrister who normally intimidated his opponents or dominated the courtroom. This gigantic monster of a feral cat before me spoke of hungry coyotes, killer hawks, and disgusting mice.

As these thoughts formed, the sound of light but steady toe-tapping arose from my left. A furry brown head, even smaller than my own, with tiny, rounded ears, popped up out of a hole in the ground. In a peculiarly deep, gravelly voice, it said, "Watch your mouth, pal. Mice are not the disgusting ones here."

I stopped and surveyed the half-acre of incredibly tall grass. "I must drag myself out of bed and get mowing this lawn."

Karl slowly shook his massive head as he listened to my rant. "Look at your environment, Kitten. Can't you smell it? Listen to the sounds. I know you heard the mice tap their feet underground. Those jays ruffle their feathers before singing from the treetops. You're not asleep. You're a young and small version of me—a cat."

This offered no comfort. I rested my back end down on the front stoop and stared at my surroundings with ears twitching and nostrils wide. I could not only smell everything, but I could hear it all, as he said.

"Why did you bring me here? And are you seriously telling me I've been reincarnated as a feral kitten?"

Karl Bunyan answered patiently, if embarrassingly slow like I was mentally deficient.

"Well, yes. You are a reincarnated human, now a cat. Not my rules. I brought you here because this is your old house. The young lady who lives with you is kind and will probably take you in." Karl tilted his head and looked closely at me from head to toe. "Given your size, you'd call yourself a runt. Good word. I like it. Yes, you're the runt of my litter, and you probably won't survive out here. The lady and her walls can protect you better than I can until you figure out whatever sent you back as my kitten and fix it yourself."

A runt! Offended, I snorted and turned my back to him, still swishing my tail back and forth, up and down. I was getting good at tail-swishing and tried to hit Karl, but my aim was off.

"Is everyone reincarnated? Are you someone else inside?" I asked an honest question. Karl exhaled from the depths of his being. His whiskers drooped. He frowned and once more spoke exceedingly slowly.

"The . . . ones . . . that . . . come . . . back . . . have . . . not . . . let . . . go . . . of . . . something," he repeated to the stupid kitten before him. Karl's large tail thumped back and forth, hitting the ground with each beat.

"Listen up. I can't help. Maybe it's something from your past. Maybe it is something in your present. But let it go. Learn how to cat. Be a cat." The wind picked up, yanking leaves ominously from tree limbs to swirl past my line of vision and into the sky.

My true worth was as the next meal for everyone around this place. What did he mean by saying, let go? And do what? Be a darned feral kitten? My head ached at the thought—or that could have been from the sun beating down on me or perhaps from my head being bashed in.

Karl added, "And to start, you could try being a lot nicer to other animals since most of them would eat you given half a chance. You were such a nasty human."

I was not nasty. He smelled.

I closed my eyes once more. Bill Hawkins, retired barrister, did not ever give up or give in. I felt it. I had a lifetime of experience that I could still access and wouldn't waste. What if I was dead? So was Clare. If I had returned, maybe Clare had as well. Maybe she was looking for me.

No. I wouldn't let go of Clare, her house, our daughter, or even my unwritten memoirs. (How would I get that memoir written with these tiny paws?)

Most importantly, Jules and I were a team, and we would not let my murderer get away.

My girl was a recent graduate from the Ontario Police College, top of her class. When she applied for a posting with the local provincial detachment, she got the job immediately. I enjoyed that she'd be working with a few good old boys who would be unprepared for the capability of my rebel girl. When she got the job, I was most grateful that she would escape the city's heavier gun, drug, and gang traffic. Was I naïve?

I hoped she would spend most of her time pulling over speeding cottagers and drunks on Highway 7. Jules was not at risk of being shot down on a Sunday afternoon just for wearing the uniform.

I had confidence in my Baby Bear. There would be justice in Crow River. I wasn't sure how I could help or even how to survive in a small, four-legged, fur-coated body. For now, Karl was the key to my future and my survival.

"Fine," I said, "but it's going to be pretty difficult to get me inside the house and away from the hawks, the wild, hungry coyotes, and the rest of the hungry animal world."

The shadow of an enormous bird stretched across the driveway. An eagle hovered above my head. I shivered at the menace of its enormous wing span. Maybe Karl had a point.

"No fear, my little Kitten." The toothy smile made my hackles rise, but his tone was more compassionate. "I'll stay here with you until the gracious lady Jules comes home. I'm betting she'll take you in. You have my good looks even if you're a runt. She likes me and feeds me. She'll take you in."

I glared. "What about coyotes and eagles?"

"No fear. Coyotes usually sleep during the day and won't come too close to the front door of a house. Same with the eagle. The ripe scent of humans is a bit much for them. Even if coyotes arrive before Jules got here, I could grab you, and we'd climb a tree until they left."

Did I trust him?

Chapter 4

I lay down on the cabin stoop, exhausted. Karl stretched out in front of me, relaxed but watchful. He turned his head to me.

"Can you do me a favour? Can you tell your daughter I prefer the canned pâté to the dry kibble? If you figure out how to meow it." He rolled over on the ground, snorting and spitting out a loud, obnoxious laugh.

"OK, wise guy. How am I supposed to convey your food preferences to Jules? And while you're at it, explain how you and I can communicate. You don't meow. Your lips haven't moved once since this began. How are we even having this conversation?"

I sounded tough. At least I thought I did. No one toys with this Hawk, all the while hiding my quivering paws under my belly. Why bother? Karl could likely smell my fear.

"It should be obvious. Have you never noticed how animals stare?"

I had not. I didn't like animals. Why would I notice them staring at each other?

"We use our minds. I read your thoughts as they form pictures in my head. Ah. Right. You call this telepathy. It develops as you grow."

I had never believed in that hogwash but had been thinking of *telepathy* right at that moment. He had read it from my mind, literally.

"Not hogwash, Kitten. We don't need to speak out loud to communicate." He grinned. "Except the bees. They dance." Karl broke into new peels of snorty laughter at some inside joke. When he finally caught a breath, he continued, "But seriously, you should have figured that one out. Even at your young age. If you're within a reasonable range, you can project out to your target. Just think. If you want privacy, try to look away and not think, or think of something unrelated. Create a barrier."

Good to know. "Why didn't you respond when you were carrying me here? Even hanging out of your mouth, you could still speak with your mind, couldn't you?"

Karl offered a quick reply. "I don't talk with my mouth full." He once more snorted out chuckles.

I turned my head away to block my thoughts from him. How long would Jules take to get home, and how much longer did I have to suffer Karl? Oh, could he hear that? Karl said nothing, and we remained stretched out in the sun together on the flagstone step as Karl began his lecture.

"Communication is an art. With humans, you must use your tail, nose, and individual perfume if you remain intact. Nose touch with them to say hello, identify scent, check the human's health, or offer a simple kiss. Rub everything with your cheek fur to assert territory and identify your preferences. Tail down means you're upset. Tail straight up means you're happy. Tail up and tip curled means you're thrilled. Your daughter will understand that much already. She has an air of experience, or maybe she's just sensitive."

My limited experience with animals was based solely on the local feral population, and I didn't know tail movement carried meaning. Would a kitten come by it naturally?

I turned over and placed my chin on my crossed front paws. "What about the meow business? How am I supposed to have a conversation with Jules?"

I had inadvertently invited Karl to continue his lecture, and he took to it like a politician at his podium.

"Adult cats normally don't meow. It's a vocalization that we use as youngsters when we want to gain the attention of our parents. Adult cats raised by humans will continue to meow because of their dependence. They don't truly grow up. Wild, feral cats don't meow. Life experience teaches them they're not babies. You'll meow when you think of Jules or any other human as a mother figure who'll care for and feed you and protect you. It should happen naturally."

Karl leaned towards me. "But there's no universal language. You and Jules will create your own language using your body, your eyes, and Jules's personal interpretation of your different meows. You may mew, mrowow, mooo, or chirp. You pick. I once knew a feral named Boop who emitted short hoot sounds or barks similar to a baby otter. He may have been raised close to their den. But you'll work it out between the two of you to assign meaning to each sound."

Jules was a smart kid, but wasn't Karl expecting a bit too much of her? Karl listened and shook his head.

"Just try distinct sounds like mews and chirps or a good, strong hacking noise, and see what response they attract or how Jules interprets them. The hacking noise usually gets the humans jumping. To attract attention, you can also use a single claw to the calf and then walk where you want her to follow. Like I said, you must learn to cat."

Learn to cat! That line had made my tail automatically swish back and forth as my ears dropped, and I grrrrred my frustration. Not acceptable. This was not communication.

"You're telling me I have to yowl, squeak, squeal, choke, chirp, and dance like a bee to get my daughter to feed me something palatable." Did I sound as snide as I felt?

Karl bristled again, with ears flat back on his head. I shivered and backed up at the sight.

"Don't ever make fun of the bees. We're all dependent on their dance. The dance is a beautiful expression of their connection to each other. They dance directions to a good flower bed, home, or danger. The bee dance is so magnificent and beautiful that it even allows them to cross over. Bees can speak to those who have passed to the other side—those not reincarnated or those who completed their reincarnated life. When the bees come back, they can talk like any other adult animal using their minds. It's only humans we need to encourage with body language. Never make fun of the bees."

All I heard was that bees could *speak to those who passed over*. Could it be true? Bees talked to the dead? The medieval Celtic myth told to me in my youth described bees talking to the dead and taking messages to loved ones who had passed over. Could they also receive messages from the dead for the living?

My mind immediately went to my sweet departed Clare, perhaps reincarnated as a kitten somewhere, too. Could I find her? Could we be feral cats together? I wasn't ready to let go of my beloved Clare yet. I wondered whether Karl knew any bees.

CHAPTER 5

It was a long day. Karl flew across the grass after a chipmunk that had raced from a hole at the edge of the flagstone front terrace. I stayed on the damaged stoop out of the hawk's gaze, anticipating Jules's arrival. Karl nosed around the entrance to the chipmunk hole, ears twitching in every direction. Watching. With his ears. I had sensed my own heightened abilities, but Karl's ears were multidirectional. Impressive.

Under the brilliant sun, I longed for my sunglasses but turned my focus on the yard, testing my newly discovered kitten sight. My front yard had become a wilderness of sounds and sights. Colours were vibrant but limited in their range. The world was saturated in hues of grey, yellow, blue, and green. The tree trunks were a darker shade of grey, and the grass was greener - if that was possible. Most shocking, red no longer existed in my kitten world. If I closed my eyes, I could recall what I thought was the colour red, but I couldn't find it with my eyes open. This upset me. What about cranberries or raspberries or even the fuzzy pink bear slippers Jules wore on Saturday nights when we watched movies?

Everything was in finer detail, and my peripheral vision was so much better. I picked up a flash of movement easily but was still short-sighted. At least as a human, I could don my black horned-rim glasses. They wouldn't fit now. Was this a kitten thing or part of my reincarnation?

I picked out a jay halfway up the tree in front of Sandy's house. It was a long way off, but the deep blue colouring struck me as distinctive. A kitten hiking on stubby little legs would take at least a half hour to traverse the distance. Four large black crows lined up in the trees along the forest edge, staring down at me. Two stately, silken grey deer watched, and grimaced from the lot west of the cabin. (They used to be brown or tan, but with my restricted colour range they looked grey.) I could sort of see the mangy fox, Everett, through the lane between Sandy's house and garage, lying on the grass. I barely caught the flick of his ears as he rested his chin on a paw but then leapt up and trotted back into the forest.

All of the animals within my sight frowned when they looked at me. What a miserable group. What's their problem? Is that what it meant to be born an animal?

Screams of sirens filled the air. The crows and the jay took flight. Lights that should have been red twirled. One crow remained behind and watched the black-and-white police cars as they sped down the road, throwing gravel to the curbs before parking and expelling two police officers. A white ambulance followed into Sandy's driveway. As attendants jumped out of the ambulance, one plain clothes (cop?) came out from between the house and garage and waved the attendants to the back.

I could no longer see but heard and appreciated the tenor of the crow's caws from the forest. A furious cacophony arose at the disturbance from the humans. The deer had already leapt to give themselves distance from the bustling confusion. One turned back and scowled at me. Did I imagine it? What did I ever do to the deer? As I looked at her, 'Darling' came to mind. Excited to know her name, I also understood with that one glance her anger towards me. Why, I wanted to ask but her back turned. I didn't catch the other deer's name.

Karl had returned, but I wanted to know the state of Sandy's backyard for myself. Before I succumbed to the temptation to sneak down the drive and peek, a scream from above cried, *keeee-ahh, keeee-ahh*. Karl pointed with his nose up at a large hawk high in the trees.

"I wouldn't go anywhere, Kitten. That hawk's noticed you."

I huddled back against the front door and turned my thoughts to Sandy's yard. I imagined the police would find my bludgeoned body. Jules would learn what had happened. I was sad for her, but once she learned of my death, the murderer could not escape. I expected justice at the hands of my Baby Bear. I could do little standing on these small, furry paws and watching from a distance. Either I could wait or be eaten. Even if I could talk, the police would never consider wisdom proffered by a mere kitten. *Meow.*

As Karl stood guard over the chipmunk hole, my old patterns from years as a lawyer surged to the fore. I started by first considering Sandy's reaction - the way she had called "No!" over my shoulder right before someone hit me. She must have known the murderer. She smiled with some awareness and she was not fearful initially. Sandy should have called my murder into the police. I wondered how she had gotten away from the murderer.

Sandy would be an essential witness. She had seen it all. And with the arrival of police it was obvious events had not moved quickly. It could not be more than a day since my death. If Sandy went through with her medically assisted death on Saturday, she wouldn't be available to testify for the trial. But knowing my body lay lifeless without peace in her backyard, I didn't think she'd follow through. Could she hold off long enough to get to trial? This would inevitably cause her unnecessary suffering, but Sandy's testimony would be necessary to get a fast conviction.

I paced the length of the front stoop, thinking. Perhaps the Crown would consider another option. With a strong forensic case to back her up, the police could take her written statement by affidavit and submit that as evidence. Not exactly testimonial evidence, but this approach could afford her the peace she desperately needed.

I sat back down on my pussy butt as the blue jay flew back to us. He landed in the tree high up and screamed, "Sandy's dead! Sandy's dead!"

Was it already past Saturday? Did this mean Sandy had gone through with her appointment with morphine? Did she leave me to rot in her backyard? Assuredly, the nurse practitioner should have noticed my corpse lying out there. Surely Sandy would have waited long enough to give the police a statement.

"Hold on," I shouted at the jay. At least, I thought I hoped shouting was accomplished by fixing a hard gaze in the bird's general direction. "They killed me. Did anyone see my body in the backyard? What about *my* body? Where am I?"

Karl looked down and like every other animal, scowled at me and then pointed his nose towards Sandy's yard. "You're already dead, son. No one cares about your lifeless body. What I want to know is with Sandy gone, who is going to continue with Everett's treatment?"

I understood what he meant. Sandy had been feeding Everett medicine for his mange, but she wouldn't be doing it now. Poor Everett wouldn't last long without someone to replace Sandy. But did I honestly care at this moment? *What about me?*

"Karl," responded the jay succinctly and in a fit of flapping. "Your kitten thinks he's dead. This one is wrong in the head. Better to put it down." The bird didn't even acknowledge me.

"I'll take care of my own as I see fit," snapped Karl. "The questions are, did you see Sandy's body, and did you see any other dead humans with Sandy?"

The blue jay stopped flapping. "No. I only saw the body of our dear Sandy laid out on the patio. Nothing and no one else, animal or human is dead back there." Then he too, flew off.

If she had been on the patio, Sandy could not have died from the injection. She must have been murdered as well. I laid my head down and covered my eyes with both paws. Something else happened, and too soon. She would not be giving any statement to the police. I prayed to Cat she didn't suffer

(Odd how I thought to pray to a Cat diety. Was I learning to cat?)

Chapter 6

An old, rattling Jeep with a Triple AAA Construction sign on its side pulled up and parked on the edge of my lawn ahead of the roadside police vehicles. The bearded face and lumberjack shirt meant Jarrod, Sandy's nephew, had arrived. I recalled his beard was supposed to be red fur. (I did think fur instead of hair. The strange thought was uncomfortably natural). Jarrod leapt out of the Jeep. A uniformed officer only momentarily stopped him.

"What's going on?" he yelled. "Where's my aunt? What happened here?"

My impression of Jarrod came from discussions with Sandy over the last year. She described him as a small-town kid with little guidance from an indifferent mother. Jarrod had left high school a bit too early to work as a labourer in construction. On weekends he was the type who drove a third-hand ATV through the trails after drinking a case of beer with a few other goons. He defined flying under the radar, but that wouldn't last long. Unless some strong male figure stepped in to take him in hand, it was just a matter of time before Jules and her professional colleagues faced him down.

Jarrod's uncle, Sandy's husband, was in prison so only Sandy was there to care about him. But she was dying.

The plainclothes officer now came out from the house and Jarrod disappeared, escorted through the front door. Already a detective on site. I approved. Even at a distance, I recognized the officer as Ewen Keens, a large-framed local good old boy. He had a serious crush on my Jules. He'd been by the house a few times but hadn't gotten past the threshold.

Odd that the nephew was there. He worked in Peterborough, where the hospital cancer centre was located, yet he was never available to take her for radiation treatment during the week. I had picked up the slack. And he wasn't available during the week to support Sandy's decision to end her life. So what was he doing here?

I kept watching for any movement, wondering what had happened to my body. Karl stared up at the one remaining crow in my yard that had not been with the other crows earlier. She floated casually down from the treetops, but again, not too close, until she achieved the top of a small pine at the edge of the drive. Karl made the introductions.

"Shelley, this is Kitten. He used to be the human jerk that lived here with the gracious lady. I learned her name is Jules. Kitten, this is Shelley. The front yard is her family's territory. They very much appreciate the leftover kibble."

Shelley was frenetic. Her body jerked as she snapped her head around towards me. Her beak didn't move, but she still frowned and spat out a pellet aimed right at my head. It struck and bounced off. If she appreciated the kibble, why the animosity? Wasn't I the one who had delivered it daily?

"*CAW!* Your reputation as a human precedes you, Kitten. We all know about you. I remember you chasing my cousins. I hope you're a better cat than you were a human. And don't you even think about eating my babies or we'll pluck out your eyeballs! *CAW!*"

I was speechless. When I was human, what did I do to the crows in my yard? Only once had I run out to scare a couple back into the trees, but that did no harm, and I had to pick up the cat dishes from the terrace. I had chased Socks a time or two, and I used a bit of water to deter Karl. But that was it. How did my reputation for animal cruelty get started? I have never, ever eaten crow babies and never would. Was it because I was now a cat? Is that something that would be expected of me? Eating baby crows? Maybe that's all she meant. Well, she can rest assured it was not gonna happen. I barely tolerated chicken. I didn't and would never eat crow.

"Have you surveyed Sandy's backyard?" Karl asked. "Jay says she's dead, but did anyone notice a second body? Maybe this guy, in his old human form?" He pointed directly at me with his right front paw.

Shelley took off like lightning. She flew straight down the drive and swerved up and over Sandy's house. She then did two low circles of the backyard and winged it back to the same pine in front of Karl.

"*CAW.* Nope. One heck of a lot of blood on the patio. Blood covered a shovel and Sandy's shell is lying there right beside it. The shovel was probably used to hit her on the forehead. No blood was flowing, but all around the head wound, there was already too much blood spilled. Also, a lot of blood rests about six feet beyond her feet. Something had to have been there to spill all that blood. Whatever it was, it's gone now. I saw nothing else dead in the area. Nope. Just one body. If Kitten was that human before, and the human is dead, the body is elsewhere. *CAW.*"

Shelley cocked her head towards me. Her eyes were piercing my brain. "*CAW!* If you killed our Sandy, you won't last the day out here, Kitten." Something about the way she said my new name made me cringe.

"No, no, Shelley," said Karl, who stepped in to save me again, placing his enormous frame in front of my small one. "I witnessed

Kitten's human soul leave the body, but I'm pretty sure Sandy stood in her yard still breathing at that point. I hightailed it out through the back forest to the feral nest. I didn't see who did it, but it wasn't Kitten. His human form was already dead and gone when Sandy was still standing."

It was too much and too confusing. Was my body gone? Sandy murdered? My tongue extended, and my breathing became rapid as I struggled for oxygen.

Suddenly, the familiar roar of my silver Beemer 7 series called to me, announcing itself as it arrived with Jules behind the wheel. She slowed and stopped at the top of our drive, got out, and had a quick chat with the plainclothes officer. He pointed to the front door, and she followed him into the house. Even from a distance, I could clearly see Officer Ewen Keens acting all puffed up as he tried to impress my girl. He didn't normally wear plain clothes or work as a lead detective. He must have been in the neighbourhood at the time the call came out over the police radio.

At least Jules wouldn't find my dead body. As much as I wanted justice and the murderer caught, Jules would have a bit more time to believe I was still here for her. If I wanted justice, I would have to get it for myself.

After twenty minutes Jules came out of Sandy's house, walked slowly back to the Beemer, and then brought it up our driveway to park.

Karl turned to me, took his big furry paw, and pushed me down once more to a prone position.

"Ok, Kitten, you're on. Act sad and hungry. Mew your heart out when she comes up, and then go with the flow. Do what comes naturally. Your instincts will kick in if you let them. But suck up fast so she becomes sappy and thinks you'll starve without her. This is your only chance. I can't be babysitting you all my life, and you'd never survive out here otherwise."

As Jules parked my Beemer (I guess her Beemer now), Karl tore off towards the west lot in the direction of the deer.

"Do you know any bees personally?" I called out, thinking that now we had good reason to use the bees. I could find Clare, but we also might discover the identity of the murderer and achieve justice by having an afterlife chat with Sandy.

"Later, Kitten," Karl yelled back as he disappeared into the woods.

Jules arrived at the front door. She is so like her mother. Jules loves this cabin and its quiet seclusion. My girl is suited to this rural life. She kayaks and, as a well-trained police officer, she knows guns. But she is a gentle soul, my sweet Baby Bear (she cringes when I call her that).

I put on my best performance. Karl was right. It did come naturally. I rolled onto my back, bared my belly, and wiggled my frame, achieving complete cuteness. I pitched my voice high.

"Mew, mew, mew, mew, mew, meeeeeewwwwww."

Jules looked down at me. I may have been terrified earlier by the sight of my fur and claws, but from my daughter's perspective, I was a tiny kitten, about six weeks old, eyes open, with the smallest paws. She fell in love with that ball of brown, gold, and black and my fuzzy little belly. How could she help herself?

Jules gently picked me up and cooed, rubbing the top of my head with her index finger. "Did you get lost from your mom, little one? Someone must have dumped you here. Poor little fella. Are you hungry? Come in with me and be my little buddy." She reached for the door handle.

"Touchdown!" I declared in my best football vernacular.

Shelley and one of her cousins roosted in the branches above the car. Two for joy. A third and then a fourth crow joined her—a girl and a boy.

Chapter 7

I would tell Karl later that I had a new name, so I could stick it to Karl. Hawk was unrealistic as a first name. It commanded the respect accorded to a dangerous, fast, strong, taloned apex predator. That was not me anymore. I had been a human hawk in the courtroom, and I would not let go of that part of my humanity, no matter my fur coat and size. Bill Hawkins was no longer; I would be known as Buddy. Or perhaps Buddy Hawk. I would find my killer and swoop down upon him and destroy him.

It had been a hard day. Now safe and at home, I couldn't stop myself - I yawned widely, showing my wee teeth. Jules cooed again as she turned to the front hall closet and retrieved Clare's soft woolen tartan shawl. She carried me down the small hall off the kitchen to my office. Already half asleep, I thought, "How dare she put a smelly little *cat* in my office." Yes, I was confused and tired and forgot that I was that smelly little cat.

"This will be your safe place for now, little buddy. You're welcome to come out and explore whenever you feel ready." Jules rolled up the shawl into a loose ball, placed it on the floor in front of the desk, and set me on it.

As I lay in my new bed, my mind raced and kept my body awake a bit longer.

Had Karl set me up? He'd brought my human self down the drive to Sandy's place. That's what started all of this. A giant moose working for Karl could have butted me dead. Coyotes or wolves could have dragged away my sorry human butt to eat in the woods. Karl and I didn't like each other in life, so why would death change anything? How much did he hate me? Who else worked with him? That crow—Shelby or whoever. She spat on me. Maybe Karl dumped me at the front door in a guilty moment of remorse. Karl and I would have a chat as soon as he came back. Then I shook my head. Get your head on straight, Hawk. No feral could have set all of that up. They're just dumb animals.

I recalled there had been a chemical odour just before I died. Something had been wrong there. Sandy had surely not called out to a head-butting moose. She had smiled but then extended her right arm forwards as if pointing to someone and yelled, "No!" I didn't think she could speak moose. And Shelby (whoever) said a shovel covered in blood lay in the yard - the obvious murder weapon. I was likely hit with the same shovel. The crow saw two pools of blood, but a large pool was quite a few feet in front of Sandy and couldn't be from her head. That's where I'd been standing.

Seriously overtired, my mind wandered. Why would Karl, or any animal, kill Sandy or kill with a shovel instead of teeth or claws? Would Karl ever work with the coyotes?

How the heck could I get justice and catch my killer while being stuck in the house? I had no ability to communicate about the details of the case, even with Jules.

I turned my nose into the shawl. Clare had been gone for months, but my kitten nose was able to pick up her strong scent. I picked up a poignant, special sweetness that used to rise from her skin as it combined with her favourite cologne. Glorious! I closed my eyes and laid my head down as if on Clare's shoulder and kneaded the shawl. Clare's smile played in my memory alongside the scent, and I once more felt her love. Let go? Never.

I fell asleep dreaming of the black sands of one of our favourite Cuban beaches, holding Clare's hand as we gazed at the brilliant red, orange, and yellow of a Caribbean sunset. I could swear I felt the warmth of her sunbaked hand. Even if the colour red had disappeared from my waking world, I could still recall and dream of Clare and the colours of our love.

It was a very deep sleep. When I woke, I'd forgotten my situation. Clare's scent was vital to my peace. In the remains of REM sleep, I sought her shoulder and moved to kiss her brow, but it was nowhere to be found. I looked around and in shock, yelled, *"Meow!"* It all came rushing back to me. My personal nightmare. Sandy had shouted. Karl had pulled me out of a woodpile and dumped me at my front door. A hawk had flown circles above, waiting to swoop down and eat me.

As I stretched awake, my sniffing nose followed a trail of sweetness to a saucer of warm milk likely laid out by Jules. As lactose-intolerant Bill Hawkins, I didn't drink the white stuff. I was more of a single-malt guy. But Buddy Hawk reacted with his new olfactory sense. I drooled and pulled myself up onto all fours. I arched my back, shivered through some leg stretches, took another sniff of Clare, and then went for the milk. I had to admit that was some darned fine cow. My belly distended. The remains of that saucer were the white mustache and goatee on my face.

A quiet buzz filled the air. I recognized the sound and immediately recognized my freedom. A search of the room led to my cell phone, dropped behind the desk, and still plugged in. I kept the sound turned off because I didn't like the disruption of bells ringing or songs chiming in a demand for attention. The phone had landed on the floor unnoticed.

Well, I certainly can't answer a phone call if all I can do is meow. But then, it happened—a miracle! The buzz followed by a quiet *ding* announced a text message. My wee right paw would fit the size of the screen on my phone. I could handle a text. I could do this. I had never set up facial recognition. I still knew my password.

Padding down from the mountain of shawl beneath the desk, I successfully swiped from left to right with that little paw. I then tapped out my four-digit security code and voilà - access to the net. I could hardly contain myself.

Merwoow!

With access to a phone, I wouldn't have to meow or chirp or even dance like a bee for Jules. I could just text her. Access to my phone would change everything. I now had the ability to communicate fully with the human world. I could access police investigations through Jules and help gather the evidence to find my murderer. When I did I could simply tell Jules who they were and where to pick them up. We would make a perfect team.

Jules might balk at her father's informal oversight of her actions or the decisions of the rural police administration, but she would ultimately accept my wisdom. I would just ensure that they all did their jobs with integrity. My wisdom should be welcome if offered with grace and detachment. In my heart, I was grateful for the distraction her job would give us both.

I tried tapping the phone icon. A text message from Jules waited for me. Typically, her texts tended to run on.

Dad. I don't know where u are but come home it's so sad Sandy from across the road was found dead this afternoon. Looks like she was struck on the head with a blunt object. I can't say more but the officer leading the investigation is Ewen Keens he said he found your credit card on the driveway. He wants to talk to u wants to know what u were doing over there and if u saw anything unusual.

It would be difficult for Jules to investigate the death of our friend and neighbour. Maybe it would be better for her if Ewen didn't bring her into the case.

Then a second text.

They've pulled me off the case cuz u r a person of interest.

So much for access to the investigation through Jules. If the police didn't find my body, coyote fodder might still be the reason. Had the forensic team arrived and analyzed the second pool of blood? They weren't acknowledging it. But then Ewen was in charge of the investigation and he was not the brightest. Nothing would be available as long as they shut Jules out of the investigation, for Cat's sake.

Why had Ewen classified me as a person of interest? And as for that moniker, he might as well have just said I was the *prime suspect*. They clearly wouldn't have evidence to point to or prove the guilt of any specific individual. Now I see they aren't even looking for someone else. They latched on to me. That's what it means to be a person of interest.

I wasn't stupid enough to respond to any request to come in. My inclination was to assume the police would say I killed her and take a shortcut to build a flimsy circumstantial case based on finding my credit card in the driveway. If they confirmed some of the blood in the backyard was mine, would they assume Sandy tried to fight back? They would hold me without bail, set a trial date, and do nothing more to find Sandy's real killer. Was I paranoid, or would they jump at the chance to prosecute a retired criminal defence lawyer? And what about *my* killer?

I stared at the text message until reality came screaming back. Hand me over? A kitty criminal? I laid my head down on crossed paws. Who was going to put a darned kitten on trial? What could they do? Lock me up at the pound? Have the vet put me down if they found me guilty? I can't hold a shovel with these front legs and baby paws! How do I testify in my defence? *Meow, meow, meow,* and *meow*? I simply couldn't hand myself in because I didn't exist any-more. That was the end of it.

But if I disappeared completely, it would destroy Jules's trust, the trust of her colleagues, and her career, as well as break her heart. And so soon after she lost her mother. I had to give her some excuse. I would need time to move the investigation in the right direction. I would need time to develop a story for myself and get her back on the case.

Swatting the reply bubble, I discovered my paws were small enough to type a response.

I intend to take a train into the city to meet old friends and assist with a murder case there. I won't give you an address. I'm not trust-ing this until we know more. I've been in criminal defence far too long to get pulled into a police station with that person of interest line.

The phone dinged.

DAD. What are u saying? Come home right now! We can clear this up don't leave me alone!

Honey, if I came in, they would hold me. It won't help your career if I come back. They won't look for the actual killer, and they'll just charge me and fire you from the force. We both know what person of interest really means. I'm staying put until you or whoever on that force has some sense. Start investigating to find the actual killer.

No way Dad. U r being too suspicious. I would not let anyone treat u that way. Besides, what excuse am I supposed to tell them? My dad doesn't trust u and refuses to come in? I can't say that! God Dad just come home!

She had a good point.

Tell them you couldn't find me, that I'm not answering my phone, and that you assume I must have gone back to the city to work on a case. They can put out an APB on me, but I promise you they won't find me. And make sure you erase this message from your phone. When you know more could you text me? Or if you want, tell them I'm in Tibet. They won't find me there.

If I have no choice u r really making this hard on me but I miss u and love u Dad.

And then, considering my actual position, I added:

Also, a neighbour found some kittens in a woodlot, and I asked them to drop off one at the door. I hope this was OK? I thought you would like a kitten to keep you company. Oh, and before I left, Sandy told me the feral cats prefer wet food over kibble.

She texted back right away.

I found the kitten on the doorstep they shouldn't have just left him there an eagle or hawk could have picked him up. I got to him in time though and he's sweet but small and likely a runt though he's long-haired and looks like a little painted lion. I'll run him over to the vet to get cleaned up and shots and look into getting him fixed. Males are very aggressive and spray I know you hate that stink. GTG. TTYL.

Fixed! My legs trembling again, and I began to pant again. I texted back.

NO! Don't fix him. That's animal cruelty. I will not allow his mu-tilation. Let him grow up to be a complete cat!!

She had stopped texting and shut down her phone. But I knew Jules would receive the message later and hopefully in time. She would check for a new text before she deleted the conversation, wouldn't she?

Chapter 8

The initial transition to kitten didn't go that well, and I was not surprised at my instinct to remain human to my fullest ability. I used to burn the midnight oil preparing for hearings sometimes up all night. Sure, taking constant kitten naps off and on all day long was bliss! But there was more to the instinctual part of learning to cat that would take some getting used to.

After another full day of napping to de-stress, a low rumbling purr deep in my chest followed a long full-body stretch to wakefulness. The fragrance of Clare's shawl of love kept me lingering.

The bizarre events to date demanded that the murderer be uncovered, but how would I influence the investigation without Jules's aid? The police needed to move in the right direction to uncover the actual killer and not sit there waiting for me to come home and hand myself in. That was never going to happen.

My phone and texting ability afforded me full web access. If I didn't have to show my pussy face or talk, I had the world at my paw tips. Learn to cat! I don't think so, Karl. My cellular lifeline would remain plugged in and hidden under the desk.

Oh, and there's nothing like reading a morning paper in the bathroom. I could stream the news right beside the shreds of paper I used as my litter. How apropos. Do kittens drink or even like coffee? That warm milk was an excellent replacement.

Thank the Cat the slight buzz or ding from my office phone wouldn't be audible in the living room and kitchen.

Then I looked from the litter, left to the phone, right? I turned left and then right, left and then right. My ears flattened against my head, and I hissed for the first time.

Litter! Oh Cat, no. At some point, Jules would come home and change the litter paper. When she went to recover the box, she would discover the phone and then remove my lifeline! I would die all over again. Or even worse, Jules could clue in that I texted from my home office. She'd question if her father was lying about taking a train or staying with friends in the city. Or would she question whether the person she texted with was even her father? Knowing I lied would hurt her. I wanted to delay her inevitable pain. Please, great Cat, not yet.

A black plastic garbage pail rested under the desk. It was not used so there was no reason to empty or move it. If only I could push the phone behind it. Could I nudge the phone with my nose? Ouch— that didn't work. I tried to shove it with my right front paw. Interesting, since I'd been left-handed as a human. That got me nowhere. I had the strength of an oak . . . leaf. The odours rising from the litter paper prodded my instincts. Karl's advice had been to go with the flow and learn to cat. Maybe he was right.

I squinted at the litter and then closed my eyes to release my inner cat. My furry frame turned to back up to the phone, and my hind feet kicked out - one and then the other, one and then the other. I choked as I breathed deeply to take in the smell of used litter, but this thought motivated the foot movements needed to push hard, crusted sand to bury an imaginary nasty cat poop. With no education, I found the action came naturally.

Success! The cell phone moved, and with my Herculean efforts, it slid across the carpet until it rested at the back of the garbage pail where it lay hidden from view—just in time. My head snapped around as I caught the sounds of the front door creaking and Jules calling out, "Here kitty, kitty! Buuuddyyyyy!"

I ran out of the office double time but couldn't gain any purchase on the pine planks with these teeny kitten claws. My body slipped and slid across the length of the kitchen floor to land at her feet evoking a peal of giggles from Jules (a joy to my ears).

"It's high time we checked you out to make sure you're healthy, little Buddy. We need to clean you up before you visit the vet," Jules announced.

I was about to get my first lessons about how to cat and the accompanying horrors they undergo.

With no place to hide, Jules had me gripped by my neck, rendering me completely paralyzed. It didn't hurt. It was natural to slump under the scruff grip. It was the same method Karl had used to carry me home. Being held high by my scruff offered a full view of the kitchen counter before Jules dropped me down beside the sink. There was a large yellow volume with black print, entitled *Cat Care for Dummies*. I thought Jules had been a natural expert.

My ears flattened at the sound and odour of musty, salt-treated well water rushing from the tap. Steam rose to my face. My human self was never much of a swimmer, but he was very much a hot tub kind of guy. Not anymore. My love of hot tubs had ended.

I squirmed and struggled for my life when Jules dunked me into the sink and began to thoroughly wash and rinse me in the shallow, lukewarm water. The smell of the soap made me gag. The rush of water past my nose convinced me I would drown by the end of the day. I began to pant and wheeze, shiver, and shake, as much from my terror as from the chill on my wet frame. Would I pass out? Horrifying!

I recalled being told that cats disliked water. This is a lesson in how to cat that I would not soon forget.

Having borne the humiliation and survived the near drowning I finally relaxed with the rubdown from a warm towel. I tucked my wee head deep into that towel to rest and forget.

The worst was over, I thought. But enter the blow-dryer. Engineered by the devil and hot as Hades, it screamed at me. The evil blow-dryer had completely compromised my dignity by the time Jules shut it down. My hair stood straight out and transformed me into a giant dandelion seedhead. Jules giggled and referred to me as her little fluff ball; a name I would not be sharing with Karl.

After such a torturous start to my day, Jules pulled out a cat carrier from the front hall closet. We hadn't previously owned one of these. She must have picked it up earlier and stashed it while I slept.

I squirmed. She shoved me in. The carrier, a simple grey prison had the essence of new plastic and lavender-scented laundry soap on the folded towel on the bottom of the carrier. This was not the preferred scent of Clare's shawl. Jules may have meant the towel for comfort, but to me it did not bode well. The towel was already associated with the bath and the blow dryer.

Jules grabbed the handle and headed outside to my beautiful Beemer. Jules had adopted my fanatical approach to car care. She maintained this thing of beauty meticulously, both inside and out. I looked forward to relaxing in the familiar territory of the Beemer. My back arched with the fear that only a cat experiences when the engine roared. Immediately, a strange tingling rose up my spine as the fur from my forehead to my butt took on the shape of an arch. The 7 Series is one smooth ride unless you have feline sensitivity to mechanical noises and vibrations. In my head, the sound came from the most beautiful engine, but in my kitten heart, the world should not shake, vibrate, bounce, or roar. I panted and hissed and *meeeooowww*ed to no avail. I would not survive this new hell on wheels, and as a consequence, a spot of poop dropped onto that towel. More humiliation.

We made it to the vet's office. Could it be all that bad? Veterinarians were just animal doctors and so would be sworn to do no harm. It's not like they would be giving me a prostate examination. But as Jules brought in my cat carrier, the essence of stress hormones from animal terror and death overwhelmed me. Jules cooed and *awe*d and petted my forehead, but as she pulled me from the carrier, I squeezed my eyes shut and shivered again. She shoved my head into the crook of her arm when I started mewing madly as we entered the examination room.

The examination room was hospital white, the metal table shiny, but the scent of fear was all-encompassing. A lab coat came into the room. Jules introduced me and my story, and the vet manhandled my frame like a stuffed toy before she brought out a needle. A slight pinch at my butt, and suddenly nothing. Dead again? Would I come back as a bug this time?

Clare held me close in my dream, sitting on our Cuban beach. We didn't talk this time. When I awoke, I was relieved to find myself in the office on her shawl. I was alive. I was not a bug. It had only been the first of many vaccinations.

A small plastic bin with a handful of fresh sand replaced the paper. I dragged myself up and wobbled my way to the back of the garbage bin to confirm that the phone remained available. I considered trying out the new litter box. If I had been fixed would I be sore in that general area? Oh, the humiliation!

Skipping the litter, I proceeded slowly, walking with my hind legs apart as far as they would go until arriving in the kitchen. Jules dropped to sit on the pine floor beside me, cooing compassionately and rubbing my forehead. I didn't purr and considered a bite and scratch would have been justified for the day from hell if she had been anyone other than my daughter.

Time to answer the big question. My eyes followed down to my nether regions. I breathed a deep sigh of relief. Thank the Cat. Still intact. Jules laughed at where I sniffed. "I'm afraid you're a bit young to be fixed, pal."

You could bet I'd resend the text message to remind her to leave me alone when I *was* old enough to qualify for the snip.

Jules got up and pulled open the refrigerator. No one can live long on warm milk. It's all fine and good, but it is not a meal that stays with you. I spied raw hamburger, which she removed from the fridge, offering me a small bit to eat.

I couldn't contain myself. Steak tartare - my favourite! A flavour to be relished. I chewed the first morsel a bit too quickly and gagged but kept it quiet so as not to discourage her. In the meantime, two more small round tartare balls dropped beside the milk bowl, awaiting my attention. It was a proper meal, as good as you would find in any of the top restaurants in the city. Organic meat always satiated my hunger; all was almost forgiven.

After I feasted, Jules and I had an hour of play. I leapt and raced at feathers on strings that she dangled just out of my reach. We pretended to hone my (never to be used) hunting skills. Eventually, Jules rendered a final pat and says, "Gotta get ready for work, Buddy."

Jules called out from the front door. "Later, Bud! See you after work."

I followed her voice, intending to wave goodbye from the dining room glass door but reminded myself not to act too human.

In the kitchen, I found another tartare ball beside the milk bowl. I would save that for a snack later. Jules had left the office door open so I could go in and out at my pleasure.

She had left the toy on the ground. My thoughts took me to the mouthy crow—Shelby? I shredded the feathers of the toy in record time. Vengeance was mine. Meow.

Chapter 9

Alone again and no longer tired from attacking the toy bird, I headed back to the office to my phone to Google the local news. Nothing was reported about Sandy and nothing about William Hawkins - whether she was killed or he was missing. Nothing.

A basic search of the most obvious suspect, the husband, revealed a possible motive and opportunity. I had originally thought Sandy was a widow. Local gossip informed Jules the husband was in prison, but Sandy had told me he'd recently been released but had not come to visit.

Googling with surprising ease, I accessed a website that is used to search property titles. Sandy's had once been held jointly with her husband. Now, ownership listed only Sandy's name. Someone would be getting the house under her will. Would that be enough to kill for?

One rag confirmed that Sandy's husband, Albert Cox, had been jailed and had been recently released. So he had the opportunity. The article described his sentence as twelve years for negligence causing death in the operation of a motor vehicle. Odd to receive the maximum sentence. He had been drunk, passed out, and struck another vehicle, killing a child. Not good, but twelve years was just too long for a first offence. Was his lawyer that bad?

The article focused on his repeated account that his wife had been behind the wheel and that he had been falsely accused. In the end, Sandy's testimony had been the opposite of his and more believable to the jury. The husband could still be asserting his own innocence and Sandy's guilt. Such a powerful accusation and consequence would undermine any marriage. I suspected the Coxes had divorced. I'd have to check this. And Mr. Cox could well want revenge if he was innocent, and after his wife so adamantly supported the Crown's charges.

Yes. Al Cox was an excellent murder suspect. The police should have been picking him up the moment they discovered Sandy. But Ewen Keens was not the brightest bulb.

I had stiffened, sitting stretched out before the phone, and got up to tour the house. There wasn't much more I could do sitting inside my office researching on a cell phone. Perhaps an escape through a window would allow me to take a little walk across the street?

First the dining room, then the bedrooms, and finally back to the kitchen for some water and the other tartare ball. I chewed. I considered. Jules hadn't left a window open. I had no access to the crime scene. The forensic results were in the hands of the police. I wanted to know if the murderer had left fingerprints. What had been the source of that chemical odour?

All the frustrated speculating tired me out. I was a kitten. I needed another nap. I tried out a new spot to sleep. The dining room held lovely, warm sunlight that beamed brilliantly through the glass of the door. With my recently acquired feline sensibilities, and drawn by the sauna-like comfort in the heat of the sun, this was much better than a hot tub. I stretched out on my belly to let the sunbeams warm my butt, still sore after the immunization needles, and yawned.

I contemplated my limitations and got a bit teary, sniffling over my position as an indoor kitty and the thought of going under the knife when old enough. I prayed to the Cat that Jules would not ignore my request to stay intact. How can they call it *fixed*? More like destroyed. You lost your masculinity. Don't get me wrong, there were no hormones raging through me. And it wasn't like I would consider any lover other than Clare. I worried whether my tiny *mew* would ever become a full *meow*. If cats could sing, would I become a bass or stay a soprano?

Perhaps I should let go and cat full time. I would never find a killer being stuck in this house and in this tiny body, even with Google access.

These thoughts vanished at the sight of Karl's snout on the other side of the sliding glass door. He carefully examined me from the tips of my ears to the end of my tail. As he got down to the nether regions he declared, "Oooohhh . . . I was worried when you left in the animal carrier. I hoped you would get the jab and not the snip. I'll have grand kittens from you yet if you can find a mate who appreciates your smaller stature. If not, then that's OK. I can always rely on your brother, Daryl."

I took it all in, surprised at Karl's plans for me. "I have no interest in mating, so don't count your grandkittens." What I really wanted right now was to look at the murder scene.

"Do you have any idea how I could escape this house?" I asked.

Karl lifted a paw and tapped on the screen outside of the window. I could see his claws come out as he scratched and started a tear and then stopped.

"This material looks pretty flimsy. You may not be able to cut it, but I am pretty sure I could. But not here. I suggest that we do this somewhere that won't be readily noticed."

Was he helping me? I thought about the best hiding spot. "There is a screen porch out back where the screens go all the way to the floor behind a couch."

We met up on the back screen porch. Karl had already started on the screen behind the couch with full claws, scratching and ripping until there was a small flap, big enough for my body to fit, though too small for Karl.

"Thanks. I'll just jog over to Sandy's place and look at the crime scene for myself."

"Are you sure you're ready for that? I can't just let you take off across the lawn in full view of the eagle. What specific route did you intend to take?" Karl frowned.

"I'll keep to the bushes. Don't worry about me." I was confident to the point of arrogance as I slipped through the screen and jumped down to ground level.

Everything was big. I'd forgotten. I walked, pushing my way along the edge of the house surrounded by long grasses mixed with weeds. There was a hedge along the side of the property that would provide cover, but I needed to traverse 20 yards out in the open to get there. If I hugged the hedge until I got to the road, I also risked running into the foxes or coyotes lurking in the forest. If I stayed hidden, I would still eventually have to cross the road and Sandy's well-kept lawn to get to the back of her property. There was no cover. It was not safe if I caught the eye of the eagle.

I would have to trust it to fate, I thought, as I ran my heart out down the barren driveway, ignoring the hedges and grasses.

It was not far before I could hear a series of repeating high-pitched screeches and looked up to see a juvenile yet still large eagle racing down the length of the drive, aiming for me. I stopped in my tracks, wondering where I could go. There was no bush or rock close by. The eagle swooped down in my direction, so close I could feel the air pressure that surrounded its frame. I was stunned, unable to move. Just then, a familiar pull on my neck sent me flying sideways out of the range of the eagle's inexperienced talons. It had missed me by an inch. Karl had scooped me up and ran me around to the back of the house, back to the hole in the screen.

"If I had seriously thought you'd take off like a fool without a plan, I never would have ripped that screen. Did you not hear me the first time I told you about the eagles? And what about the coyotes? They should be coming out to hunt very soon if they haven't already. What were you thinking!?"

I wasn't thinking, but Karl knew that already.

"So, you say I have a brother?" I had hoped the original conversation would be a distraction. Karl looked down at me, took a deep breath, and sighed as I jumped up to the hole and crawled back inside the house.

"Yeah, he was the only other one I could save from the coyotes at the woodpile. I have him stashed in a barn." Karl stretched his legs and neck and smiled broadly. "He's quite a strapping fellow and already eating mice and voles which he catches himself," Karl bragged about my brother. He had never stood so tall when speaking with or about me!

My tail flicked back and forth. I had the sign for irritation down pat. With a human father, I did not need Karl's paternal approval. Daryl's actions didn't impress me. My so-called brother was obviously not reincarnated if he was eating live rodents. Disgusting! I preferred my steak tartare. It wasn't a question of taste but of class and the expression of my continuing humanity.

But Karl had also implied I just wasn't cat enough to find a mate. I needed to stand up for myself. My tail flicking gained in speed as Karl turned his back to me and looked out at the river.

With his back turned, he could likely still hear me, even if he could not see me directly.

"Does Daryl feed you too? Like Jules and I feed you? Does he save you a mouse or two?" His lack of respect put me off. I had made an effort to provide for him. He utterly failed to appreciate my giving nature. If I didn't calm down, I'd flick my tail right off as I stood breathing heavily and sending my own small snot balls all over the screen.

"And you don't value or even recognize my intellect. The amount of kibble was reduced, and Jules introduced more of the wet mush you said you liked so much. Did I get the credit for working on your behalf? I simply informed her of your preferences, and I didn't need to dance to do it." I could brag too.

That got Karl's attention. He whipped his head back and stared hard into my eyes. "How were you able to pull that off?"

"You don't believe me! Hah. I texted her." I figured he wouldn't understand that and would be even more impressed when I explained. I continued staring at him speaking slowly. "A . . . communication . . . machine . . . that . . . humans . . . use. A . . . cell . . . phone." Now it was my turn to treat Karl like the fool.

Karl perked up and lifted his head to stare me down. It was a bit creepy until I understood he was reading me. "Fascinating. Have you tried using Google or other websites to find Sandy's killer?" Karl was a quick study and a fast mind reader, pulling all the background out of my mind. He anticipated the usefulness of my discovery and quickly brought me back to what I should have been working on instead of sunning myself and mewling like a moody runt.

I explained the phone's limits. "The cell phone may be helpful in researching the background of possible suspects. It can inform our analysis of motive and opportunity. But it doesn't give us reliable evidence of identity. I need to get on location for that. I was trying to see the murder scene to look for clues. The police should have gathered forensic evidence."

"Maybe we could go look at the backyard together?" Karl said without conviction.

"Not wise right now," I said. "You barely saved me from eagle today. I'm not sure you are equipped to protect me and battle all coyotes coming out," I replied. There was also the possibility that if it was a coyote, Karl would take off to make his own escape, leaving me as fodder.

Karl probably read my thoughts and didn't defend himself. Rather, he turned a few circles and then lay in the spot of sunbeam he'd chosen. A chipmunk slipped from its den not four feet away, and like lightning, Karl ran off giving quite the chase, zigging right and zagging left until the creature dipped back down into another hole. Karl then returned to his spot in the sun.

It was time to clear the air. "Why did you bring me to Sandy's when I was still a human? Did you see who killed me and Sandy? Or were you part of it?" I wasn't entirely sure how to read whether a cat was lying or being truthful by its facial expression, but I took the shot.

"My intention was to show you the type of food that Sandy left out to inspire you. Then the chemical stench hit me, and I hightailed it back to the woods - fast. I recalled that same stench all around an abandoned trailer in the back lot behind Sandy's place. I smelled it myself."

Karl didn't move a muscle, and he glanced upwards as he sought the memory.

"A feral colony tried to take it over two winters ago through a rust hole in a wheel well. They were all found dead together inside the trailer. They weren't wounded or eaten or harmed physically. We suspected poison killed the clowder. Humans burned the trailer down."

Karl stopped for a moment and then looked down at me.

"Nope. I wouldn't hang around and have the same poison take me out. So, no. I didn't see who killed you and Sandy. Stick that where your tail sits high!"

His facial expression and the intensity of his eyes were no different than when he spoke earlier of his affection for Jules. If you could read a cat's expressions, then he had passed the test.

We could come back to the chemical stink later.

I also remembered the bee mythology. It would be much easier to identify the killer by getting a bee to the other side to ask Sandy, who had killed us. Jules would follow up and find the necessary proof to rocket her into detective status.

Karl had curled himself into a large fur ball in the sun. I had to get out the next questions before he fell asleep on me.

"Karl," I asked, "do you know any bees personally? Ones that can travel to the other side and back? You were talking about that earlier. I hoped to rent one or whatever it is you do."

"Rent?" He rose and snarled as he shook his head. "What is wrong with you? You don't rent animals. You obviously have not started to think like a wild animal yet. But even your past life human self would know better."

I hid my recollections of a local riding stable with horses for hire. Karl didn't understand the human way. To distract my mind and create a privacy barrier, I took a couple of swats at a fly that had landed on the other side of the screen. The movement and *bop* sound would scare the fly. It was a perfectly harmless action no different from when I had chased Socks or the crows in the front yard.

Karl watched my antics until the fly gave up. He then picked up a small stone and flipped it back and forth between his front paws as he taught the lesson. "You shouldn't ask for help from another animal. It's poor form to request help from any animal, be it fur or feather or even a bug. But if you must have help from a bee friend, you explain the necessity and ask for kindness. You bow deeply and call him *sir* or *master bee* and make no direct eye contact. You must be respectful and submissive. Something to offer a bee, like honey or sugar or a fresh flower would be welcome. It's not a trade. It is to be offered as a gift to support their survival. The offer creates no obligation."

How was I to know? I was just a kitten. This was getting complicated. "My sincere apologies to all animal-kind but please contact your bee friend for me. If I can't view the site, maybe your bee can find out the truth about my murder and the death of Sandy."

I attempted to explain it all to Karl (likely unnecessary, since he could see into my mind). "Don't you see? It would be easy to ask Sandy who killed us. She saw someone and tried to intervene. It was the last thing I remember. She could name or at least describe him. This would complete the investigation in a flash. And no eagles."

Karl let the stone drop and quietly shook his head slowly from side to side again, murmuring the feline equivalent of tut-tut. He was losing his hard-won patience.

"I know bees. Lots of bees. I'm not calling one in if you plan to embarrass me. First, don't offer to rent them. Be respectful. Are you even capable? You can't expect them to go back and forth at your request on a whim. Prepare a gift of flowers or honey to give them strength. How are you going to do that?"

I rolled my eyes. I knew it was too dangerous to be outside, but my life was pretty much over if I was to be locked up in a house.

Karl sighed and tutted again and flicked his scraggly tail. "I'll be there to do all the talking. My bee friend may help even without an offering. The request must be important to all animals, including the bee population. As well, you can only make one request. Don't expect more than one free shot. I'm not confident you would show appropriate respect. I'll have to do this for you."

Got it. Treat the bee like a Superior Court judge and hope he's in a good mood. If I could request only one trip, I hoped the bee would talk to Sandy, but maybe he could also check on my wife, Clare. I would just slip that in.

Chapter 10

Buuuzzzzz.

A giant bumblebee butted the sliding glass door. I mean huge. Did I still suffer from an allergy to bee stings in this small kitten's body? A bee that size would put me under fast. Best not to make him upset. Fortunately, I was isolated on the right side of the glass.

Karl was sitting about a foot from the glass. He bowed deeply with both of his front legs. As he turned back to me, Karl formally introduced Bumbler as the bee circled his head. I was on. I moved as close as possible to the glass and mimicked Karl's bow before beginning my presentation.

"Good afternoon, Mr. Bumbler. I would greatly appreciate it if you would assist me in obtaining information from the other side." I held my bow a bit too long, but a little extra time in prostration should help to emphasize my sincerity.

Then I lifted my head slightly and tried to ingratiate myself by smiling broadly. Bumbler still buzzed circles around Karl's head. Karl kept still, showing no emotion or movement. Hopefully, I wouldn't screw up.

"You may know of Sandy's demise. The human who lived across

the street. I was a human then and was killed at the same time. I didn't see who did it. If Sandy remains on the other side, she might identify the murderer. Whoever killed me likely also killed Sandy," I explained. "Also, while you're there, please ask for others who may know me. My wife, Clare, may be there. If she is, would you ask if there's anything she needs? I love her and miss her, and I want to ensure her comfort. Oh, and can you ask the dead me if I have any information?"

"Buuuuzzzzzz buz uzzzz?"

I did not understand the bee. I don't know if it was my young age, inexperience, or if bees block their thoughts by buzzing.

Bumbler landed on the terrace and suddenly flew right into the glass in front of my nose, twice. I couldn't leap back fast enough and was about to speak when the bee landed again. He turned his butt to me and wiggled it. I didn't hear what he was thinking, and I didn't know what the buzzes meant, but I could guess by his rude behaviour. Karl stopped me before I made a snappy comeback, raising a paw directly in front of my snout as he turned back to Bumbler.

"I know. You don't have to tell me. I'm sorry, Mr. Bumbler. I agree—Kitten is both rude and stupid. He doesn't yet appreciate that he's actually here and can't also be on the other side at the same time. He's only a kitten. Please be patient."

"Buzz uzzzz?"

"It should be safe. This is his daughter's home. She's a human police officer trained to catch killers but is kind to dumb animals like Kitten here. He'll survive under her roof."

I glared at Karl as the bee raised himself into the air and circled around Karl's head again. Karl continued. "More to the point, you'll recall Sandy used to leave out clean, cool sugar water in a dish for you and your brethren. I think we were all treated well at her house. The murderer has taken Sandy from us. He didn't eat her or take her nectar. The killer should pay for such an ugly and cruel murder, even by our laws. I'm sure you would agree."

"Uzz uzzz buuuuzzzzzz." And Bumbler left.

"It'll just be a bit," said Karl.

Karl and I moved back to the front of the house, away from the broken screen and to the sun-drenched flagstone terrace. I felt safer behind the solid glass of the dining room doors.

I lay back in the sunbeam that had become my private sauna. The perfect spot as the sun crept across the floor of the dining room. Karl lay outside in his spot, a larger sun-drenched area, and in no time, he was snoring. I decided to wake him up, turning back to our discussion.

"Why couldn't I understand your bee? And how does he get to the other side?"

Karl swatted at a fly that bounced and buzzed against the window. "See that kid? Flies buzz and you don't understand them either. You're young and Bumbler wasn't prepared to lower himself to speak directly to you. He blocked you. That allows him to talk behind your back when he is in your face."

Lovely.

"As for how he travels, no one knows. Trade secret I guess."

We two lounged in the moving sun spots without speaking. It only took about ten minutes for the bee to come dancing back, buzzing excitedly. Karl raised his head, yawned deeply, and eventually turned back to me.

"Sorry, kid. Bumbler says Sandy's not there. She was reincarnated like you, and at about the same time. The bees are most interested in finding her. She did consistently leave them sugar water, and they want to offer support to protect her in her new incarnation, if that's still appropriate. It depends on what or who she is now. The bees are out looking for her, but she could be anywhere and anything in the world. She could even be a fly if she did a serious wrong during her life. Just don't get your hopes up."

Sandy was well prepared to let go before she was murdered. Yet reincarnated? Why? She had to learn something? She had to repay a debt of some sort? I probably would never know.

"And my wife? Is she somewhere back here too?" I asked this quickly with growing excitement.

"*Z.*"

The bee sat down in front of Karl. That can't be it, I thought. One *Z*?

Karl translated. "Bumbler says she remains on the other side. He found Clare to be a lovely being. With everything resolved and having said her goodbyes, she let go of life and is now established happily on the other side. Clare keeps an eye on you and Jules all the time and will always be close to help. But she wants you to let go yourself. She wants you to learn to cat so you can join her someday. She loves you and will wait until you're finally ready to join her."

It felt like Karl was pushing his own agenda.

"The bee said all that with one *Z*?" I asked attempting a smirk with my snout.

"*Buuuuuzzzzzz buzz.*"

"Also, Bumbler says some creep named Daniels showed up when he arrived looking for a friend of yours—Franny. Daniels was immediately shifted out and down - if you know what I mean."

I snapped to attention. Fran?

On my last day before retirement, the Crown Attorney had called me to wish me luck but also to break the news that one of my clients, Fran, was gone. He asked if I intended to take the defence as my final case. At the time I sat comfortably in my profession. It was not necessary to accept everyone seeking my service.

Fran was known as the mother of mobsters, working as a bookie, handling substantial accounts for local heavy hitters. After so many years, she had become a friend. Fran had been murdered outside her home - run down by her own car with her husband, Charlie Daniels behind the wheel.

Daniels was a small-time hustler - a greedy nobody who reeked of nothing going nowhere. He was always searching for and never finding the next sleazy deal. He had no legitimate skills, criminal or otherwise, and wasn't even a good liar. His rap sheet was as long as my arm, but it was all petty. He would have run her down for the insurance money and her "book" which would have implicated her clients.

The thought of Fran's murder was crushing to me and so the thought of Fran's murderer wishing to retain my services was ludicrous.

Now, it was with great joy I learned justice had caught up to Daniels. But if Fran wasn't up there?

"Is Franny on the other side?" I directed the question directly to Mr. Bumbler. Karl again raised a paw to the height of my snout, once more intervening to stop my questions. Bumbler buzzed off, showing speed that rivaled a Beemer in the passing lane of the autobahn.

"Nah," said Karl. "Fran's been here for almost a year. She's a pal. We call her the Nose."

I jumped up and down with excitement like a dumb kitten. What were the chances that Fran ended up reincarnated in my neighbourhood? Had she been monitoring my retirement over the last year?

"Is she another feral?"

Karl tipped his head to the left. "No. She's a fox. She had hoped to have a litter with Everett so long as Sandy was able to cure him enough to allow them to get close safely. But with his mange, we all stay away from good old Everett. The cure won't be happening anytime soon now that Sandy's gone."

My head was spinning. I settled down on my belly with my front paws crossed.

Clouds had covered the sun and my sunbeam, but they had moved on by now. My sauna returned to the dining room as it left Karl's spot. Karl got up, stretched his legs, and shifted closer to the dining room door to pick up the last of the sun before it left the terrace altogether.

I was relieved to know Clare was OK. She didn't get reincarnated but could watch over us (if Karl hadn't made it all up). Sandy was back somewhere. Who knows where? There would be no help from that direction.

There were no simple answers garnered from the other side. I would have to rely on more traditional investigative techniques. Fran would know how to help.

I explained my interest in the fox to Karl. "Fran is a long-standing family friend. I'm excited at the possibility of seeing someone who actually knows and can understand the real me. She also has direct experience with crime and investigation."

I turned my head away from Karl, hoping this would help to block my thoughts from him. But I was too excited. Fran knew how to help me, and she was in the neighbourhood.

"You want contact with someone that will help you avoid learning to cat?" I swear Karl smirked.

A fox. Of course, Fran would secure a fox. How is it I drew Karl's runt kitten? It was how my luck had been going recently.

I had read about foxes from the Japanese Kitsuné stories told by my favourite fifth-grade teacher. Fran fit the mold.

In her human incarnation, Fran had had many skills you'd expect of a fox. She was a naturally mischievous and magical fox spirit able to control and influence humans.

Fran had been a major player in the gambling scene and had made wads of cash for herself and her bent-nosed backers. She was a brilliant statistician, estimating lines and point spread to advantage. Fran wasn't just a strategist; she was also charming, brighter than most, and resourceful.

Fran had been a bit of a loner, able to evade the police and any convictions for her crimes for most of her career (with a little help from her brilliant defence attorney). Witnesses against her in court disappeared so her backers wouldn't lose her skill set to prison. Yes, a Franny fox made sense.

So how did this older criminal lawyer bearing the nickname, the Hawk draw the runt card? Who would play such a cruel trick on me? To be brought so low.

But oh, it would be so nice to speak with Fran and gain from her experience in both lives. Jules could be encouraged to restart Everett's treatments if he was truly worthy of my Fran.

Karl lay there in the small remaining patch of sunlight and made no comment. Was he listening in? I got up and paced. I had to make my case to Karl. If he had been listening in on my thoughts, he wasn't offering to help me yet.

"Karl. Franny and I go way back. She would be a real help in my investigation of the killer. I know it. I'd like you to contact her for me. I'd love to reconnect," I said with an expectant smile.

Karl was getting close to a nap but suddenly lifted his head.

"Not on your life, Kitten. I said she was a friend, but it's a cautious relationship." Karl stared out at the road. "She has an excellent nose and can sniff out dinner even under a pile of snow. We both like our rodents, or rongeur, as Franny says, but it's also known foxes chew on kittens if they are hungry enough."

Karl looked back at me. "She and I, so far, have a mutual pact. I leave her future pups alone if they're ever born. She agrees to stay away from my kittens. But you can't fully trust her. No matter what we've agreed to or even if she likes you, she's still a fox. Her intended mate is also a large, hungry fox. Where one is, the other is close by, and I have no pact with him. There can be no trust until you're much bigger. God knows how you'll be reincarnated the next time around if she or Everett eats you. Nope. You are staying in that house."

I pushed my body sideways against the glass and purred feigning an appreciation for his concern, but I wouldn't give up. I tried to reason with dear old dad-cat.

"She won't gain access to the house. There's no way Jules will ever let me out to be eaten by coyotes or friendly foxes. Couldn't you bring her to the window? It's purrrrfectly safe." I purred and rubbed again in front of his face. "Maybe we can put our heads together about the murders. She dealt with lots of them in her old life," I said, using Sandy's death as the lure to get my way.

Then I pulled out the big guns. Eyes as wide as possible, smiling ever so sweetly, I cried out in my most syrupy sing-song manner, "PUUULLLEEEAAASSSSE." (Heck, it always worked on me for Jules when she was a kid.)

Karl furrowed his brow and shook his head. "No."

Just when I revved it up for a second plea, a small, beautiful fox peeked her long snout around the large spruce tree out front. I assumed the fox was red in colour, though it was a colour no longer within my palette. To my feline sight, the fox was grey. One dark ear rotated towards Karl's position. As she trotted up, I recognized those magnificent blue eyes. Could it be? Franny?!

CHAPTER 11

"Mon Cher. I smelled a chaton. This is one from your litière?" A beautiful small fox spoke to Karl in a phoney French accent as she sidled up to my feral father and the glass door. Karl placed his body between her and me even though the glass protected me perfectly well. The fox stretched her neck, peeked over his shoulder at me, and burst into a brilliant smile of recognition.

"Hawk! As I live and breathe in my new den, is that Mr. William Hawkins?" The fake French accent had disappeared.

"Is that you in the teeny fur suit? You should have been a judge by now. Not a runt kitten in the middle of nowhere."

"Fran, Fran, Fran!" I jumped with stupid kittenish glee once for each repetition of her name. "I can't believe it! The Queen of the Book. Mother to Mobsters. Cook to the Crooks. Finally, someone I can talk to."

My reflection in the door's glass revealed a smile that stretched bright and glowing from ear to ear. "You know your murdering husband is also dead now. A bee said he passed over and then went south. Deep south and I don't mean Georgia."

Fran smiled wider and winked.

"I talked to Bumbler myself," she said. "Daniels got what he deserved, trying to make money off my books by blackmailing my old pals. He should have known better than to mess with the mob."

Karl had been listening but now let out a low growl, playing the protective father to which Fran retorted, "Settle down, big fella. We have a pact. I heard about your litter, and I'm sorry. Our agreement remains intact. I would not and did not touch them."

Karl grimaced. Fran continued.

"Seriously, I know Hawk. I wouldn't hurt a hair on his now furry little butt, even if he smells like cotton candy. Besides, I can't get to him through all that tempered glass, so relax."

"Just so we're clear," said Karl. Fran nodded and then stretched out, placing her front paws so close to Karl that he winced and backed up a few steps. Karl's back fluffed, and he snarled.

I turned to Fran and laughed.

"You will, of course, remember when I tried to talk you into getting a gaming license to make your business legal." I looked from Fran to Karl. "I told her she should incorporate, eat up the profits through salary, and all she had to do was establish her operations as a charity."

Karl was mute and disinterested, but Fran had laughed then and laughed again now, though with a quirky fox chuckle.

"The only charitable donation I would make was to my own wallet. My backers were not exactly charitable sorts either," said the fox.

"At the time, you said it felt wrong," I said, and I fell to the floor laughing and holding my front paws to my belly.

Karl was not just stoic; he was at a complete loss. He could have learned but wouldn't take the time to understand the meaning of words like *gambling, incorporation,* or *charity.* He moved on to the principal subject. "We have news about the lady across the street. The one who was trying to help old Everett, your boyfriend."

That got her attention. Fran went still. "Only just got home. What's up?"

Karl and I caught Fran up on the local events since her rebirth as a fox. This included my move to the neighbourhood, the death of my wife, Sandy's death, my death, and the disappearance of my corpse. I told her about the experience of arriving to find out I was a kitten and introduced her to my new name. I added that Karl had duly delivered me to the hands of my OPP daughter. Finally, we explained the failed attempt to investigate using the bees. I added that my one advantage was access to the net through my old cell phone. Fran understood what that meant.

Her snout dropped in a futile attempt to hide the welling tears as she murmured, "Haven't you guys been busy." And then, "My poor Everett." She stood up on all fours as if she was about to leave.

I couldn't let her go. I needed her help, and she understood life in the human world and this one so could serve as my translator into the wild world. Karl's previous warning that you didn't rent animals or trade for them—you showed respect and kindness—ran through my mind. I trusted Fran's instincts. If this Everett was who she wanted to mate with, that was good enough for me.

"Wait, Fran," I called. "I understand Sandy used to give Everett medicine. I wanted you to know that I can use my cell phone to text Jules and have her take over his treatments if you would like."

Fran shifted her snout to point back to me and responded, offering a soft-eyed, grateful half smile. "Thank you, Hawk. Or should I say, Buddy? Have you had the pleasure of meeting Everett? He is so completely different from Daniels. A true gentle fox. He's so kind. And smart, as . . . as a fox, hah, hah. I know once Jules treats his coat and skin, he'll be as handsome on the outside as he is on the inside. Thank you."

But then Fran added, "That will not last forever, you know, Hawk. Your daughter will find that phone eventually."

My instincts were right. This was the first that anyone tried to warn me of the risk I was running by relying on that cell phone. Fran recalled her human life, but I didn't want to face reality right now.

"It's plugged in," I answered. "If she finds it, I'm still a cat in her house. In the meantime, we must find the killers before the cell phone becomes obsolete."

I turned to Karl. "How 'bout we try some old-fashioned investigating? The first stage of any serious investigation is to review the site of the murder and bring in a forensic team. But without the police reports, we'll have to inspect the scene ourselves."

I then invited Fran to be the lead. "Your nose might sniff out clues. You have good eyes. You could carefully evaluate the murder scene before it's disturbed and you lose any scents."

Fran's large eyes grew and she stared with intensity when she looked back. "Remember, pal. I said I don't do charity."

Then suddenly she smiled. I thought I caught what sounded like a chuckle. "Nah. Don't worry your pussy butt. Anything for Sandy and you, Hawk—I mean Bud."

And with that, Fran was off, galloping down the drive towards Sandy's backyard. Fran knew exactly what I wanted. Finally, some action!

I was going to reinstate Everett's medical treatment, and maybe there should be a bowl of sugar water left out for the bees as well. I'd have to remember to text Jules.

Karl and I lay back down in our now shady spots waiting for Franny's return.

I returned in my mind to the strong chemical odour in Sandy's backyard. How had that smell related to the death?

Before the clouds had even cleared the sun, Fran streaked back across the street, panting to get her report out. She had picked up the scent of blood from Sandy, and she already knew my human scent from our prior life. (She had both a good nose and an excellent memory.) But there were scents of other people at the location that she didn't recognize.

For sure, one would have been the killer. But how to tell the difference between the killer and the police or the forensic unit? Fran was too new to the neighbourhood to help identify anyone specifically.

I asked if she'd noticed a chemical odour. A shudder ran through her shoulders as she replied, "Meth lab."

Chapter 12

I nearly jumped out of my fur at Fran's news.

"Who? What? How would you know that? Are you sure? Are you saying Sandy was a drug dealer? Impossible!"

I brought some experience to the field having dealt with the drug trade as a criminal defence lawyer. Pretty ugly players had supported Fran's human life and business interests, but I never suspected either Fran or Sandy would be involved with drugs - let alone cooking crystal meth. Fran cooked the books. She worked the odds. If she'd been smart, Fran would have avoided the drug trade, which was traditionally full of idiots.

As for Sandy, she could not be a drug dealer. Period. She had been in her mid-seventies and a knitter when she died, for Cat's sake. Sandy cared about all the animals in the neighbourhood. She was quiet. She had no one odd hanging around her place, though that nephew was a bit of a loser. But really, neither of them fit anyone's picture of a kingpin drug lord.

It turned out Fran had extensive knowledge of the subject.

"My clients made money in different ways. I picked up enough on what was going on, staying away from that side of the business.

It's well known that this area is the source of a lot of meth production that has been finding its way into the city."

Fran was confident in Sandy's innocence.

"The meth stink at Sandy's is new and confined to the shed. I knew Sandy well. She tossed hamburgers with medicine to Everett. I rid her yard of vermin as a thank you. That brought me close enough to get a whiff of Sandy and the house. She didn't wear the stench of a person running a meth kitchen. I never picked up the chemical smell around the rest of the house or even around the shed before today. The dude who offed you both was likely the one setting up a kitchen and hiding his stuff in that shed. There was one person's scent at the scene that I didn't recognize, and that is the one that had the stink of meth on them."

Fran was done with her report. She crouched low near Karl. I didn't speak, but they probably listened to my thinking process as I paced.

The meth was connected to someone else. It had to be. At the time of my death, the shed was behind me and so was my killer. If we were going to identify this mysterious person, we'd need more help, human or otherwise.

I recalled Karl saying he smelled a similar scent that had poisoned a feral colony. Could that have been a meth lab as well?

"Was the chemical smell the same as the one in the trailer?" I asked him.

He responded curtly, "Yes. I didn't know what it was at the time, but it was on the lot immediately beyond the woods out back of Sandy's place. The trailer was burned a couple of years ago and the humans removed the shell last spring."

With my phone and access to the internet, I had a way to find out who owned the lot.

Karl snapped, "Why don't you just Google it?" That wasn't quite how to do it, but I wasn't going to explain this to an obviously angry

Karl. He had been unusually quiet until he offered his short, snappy suggestion. This spoke to a growing shift in his normally carefree and callous temperament. He usually looked bored all the time, yawning, lying down, sleeping, or walking away in the middle of a conversation. But now he had been sitting at attention and had been deadly silent. It reminded me of his intensity when he would stare at my human self from the flagstone terrace, judging me through the dining room glass door. That was it. He was judging me once more.

Fran trotted back to the grass out front and stretched her lanky body out in the sunshine. Karl didn't move but I would deal with him later.

I trotted back to the office to conduct a quick title search of the lot at the local Land Registry Office. I got a name. I would pass this on to Jules, but since the meth kitchen had obviously been shut down at least two years ago, and with the trailer gone, I doubted this would be helpful.

I returned to the dining room to plan the next steps with the others. Fran had crept behind the silent Karl where she lay half-hidden from my sight. But I was back to pacing.

Only a coordinated effort of animals with useful skills and abilities would let me draw any more information from the crime scene. I got excited at my own thoughts and danced a bit of a circle. I had access to some animals with differing skill sets. A more experienced nose? Perhaps air patrols from the crows could be employed though I didn't exactly get along well with Shelby.

Karl then snapped again, "Shelley," correcting me. "Or why don't you rent an eagle?"

I ignored him but his tone and demeanor indicated something was definitely wrong.

Older noses would have a greater chance of identifying specific individuals who left their smell in Sandy's backyard. Maybe Everett's nose was old enough. I'd have to ask him.

I noticed Fran now had her snout right down, hidden behind Karl's swishing tail. I couldn't even catch her eye. I was dancing and twirling and pacing, absorbed in my planning. But something was off.

Karl had been too quiet and too snappy and Fran was hiding.

I finally gave in."Is it Fran? Are you angry she's here to help me? What's wrong now?"

Karl turned away from me for a moment as Fran skipped backwards to make room for a big, angry feral cat. We waited. He dramatically turned back and maintained his silence for a good long minute. Finally, he spoke.

"Did your experience with Bumbler not teach you anything?"

(He meant the rent business.)

"In addition, Kitten, all you can think about is your own murder. You keep reminding the world that no one is looking for your murderer and that Sandy was not the only victim. Now you want to rent all of us and for strictly human business?"

I was right about the rent business, but there was more to it.

"Neither of you cares about the other murder. Remember my litter? There were once three kittens," said Karl.

"There were no other kittens when I arrived in this fur," I declared. That made me wonder what had happened to the original personality of the kitten I inherited. Somebody else wore the fur for 6 weeks before I arrived.

Karl was listening.

"My original kitten was shoved out into a different incarnation as you took over," said Karl. He then turned to Fran just as three of Shelley's family arrived in the tree above his head, followed by a fourth.

"But you knew this, didn't you, Fran?"

The fox ducked low and turned her head away. Karl turned back to me.

"Only you and your brother Daryl are left. What about your sister Floosy's murderer? Do you even care about your sister? Do either of you care about your fellow animals?"

Floosy? I hadn't known that I had siblings or that one was missing. I'd talked a lot about my daughter. Karl had said nothing about his. Did he not have the same relationship? Things could be different in the animal world. My eyes widened as I leaned towards Karl.

"I didn't even know there were any other kittens, let alone a sister. And what kind of name is Floozy?:

"Not Floozy like some painted-up human. It's Floosy. And I named her," said Karl. "You humans keep attaching human names to every animal you see and when you do, it sticks. This time, I beat you to it and came up with my own."

"Floosy isn't even a name and Daryl the feral? There's a name and a half!" I said.

"You pronounce it Dareyel," responded Karl.

"You made that up. I heard you correctly the first time."

I was avoiding the real issue and had to admit that even if I had known Floosy existed, I wouldn't have placed the death of an animal above, or even equal to, the deaths of humans. Was I demonstrating human privilege? I didn't recall Karl ever mentioning anything about family but he was right. Humans would not treat her murder with the same gravity.

Of course, Karl listened to it all and went for my soft white underbelly. "How do you expect any animal to offer help to find human murderers of humans when you don't give a cat's toot for animal murders or the punishment of their killers?"

Karl was right. If I wanted help with the investigations, I needed to win over the animals. Right now, except for Fran, they all hated me. I couldn't ask, and I couldn't rent them. I was going to have to do something grand to gain their support.

Karl growled deeply from his chest as both his eyes narrowed and his ears fell back flat against his head. "We know it was those coyotes who took her. They should be driven out."

His bald hatred surprised me with its intensity. If he already knew who the culprit was, what more could I do?

I tilted my head to the left and said, "I don't think I'm big enough. It strikes me that coyotes are at the top of the food chain." I didn't mean to sound snarky, and hopefully Karl knew my intent.

Karl slowly turned back in my direction. "Walter."

Franny immediately leapt from behind him and faced Karl, her blue eyes wide and a frown on her snout. "Walter? Are you crazy? You don't want to waste his time. You know he'll never lift a paw against those coyotes unless Session is held first and then only after we prove the coyotes were the killers. Even then, Walter won't punish any coyote unless you prove it's necessary to protect his cubs and not just the rest of us."

Karl snorted, "If his lordship, Buddy, wants help from us, he can repay in kind. I know Bud's mind and his background. He knows legal processes and so he can run Session and use his skills to present a reasonable case - strong enough for Walter to take action."

With that, Karl took off, still in a huff with Fran trailing behind. "Fran and I will scent out the feral den in the morning to confirm the murderer's identity." With that, they were both gone before night fell and the coyotes began to hunt.

We would be investigating not two but three murders, and I needed to be a major figure in the new animal investigation. And if I argued successfully to drive out coyotes for the good of all, I would secure the indebtedness and aid of the animals without the need to rent them, as my dear old feral dad would say.

I didn't know any animal named Walter or what Session was or how I would prove the guilt of a coyote. And I could not trust Karl right now. What mischief was he up to?

Chapter 13

Fran and Karl would be gone for the night. I returned to the office to check in with Jules by text before sleeping. Part of me hoped Jules got her hands on the police forensic report. Did they know about the patches of blood that remained on Sandy's lawn? How could an experienced cop miss it? I lay on my belly in front of the phone and swiped, opening the text bubble to Jules.

How is that investigation going? Any leads on the murders? Are they still expecting me to come in?

Jules didn't take long to respond.

Murders? Do you mean Sandy? As far as I was told there is only one. No one will tell me a thing. What r u talkin about.

Sorry, honey. I meant the single murder of Sandy. How's the case looking? Any leads yet?

Don't know I'm persona non grata been pulled from the case and denied any access because of conflict of interest. That would be u Dad. But I saw a shovel pretty sure that was the murder weapon. Had blood all over it. Will try to squeeze some info out of the investigating lead Keens. I don't get how he is lead. Guess you have to be born here.

Isn't Keens the one who keeps asking you out to the Legion? The good-looking one?

Yeah don't get ideas Dad something's wrong with that one. U know the kind of guy that pulls legs off of frogs during recess? Ewen is popular at the station he has an in with the local losers. He gets info on what's going on in the underbelly of this town but he's about as smart as a bag of rocks. He's supposed to be in charge but pulled a real rookie move at Sandy's forgot his blue gloves and picked the shovel up before it was bagged and tagged.

My lids snapped open, and my eyes almost fell out of my furry face at the thought.

All looks, no brains. Had he understood the prints of the actual murderer would be smudged by his stupid paw print?

Good one Dad. Paw. LOL. No he's not the brightest bulb on the Xmas tree. Forensic team had a fit. At least Keens doesn't believe you're the murderer. I'll throw him a bone and maybe go for a coffee.

I asked about the chemical odour. I wouldn't expect a drug lab to be set up at Sandy's or that a drug lord hung around with her. This was high-end rural living, and we were in the country. I believed everyone in the countryside lived clean, healthy, and happy lives with homemade soup. A lab boxed in the garage meant one person at the scene of the murders carried the stink of drugs on their body, so maybe the smell could be traced.

Hon. This town is a bit of a sleeper with farmers and kayakers. But are you aware of any drug dealers working up here? It pertains to a case I'm dealing with back in the city.

Again, she came back fast.

I didn't want to worry u but yeah this area has lots of guns and drug traffic. We busted a meth lab at a house in town a short while ago a sting operation with the Kingston police.

Is Keens on that one?

NO. Some people wish he was and could use his local contacts to help. I might have to buy the coffee to see what I can get from him. The lab disappeared it was gone by the time we arrived. Someone must have warned them they moved the equipment. All we got were traces of meth and some fentanyl. The landlord is in Florida so we charged the renters but they were just some old '60s stoners probably couldn't maintain their own pot plants let alone manage a substantial operation. They were probably just getting paid to sublet part of their space.

And Dad, you'll like this Ray Tickborne is the defence attorney. Remember him? Had that wee problem with cocaine, cleaned up moved out of the city to escape the lifestyle? He set up a criminal practice in Belleville.

Ray was not atypical. I knew a few old-school criminal lawyers who got too close to their drug clients. Ray bought into the myth that some drugs can enhance performance with a snort or two. Realistically, how do you deal with the worst of society and not become jaded? Clare and Jules had grounded me. Ray had no one except the wrong friendships. In the end, he got smart and removed himself from the scene to clean up before he destroyed himself.

I tapped back.

Hopefully, Ray will pull out the names of the real culprits when he questions his clients. Maybe they can offer some names on a plea. If you find out who was cooking and transporting the product, let me know. It may relate to a case I'm on. Oh, and if you think it would help, I could give Ray a shout and try to nudge him in the right direction for you.

No Dad I've got it. I can talk to Ray it's my job. Let me do it. Stay out of it. Promise.

That girl was testy. She didn't have to know what I did. She would thank me later.

I know you can do your job, Honey. Also, I did pop in to say goodbye to Sandy before getting on the train. It was my last chance to spend time with her before her procedure on Saturday. SANDY WAS ALIVE AND WELL when I was at the back, but a weird aroma wafted from the garage and it reminded me of the smell of a meth kitchen. I'm no expert, and I suspect your people have already followed up on that.

They can't take me off everything. Keens said he uncovered evidence of a possible meth lab stored in boxes in Sandy's garage. Problem is he charged into the garage and discovered the equipment. Idiot put his big mits all over everything. I'm not sure what I can do with this.

But the two meth kitchens had to be related. Only one person could have been running such a substantial drug operation in a small community (if Fran was to be believed). There would be no room for competitors. The likely location that hid the town meth lab was Sandy's shed linking the two cases together.

If someone got smart and offered a plea deal to the renters for the names of the real kingpin, we might identify our killer at the same time.

I rolled over and stretched out for a minute before going back to the text bubble. How would Sandy miss someone moving a drug lab in boxes into her shed? She must have known, but I still couldn't believe she had been involved.

Jules. Have you considered nudging the Crown to offer a plea deal to the couple that was renting the house where you expected to find a meth lab? Make a deal for lesser charges or a lower sentence if they offer the name of the person running the show. It's just a thought.

Obvs Dad we r on that already. My boss is still pushing me to get u in for questioning on Ewen's case. Can u call them and just talk or do a Zoom call? Do you still have your train ticket it would support an alibi. I'm getting worried about you it's lonely around here. There has to be a better way to handle this that doesn't involve you hiding in Tibet.

I can't come in if you won't let me out of the house. I imagined myself trying to meow my position through the phone. *"Mew, mew, mew."* Zoom this puss face? How would that be helpful?

I am not setting myself up to have a call traced. You can tell them I'm not available and not answering my phone. As far as you know, I'm off to climb Everest and will call from the peak if it has cell service. That should hold things for a while. And don't forget to erase these messages. We wouldn't want your sergeant to uncover your involvement in this conspiracy to support my continued freedom.

I imagined she held her head and sighed at this point. I had that general effect on her.

This is a lot of pressure how will they trust me at the station if this is how I start this job? But I'll keep up the pretense for now you owe me big time Dad. I'll just call you next time and come home soon miss you. TTYL

This would not last. I needed to come up with something. Would I have to learn to cat and give up? Let her think I jumped off that mountain. They'd never find the body in Tibet. But that would also mean I died. At that thought, my heart ached for my daughter. Would she ever be able to move on if I just up and disappeared? It was too soon after her mother's death.

I lay down on Clare's shawl again and shut my eyes. They promptly snapped back open. Where *was* my body? And where was Floosy's body? Perhaps Floosy was eaten by coyotes and maybe I was too. Or maybe bodies were yet to be uncovered?

Entrenched in these sad and gruesome thoughts, I got up again and went online to research the correct treatment for Everett Fox. Jules would have to pick up ivermectin at the local vet to add to tasty meatballs. I didn't know how long Sandy had been treating him, so we would have to start over.

I opened another message bubble.

You need to purchase ivermectin from a vet. Sandy used that drug to treat that mangy fox from across the road. I think we should fin-ish the job in her memory. I've read that you add it to meatballs and feed him each day for three weeks and then once every ten days for another month or so. Also, while you're at it, can you place a bowl of sugar water outside for the bees? And don't call. Just text. I have poor service and the calls get dropped.

I hoped she wouldn't erase the earlier messages from me before she read that one. I'd check at a later date.

I hoped my excuse for not calling to talk was sufficient.

CHAPTER 14

Clare's shawl called out to me for a quick forty winks and perhaps some advice. If I dreamt, I didn't recall.

When I awoke, the smell of fresh well water and steak tartare drew me out to the kitchen. Jules must have slipped home at some point. I made a quick trip to the dining room to search for signs of Karl or Franny in the yard. No one yet.

As I leaned back on my tail, patiently waiting, Socks, the singing grey-and-white feral, came by to check the empty kibble bowl and then left without a sound. Not in the mood to sing? Come to think of it, I hadn't been blessed with his caterwauling since my reincarnation.

Shelby or Clam Shell (whatever) swooped in for a bite of kibble too. I tapped on the glass door to get her attention and waved hello. She glared back with beady black eyes and flew away. Not even a caw. I shook my head. Seriously? What did I do? Chasing a crow away from the house once should not deserve the social death penalty.

Two deer graced the front lawn, elegant and grey. My kitten ears twitched, and I tried to pick up the sound of their hoofs as they strode elegantly towards the road along a well-worn path that brought them through my lot. Nadda. The path continued across the road and along the side of Sandy's lot to the forest beyond. The deer and I had seen each other when I had been human. The last time I saw the smaller one, Darling, she had scowled at me with real menace. I hoped now they were used to me as a kitten and would come over and formally introduce themselves. I was lonely and wanted to ask Darling what my prior human self could have done to cause her ire. But this time she followed her sister without looking back, disappearing into the forest.

Why did the animals hate me? And how would I find my killer or Sandy's or even Floosy's? I knew nothing of the wild world. It didn't want me. I lamented being stuck inside, an indoor kitty, alone.

I was about to turn back to the office when out of the corner of my eye, I caught sight of Karl emerging from the west wood. I batted repeatedly on the glass of the door to attract his attention.

Karl trotted across the lawn to the front terrace and faced me with a broad, toothy sneer. "Fran picked up the stink of a coyote. The pack killed feral kittens last year and got away with it. This time, we got them," declared a triumphant Karl.

In his eyes, they were responsible for everything wrong in our little neck of the woods. But I also trusted Fran and knew the other animals respected her sensitive and reliable nose.

"OK, but did she pick out an individual? I didn't think coyotes ran in packs."

"Google it," Karl retorted. (I later learned they might run in packs or hunt individually.)

"My point is did she identify anyone in particular? Or anything or anyone else? How many coyotes are even running in this neighbourhood?"

Karl snarled back, "The pack is five strong. We know them to be kitten killers. All of them. We lost litters last year and in past years. Everyone knows they did it. This time we have the evidence. I'm going to get Walter and call for Session."

I didn't know how Session worked or what they expected of me. I called after him. "Wait! It's too soon. You can't condemn all coyotes for the actions of an individual. That's not justice. It's not fair or right. I haven't even spoken with Fran. What am I supposed to do here? What the Cat is Session?"

Karl ran like a streak of brown lightning towards the back of the house to the riverside. Rumour had it that a bear's cave had been found down by the river. Walter's home?

What was Karl hiding from me?

I knew he could not be objective and he was trapped in preconception and false logic. Kitten deaths in the past by coyotes would be formally classified as character evidence. That type of evidence could not be used to infer guilt unless there was a clear, distinctive pattern to the murders, other than the type of victim. Karl had offered no facts that would unify the events. No, this would not hold up in a human court. Animal court shouldn't be different but then who said it had to be just and fair?

I guessed Session to be some sort of kangaroo animal court and assumed he expected me to act as some sort of prosecutor.

The prospect of getting back into a court was enticing, and the kitten in me drooled at playing the Hawk once more (though that name was not based on a killer instinct, but on my peculiar style in front of a jury). I had stood tall in my courtroom, waving my arms at the Crown's allegations about my clients and shaking my fists to demand acquittals. The resultant flapping motion was always a sign that I thought I was about to lose the case. It was theatre at its worst, and I was the lead actor. The flapping Hawk.

I had not done a lot of jury trials pre-retirement. Most people came through my office guilty. They knew it. I knew it. The Crown and police did a fine job proving the charges. It was no longer about justice. All that was left was to negotiate the sentence on a plea. I traded my once-renowned advocacy skills for the art of the deal. I argued for reduced sentences agreed to in the back rooms to honour my clients' life challenges that led to their crimes. By the time I retired, my high horse bowed its head low.

I didn't know the process or the laws. If Karl wanted me for my human skill set, I had to think like the lawyer I used to be. I didn't think plea deals would apply to the coyotes. It was not long before I realized it all would depend on Fran.

Was there a smoking gun? Had Fran excluded other scents or other animals? Had she identified a single perpetrator? Even if there was good evidence that a particular coyote or his mate was responsible for the fate of last year's lost litter, this was not relevant to the present. Again, it's evidence of character and that's not enough.

One thing I understood was that in the animal world, identification relied primarily on scent. It was as good as DNA. But evidence of a specific bit of fur or even a witness could corroborate Fran's interpretation. Someone who saw them take Floosy would be a real asset. Someone who had overheard something peculiarly damning, like an individual's howl. Or maybe someone would admit that Floosy had been a tasty treat. It had to be information from a source so convincing that it increased the probability that the accusation was truthful.

Last-minute confessions happened only on TV. I was sure coyotes probably wouldn't admit to Floosy's murder or disappearance. They wouldn't want to face the judgment of an angry bear named Walter.

I paced back and forth before the dining room door. It was a busy night and an almost full moon. Coyotes would also be out hunting. A statement from the accused would be handy, so I strained my neck at the window searching the growing darkness for a four-legged shadow on the prowl.

With my questionable kitten night vision, I saw Jarrod Bailey, Sandy's nephew. He arrived in a jeep and hopped out, jogging straight through to the backyard with a six-pack of beer. The kid landed in one of the white plastic chairs at the firepit. He leaned for-wards, used a blowtorch to light the fire, and then quaffed his beer. He seemed harmless enough.

Despite the flames, it was hard to pick up anything more than a vague movement in front of Sandy's. Still, I could have sworn some-thing like a large dog ran across Sandy's front yard right behind a cat. Maybe Socks. The cat leapt up a tree and disappeared into the upper branches. My distance vision was no longer what it used to be and the doggish silhouette disappeared quickly.

It didn't matter. Coyotes wouldn't come close enough to the house to allow me to even ask for a statement. Besides, I didn't know what to ask. "Did you kill kittens?" Like I'd get an answer to that one.

What was Karl up to? I needed Fran.

Chapter 15

Back in the office, I pulled out my phone and did a quick check for Facebook cat videos. I hoped they would be an excellent way to research how to be an indoor cat. They were embarrassing, to say the least. Learn how to cat? Pffff.

I finally hauled myself onto Clare's shawl and, with eyes closed, allowed her sweet wisteria and jasmine scent to envelop my body and soul. I fell into a dream and called to Clare. I wanted to tell her of my fear of how this would end for our daughter. My poor darling daughter. She had lost her mother. Now she had lost her father.

Clare's bathing suit was the whitest. Her hair had grown long - the way she'd worn it when we first met. Her skin was golden-tanned. Her smile eclipsed the magnificent setting sun at the edge of the horizon, as brilliant as the diamonds of light kissing the waves. She had always been a beauty. I could relax in this dream and find peace in her eyes. She laughed and splashed, dancing along the waterline. I could stay there all day. She finally came up from the water and dropped beside me onto her towel.

"You're going to have to tell her the truth." Clare looked into my eyes and chuckled. "I would love to be a fly on the wall when she finds out you're a kitten and that she almost had you fixed."

I stopped rubbing my heels into the sand.

"I love you, but you're crazy," I said. "There's no way I can tell her I'm a cat. She wouldn't accept it, or she would think she'd gone nuts herself. Or worse still, if I could prove it and she believed me somehow, she would have to accept me as dead and gone. She just lost you, my love. We can't do that to her again so soon. She still needs her father."

Dropping to my back, I let my shoulders relax into the sand of my dream. Just speaking to Clare comforted me. She could solve all my problems. When I shared them in the past, she always had the right solutions. I wasn't ready to hear it this time.

Clare rolled onto her side. The aromatic scent of suntan lotion caught my attention when she planted a quick kiss on my forehead. She smiled brightly. "But Hawk, she won't have lost you. You two are the team that you always were. You're not doing cat very well. You're not letting go of your old life or me. You might as well do Hawk for a bit and not do cat until you think she's more settled. But with you, even as her cat, she'll still have the best parts of you, wrapped up in a small ball of fur. She adores cats. How could that not make her happy?"

I closed my eyes and experienced Clare's gentle touch again on my forehead, but when I opened them, a gigantic Jules loomed over me. She stroked my furry forehead with her index finger so gently, like she was touching a butterfly's wings.

"Hey, little Buddy, time to wake up. Do you want a bite of dinner? Maybe watch some TV tonight? *Gladiator* is on again. Dad loves that one, but he isn't home, so you're my partner for tonight. Glass of wine? A saucer of milk? Rome in all its glory? What do you say, Bud?"

Just as I was about to mew my approval, a knock at the door brought Jules quickly up from her crouch. She scooped me up with her left hand, drawing me up to her chest, and as we arrived at the front door, she popped me onto her shoulder. When the old oaken door opened, Ewen Keens stood there tall and in full uniform, holding his hat at his side like some gentleman from a previous century. Pearly white teeth glowed above a sculpted jaw. His pretty-boy blue eyes shone at Jules. His big, dumb, expectant smile was easy to read. Jules didn't want to encourage him and tensed.

"I thought I'd check on you and see if you were interested in grabbing a beer at the Legion tonight. Have you had dinner? They have a fish fry. On me?"

She wanted his help with local contacts that could move her drug case forward, but I didn't think she'd date her way into accessing the information. Too crass for my girl.

Jules looked back at me and the TV. "Oh. I'm so sorry, Ewen. Can't do it tonight. I have a movie date. But let's grab a coffee in the morning before shift."

It thrilled me she wouldn't leave me alone on movie night, even if I was just an excuse to avoid this doorknob of a human.

"Sure, sure." His smile dropped and his chin lowered as he accepted her invitation for morning coffee. "I'll be in by eight tomorrow. Nice kitty cat you got there." And with that he flicked my ear with his index finger.

"Hey!" Jules exclaimed.

"Mew!" I hollered. That hurt! What a jerk!

Ewen offered a quick apology. "Oh Oh...I'm sorry. Poor kitty. I'm sorry. I didn't realize their ears were so sensitive. I thought they were more like fish lips, you know, all cartilage?"

Was Ewen being sincere? "Call my ears fish lips," I hissed.

Jules shut the door, then cooed as she checked my ear for signs of damage. Only my pride was hurt. It's a good thing the door closed when it did. My claws were tiny but mighty.

We headed for the living room to settle in for the night.

"Where are my gladiator sandals?" Jules said. She referred to the fuzzy pink bear slippers she always wore when we watched TV. I tried to be helpful. I stuck my head under the couch and spied the two beasts well within claw's reach. One came out with a swift pull. The second had to be batted a bit before I could get a good grip on the heel. When both were out, I stepped back and waited for Jules' praise. Only then did I realize I might have blown my cover.

Jules stood staring down at me, frowning. "Who are you, cat? That's too weird."

I had wanted to be thoughtful. Stupid mistake. She might throw me out if I acted like some creepy psycho kitten.

I quickly started batting the left slipper hard, snarling and pushing it across the floor, biting and *grr*ing to sell that it was another random toy to me. Jules followed as I flipped and flopped the slipper into the kitchen, then finally caught up to me and picked the slipper up.

"Not a toy, Buddy," she said as she laughed at my antics. Thank the Cat she bought it.

It was glorious sitting on Jules's shoulder, our heads and hearts together. I hadn't snuggled with Jules for many years. This time, I was the small one in the snuggle, but *Gladiator* was still my favourite movie. Jules brought a burger and a beer from the kitchen and a couple of raw meatballs for me. This reminded me to check in with Jules in the morning regarding whether she'd received my message about Everett. He'd be needing meatballs too. And the bees needed their sugar water.

After the movie, I enjoyed another peaceful nighttime slumber with Dream-Clare still trying to persuade me to come clean to Jules. I remained unconvinced that she should be told about my furry status. I'd rather pretend to move permanently to Tibet. And so long as the phone remained plugged in, my charade could continue for many years.

As long as no one found my body.

Chapter 16

I woke to a lovely morning. After completing my ablutions, I trotted to the kitchen for a bit of tartare. Tasty as usual. In the dining room, the clean fresh air that wafted in through the dining room surprised me. The glass door was open with a screen in place. The glorious smell of the yard and trees and mice and foxes in the rain was exciting. It made the fur on my back fluff up a bit.

Jules jammed her hand into the pockets of every coat in the hallway at the front door before emptying her purse onto the table. "Cripes. Where are they? I'll be late for work. I must have dropped the car keys outside," she muttered to herself. Jules ran to my office, presumably to grab the spare keys from my desk drawer.

Five of Shelley's family lined up above the bush. I was getting used to the hints that they offered. With my slightly deficient daylight kitten eyes, even I glimpsed the silver glint of the keys under a bush beside the driveway. I had no way to tell Jules and no one to help show her where they were. After the slipper incident, I wasn't about to point to those keys.

Jules carried a bag of meatballs outside—she must have picked up Everett's medicine and prepared the doctored treats. She dropped off some canned mush and kibble at the usual spot on the terrace for the ferals. The odour wafted through the screen into the house. I must admit I had acquired a taste for the delightful mush with a fragrance now reminiscent of salmon in a lemon dill sauce.

Jules headed to our Beemer but pivoted when she saw that Everett, the mangy fox, waited at the edge of the forest to the west. Jules drew out a meatball and lobbed it to him. Everett knew the drill and leapt to snatch it in midair, followed by another.

The sound of slavering jaws woke me from a sun-drenched doze in front of the screen.

"Fran! Stop! That's Karl's food!"

Fran raised her head, smiled with her perfect white teeth, and winked at me. She leaned into her meal and growled with pleasure, savouring each mouthful before she spoke again.

"It's OK. I met him about an hour ago. He landed a nest of squirrels and is full. I couldn't let this lovely breakfast dry up and go to waste."

"What do you mean, landed a nest of squirrels?" I asked nervously.

"He found a nest of squirrel pups and ate them for breakfast," she replied casually.

Fran's long tongue slowly rounded the inside edge of the bowl to catch that last glaze of mushy flavour. Or was she thinking about Karl's meal and imagining the pleasure of eating wild game? Did I count as wild game?

I stepped back from the screen. I was uncomfortable with the whole predator thing. Karl didn't need squirrels when he had salmon in lemon dill sauce delivered on cue. I set my opinion aside because this was my chance to get the scoop from Fran. I needed to better understand what the animals expected of me in Session and how to achieve justice in that context.

"OK. Hold your horses. This is getting confusing."

I stepped back farther, acutely aware that only a screen separated me and a ravenous fox. I prayed to Cat, Karl's food had satiated her appetite.

"Why is *that* not murder? Explain this special rule that lets Karl get away with hunting and eating squirrel for breakfast without being run out of the neighbourhood by a large, angry bear. How are you culpable for a breakfast of feral à la carte but not squirrel takeout?"

Looming over the now empty bowl, Fran huffed and glowered at me before replying, "Who says it's murder to eat a feral?"

I replied, "Karl seems to think so if you happen to be a coyote."

" I know what Karl has told you, but it depends."

Why were they all so coy with me?

"Depends on what? Don't play me, Fran. Karl said nothing about my job in Session. I have to understand this. I need help."

Fran had finished breakfast and began her lecture while maintaining a respectful distance from the screen.

"I'll explain in legal terms you'll get. In human courts, there are specific defences to a charge of murder. I used to follow you in court to witness your performance in my prior life. One day, you explained justifiable homicide as part of your defence argument. You were fabulous, by the way. With all the difficulty with my loser of a husband at the time, I found this an interesting subject, so I did some research after your trial. You were my inspiration."

Her flattery drew me closer to the screen. Inspiring her to kill her husband was probably not my best work. I became acutely aware of the flimsiness of the screen between us. I recalled her deep growl as she had wolfed down Karl's breakfast; I wondered if she would growl as loudly when chewing on a kitten. The fur along my back stood up as my spine tingled.

"We make similar arguments in the animal world to justify a killing, but they're all based on a single principle - justifiable predation."

Fran's comparisons to the animal world captured this broader principle.

"If people kill in self-defence, whether of themselves or another innocent person, the victim must be in imminent danger of death or grave bodily harm. The victim must only use equal, reasonable force against their attacker. Animals don't limit how much force is justified to protect ourselves. It's all fair game, so to speak."

Fran cocked her head. "Another example which I admit is confusing is human warfare. Soldiers are only guilty of murder if they target the innocent or people already injured who can't fight back. The animal world is always at war. You protect yourself, your mate, pups, kits, or cubs from predators. You have an absolute right to kill your prey to eat or feed your mate or your offspring. In all instances, this is referred to as the defence of Predation."

"There are exceptions that it is important for you to understand," she said as she stood up and moved a step closer, hopefully only to emphasize what she was saying.

"If the victim is not natural prey for your species, you must have evidence of a substantial food shortage. Only then can you justify expanding the hunting territory or your palate."

She added, "It's also different for crazed killings. By this, I mean that sometimes an animal kills because of mental disease from something like rabies or poison."

I didn't expect this to apply, but curiously I wondered if animals were offered psychiatric care or if they were simply put down. Fran answered my thoughts.

"No. No one locks them up or offers medical treatment. Animal justice tries to ensure the crazed one is held accountable even if not mentally responsible. Larger predators like Walter safely put them down to ensure that their crazed activity doesn't continue. Sometimes we've even enlisted the help of humans with their guns and needles if it is too dangerous for Walter."

Fran was an excellent teacher. It made sense (from an animal's perspective) to simply limit the ongoing risk. But again, I didn't expect this to be an issue with the coyotes.

"Most of our predators around here are omnivores," Fran continued. "Walter can eat anything. His natural preference is for nuts and berries and sometimes fish. He'll rarely kill animals for food. It's not unknown or unacceptable, but it's not a preference. If he kills a coyote for food in the middle of a berry field that's packed full and ripe or right beside a salmon spawn, Walter would be considered crazed. It raises a question: Why would he waste his time on a coyote that would fight back when his favourite food was there for the taking without attracting harm or injury?"

This made me wonder more about Karl's breakfast when he had canned salmon waiting. Maybe Karl was a little crazed. Again, Fran listened in on my thoughts. She stood up and took another step closer to me.

"No. We do not consider canned cat food to be prey. It doesn't count."

The lecture continued. "Like bears, coyotes are omnivores. They focus the hunt on live rodents, gather fruit and insects, or eat larger carrion. But they're also known for nibbling on cats or small dogs. Feral kits are the size of a small to medium rat and are not unnatural to their diet."

Fran took a step closer to the screen. She got a bit too close. "Like coyotes, I also hunt rabbits, rodents, birds, and frogs and eat carrion if it's lying there all juicy-like. If it wasn't for our formal agreement and the wealth of mice, squirrels, and birds around here, I suspect Karl would lay charges at my feet. If he tried, I would raise the defence of Predation."

She was implying that I could be the next meal. I quickly wiggled back about three more paces, wanting to add a bit of distance. Much farther and I'd be behind a chair leg.

Fran's explanation left me wondering - Karl's denunciation of the coyotes wouldn't hold up. If they did kill his kitten, it was simple predation. How would he get away with this? What did he think I could do?

As for the process, Fran again described Session in terms I understood so I could play my role in this charade.

"Interested animals will group together for Session. One animal is to act as the Protector. That role sort of combines prosecutor, defence, and investigator. The Protector is not supposed to prosecute the murderer but to prove guilt while protecting the accused from being unfairly condemned. To honour the role of Protector is to uncover the truth and achieve real justice. You must be objective and logical. In the end, Walter is the judge and executioner."

I considered Karl's expectations. With my penchant for justice, did Karl want me to act as the Protector at Session, or did he just want the coyotes run out of the forest, or worse? Was he counting on my lack of experience and failure to raise the defence of Predation just to get the coyotes condemned?

"Session begins once the animals arrive," Fran went on, "and as they do, they're under Walter's protection. You can't have various predators within paw's reach without encouraging a good old-fashioned slaughter. Walter is the guard against that."

As to how the actual Session proceeded, Fran explained: "You can question anyone who shows up, and they must answer formally to the group. Walter punishes anyone offering a falsehood as if they were a murderer. In other words, liars will be driven out of the forest, and if they refuse to leave, he executes them on the spot. If you don't want to be caught in a lie, you don't attend."

I paced. Fran paced alongside me, mimicking my movements and watching me like a predator. A shiver rose from the base of my tail and crawled to my neck.

I knew now where this was going. Karl would lead the testimony with innuendo and his subjective interpretation. What about Fran? Would she also condemn the coyotes? I stopped and turned back to Fran who also halted. "Karl has told me that the coyotes were known killers and that the scent of the coyote pack was at the feral nest. He intends to give that evidence."

Fran cut me off. "Uh-uh—wait." She raised her right paw into the air. "Karl said the pack should be driven out. He did *not* say he or I sniffed the entire pack at his den. His opinion on sentencing and guilt is not a lie."

She was right. And I also would have to be careful what I said, or I'd face Walter charging at me through the dining room glass for misrepresenting Karl's statements.

Fran then addressed her primary concern - mob rule.

"Karl has been pushing to remove the coyotes from the area since before I arrived. He rallies the other animals and blames the coyotes for everything. So far, no one has felt the need to bring Walter in, and I think Karl has nothing. But he's repeated the ridiculous stories about unwarranted killings so many times that I think others are believing him. He's been scaring the others to support him and says that he wants to make our forest safe again."

Fran lay back down on the terrace.

"There has never been a Session on or an independent investigation of Karl's charges. He holds his own court, and many of his mob have stopped asking for the truth. They just bounce their heads in agreement with whatever he says. But not one of them is big enough or aggressive enough to deal with the coyotes themselves."

Karl was risking a dishonest claim in front of Walter. A follower and member of his mob would be impressed and he would maintain his top cat position in the forest.

Fran laid her snout on top of her paws, her front legs bent at the elbow like she was lying on the carpet watching TV.

"Honestly, Hawk, the comparisons to the human political scene are too close for comfort. Think about it. Karl claims he wants the forest to be safe for the smaller animals again. Isn't that familiar? But it's not just coyotes that are predators. Karl himself is one. The mob forgets this as they listen to his exaggerated claims or his insistence that he is just another victim. I only hope you can have some influence. If Karl succeeds at getting coyotes removed without proper justification, I suspect it will only be the beginning. Karl and I compete for the same food. Could I be next on the hit list?"

I understood her concern and would think about how to approach my role more carefully. I needed ammunition. "You also nosed around the feral den. Did you find evidence damning a pack of coyotes? You can testify as well," I pointed out.

Fran frowned at that. "Karl has already threatened me not to waste his time in Session. I am told to back him up or not to show up. I'm to keep it short if I'm there. I need you not to ask the hard questions if you have nothing else to back me up. Karl will be after me if I don't toe the line. It would be best if you won the animals over to you before I testify about everything I found. If his mob doesn't back him, I won't either."

I assumed the animals that expressed their disdain for me were those that had been recruited into Karl's mob. My undeserved reputation was based on innocent actions towards them. Sure, Karl and I weren't on the best terms, since he was the primary recipient of my shenanigans. I had hollered at him as he dug through our vegetable garden to defecate. Another time, I chased him, spraying him with the hose. But I also put out his kibble. Seriously. I wasn't all that bad. But had Karl been slowly drumming up a mob against me?

Karl's actions were too familiar. The worst of politicians used fear that created prejudice. False and unrealistic promises fed the righteous loyalty of a follower. A dish of frightening tales is served to those who need someone to blame for their miserable lot in life.

Since becoming a kitten, I had been spat upon and threatened by Shelley the crow. Darling, the deer, expressed malicious intent with her eyes. I was not imagining it. None of the other animals ever came to the terrace to talk. Was Karl behind it all?

Was he now cornering me to put a false case before Walter? Did he expect to manipulate my ignorance of animal law? From what Fran explained, I'd risk Walter's wrath and was placing myself at risk. Is that what my dear old dad intended?

But I still needed to win the animals over to get help to find who killed Sandy and me.

"Fran. Did you find evidence of the coyotes attacking the litter in the feral nest? Karl said he had clear evidence that demanded Walter's attention."

Fran dropped her snout, sniffing the ground to recall her involvement.

"Karl and I went to the feral nest. I found no scent of fresh blood. I picked up the smell of a coyote, but only a lone bitch who had recently birthed. Even with a wealth of rodents in our area, with new pups to guard and feed, she would have been justified in raiding the feral nest. It would be a convenience kill allowing her to return quickly to protect her own pups. Rodents would have given chase and so would have taken more effort and time. Frankly, I feel her actions were a legitimate, justified predation. Any wild mother would agree."

Karl was justified in dining at the squirrel's nest. Momma Coyote had not been any different. "She was alone then? No other coyotes?"

Fran again caught my eye.

"No. No other coyotes, but the bitch was not the only predator at the nest. Karl doesn't want you or anyone else to know about the others. I scented a porcupine, a pair of raccoons, and a skunk, all of which would hunt in the area and at a feral nest. All are also members of Karl's goon squad. Some you've never met."

Interesting. I could use it if any of these other hunters showed their snouts at Session.

"I also spied a hawk in flight overhead," said Fran.

They were predators, as Karl had drilled into me from the start. Fran continued.

"I thought maybe he witnessed something. That hawk swung down low but kept quiet. He may not be willing to testify but remember, you can question him if he shows up at Session."

Fran identified one final perpetrator or at least a possible witness.

"I also got mocked by that vicious, nasty, spiteful red squirrel. He challenged both of us with a flick of his tail from a branch above the nest. I tried to question him using your methods, but Red didn't respond. He waved his butt at us as he laughed. Reds are nasty. Don't trust them. He may be a squirrel, but they are the only ones that eat other squirrel babies. Just nasty to eat your own."

Fran had established that all these animals were natural predators with opportunity and motive. All could claim justifiable Predation. Feral nests were fair game. Feral and squirrel nests held precisely the same temptations if you were a natural predator of the species.

"One last thought you need to consider." Fran had another surprise for me. "Female cats don't mate for life. Rather, all males will vie for attention when one goes into heat. Once she births and is nursing, she no longer goes into heat until there are no kittens to nurse. So, while fathers may help to protect their young, other male cats will sometimes wipe out a litter if they gain access. They do this to bring the female back into heat quicker. Charlotte, the Queen, your mother, would have a right to attack and kill any male cat threatening the nest. By the way, has anyone seen Charlotte?"

I'd had no idea my cat-mother was named Charlotte or had achieved statehood. I don't recall meeting her and no one spoke of her. Should I bow down low in prostration before her? I pictured a tiny cartoon golden crown and chuckled.

Like a light bulb, it suddenly clicked, and I thought, where is Socks? "If I understand you correctly, Karl has been climbing the wrong tree. He's been blaming coyotes when any number of predators, including Karl's pal Socks, could have been involved, and none would be culpable for hunting the nest."

Fran shook her head. "Not Socks. He has no motive for killing Charlotte's kittens. He has no interest in Charlotte."

"Why is that?" I asked.

"The local animals think a family may have dumped him at a young age. A feral that has been fixed also has the tip of his ear cut off. Socks' ears are both intact, but he's been snipped if you know what I mean." Fran said this with a wink and a broad smile. "He was dumped as an adult after his humans had him snipped. But if you ask me, it has more to do with his special friendship with Karl. He's a boy cat that likes boy cats instead of girl cats. Karl mounts everyone to let them know he's the boss. Socks is in love. Sure, there are many examples of bisexual animals, but cats? Not so much." Fran watched intently for my reaction. "Don't tell anyone."

My head snapped back. "Socks is gay?"

Chapter 17

For mental privacy, I trotted back to my office, where other animals could not read my thoughts, to work out my plan for Session.

Karl shouldn't be allowed to incite his mob against anyone who didn't fall in line. My sense of justice guided me. If this was all true, Karl had to be stopped. Fran would not be backing him up. She needed me to get him under control to stop this mob action before he could do actual harm to either Fran or even to Socks. She might not like my approach, but Fran would play a critical role in Session.

If I lost the mob, I could still rely on Fran and maybe Everett and Socks to help me with the investigation.

When I came back to the dining room screen, Fran twitched her ears towards the road. Karl swaggered up the drive, leading an impressive array of animals in his wake—two deer, a skunk, a porcupine and her pup, and a huge old beaver trailing a very large, dry tail. At the very back, a rough-looking Everett followed at a safe distance. Shelley the crow and her extended crow family flocked above. Session would start once the last animals and Walter arrived.

"You have a few friends with you today." I acted impressed. Fran backed away to the side, hastily removing herself from the main group while maintaining eye contact with me.

"Yes, Kitten, and there are many more, but we can't wait to start Session. It's time to bring the case of my missing Floosy to Walter," shouted Karl.

He spoke and slowly turned to better address the assembly of animals behind him.

"It's time to drive the coyotes out of this wood. They are murderers, and we have the witness of a reliable snout to support our case."

Karl flicked a paw towards Fran. The crowd cheered him on by flapping wings and tails or jumping and stamping and dancing back and forth.

I knew there was no case to bring to Walter. The mob had to learn the truth to put a stranglehold on my dear old feral father. I would stop the unjust coyote hunt and talk the mob into helping me investigate the human murders. Time to flex my human skillset.

I began with Karl. "I am not Kitten. I am Buddy Hawk. Please refer to me by my correct, human-given name."

I then turned to the crowd to remind them of their love for Sandy. "I thought we were supposed to be hunting Sandy's killer. Many of you were treated very well by her."

At the back of the crowd, an underweight Everett sported crusty, flaking patches all over his skull. He'd lost fur in large sections over his back and displayed open sores on his legs. Thank the Cat, Jules had taken over the medication. Everett had received at least two of his meatballs already.

"Sandy had been feeding you medicine for your mange. Doesn't she deserve justice?"

Everett bowed his head low and then lay down on his belly in silence. He was onside.

"I know Sandy had an apple box at the back of her lot." It was my turn to glare menacingly at Darling the deer, and her sister. She turned her head and blocked me from reading her mind.

"Sandy left sugar water, fruit, nuts, and seeds out for everyone. How have you all forgotten?" I raised my voice and punched my paw into the air (the flapping hawk returned). "Why aren't you trying to find her killer?"

Many of the animals looked back and forth at each other and to Karl for his direction. Karl glared at me.

"This concern of yours is not relevant to this Session. Humans handle humans. Our responsibility is to deal with animal murderers and right now, to deal with baby-killing coyotes. That's all we are here to do."

I raised both paws onto the screen door, my eyes squarely focused on Karl while demonstrating my newly gained knowledge. "You're not trying to say that you don't use humans to deal with animal murders? You know human hunters go after and put down crazed or dangerous animals." Some of the crowd nodded in agreement. "Why can't we use our animal skills to assist humans in tracking down Sandy's killer? We all owe her a debt. High time, we all paid up."

The crowd mumbled and shifted nervously. Karl scowled back at me. His right paw flashed up to the screen within an inch of my face and smacked a fly. I fell back quickly and the fly fell dead on the ground. (I wondered if that fly was a reincarnated Sandy).

"Fine," Karl said. "We'll talk about it. But first, you must present the case against the coyotes for killing Floosy. Get on with it."

And just as I opened my mouth, a very large Walter the bear ambled up the drive.

"*Caw!* Session is called!" shouted Shelley from a tree at the edge of the drive where she clustered with her 9 cousins.

Walter settled close, but not too close to Everett at the very back of the crowd. Walter was large, well-fed, and round, with a heavy coarse coat of black fur and a long snout. A good three inches of his thick yellowing claws were visible at the end of his paws.

Though the bear would stop any carnage, it had no effect on the mounting fear of a single mouse who screamed before diving into his hole. "I can't take it. There are too many of you. Walter can't protect me."

The animals had gathered in the driveway, and the most important speakers were closer to the terrace, where they would stand to offer testimony. (I can't imagine what the neighbours would think about such a menagerie in front of my house. Thank the Cat, the lots were huge, and those on either side of us were vacant.)

The shuffling and mumbling of the crowd ceased. Silence struck without a single chirp or growl. Karl stood close to the dining room door. He faced the crowd as he introduced me as the Protector. A string of complaints roared up from the mob: "He's a killer himself . . . He uses rat poison . . . throws rocks at animals . . . sprays us with water . . . Don't trust him. A Protector must be fair to us all."

None of the claims were true except perhaps the one about spraying water which only applied to Karl. Some implicated Sandy's suggestion that I use poison. I would not be bringing that up if I wanted help in my investigation. But it was clear that Karl was the source and had harmed my reputation. He had betrayed me. It was not the behaviour of a loving father.

I felt perfectly suited to the role of Protector. In my previous incarnation, I had mediated the competing forces of lawbreakers and lawmakers. I enjoyed holding the government and police to account without attracting their ire (for the most part). If the police or Crown got sloppy and got away with it, anyone could have ended up unjustly convicted. Sloppy policing meant your innocent life ended from behind metal bars. In my books, integrity meant we protected the innocent as much as we defended the guilty.

The role of Protector was a natural fit. In Session, I would bring justice to bear (no pun intended) on the guilty, but I would protect coyotes, as dangerous as they were, from unfair charges.

Perhaps I could find some justice in this new world.

I began with my formal response to the mob yelling over the heads of the crowd.

"Who has spread these lies about me? I didn't ask for this. Karl appointed me. Would he appoint me if he had any complaint about my behaviour? He knows I don't harm animals. I have not thrown rocks at any animal during this or my past life. I have never in my life used any rat poison or any other poisonous substance on this property. I demand to know who found poison on this property—precisely where and when it was located."

The mob went silent except for mumbling and light coughing. I had raised doubt in their minds.

"Not one of you can name a single animal harmed in this way by my hand. And as for the allegation of spraying water, I am guilty of taking the hose to Karl. He deserved it and knows it."

I had grasped animal law and guessed what would make a justified response to a competing male.

"Karl himself appointed me Protector, because he knows it was my right to hose him with water when he placed his territorial mark on my front stoop. *My* stoop. *Not* his stoop. He had no right to claim the territory. I had every right to clean off his scent and reclaim my own. As a personal matter between us, it is no one else's business."

I sounded pompous, but mumbles arose in response, and heads bowed in gestures of approval.

"Finally, I am not here to chase coyotes." (Admittedly odd, coming from the mouth of a kitten.) "I am here to protect their rights to live as animals. Their freedom from persecution is your freedom from persecution. That is the true role of a Protector. What other complaints do you have about my appointment as Protector?"

Silence again. I had achieved a measure of support from the mob and legitimized why I would have been using a hose on Karl. He was losing credibility. Time to move on.

As the Protector, I had the authority to ask anything of anyone in the group. Some animals in the crowd had been to the feral den and Red, the nasty squirrel, hung on the branch of the closest tree. A hawk flew in and started doing figure-eights. Was he the same hawk that had been at the den? Karl moved back below that tree, and the red squirrel started wiggling his behind and aiming for Karl's head. Both were witnesses to Fran's investigation.

Walter lounged quietly on the front lawn from a distance. A hush set in.

CHAPTER 18

I opened with a statement of high principle. "As you say, Karl, we require all the facts. The investigation must reveal the truth of the matter openly and honestly before all gathered here today." The group was likely aware Karl and Fran had scented out the scene of the alleged crime, so we would start at that point and see where we ended.

"Karl. Please come forward to the terrace."

He did. More animals had arrived, and they kept back a bit, scattered on the drive and lawn or in the trees. I continued.

"You have requested this Session to determine if Walter should execute an order to remove the coyotes from the forest. When you went back to your den for Floosy after delivering my brother Daryl and me to safety, can you tell us if you picked up any scent at the time?"

Karl responded with a firm "Yes. Coyote scent. The coyotes took and ate my Floosy."

He wanted the entire pack expelled. I understood. If coyotes went for my Jules, I'd be after them all as well. But I kept to the job and went for the kill.

"How many coyotes did you smell?"

"I'm not sure," he answered.

Ha. A familiar response. Karl's eyes shifted downwards. Typical. He was thinking hard. Liars became uncertain in the face of hard questions. I pushed onwards.

"What do you mean, you're not sure? You can tell, can't you? Coyotes don't all smell the same. Did you smell at least one coyote?"

"At least one."

"More than one?"

"I'm not sure."

Karl was obvious and too evasive. He kept looking down, hiding his face from me, hiding his thoughts from the crowd and from Walter.

"Sir," I challenged. "I don't understand how you cannot be sure. Did you smell Floosy's blood? She's your kitten. Surely you know her scent? Surely you can answer that?"

Karl looked up quickly. "I didn't smell her blood, but I wouldn't if they grabbed her up and took off to eat her elsewhere."

Darn. He'd got me there.

"All right. We'll assume Floosy remained uninjured while still at the den. Did you pick up any other scents at all? Were other animals or predators sniffing around the area?"

Karl stared at me fixedly.

"I don't recall."

It was another very typical evasive response from a liar. There's no Bible for animals to swear on. The penalty for lying in Session was immediate execution by Walter. So how do you avoid lying? The animal court method didn't differ from what I had expected in a human court. You simply didn't recall. That way, even if the animals could read his mind, he technically had not stated a lie. Karl was the master at blocking what should not be heard.

I tried to sound patronizing and set him up to destroy his credibility. I imagined this sounded silly coming out of one of the most petite frames in this group.

"Excuse me? You were searching for your *missing* child, intent on sniffing out a predator. You expect us to believe you don't remember? You don't recall if you smelled any other animal or even the number of coyotes? You *are* a feral cat, are you not?"

Karl made a slight raspberry sound through his lips. "Pfff. Obviously."

I surveyed the assemblage of animals, slowly catching their attention one by one. I hoped they could see me and hear my challenge to Karl. Until that moment, I hadn't realized that with experience, you didn't need to make eye contact with another animal. You only needed to direct your thoughts outwards. I tried to do both.

"We know that feral cats have a keen sense of smell, so where was yours on that day? Can you at least recall that much?"

"I must have had a cold."

Aren't you the tricky one, I thought, sending out my thoughts clearly. Not quite a lie but an interpretation? Speculation?

For effect, I dropped my kitten noggin and shook it back and forth slowly.

"You must have had a cold, or you had a cold? Which is it?"

Walter let forth a low growl that rumbled from the back. "Move on."

I turned to the crowd and asked if the crow or the deer had been in the area that day. The deer stepped up, and the crow flew forwards to the terrace, but both denied involvement. Shelley spoke for her whole family. It was credible. The feral den wasn't near Shelley's territory and nowhere near where Darling and her sister would have grazed. Others were more important to challenge in the animal mob, but not yet.

"Fran. Can you join us on the terrace?" The terrace was getting crowded. Those that had answered questions did not return to their original places. Fran had to skirt around the deer's legs and race past Karl until she was in front, facing me.

"I think we can all agree that as a fox you have a very keen sense of smell. In fact, don't you have a reputation for having one of the strongest noses among the animals?" I asked.

Fran stood right before me and blinked. "Yes," she replied.

The group murmured their agreement. Even Walter tipped his head. They formally recognized the reliability of her snout, so I went on questioning.

"Did you attend the den location to investigate Floosy's disappearance?"

"I did yesterday," she replied.

"Did you smell coyote?"

"I did. But only one lone female."

Good girl, I thought. You know where I want to go with this. It was time to push Fran.

"I understand it is an absolute condition of participating in Session that you tell the truth."

Fran smiled behind her reply,

"Yes."

I forged on.

"Did you smell any other non-coyote predators at the site?"

Karl immediately stepped in front of Fran and intervened.

"I object to that question. We're here to determine the fate of coyotes. I smelled nothing else, so that's all that matters. Fran shouldn't answer the question."

I turned to Karl. A fast learner. He had picked up the art of the objection from reading my mind. Was he protecting someone in his mob or his version of events?

"I disagree, Karl. We are here to uncover the truth, and you already admitted your nose was unreliable. Remember: *you* had a cold."

Fran slipped in her answer before being cut off again.

"I could smell a porcupine, a pair of raccoons, and a skunk."

I scanned the contingent. No raccoons but a porcupine and a skunk were in the crowd, and neither looked concerned. Perhaps they weren't the same animals, or Karl was trying to protect their involvement. But why, when it was his own daughter who had disappeared and had possibly been eaten by one of them?

Fran continued. "The same porcupine mother and skunk attending Session today. I can smell them from here."

The mob turned as a body and gazed at the two as they shook their heads and blinked rapidly back at Walter and then to the front at Karl.

Once more, Karl piped up.

"Hold on. I'm still objecting. Even if my nose was not the best on the day Floosy disappeared, Fran sniffed only yesterday. It was long after Floosy went missing. These other animals likely walked around the den area long after the coyotes took my kitten. These others are friends of mine. They might have even helped to look for Floosy for me. But Fran was too late to sniff out the den for murderers."

Walter nodded approval at Karl's reasoning. But that still left me with the most important point to make in the coyotes's defence. Karl hoped I didn't have a good understanding of animal law. As Karl snorted and frowned at Fran, she held her head high, and I pushed on.

"Could you tell when the others had been on location?"

"No," Fran answered honestly and Walter settled down.

"Was there anything odd about the coyote scent?" I asked.

"Nothing I would call odd," she responded but then tipped her head to the left.

"Her scent was unmistakable - a blend of her own musk and the fresh, earthy fragrance of her newborn pups. They don't smell like separate animals but smell like they're part of the mother when they're first born. A weak nose with a cold could miss it."

She had taken a shot back at Karl but gave him his out. But she was obviously ready to go after him and support my line of questioning.

"So - only one coyote and a recent mother?"

"Yes," Fran answered bravely, and standing up to Karl. I had to support her and push her further.

"Would it be unusual for her to hunt a feral den?"

Fran offered a more considered response. "Not at all, particularly if she was pupping close by with little time to hunt. She wouldn't leave them alone for long. Few mates will puppy-sit while the mother hunts."

I scanned the group, then glanced back at Walter. High time to sum it up, finish with this kangaroo court, and get on with my proper investigation. The longer this went on, the greater the delay and the more likely human murderers would escape justice.

Karl had moved back under the tree on the edge of the terrace, glaring at me.

"Karl, why have you insisted on calling Session? Why should all coyotes be driven away from our woods? There's nothing to suggest this was a crazed killing. Where is your smoking gun?"

The confused eyes of the spectators squinted at me.

"What's a gun got to do with it?" roared Walter. "Get on with it."

I wasn't going to argue with a bear. I turned to Karl and showed my disdain, which came out like a kitten smirk as I forged on.

"My second point is that Karl's charge is based on a logical fallacy."

The audience stood stock still, flabbergasted. Their silence became menacing. You could hear a pine needle drop. Walter frowned.

"I am referring to the axiom that says it is faulty to relate causation to temporality." All eyes glazed over. Low growls began, and Walter issued forth a steady grumble. I tried again. "Just because something occurred before an event does not mean the first caused the second!"

This was going nowhere. Karl smiled slyly, less like a feral and more like a fox. I had forgotten my audience and was at risk of shoring up Karl's position and having a large bear charge through the dining room screen door. Walter took a few steps forwards, and the crowd cleared him a path.

"What I mean to say is that because a kitten disappeared after a coyote walked in the area is not proof the coyote had anything to do with the disappearance. It is also not proof the coyote worked with the skunk or the porcupine, even if their scents were also there. On top of that, there is still no evidence of the murder of any kitten."

The mob sounded a unified sigh of relief as the skunk and porcupine danced and hollered their approval of my logic. The bear stopped moving forward, listening.

I turned back to Karl again.

"Karl, consider this. You agree Fran has a better nose than your cold sniffling and running one. There is no evidence of the whole pack of coyotes in the area. You both scented a single coyote and with her peculiar scent, we know it was a mother recently pupped."

Just before I got to the big finish, a large male coyote suddenly skipped across the front yard, confidently landing right beside Walter. I had wondered where the coyotes were and if they would attend. Well, it's better late than never.

The coyote spoke. "Rabbits, voles, mice, chipmunks, squirrels, and feral cats are all a normal source of sustenance for our clan. My mate had every right. There's no crime in normal predation! I call foul."

He growled and bristled. Good timing, I thought, though he'd taken my punch line. But it thrilled me to have support for the big finish. I tried to mimic his growling by hissing as loudly as possible when I picked the argument back up.

"*Hhhhhhiiiisssssssss*. As our new friend in the back points out, how is this not legitimate Predation? What did you think you were proving with your testimony concerning the coyote mother? Where is the evidence of a crazed killer? Should a coyote mother not have the right to hunt efficiently to feed her pups?"

And then I finished with the slam dunk, standing on my hind legs with front paws spread across the screen, trying to wave them and flap like in the old days. My claws kept getting caught on the screen.

"We must have justice, but what is that? Session recognizes the legitimacy of Predation by all animals. It is justice as much to protect the coyote mother as it is to protect the interest of Karl and his kittens. She has a right to eat and feed her young. If Floosy is lost, so be it. Are we not animals?"

I tried to flap my front paws but again got stuck on the screen. I was no longer the flapping hawk but the spread-eagled kitten. It's a wonder they didn't all burst out laughing. But the crowd returned to life, humming and chittering approval. The porcupine and the skunk left quickly and quietly. The coyote father yipped twice and then bounded off back into the trees.

Did the group finally grasp the truth about Karl? He had already retreated to the edge of the lawn, probably getting ready to take off if Walter got angry. Before I could demand that Karl justify wasting everyone's time, my speech was eclipsed by raucous howls of laughter from the red squirrel rolling around on another branch above Karl's head.

It was distracting and rude. I confronted him.

"What's so funny?"

Even Walter's snout turned to the source of this intrusive chattering.

"You're all so full of yourselves. You with your Session and all this arguing about food. Did anyone think about checking with Karl's mate? Where is Charlotte? No one asked. Karl has never mentioned her. Is she alive? I'll tell you. That's her right behind you, isn't it?"

The laughter climbed in pitch as the smoking gun was revealed.

The most beautiful pure-white feral cat swayed her full thick tail gently and suggestively as she came trotting down the driveway. In her mouth, she carried a small black-and-white striped kitten. She held her by the scruff, swaying boldly past Walter, past the crowd, and up to Fran and me at the dining room.

Karl had snuck around the crowd to come up front. She dropped her bundle. He sniffed at it and exclaimed loudly. "Praise the Cat. My baby is alive? Or are we witnessing another reincarnation?"

Charlotte was quick off the mark. "Don't you dare," she snapped. "Our baby has to finish her first life before moving on. You're not fooling anyone."

The fur on her back rose as she hissed and growled while batting the top of Karl's head as fast as a succession of bullets out of a machine gun. He crouched low under her blows.

Charlotte's rhythmical interrogation followed the tempo of her bullet bats.

"I had to learn from Red"—*bop, bop*—"a nasty squirrel"—*bop, bop*—"that you were looking for Floosy?" *Bop, bop, bop.* "Did you think to ask me where she was?" *Bop, bop.* "Did you even try to find me? Bop, bop.* Of course I was hiding her." *Bop, bop.* "After a quick hunt, I returned to my den. *Bop, bop, bop.* I found Daryl gone." *Bop, bop.* "Why did you take Daryl out of the nest? *Bop, bop.* I followed his scent and found him stashed in a barn!" *Bop, bop.*

Karl was still ducking but tried to respond.

"I couldn't keep babysitting, so of course I took the biggest of the boys to stash for safekeeping. I figured if anyone went after the nest, the runt and the girl could be sacrificed."

He thought he was being reasonable?

"Sacrificed for what? What was so important that you had to leave them?"

Charlotte's eyes were almost glowing as her hackles rose even further.

"Lunch," whispered Karl.

He quickly lowered his eyes and ducked his head down, correctly anticipating the next series of power blows on top of his head. They did follow—nine bopping blows in succession with emphasis on the last before Charlotte stopped.

"I came back and grabbed my girl and stashed her," Charlotte said. "You know she's too spoiled to survive on her own. When I came back the runt"—that would be me—"was also gone. You lost the runt to the inside of this human habitation. And you didn't even try to find me? Or your daughter? What is wrong with you, Karl?"

Charlotte struck him one last time - hard.

As the family reunion progressed, Walter lost interest and left. And when Charlotte stopped batting Karl, he and most of the group dispersed quickly. The queen then turned to Fran.

"What's your involvement in all this, girlfriend? I know you. Are you behind all this trouble? What trick have you been pulling on my kittens?"

Fran blinked twice and lifted her chin.

"We have a pact. I wouldn't break it. I was having a bit of fun with your mate. Karl's been full of himself lately, so I've been talking to the runt and set him up to take Karl down a peg. It was fun. You would have enjoyed it."

Fran had led me on about Karl. Had she tricked me somehow? I didn't understand. Karl deserved the treatment I dished out during questioning. He unjustly targeted the coyotes. Fran had pointed out he manipulated the group; he had turned them against me. Fran's comment made little sense. Was there ever an actual mob? Did Karl even need to be taken down? Was Fran, the trickster fox, trustworthy?

Queen Charlotte huffed twice at Fran and then winked at her. One paw pushed down hard at the back of Floosy's neck as the little thing squirmed and squiggled to escape. Floosy had to be the most beautiful kitten, marked like a teeny white tiger but with long, silky hair and the biggest eyes. Then the queen turned to me but spoke loudly enough for all to hear. "Who is that inside of my runt?"

I guessed she referred to my pre-reincarnated human self, so I introduced myself. "William Hawkins, Your Majesty. My human family and I moved into this house last year. Someone recently murdered me, and Karl says my soul entered your kitten's body. He dropped me off at home for my daughter to take me in. She calls me Buddy." I rambled like a stupid kitten again. But she was majestic and forgiving.

"Ahhh. OK, Buddy. Nice to meet you. Karl did that for you? Surprising. He hated your human self with a passion. All he ever talked about was getting even with you for some water incident. I guess fatherhood eventually won out." Charlotte blinked delicately.

"Karl showed unusual wisdom in providing a warm, safe home. Jules takes good care of you?"

"Yes, she does. And she has also been feeding Karl and Socks for a while."

"I'm glad for you. I may take you up on that, but for now I need a favour. This is your sister Floosy. She is a genuine silver, and this makes her special. Unfortunately, she knows it."

Charlotte gestured gracefully with her right paw towards the new kitten that she stomped with her left paw to keep the squirming kitten in place.

"Feral life doesn't suit Floosy. She won't survive out here. She's as lazy, spoiled, and foolish as her father. Will your human take her in as well, do you think?"

One look at those enormous eyes and Jules would crumble.

"I'm sure of it," I said. "And you're welcome to come by for a visit and a bite to eat anytime you like."

As we chatted and waited for Jules to come home, the last remnants of the crowd slowly dispersed. I hoped I had gained the support of the animals to get moving on the investigation into Sandy's and my murders. I needed them.

As we waited, a police car pulled up into Sandy's drive. No one got out. I could see it was Ewen again. He sat inside the squad car for a good half hour. Was he now stalking Jules? At least he wasn't disrupting more of the evidence on location.

The clock ticked. It would be dark soon. Coyotes would be out hunting, and they knew now where two kittens were residing.

Chapter 19

Both Fran and Charlotte, hawk-eyed and ready for action, crouched behind a bush discreetly guarding the little kitten. The coyotes could get past them, but Charlotte could climb a tree as quickly as Karl, with or without a kitten in tow. Fran was losing interest and kept turning her head west to the forest. I think she wanted to get her own hunt started.

I politely asked Shelley the crow (I remembered her name!) if she would collect the Beemer keys Jules had dropped under a bush in the yard and deliver them to the front stoop. I had at least won some respect from the crows. Shelley had a glint in her eye drooling over the shiny keys, but she obliged before the family flew off. She owed me for the kibble.

I directed Floosy to place her butt down beside the keys. The sun, glinting off the silver, would ensure that Jules's attention would be drawn towards the keys and the kitten, in case Floosy didn't do her job. I could return the Beemer keys without drawing attention to myself and also put Floosy in Jules's line of sight.

"Is it like making an offering to the bees?" Floosy asked. Darn, my sister-kitten already had more experience about how to cat.

"Sure, sure. Whatever," I replied.

Maybe she would get the job done after all. I watched from a window in the front hall beside the door. When the Beemer pulled into the drive Charlotte and Fran scattered like the wind into the forest. At my suggestion, Floosy lay down on the stoop and pretended to paw at the base of the door as she *mewed* and *mewed*. Just as Jules walked up to the stoop, Floosy dropped onto her side with her eyes closed, sighing but too quiet. What an actor!

Of course the glint of the keys caught Jules' eye right away, and then the prostrate kitten came into her view.

"Oh my God. Look at you. You sweet little thing!" Jules fell in love instantly.

Floosy opened those enormous eyes and stared up at Jules. A *meeww* followed by a very small *hisss* (she *was* a feral) hooked my daughter. Jules gently lifted the kitten with one hand, tickled her behind the left ear, and then brought her into the house.

It started off innocuously. I witnessed Floosy's limited introduction to the house. They passed through the dining room and kitchen and headed directly to my office, introduced by Jules to Floosy as the *safe* place. Floosy, too new to everything house-related, flattened her ears against her head as she snuggled her snout deep down into the crook of Jules's elbow. It had been a distressing day, and when Jules set her on the shawl Floosy cried a couple of faint *mews*, hissed twice, shut her eyes, and immediately fell asleep - on my bed and in my spot.

Initially, I had felt sorry for her appreciating that the space and smells of the house would be unfamiliar and perhaps even a bit frightening. As the day progressed, I came to understand the challenge I faced sharing my home and my Jules with this little monster.

Floosy's bath went about as well as mine complete with the hellish blow dryer. She screamed and slashed at Jules. The blood wasn't Floosy's. Yes, tiny but mighty were her claws.

I didn't join them for the trip to the vet, but I'm confident a needle in her behind wasn't pleasurable either. Floosy's stamina was impressive, though. She was wide awake when they came home, so she hadn't passed out with the first poke as I had. Jules released her from the carrier, and she casually strode out lifting her snout and sniffing the air curiously. Floosy was OK with it all.

Jules started her spa treatments (petting) which were suited to such a spoiled royal pain in my butt. Floosy had already claimed my bed and now claimed my daughter. Jules brushed and stroked and petted as Floosy purred and stretched and rubbed her forehead against Jules's hands. They became fast girlfriends.

I didn't need petting or brushing, thank you very much. I preferred more intellectual pursuits.

That spa treatment continued for over twenty minutes! Finally, Jules left the office to answer her phone. Floosy ran after her in pursuit of a repeat performance by the soft-bristled brush. Jules stood in the kitchen on the phone. It sounded like Ewen Keens was at it again.

"No, really, thank you so much, Ewen, but it's not a good time for me with my dad gone and the new kittens to attend to," she said.

I didn't mind if she threw us under the bus as an excuse to avoid a bad date.

"Yes, I have two now, and they're very young. I can't leave them alone for too long."

It was getting boring for Floosy who walked back to the office, "Blah, blah, blah. Why does she talk into that long black thing when she should be brushing me?"

I tried to dumb it down, given her age and all. "It's called a cell phone. It's a human gadget that lets her talk to other humans. Right now she's talking to a guy who wants to be her boyfriend."

"Does she like him? Is his fur soft? How's his nose? Is he a good hunter? Has he brought her any mice?" Floosy asked.

"I doubt it," I answered. Remembering his finger flick of my ear, I added, "And he doesn't like cats much."

"I'm bored," Floosy declared.

She was cranky and pulled herself up onto my well-worn reserved spot-on Clare's shawl. "What's reincarnation?"

"It's when you come back as a new person or animal or bug or something because you didn't finish something in your life." I wasn't good at explaining this. "I used to be a human in this house. I was Jules's father, but some stranger killed me and I came back, reincarnated - into your brother's body.

She looked a bit confused.

"Why did our dad ask if I was reincarnated?"

Karl had been trying to cover his own tracks for the Session fiasco. It would be difficult to explain that to this kitten.

"I'm guessing Karl didn't want to admit that you were alive all along when he took off and left you alone for the coyotes." That was accurate, but it was mean of me to dump the raw truth on her. I regretted saying it as soon as it was out of my mouth. How much would she understand? I waited.

Floosy stared at me with those enormous eyes. They glistened, and then she turned her head away from me but spoke. "When you were human, you didn't take off on Jules, even after you died. You wouldn't ever leave her alone, would you?"

"No." My heart broke for her at that moment. I promised in my mind that I would be nicer and make up for dear old dad's failings. "But I think it is different for predators. The struggle for food in the wild is pretty intense. I don't think your dad meant anything by it."

To prove my promise, when Jules offered us something to eat, I graciously allowed Floosy first dibs. Big mistake. An evil little being lived inside that black-and-white fur. I had sworn to be nice, but when food was out, she had the instincts of a ruthless killer. Flo was unmatched by anything I had ever witnessed in a courtroom or in the back streets of the city.

When Jules laid out the tartare, Floosy scarfed down all the food, including my bits. Jules witnessed it and forgave her. I tried to be patient. Jules pulled out a can of salmon. She would make sure I didn't starve to death. I honestly drooled at the smell. Floosy also smelled the mush for the first time and closed her eyes at the perfume. She had been raised on mother's milk and mice and baby voles brought by her mother, the queen. The canned mush didn't run or play or bite. It was no fun, yet it smelled glorious.

I nosed the edge of the can to nab a quick, gentle lick to demonstrate proper food etiquette. Foolish me. After finishing all the tartare, Flo leapt over my head, landed her backside on the nape of my neck, and pushed my snout down into my dinner. When I raised my head, the slimy pink goodness covered my nose, whiskers, and chin. Floosy then used her hind legs to slap me backwards away from the can. She wrapped her paws around the can's perimeter and chewed languorously, eyes closed, broadcasting her delight with a low growl followed by a deep purr.

I was dumbfounded and watched her carefully as I licked off the slime. I slowly shifted my frame to the other side of the can, intent on finding a niche and some sustenance without prompting another attack. Still, Floosy would not share. It wasn't in her nature. She lifted her head, glared at me, released a loud warning hiss, and swatted at me with her dominant right paw.

If this was her reaction to her first domestic meal, would I ever eat again?

"Enough of that," declared Jules.

She picked up the can, found two white ramekins, and split the remains of the food adding extra to my dish. When she placed them down on the kitchen floor, she separated them by almost two feet, keeping us at a reasonably safe distance.

Floosy was a true feral predator.

I still tried. After the meal, I educated her on the proper use of the cat box though she seemed to take to that naturally, after which she happily took a nap like the princess she knew herself to be.

We introduced Floosy to the rest of the house before Jules left for her evening shift. Jules held her and walked around each room that she would allow cats to access. This meant a walk through the hall to Jules's bedroom but not inside. Bedrooms were off-limits, even if the doors were usually open. Jules didn't want cat-box paws on any pillow.

"Don't go in there," I said. "That's Jules's private room for sleeping. No cats allowed."

Floosy glanced into the room and then turned, smiling at me. Rules were not something Floosy would follow, even if she understood them. She would definitely test my patience.

We walked back to the large living room. Floosy stared upwards, fascinated by the beamed ceiling.

"How do you get up there?" she asked.

I ignored her. The tour did not include two other bedrooms with closed doors (no longer used). Floosy already knew of my office, our bed, and the shared cat box.

Jules dropped Floosy back in the office and went to get ready for work. I stayed to take care of my wee sister-cat. I thought a bit of exercise was in order. I tried to play tag, bopping Floosy lightly on the top of her head like I'd seen Charlotte bop Karl. Maybe I had misinterpreted the scene between Charlotte and Karl? I paid for my actions with a growl, hiss, and a swipe of her needle-sharp paw across my ear. *Meow!* Not my ear again! Floosy didn't like that game but settled back down quickly.

"Let's go outside. You got any mice around here?" she asked.

"We can't go outside. We're stuck in here. Besides, it's too dangerous, and there are no mice to chase."

But then I got creative. "Have you ever been on a snipe hunt?"

Floosy bullet-bopped me with questions rather than her paw.

"What's a snipe? Are they fun to chase? Are they good to eat? Can I catch one? Are they inside the house? I thought you said we couldn't go outside?"

This had the potential to get rid of her for a while.

"It's small and black and furry but odd, like a cross between a bunny and Red the squirrel. But it's a bird and doesn't fly."

Floosy had settled onto her belly with her front paws under her chin listening intently. "But we can't go outside, you said."

"No, but this is a creature that runs around the inside of the house. It likes to stick to the corners of dark rooms. And it's nocturnal."

"What's nocturnal?" she asked.

"It means awake at nighttime. Snipes like to come out at night, and you'll find them in dark corners hunting for flies and spiders," I explained.

"Is there any particular hunting strategy I should use?" she asked.

"Just follow your natural instincts. When humans hunt snipe, they do it with a pillowcase, but that's because they're not proficient hunters. I'm sure you'll do fine. They're small, like large mice or little rabbits." I had bamboozled her. It was fun playing the brother rather than the father.

Floosy crept silently, crouching low as she left the office and the comfort of the shawl, and proceeded out into the dark of the living room, hallway, and restricted bedroom to hunt the mighty snipe. I settled into my spot.

An hour later I woke to Floosy looming over me. I heard her announce that she had not caught a snipe yet. (Since they didn't exist, she never would). She accepted this as her own failing and lay down on the shawl. She was immediately asleep perhaps from the stress of transitioning to the indoors or from the excitement of the snipe hunt.

I stood guard over my sister-kitten to give her a sense of security. I could be both a brother and a father if needed.

Chapter 20

I finished my evening playing poker on a casino app, accumulating a total of $3,004,761.03. I wished these were real winnings, but even with access to my bank account through the phone app, I would never gamble with my hard-earned cash. And where could a kitten spend 3 million anyway?

A jog to the dining room door rewarded me with more good news. The animals had arrived to lend a paw, hoof, or claw. Everett, Fran, Socks, Shelley, and Darling lined up on the terrace. They had each enjoyed Sandy's generosity.

Darling, being the youngest, couldn't wait to speak. Her front legs danced back and forth.

"I can help. Sandy used to leave out tasty apples and pears for me and my sister to eat. I miss those treats and Sandy. It isn't right."

Socks's recollections were not of Sandy.

"You didn't have to chase me or make fun of my singing when you were human. I know you didn't actually intend me any physical harm, but it hurt my heart. But I'm still willing to help. From what you've said, Sandy didn't choose to leave us at the hands of strangers. I will do what I can."

Shelley piped up. "I'm here to offer air patrol. Nice that someone appreciates what my family can do. Together, we are a fantastic fighting force so we can act as air security as well. If you tell us what you're looking for, we can do a comprehensive search by air. Karl shouldn't have made you out to be a killer, and I think we understand you better now."

Fran spoke on behalf of herself and Everett. "We foxes are here to help. You know what Sandy did for us. That killer is owed some payback."

Karl was not with the group. Of course, he blamed me for his embarrassment at Session. He had wasted Walter's time, which no one wanted to do. Queen Charlotte's paws had rendered humiliating blows. She not only showed up with Floosy in tow, but she put Karl squarely in his place in front of the entire gang. I bet he would seek revenge against me, but I didn't care. Time to get serious and uncover the murderer with the help of these locals.

One good thing about animals is their ability to pick up a specific scent which is as distinct as DNA. If only animals could testify to their results. But if we identified the murderer's scent, alternative ways would present to prove guilt to the humans. (I surprised myself, referring to people I know as "the humans").

"I appreciate your help with this investigation. I'm sure Sandy would as well. I'll do a bit of research. Could you re-sniff Sandy's backyard? The first time Fran sniffed, she didn't recognize everyone, but she hadn't been here long. See if you can pick out anyone specific who was in the yard, around the shed. If you don't immediately recognize anyone try checking around town for similar scents. Maybe we can trace the killer that way."

I tilted my head towards Socks as I recalled, "You've been here for a few years."

"Yep," he replied.

"Do you know any people in the neighbourhood Sandy visited other than my wife and me? Did she have local friends?"

Socks was thoughtful for a moment. "Most of the people here didn't care for her much. I could tell because they avoided her when they were out walking. While they visited each other, they never visited her. I don't know why. She was very kind to the animals, but the only human she would talk to was the one that lives in the big house with the three garages east of your place. The people in that house only moved here about four years ago."

That would be the Reid house. Jules would need to cozy up to Mrs. Reid. I'd raise this in my next text.

We agreed to meet the next day to review what they had found and plot out the next steps. The group left to start their search.

Sister-kitten was asleep again in my spot after a night of snipe hunting. I struggled with the desire to wake her with a swift bump right off the shawl. But once awakened, she would only start annoying me in her usual evil-sister fashion. I wasn't up for torture.

The online casino app called me. Playing the slots helped to focus my mind on the murders and our investigation.

Whoever killed Sandy also killed me. The MO was similar as was the profusion of blood in the yard that Shelley had described. But who would want us both dead? I didn't think we shared a common enemy though Sandy appeared to know and smile at my murderer right before the deed was done.

I had too many disgruntled clients and angry victims of clients, and as far as I knew, Sandy had no connection to any of them. Also, how would they catch up to me in the middle of nowhere so far from my old turf? The phone number was unlisted. The change of address was to a box in town. If someone wanted me dead, they would have attacked me on my property rather than Sandy's backyard.

It would be more productive to focus on Sandy. Maybe I was just a happy accident. Who would want Sandy dead?

The winner's circle award dinged repeatedly from my app. My paw continued to swipe the wheel mindlessly. The dings woke Floosy, who crouched down with her front paws and stretched out her back legs, one after the other.

The murderer would have to be strong enough to kill me with a single blow to the back of my head and then Sandy right after. That sounded like a powerful male. As much as I wouldn't want to dismiss a potential suspect based on their gender, the mechanics of this crime signaled an excess of testosterone. Women committed few murders involving hands-on physical violence. The female gender tended towards offences that require planning, cunning, subtlety, and sometimes a knife, poison, or a gun. Not a shovel.

Ding, ding, ding! More fake money.

"What's up, Jerk Face?" said Floosy.

I could smell her breath as she yawned, peering over my shoulder at the screen.

"What's with all the noise? Can't a girl sleep in peace?"

"Not if she sleeps on *my* spot on the bed," I answered without turning my head.

She likely didn't hear me being too young to pick my thoughts up without seeing my eyes. My paw swiped the wheel again. And again.

I recalled - Sandy had not run away when the attack began. She was likely killed by someone she knew, but she had few friends or family. She tried to stop the attack on me by simply calling out to the killer to stop right after she smiled at them. I was confident she knew the killer personally and was unconcerned about the potential danger to herself. If not family or a close friend, perhaps a business partner? The meth lab was relevant even if out of character for Sandy.

This was turning out to be a really ugly killing - hard blows face-to-face from someone she probably trusted. The murderer would have to be a genuine psychopath. That also fits the personality type of someone deeply involved in the nastier aspects of the drug trade.

Suddenly, Floosy pounced on top of the phone, pushing it out from under my paw. If she pushed too hard, it would pull out the USB charger cable. "Stop!" I hissed at her. "You'll unplug it." My ears lay flat and my fluffy back told her I was serious. "Back off, *now*."

"No." Floosy rested her pussy-butt right on top of the screen.

"Now, Flo. You know that phone of mine is no fun. You said so yourself. It doesn't run, chase, or fly. If you get off and leave it alone, I'll give you a treat that I've been hiding for myself later." I wasn't above bribery.

"What kind?" she snapped.

"Chicken squishy, and you have to leave me alone for a while."

"Done." And she got off the phone.

I flipped off the app, nudged the phone back slightly to take the tension off the USB cable, and then shifted my back to Floosy, so she would not discover my stash under the shawl. I pulled out my last treat and flipped it backwards into the air to her. Flo leapt and caught it midair. She had a kind of killer grace about her. With chicken squishy in her mouth, she trotted out of the office.

I guessed she was off to hunt for the mighty snipe again.

CHAPTER 21

The sandbox had been well used and not yet cleaned. That was odd. Jules hadn't come home? What did that mean? I suddenly felt worried for her but also vulnerable.

I had to suffer the indignity of using the dirty box anyway. I couldn't afford to cross my legs without knowing when the box would be scooped. Then, off to the kitchen where I was disconcerted to find only dry kibble filled the two little ramekins. Kibble. I tried it and now understood Karl's preference for mush. My teeth were scraped clean with each chew, but the flavour did not impress.

This was all very worrying. Where was Jules? I strolled through the house searching casually for her. It was wise, also, to check the house in the morning to ensure Floosy's snipe hunt hadn't destroyed anything. The house was in order, but empty of Jules.

I returned to my phone in the office in time for a new text from Jules. The *ding* drew me in, and I felt relief immediately hoping to understand what had distracted her from her cat box duties.

Dad I had an early coffee with Ewen before work. I'm doing a day shift this week so I'm frazzled with the shift change but I can assure u never again. Don't be expecting anything more from that guy all he talks about is four wheelers muscle cars and hunting. He buys me a coffee and then chooses a seat in front of the mirror wall and watches himself when he's supposed to be talking to me. He's such a dork.

OK, Honey. And?

So I wormed info from him while he was distracting himself LOL he admitted the forensic analysis confirmed Sandy's garage contained the mechanics of a complete meth kitchen. It was used recently based on evidence of residual product. Ur sense of smell is amazing how did u know it was meth? What have u been doing all these years LOL

Trust me. I have not been cooking meth or making or taking any other drug. Just something someone told me once on a case.

Ur really going to be that vague? LOL so I talked Sarge into making Ewen give me limited access to the murder case cuz it could be related to my drug case. And ur now an unofficial person of interest in my investigation as well but I get to remain on the job and with the drug squad. So now ur a murderer and a drug kingpin u better stay in Tibet for a while until I can get this solved. I'll keep clearing yr texts from my phone for now.

Great, Honey. Let me know what you find out. TTYL.

There would now be some access to the evidence for Sandy's and my murders. That was good to know. No—it was great! Now I could really involve myself. And a direct connection between the two cases would help to identify the murderer.

I lay on the floor in the office with my enthusiasm renewed and snapped open my casino app.

Sandy had no blood family left. She had that loser of a nephew by marriage - Jarrod. He visited before and after her death. Not to mow, mind you. The grass kept getting longer. From what I'd witnessed, he wasn't the most reliable help either with yard work or the cancer treatment appointments. He played to his strength, which was drinking beer around a campfire from what I could surmise.

Sandy also had a husband—I assumed ex-husband in the circumstances. We would need to make sure there were no other relatives. Maybe the Reids would know. Jules would have to ask Mrs. Reid.

If Sandy had an online presence, it could help me to figure out what was missing in this story. I opened the phone and started a Google search for Sandra Cox. I found obituaries and a story about a murderer living in the wrong country. Reviewing the many Facebook profiles finally took me to the image of my Sandy.

Like so many of the over-seventy crowd, Sandy had only recently joined Facebook and had a very brief history. Being new to social media, her settings were still public. She had twelve friends in total, all from the Oakville area where she had grown up. Likely all old school chums. There was no mention of a husband. She followed a local wildlife rehabilitation group and the usual funny animal videos on YouTube.

The FB posts included her report of the successful closure of the sale of her family home in Oakville. Interesting. I checked the House Sigma app to learn the house went for 1.2 million. Just before I died, Sandy had told me she intended to leave a fair portion of the sale to an animal shelter. This was enough to start her own bloody zoo.

That kind of money suggested a motive. Who benefitted under her will and were they aware she was about to give a lot of her money away? It's an old adage but true - when chasing down a murderer, it's always wise to chase the money.

Floosy appeared out of nowhere with a sloppy wet chin and crawled onto the shawl. She was going to get my spot wet. I'd take care of her once I had finished my research. When I turned back to the phone, she was already snoring.

A Google search of the local papers revealed another article about Al Cox's release from prison. He was imprisoned after his own wife, Sandy, had testified against him. It referenced a much earlier article about the original trial, which I also found. It reported the couple had been at a party and suffered an accident on the way home. The accident had involved a head-on collision and charges of negligence causing death. The Cox vehicle had crossed the line into oncoming traffic. A child in the other vehicle had died. The severely injured mother lived. Sandy and Al flew from their vehicle yet survived relatively unscathed.

The article also reported that Al Cox had an extremely high blood alcohol level of 0.30 percent - over three times the legal limit. That should have been enough alcohol to make him black out and stay out for hours.

He couldn't have driven at all with that much alcohol in his bloodstream.

Maybe he had downed the last shots quickly at the last moment before leaving the party. Blood alcohol levels increase slowly. He may have been lucid enough when he first got into the vehicle, but he would have become more impaired as he drove until he became unconscious. I had used that argument to get people off drunk driving charges when there was a long delay before my client faced the breathalyzer. High blood alcohol levels obtained late in the process were evidence of lower levels previously when the individual had actually been driving (So the argument goes).

I was about ready for a break. Floosy continued to snore behind me. Soon I would launch my attack and shock her awake. Heh, heh, heh. I chuckled as I played the scene in my head.

The thought of Al Cox driving impaired brought me back to the meth lab. There was a lot of lore surrounding meth and how it killed people. Some overdosed and jumped off buildings trying to fly. But most often meth deaths occurred during accidents from impairment while driving motor vehicles. Even if alcohol was the cause, could meth have been involved as well?

Meth would have shown if blood tests were taken, even if it was not the cause of the impairment. That drug was not mentioned in the article or any other reporting about the trial or cause of the injury. The proverbial square peg did not fit into the round hole.

I got up from the phone, stretched, and ran out to the kitchen for a quick drink of water. When I came back, Floosy had rolled onto her face still asleep but no longer snoring. Back to the phone.

The reporter assigned to the courthouse provided more details in his article. The accident had occurred at night. The mother in the other vehicle couldn't identify who drove the Cox vehicle. Sandy said she had crawled to the side of the road and passed out. She couldn't remember where she'd landed. Al had landed somehow on the opposite side of the road from the driver's side and had no recollection of anything. The placement of Al's injured body contradicted the claim that he had been driving. Sandy was awake enough to crawl to a location that confused the issue.

The case had depended on the whims of a jury and the testimony of the Crown's star witness, who turned out to be Sandy Cox. The only thing Al said he recalled, which he had repeated, was that Sandy had taken his keys from him before they left the party. He couldn't have been driving. He had passed out. But Sandy had denied taking the keys. She said Al had been driving, and she had not been able to stop him. In the end, the jury believed Sandy's story. She sent him away to prison for twelve years.

How would it feel if your wife betrayed you by testifying against you in a criminal trial? That was an excellent motive for murder. Would Sandy do such a thing? She was kind to dumb animals, but also a bit of a contradiction when she brought out the poison. I really didn't know her.

"Hey, Loser, wanna play some soccer?" The squishy ball hit the back of my head. My evil sister-kitten was awake again.

"No, not now."

Would Clare have testified to make sure I went to jail if I drove drunk? If she did, it would have been to make sure I was locked up and not able to harm anyone again. Would she have lied to protect me or would she support the justice of my conviction over my freedom? I'm sure she would have died for me if necessary, but I don't think she would have gone to prison for me.

My head was spinning. No use comparing Sandy to Clare. They were different people with different relationships with their respective husbands.

If I were the one with no recollection of the events, I wouldn't be angry at Clare's honest testimony to my guilt. If Al resented Sandy's testimony, would he have wanted revenge enough to kill her?

Finally, following the money, would he profit from her death? There was a will. Sandy had mentioned she intended to meet with her lawyer to change and resolve something with her estate. Did she plan to remove her husband from the will if he was still a husband? Was it to include the wildlife centre donation? Did the husband even know if he was in the will or that Sandy had intended to donate the bulk of her money to charity? Did he know she intended to die under the MAID program?

Floosy had moved off the bed and now took a threatening stance in front of me and the phone. She intended it to be distracting, but I forged on.

The more I thought about it the more the 12-year sentence bothered me. Al got the max, which was too high for a first offence. His lawyer had made a mess of it. The Crown prosecutor must have argued for the max because Al failed to show remorse or take responsibility. If you were innocent, would you? But the sentence was still too high. There should have been an appeal.

Worse still, Cox had served the full sentence. That never happens either. He should have been out in one-third of his time for good behaviour. The parole board would release even a complete jerk at the two-thirds mark – out for sure after eight years. For twelve years, he refused to admit guilt or remorse. Was he belligerent to the board members, or did he threaten Sandy?

If he was innocent, would he have suffered over Sandy's behaviour? Twelve years of resentment would build a powerful motivation. But for what? Divorce? Murder?

I reassessed my judgment of Sandy's character. I had seen contradictory signs that she was cold and not afraid to murder animals she claimed to love and care for. Was she so cowardly or selfish enough to lie under oath? Al would have been passed out - not driving – just another victim of that accident.

"Lying is easy," said Floosy. "The dead lady would fib to keep herself out of trouble. Anyone would. What's wrong with that? What's your connection to this dead lady?"

Flo had been listening to my thoughts? Her response didn't actually surprise me, but her growing ability to read my mind gave me concern.

"She wasn't a spoiled, selfish little kitten like you. That's what's wrong with that."

This kitten had quite an evil streak. Is that what Queen Charlotte meant when she compared Floosy to Karl?

I recalled when Clare left us to rest in the local cemetery, Sandy brought over a generous pan of lasagna to the house, bless her heart. Jules and I watched the cheese harden. The funeral lasagna made it to the bin. Sandy watched out for the two of us. I owned her. But I had to admit, something was off about her.

If Al knew Sandy had cancer or that she had already planned to end her life by choice, really, what value was there in speeding up her death by a few days? If he was in the will, a few days made no difference. If he wasn't in the will, there was no need for revenge since Karma was taking care of that for him.

I tried to access the divorce records through the online courthouse portal but found nothing. Sandy and Al were probably not divorced. I found no application or declaration filed anywhere connected to where they lived. Jules would have to track the answer down.

"What's a deeevorce?" asked Floosy. She sounded silly. But divorce was not a term that applied to the animal kingdom. She had never heard it. Or she was just being a silly puss-butt.

I explained, "It's when you dump your mate."

"No big deal. Why is that important? What's it got to do with the dead lady?" Floosy just wanted attention. If I didn't respond, she would nag me until I answered her.

"If you must know, I'm trying to reason who would most want the lady dead."

"Oh." Floosy turned her back to me and trotted once more out of the office.

Next, the trailer property. As Karl had said - "Google it."

The drug connection was foremost on my mind. The drug trade went hand in hand with murder. In such a small community, a meth lab would have to move around a lot to avoid detection by the police. It must be hard to keep secrets in a small community. My hypothesis was that it was too easy for the police to notice a large operation with too many players. The nosy neighbour factor played a role. And there would be little patience for competition between different drug lords. It would be obvious if new management moved in.

The boss likely worked almost alone with no competition, and maybe he or she had a special connection to the community that helped to keep matters under control.

Were the feral deaths in the trailer connected? From my research on veterinary websites, I learned crystal meth was exceptionally poisonous to cats. The lost feral colony could have picked up meth residue on their paws and fur because it would cling to all the surfaces of the cookery. Residue would be all over the counters and floors. It would transfer to the cats' mouths when they cleaned themselves. Food brought in would pick up residue, and with the small body size of the cats, even a miniscule amount of drug residue would have devastating consequences.

I wasn't the old Bill Hawkins anymore. Feral cats were now my brothers and sisters (though I wasn't overly pleased with Karl at the moment). I wore the fur coat myself. I now understood the sad tragedy of the colony deaths. I found no article in old papers or local blogs about the loss of the colony. The humans burned the trailer to the ground. That had been the end.

A simple title search showed the property had been owned by Robert Hall, a name, thus far wholly unconnected to Sandy or her death.

CRASH. Something fell and smashed in the living room. Psycho-kitten!

"Floosy! What are you doing out there?" I yelled my thoughts out to her.

"Snipe. It got away. Nothing broke," she called back in reply. Good old snipe hunt, I thought. What had she seen? Certainly not the elusive (fake) snipe.

One last job. I would send a text message to Ray Tickborne who was the lawyer acting for the town renters presumptively charged in Jules's bust.

Why was I even contacting him? I wouldn't gain much insight

into my death or Sandy's directly through him. I didn't expect Ray to blab confidential information about his case. But I'd promised myself to help encourage a plea. I could nudge him in that direction for Jules.

Ray. Hawk here. How's it going, pal? I heard you settled well in Belleville. This is not an official inquiry by any means. Just an old friend with concerns. I'm retired now.

His reply came promptly.

Hawk? Wow. Yes. All is great. I have a busy practice again, and AA is the best part of my life now. And you retired. If you're bored with retirement, you can come work like a dog for me in my practice. I'm really sorry about Clare. She was such a kind and generous lady. I'm sorry.

Yes, well, I am truly and fully retired and won't be joining your practice. I'm living with Jules right now. We're in the country only about an hour north of you. Jules got accepted by the local OPP detachment and is loving it. Say, she mentioned you have a case up this way.

Yep. Got a couple. I can guess which case you're thinking about. I have Jules as an arresting officer on one of my cases. I'm working on a classic Hawk-move as we speak.

I knew exactly what move he meant. Ray would try to scare his innocent client into giving up the true guilty party and offer evidence for the Crown. It was a hard boat to row when your client believed the guilty party was scarier than the thought of going to jail.

Well, that's just what I was going to suggest. I happen to know you'd be greeted with open arms up here by the police for your Hawk-like approach to that case. I'll ensure Jules gives you enough time to get your clients dancing to the right tune. GTG. I have another call.

I got off the phone quickly, realizing that I had been about to offer to meet him for a drink to catch up on old times. Not only would such an invitation be contrary to his participation in AA, but the fact remained - I was a *cat*. *Meow*. I had to keep reminding myself of that fact.

Ding, came the sound from the phone.

Dad great news just got a message from Ray. He wants to meet with the police and crown to discuss his client's options. It looks like he wants to plead and make us a deal I'm betting he's willing to offer up the name of the person behind the meth lab. I'll let you know what he offers if you still need the info.

One step closer . . .

CHAPTER 22

The front door slammed. Jules was home.

As I backed away from the phone my behind ran smack into Floosy's face. She quickly landed a little nip, barely missing my intact jewels but still sending me flying straight up into the air above the tartan bed.

"MEEEEWWWWWWWW!"

I must have screamed. Jules came running in to find I had landed sprawled half off the shawl facing the practiced stance of Little Miss Oh-So-Innocent. Flo had stopped puckering her mouth and squinting at me. She stretched her eyes wide at Jules, snout raised into the air, attracting *ahh*s from my daughter. *"Mew"* came a soft, tiny sound of innocence. When Flo turned back to me, she hissed viciously. Jules knew Flo meant to blame me for some unknown injury. How dare she!

"Poor little thing. Is Buddy bothering you? Is it time to get him fixed?" Jules stroked Floosy's forehead. "I'll get you a treat, Sweety. Would that make it all better?"

And how dare Jules? Was she letting Floosy get away with it?

Floosy looked triumphantly back at me. She flicked her tail

straight up into the air to show her joy. "Let that be a lesson to you, Bud. Don't cross me, or you'll be hawk bait."

I flicked my tail back and forth a few times, to warn her punishment would be forthcoming. I would give her something to hiss about.

"What does she mean when she says she'll get you fixed? Are you broken?"

No answer to that one. I would give her no ammunition. She was enough of a hellion already. But the question served as a distraction from an all-out war between us.

Then my Jules, a trained professional, turned to me and winked. "Don't worry, Bud. She's not fooling me for a second." Jules had heard my scream. She was well aware of who had the best spot on the shawl and who lay awkwardly half off the bed. "So, treats all around." As she caught my eye, I turned on my own pathetic purr. Floosy wouldn't be getting anything past my cop daughter, I thought proudly. "Hawk bait. *Pfff.*"

Jules went to retrieve treats.

Floosy turned back to me sounding annoyed. "Tell me again, what is that thing you were batting? It doesn't look like much fun. It doesn't even try to get away," pouted Floosy. "Is it the snipe?" she asked hopefully.

"It's called a cell phone. It's not a toy. It's the same device Jules used to talk to the guy who wants to be her boyfriend. Remember?"

She was bored and summarily replied, "Whatever. What do you think *you're* doing with it? You're a weirdo, but you're not human."

"I am, or at least I used to be human."

"Whatever," she repeated after a long, wide yawn and pronounced even my weird human traits were "borrrrringgg."

She asked nothing more about the phone or my humanity but continued relentlessly to pepper me with questions focusing on her self-interest.

"How often are we fed around here?"

"Twice a day," I said.

"Have you got more treats stashed? More chicken squishy?"

"When Jules is off treats come more often," I said. "I have no more stashed away."

"Off what?"

"Work," I said.

"Whateverrrr. Do we have to share the cat box? I should have my own. You stink."

"Fine." I was getting tired of this. I turned to walk away to the kitchen for a change of scenery that didn't include Flo.

"I'll tell Jules to get you your own litter box."

She skidded across the room to land in front of me.

"When?"

"Later. After Jules leaves," I said.

"Do I have to bathe in that awful water again?"

"I don't think so. The intention was to ensure you had no bugs on you to spread into the house," I explained.

"Do you get bugs?"

"No. I don't go outside. Bugs are outside," I said.

"Lick me? I feel scruffy." Flo rolled onto her back and presented me with a view of her belly. Was she trying to be vulnerable? She opened up her eyes as wide as they could go, taking on the usual "I am cute" expression. Did she think that was all it took?

"No," I said.

"I want to be brushed a lot. It's nice. How often do I get brushed?" She spoke while remaining upside down.

"No idea."

"Tell her I want to be brushed. A lot."

"No. You'll have to figure it out for yourself," I said.

Flo stopped nagging me and rolled back onto her feet. "Do I have to share this bed with you?"

"You're more than welcome to find someplace else to sleep, but I'm not moving. It's my bed and my former mate's shawl. Feel free to leave," I said.

"Where does Jules go when she's not here?"

I offered the shortest explanation. "I already told you. She goes to work. She's a cop."

"I don't know what that is. You're boring me again."

Jules saved me by walking in with a couple of chicken squishy treats and a soft-bristled brush. Floosy's eyes grew to an enormous size again, and Jules began the bristle massage. Flo purred so noisily. I could barely hear myself think.

"Oh, my. You certainly like brushes, don't you, little girl," cooed Jules.

"You got a touchdown," I declared.

"What's touchdown?"

"Forget it," I said.

"You're really boring today."

If Floosy was an example of what it meant to accept your nature—to go with the cat flow, so to speak—then I would not be letting go of my humanity anytime soon.

It struck me that Flo should have been able to read the answers to most of those questions by reading my mind. Was she too young to communicate like the other animals, too lazy to focus, or did she enjoy being an irritation?

I turned my head away and refused her access to any thoughts for the rest of the day. Still, it was a rousing day chasing the fake bird on a string and the small rubber ball. I showed off my soccer expertise. But as the day progressed, Flo grew better than me with the ball. She had a natural killer instinct that I lacked. Demon-kitten on the field.

I returned to the shawl, hoping to catch up with Clare again. The beach. White sand. Clare turned and laughed. "I like her." Could she honestly be referring to Flo? I shook my head slowly and fell asleep on the beach.

A check in the dining room revealed no one was around. Odd. A police car was parked on the side of the road past Sandy's place. Jules hadn't noticed it. I suspected that boob Keens was lurking around again to catch sight of Jules. The door opened, and sure enough, Ewen stepped out and walked towards the house.

Jules needed to be forewarned. *"MEOW!"* I yelled. Jules came running, looked at me, and then outside. Ewen Keens approached the front door.

"I don't know how you knew to do that, Buddy, but thanks for the warning," Jules answered the door. I returned to the office to avoid another ear flicking. He talked his way in for a cup of coffee. It was painful to watch or even listen to his fawning attempts at courtship. His Old Spice cologne wafted throughout the house. Who wore Old Spice nowadays?

The coffee was short-lived. Jules bowed out early, because she had to leave for work. Keens did not continue to hang around, thank the Cat.

CHAPTER 23

Most of the gang arrived outside the dining room. Everett was missing. Darling and Fran came up to the window. I assumed Shelley was part of the large grouping of crows that filled the trees in the front lot. Too many to count.

Floosy had followed me to the window, curious and murmuring behind me, "Who are these losers?" I ignored her put off by her attitude.

Socks moved from behind Fran to the front of the group. He stood proud and tall with his dusty white feet and flexed torso showing off those prizefighting muscles under sleek grey fur. He turned his head slightly towards Flo and flashed her a smile and a wink. I swear Floosy literally fell over swooning and humiliated herself by drooling on the floor.

When Flo got back up, hiding her eyes and lowering her snout in her embarrassment, she took off like greased lightning, slipping and sliding across the kitchen floor back to our bedroom. We losers had the last laugh.

"Do you have that effect on all the girls?" Fran and I laughed. Some eight and then nine crows calling out light chuckling caws from the trees: A wish, a kiss, and something not to miss? Even the crows knew his leanings. I think Darling was too young to understand. Socks flipped his tail up and curled the tip as he tipped his head slightly with a glint of humour in his eyes. I chuckled, but it was time to get down to business.

"Please proceed with your report," I said.

Socks hunkered down on his haunches, back straight as an arrow, showing off his length. He started by offering a personal comment before getting into the formal investigative report. "Were you aware Jules smells much like her mother?" Socks became wistful. "It's not the scent of perfume but of her skin—like wintergreen combined with irises. Lovely. I thought you'd like to know." I offered Socks honest gratitude as I bowed my head. I hadn't known Socks had such a sensitive nature or nose. He was kind to share this with me. I, too, became wistful. Scent meant so much in the animal world.

Socks then explained that they'd all had a good sniff around the property. He and Darling picked up various scents, but these were likely left by the police and Jules. It was, he admitted, a confused scent mess.

Darling chimed in excitedly, tapping her hoof and repeating, "Me next," a few times before we all stopped to give her our full attention. Darling lifted her small chin confidently. "I've figured out who did it. It is that awful human kid who comes here to race his ATV all over the roads and trails like he owns the place, scaring everyone. He has tried to run down animals in the past and aims for garbage bins every week. He probably ran down you and Sandy."

Shelley chimed in, "*Caw!* No. I roosted in the trees when the police were all around the yard. A shovel lay on the ground with so much blood on it, it was surely the weapon. Besides, an ATV leaves tracks. There were none."

I recognized their agreement, expressed by hums and head bobs throughout the crowd.

Everett finally arrived but hung back. His medication had not taken full effect yet. Socks stepped up again.

"Make room so Everett can come forward. Fran's nose is sensitive, but Everett has more experience and a broader knowledge of the local scents."

Everett carefully moved forward as the others spread out respectfully. No one wanted to catch his mange or hurt his feelings.

"Yes and thank you, Socks, for your kind introduction." Everett presented himself formally and called to mind an old British professor I had for torts in law school. He had class.

"I appreciate your patience with my present ailment and the opportunity to assist in this venture." Turning towards me, he added, "And thank Jules for restarting my treatment. I recognized the medication in the lovely meatball last night."

He raised his head up towards the treetops as if savouring a fine vintage wine.

"Organic yearling. From the Jones farm in the next county. South field. Brown and white cow. Lovely texture and flavour."

If I didn't say it before, it bears repeating - I did like this fox. Fran's wide-eyed, transparent adoration for him was simply because he was the antithesis of Daniels, her human husband (may he rot in you-know-where for killing his wife, the human Fran). Where Daniels was incompetent and dishonest, Everett was accomplished, wise, and kind.

Everett offered his analysis.

"I picked up several recognizable scents of local police officers, but these were not mixed with the scent of your human blood. One that was close to Sandy was her nephew, the one you call Jarrod. There were two scents in the back close to the shed, more intense, and both were mixed with the scent of your blood, not Sandy's."

Now we were getting somewhere.

"I did recognize both of these from the past, but I can't yet put names to the scents. But they are definitely connected to the chemical stink from the shed. One of the blood-mixed scents was very similar to one connected to a black-and-white vehicle I saw a few years back. And that same chemical smell, meth you call it, was also related to the same black and white vehicle. Both the scent and the vehicle were at the scene of the feral colony deaths in that old trailer from the lot behind Sandy's house."

It sounded like one of the two mystery scents had been a police officer, but we knew they had arrived later. Maybe Everett had the timing off.

Everett raised his snout to me and asked, "Are all police vehicles black-and-white?"

Everett was uneasy at the thought that his word could condemn someone innocent. He didn't want to get this wrong.

"I caught the lingering scent of Sandy and William Hawkins, both powerful because of the copious amounts of blood. Hawkins' blood scent mixed with the scents of two unknown persons, not the police. I don't think I could be wrong on this unless the police themselves removed your bleeding body."

The police didn't even know I was dead.

Everett was quiet for a minute, concentrating, and then he lifted his snout and continued.

"I can age the scents as well. The two scents that were mingled with your blood both moved together to the front of the house and along the driveway. The body of William Hawkins had already disappeared before the police arrived."

Everett was not done.

"Jarrod's scent is all over the property. He had been going to the house, front and back, for a long time. His scent shows he was in and out of the shed. He visited Sandy and even did a bit of yard work, so his scent is older than the police scents. But it is fresh at the back, and I am pretty certain he arrived before the police arrived, though his scent is not mixed with William Hawkins' blood."

"That's all I have at this point." Everett bowed and backed away keeping his distance from the rest of the crew. I thanked him.

That was unexpected. Three people out back: Jarrod, maybe, and two unknown people mishandling my corpse, while carrying the scent of meth. All were there before the police arrived. If Jarrod had been there earlier in the day before the police arrived, it's possible he was a witness. But wouldn't he have said something if he had been there?

Fran and Socks moved back to the dining room window. Darling had lost interest and stood in the front lot nibbling on some grass.

Fran raised her right paw above her head and cut off my thoughts.

"Who called in the death? How did the police know to go to the house? Someone saw something. It must have been Jarrod."

And where did my body go? Wouldn't a murderer let the bodies lie where they fell? Why move my body, but not Sandy's? Did someone want Sandy to be found? And not me? Or did the police arrive too quickly?

Everett called from the back. "Hawkins was dragged on something else to the front driveway. The scent was lighter than it was in the back. No blood stains were marking the driveway anywhere. But the scent was unmistakeably your blood."

So I had been rolled onto a blanket or cardboard and dragged out front without leaving a blood trace. They found a credit card in the driveway. My body was there. But where did I go?

Floosy had gathered herself together and wandered back into the dining room as we were talking. She moved in beside me for a better view of Socks, quietly smacking her tail against my butt to get my attention, and then murmured in my ear, "Isn't he gorgeous?" I ignored her.

"Everett is reliable," said Fran. "If Jarrod had arrived earlier, he might have called in the death. But he's a coward. I know cowards. He's like my husband Daniels. I bet he came around earlier, found

Sandy, and called in the death, but then took off. Or, if he had been there at the time of the murders, I expect he would have run away, too afraid to implicate the others. If he saw the murders, I'm betting Jarrod is running scared and knows the other two people."

Socks caught sight of the chipmunk den entrance left of the terrace. He quietly moved to crouch beside it, in case the inhabitant tried to leave. Flo, likely evaluating his skills as a hunter, sighed deeply. But she had been listening while drooling and spun quickly towards me, frowning while repeatedly batting my behind with her swinging tail. She always had a killer instinct, but her sudden participation showed her abilities were growing. She had carefully listened to my thoughts and those of the other animals around her.

"You bunch of losers. Isn't it obvious? If I were the murderer and wanted to shift the blame from myself to someone else, I wouldn't want that to be found. As long as the police don't know your human self is dead, you make a great scapegoat. At least, that's what I would do."

Flo had employed that particular strategy in our day-to-day interactions. She had become a master at shifting blame. But she left me wondering. Was she born evil? But she made sense if that credit card had been left intentionally in the driveway. This one fact would have the police classifying William Hawkins as a person of interest. It was easier if you hid or dumped the body.

Hold on, I thought. We don't want my body found! I didn't need to clear my name. I was dead anyway. Jules would be hurt if I eventually was blamed for the murder and never surfaced, but she would also be hurt even more if she discovered the father on the other side of the text messages was actually dead and that I had become her reincarnated kitten.

"We need to focus on Sandy. The location of my body doesn't matter."

"We can leave the analysis. Fan out and see if you pick up any of the unknown scents around town. We want to find anything that would help to identify them." Heads bobbed and there was humming again in agreement.

"Also, report back to me as fast as possible if any of you happen upon the body of Hawk. We don't want to bring that forward to anyone else too soon." It felt natural to refer to Hawk as someone other than myself. Was I learning to cat?

I recalled watching as a kitten, waiting for Jules to take me in. Jarrod had arrived while I was on the stoop. I wondered why he didn't identify the murderers directly to the police, then. He just casually drove up in the work Jeep. Jeep! I was about to turn away and stopped realizing Sandy's car was missing. Sandy had parked her candy-apple red 1967 Camaro in the driveway when I had crossed the street, alive and human. It wasn't there when the police arrived or when Jarrod arrived. It hadn't returned.

"Do you all remember the big metal box in Sandy's driveway?"

I forgot they interpreted what I meant by reading my mind. The group looked back and forth at each other, then carefully in my eyes and nodded a yes.

"You mean the Camaro?" asked Socks. "Now there's a hot number." How would Socks know how hot that car was? Was he reincarnated as well? Were they all just reading my mind?

"Yes," I replied. "That car disappeared just like my body. Maybe it was used to move my body. Do you think you can find it, Shelley? Could you ask your family to spread out and do an aerial search?" Did I get her name right this time? I breathed a sigh of relief when she didn't react. Thank the Cat.

"Got it, boss. *Caw.* One Camaro." She called me boss. I liked that.

Chapter 24

The familiar *ding* sounded a text message. I leapt from my bed, hoping for a new clue or at least a lead. But this time Jules was in the living room with CNN playing on TV in the background. Responding to her text before she left for work could be risky but it was worth a quick look.

Don't get mad. I got another kitten a sweet little thing. She's probably from the same litter she's only slightly larger than Buddy. I'm working so much and u aren't around I thought Buddy needed someone for company. She's just a sweet little white fuzzy wuzzy. What should I name her? And how are u? How's Tibet or where ever? When r u coming home? They've stopped asking about u at work.

I typed back.

Tibet is cold. I'm staying. What does that mean, they've stopped asking about me? And call her Fuzzy-wuzzy.

Heh, heh. Floosy would hate that. Just a bit of revenge.

I don't know why u r not on their radar anymore maybe they have other suspects to follow. If I learn anything I'll let u know. Fuzzy-wuzzy it is TTYL

I shut down the phone and trotted out to the living room. Jules had switched off the TV and had requested easy jazz on Spotify as she lay back, her eyes closed, an open book lying across her chest. I jumped up to the arm of the chair for a better view of the title - *Cat Care for Dummies*. What? Did she still have that instructional manual? Waste of time if you ask me. We are inscrutable.

I hopped down to search for Floosy who was nowhere in sight. That was a bad sign. What mischief was she up to? Snipe hunting should be a living room activity late at night. I hadn't seen or heard her in some time. I walked down the hallway following the sister-kitten's scent, eventually finding my way into no-man's-land - Jules's bedroom.

"Floooooooosy. Where are you? Flooooooooo," I called in a whispering mew. There was nothing under the bed or on it. For the life of me I couldn't find that kitten anywhere. Had she escaped the house?

I saw Jules' sock drawer was ajar. It wasn't open enough to allow escape assuming Flo had found her way in there earlier when the drawer was wide open.

"Flooooooo!" I meowed louder, finally rewarded with a small kitten cry of fear and sadness issuing from that self-same sock drawer. Was she crying? Tiny mews were calling to me and picking up speed, followed by a faint rancid smell that wafted down reminiscent of the litter box.

I stopped whispering. "Flo. Is that you up there? Did you fart?"

"What if I did? Buddy, I'm stuck in this box full of lovely soft rocks. I'm starving. I'm thirsty. I have to go pee. I need water. I'm gonna die. Get me *out*!"

What a drama queen. She couldn't have been stuck for more than an hour at best, or maybe two. There was no risk of starvation or death.

With my sweetest voice, I answered like any brother would. "You got yourself in there, so you can find your own way out. You won't ever escape. She'll never find you. Yep. You're going to die in there. Serves you right sticking your nose in other people's drawers."

"Mew, mewww, mewww" came the muffled, whimpering response.

I gave it a minute and started having misgivings. I may have gone too far. Was she crying? Indeed, she wasn't used to the environment or my peculiar form of brotherly love and humour yet. I'd never had a human sister, but I knew how to be a compassionate father figure. "It's OK, Fuzzy-wuzzy. I'll bring her back here and show her where you are. I won't let you die."

"What do you mean, Fuzzy-wuzzy? What's a Fuzzy-wuzzy?"

"That's what I told Jules to name you."

"No!" Floosy exclaimed.

She didn't whine or cry, but she utterly rejected the very concept of her name change.

"I swear, Buddy, you'll be hawk food. Get me *out of here* and give her my *real name.*"

I trotted off back to the living room without answering. Jules opened her eyes and lifted her head. "Hey, little Bud. Sorry about that. Are you and Fuzzy ready for dinner?"

I recalled the oh-so-eventful day when I had died and how Karl had enticed my human self over to Sandy's yard. Mimicking the action, I hopped up and down and then took a few steps down the hall towards Jules's bedroom. I stopped, turned, and shouted, *"MEOW!"* (My voice would eventually drop an octave, and this remained a cause for concern. There may still have been a plan to have me fixed.)

I marched back to her feet, turned, and started over again. Just as with me, it took three times doing the Karl dance before she caught on.

"You want me to follow? OK, little Bud. Show me . . ."

When we arrived in her bedroom, I stretched my front paws up onto the front of the dresser. I then nosed at the partially open drawer. Flo let out a tiny, plaintive mew.

"Oh, my God. Poor little thing! How long have you been in there? Come here, Honey." Jules pulled open the drawer and grabbed the little white fluff. "Aw, you're such a honey. Maybe that should be your name - Honey."

Flo was not happy with me. "That doesn't sound like she called me Fuzzy-wuzzy, you jerk." She turned back to Jules, feigning exhaustion, and mewed oh so weakly to reflect the unbearable suffering from her starvation and all that dying (while surrounded by sock rocks for about an hour). She purred like a hot rod that had lost its muffler as my loving daughter carried her off to be hand-fed, watered, brushed, and put to bed—my bed.

I followed behind utterly ignored. No fanfare for the hero who saved the day. No pats on the back for using my nose like a cat. No thanks from little Miss Nibs.

Chapter 25

Karl appeared outside and started eating. I pawed the glass and then smacked harder to issue a light *thud, thud*. Karl ignored me. I didn't exist. He licked more slowly (if that was possible). The grass grew at least an inch before he lifted his square noggin.

"What's wrong now?" I asked. "I haven't seen you since Session, and you didn't show up to offer your promised help to investigate the human deaths."

"What's wrong?" Karl stared so hard I thought it would crush my brain. "All I have ever done was help you. How am I repaid? You repeatedly and intentionally tried to disgrace me with your lawyering and tasteless questioning. You were absurd using your human courtroom tactics in an animal Session."

I listened, but I wasn't getting his point. He was the one at fault. Not me.

Karl snarled sarcasm. "What part of the role of Protector did you not get?" He held my attention with a beady-eyed look of disgust. "You showed disregard for us all by your misuse of Session to embarrass me in front of my peers. Session is not about humiliation. It's about protection. Did you protect me?" His eyes were like bullets.

"They used to respect me and my opinion. Now I walk alone because of you."

I didn't respond directly but simply opened my mind to him. Admittedly, I was rough on him when I questioned him during Session, but he pulled the "I don't recall" crap to avoid answering my questions. I had no patience for it. I let him know without a doubt how I felt and then stood at attention as I lowered my eyes to remain silent while I listened for his response.

"You don't understand, do you? You're thinking like a human, not an animal, and certainly not like a cat. What's wrong with you? If I had told a lie during Session, I'd be dead by Walter's claws. That's the highest rule of Session. You knew that. The only way to avoid death was not to remember. Everyone could read me and would have known the truth without my stating anything and without your courtroom tactics. You placed my life in jeopardy. Everyone else was OK with getting rid of those coyotes."

I didn't see the distinction. What was I there for if everyone had read his mind? Why question anyone? Why even hold Session? If most of them were already aware of the truth, why were they backing Karl?

"As an animal, I may do what I can for food, for my offspring, and for my mate, including calling Session to rid myself of coyotes who compete for prey and who could steal my kittens. Yes, they have a right to eat, and so do I. I have an equal right to eliminate them, even through Session. I'm not a natural predator of coyotes. I'm not crazed but I'm smart. Session was the only way to get them. I took a shot. I lost. We could all move on if you would start to cat and show me the respect I'm due for my creativity. I am a predator."

Maybe I didn't understand Session or animals or how to cat. Perhaps he had been making an intellectual predatory move on the coyotes by using Session to stage the attack.

I had been listening too much to Fran. She was the one who had steered me. Fran implied Karl was running roughshod over everyone and behaving like a political authoritarian. It was Fran who'd suggested Session would be the place to call him to task.

How much did Fran want to be rid of Karl? She was a fox and in competition for prey with the feral cats. Did she fox well? Was the whole setup another predatory move? Fran had admitted to Charlotte in front of everyone that she had used me to run a play against Karl.

I was finally understanding.

"I expected more from my kitten," Karl continued. "I have only been helpful to you and without even being asked."

He hadn't exactly been helpful when he tried to turn the others against me. I'd been spat upon, glared at, and ignored by everyone until Fran came along. Karl had been behind the exaggeration of my misdemeanours when I was human.

"You were a nasty human," Karl said. "I didn't like you any more than you liked me or Socks. But that was before you were my kitten. I would have turned them around with a bit more time so they'd support you. Your actions as a human shouldn't have mattered to the other animals once you were feral yourself."

"How did you help?" I was now directing my thoughts outward to Karl.

Karl turned circles three times before settling down on the terrace with his paws tucked under his chest.

"Let's look at what I've done. I arranged for the bee against all rules governing courtesy. You wanted to use Bumbler for emotional gain. It's utterly wrong to ask another animal to involve themselves in your affairs or difficulties when it has no impact on their lives, food, or habitat. Animals don't buy, rent, or use each other. It's hard enough finding food and avoiding becoming lunch yourself."

I mirrored Karl, turning three circles myself, and then curled into a ball in front of the dining room door. I forgot to tuck in my paws.

"I also told you about the trailer, the history of the lost feral colony, and that the smell at Sandy's shed was the same as the smell at that trailer." Then Karl squinted at me. "From the start, I warned you that your good friend Fran was a risk. She's a fox. I only tried to warn you away from getting eaten. I should have discussed with you what foxes were like. My contract with her to protect pups and kits is not reliable. Your friend has learned to fox. She knows how to compete for food with feral cats, and that includes helping herself to a diet of kittens if available.

"Yet you wouldn't listen to me. You have been a fool to ignore the reality of your existence."

Karl pulled his paws out from under his chest and laid his chin down on them. He was almost teary. Cats don't cry tears (real cats, not reincarnated ones).

"You refused to learn to cat. I had to drop you at a house to become a prisoner to the humans because you're a runt and would never survive without their help."

I stared back at Karl with his crocodile tears. He thought I was a prisoner? It was a luxury being in my home with Jules as my caretaker. And after Charlotte's diatribe at Session I learned I could have been coyote cub dinner, all because Karl flaked out on babysitting his offspring, taking time for a bite of lunch. How was that being helpful?

I didn't state this, but I thought it, hard, and he clearly picked up my thoughts. That brought him to his feet. Karl stood up as if he was about to leave.

"We are animals," he responded. "I did save your furry butt from one hungry female coyote. It was also perfectly reasonable for me to move Daryl first as the largest and strongest male of my litter. I can only move one at a time. I came back for you and delivered you to safety. Even Floosy was prioritized by her mother. We're animals!"

Karl turned as if to leave, but I wouldn't let it go. Karl had originally brought my human self to the back of Sandy's house and then had taken off right before I was murdered. Was this a setup? Oops. I hadn't meant to share that thought, but it was too late.

Karl turned back quickly. He stood tall and utterly still with his ears flat against his head.

"You think I set you up?" Karl was yelling in my head now, and I stood and backed up a foot quickly.

"You're a bigger fool than I thought! How do I control how humans treat humans? How would I accomplish a human death? I would never work with a coyote or a moose. It's not possible. Yes, I can read your mind and know what you first thought—that I had hired a moose to strike your human self down and the coyote pack to eat the body, to get rid of the evidence. Ridiculous! Thinking I would have been involved in your death in any way is absolute nonsense."

"Kitten. You take credit when it's not yours to take. I told you about Everett and his mange to protect you from getting it yourself. I told you about Fran's interest in having pups with Everett, which couldn't be fulfilled unless someone took over his medication. You got points for passing the need for medication to Jules, but who told you about that need? I nudged you in that direction for all of our sakes, but you took all the credit with Fran and Everett."

That last statement took me aback. Karl was right. I didn't know how to cat. I was still clinging to my humanity. I enjoyed my so-called prison. Being stuck as an indoor kitty was supposed to be abhorrent to a feral. But Karl had been an ally. Maybe my hatred of feral cats had carried over into this incarnation.

Maybe Karl wasn't the evil mob boss Fran made him out to be. In retrospect, the so-called mob was easily controlled. Turning them before and during Session had taken little effort. My speech before Session started wasn't all that special. I had to admit it. Fran likely had her own predatory agenda against the ferals and had learned to fox. She set me up.

Karl wasn't done.

"And finally, I think you should apologize to Socks. You always made fun of his singing when you were a human. We all knew. No, he doesn't caterwaul. Yes, they are songs. He has stopped singing because of you. He used to sing the most beautiful arias. Humans refer to the style as operatic. Socks was also reincarnated, and in one of his previous lives he was an accomplished tenor. His 'Nessun Dorma' would bring you to tears."

I had called Socks's singing caterwauling. Was he actually singing?

"Fran said that you didn't like him, and he had to hide his true nature from you."

Karl was taken aback.

"Nonsense. He is a rare creature who sings magnificently and is abundant with his love for everyone and all species. I'm lucky to have earned such a rare friendship with such a beautiful soul. Yes. I know he is in love with me, but he knows I am with Charlotte for now."

Karl stood, strode boldly to the food dish, and flipped it over with one paw revealing my dark brown leather wallet.

I gawked at it and at Karl and then screamed a resounding *"MEEEOWWWWW!* Where in Hades did you find that?"

Before Karl could answer, Jules came running from my office with cat brush in hand. Karl scurried back behind a tree, and I crouched down staring at my wallet. Jules followed my gaze, and flew out the front door to retrieve the item that we both recognized. Karl stretched his head around the tree, and Jules stared at him and then offered what appeared to be a thank-you nod. That was odd!

When she came in, Jules dropped onto a dining room chair and opened the wallet. She pulled out my driver's license, my Bar Association ID card, and the other credit card that had shared a spot with the one the police had found on Sandy's driveway. She gaped at the cards and laid them on the table individually.

My tail twitched quickly back and forth. Where had Karl found it? Was my body going to be discovered? What was I going to do? Jules was going to find out!

Jules moved to the living room to her cell phone, where she texted first and then called in to work. I couldn't go and check the text yet. I could barely contain myself.

"Jack. Are you still on the Cox murder?" asked Jules into the phone. "Well, a feral cat showed up with my dad's wallet. It has his ID. I'll bring it in if you want it?"

From my location in the dining room I couldn't pick up the response from the person she referred to as Jack.

"Fine," she replied. "I will and shut your pie hole. My dad is not a feral cat. I don't know where he is, and he did not hand me the wallet. His last message to me said that he was traveling to Tibet. Tell Ewen he can bugger off."

Jules hung up hard, if that's possible, on a cell phone. She stared down at the phone for what felt like forever. Whoever Jack was, he had made a crass joke about the feral's identity, but it implied Ewen was behind a claim that my daughter was lying or hiding her father. Why didn't they trust her? Was she also being set up by a human predator trying to start rumours that would get her fired?

I recalled Jules's text, and anticipating that it was for me, I scooted back to my phone.

Dad do u know where ur wallet is?

I knew to keep up the pretense. We weren't done with the investigation.

No, Dear. I lost it before I left for the city. I've already called in the credit cards. I've been paying my way with e-transfers. Why do you ask?

She remained quiet for a few moments.

That feral Karl just dropped it off. God knows where he found it but I'm taking it in to work. They want it I don't know why. My guess is they're checking for prints which strikes me as a waste of time.

Interesting. Whoever killed me would have handled the wallet. It was worth checking.

No, dear. It's not a waste. Someone may have pickpocketed me. Whoever did it could be the one who left my card on Sandy's drive. Prints could identify a suspect who isn't me, or at least a witness. See if you can find out who's been handling my wallet.

I'll ask but they're still keeping me out of the loop on anything that has to do with u.

While I had her attention, I added:

It would be worth asking about Sandy's will and if she had any other relatives besides Jarrod and the ex-husband. Sandy's friend next door could know and help.

Even the most amateur sleuth would recognize it was time to follow the money. Jules sighed slowly and deeply from thedining room.

Way ahead of you. I can't get the information at work but I talked to Mrs. Reid. She's the executor of the will. My precinct picked up a copy. Sandy had an appointment with her lawyer to make changes because of the sale of the Oakville home. The house was to go to Jarrod money still in her accounts and any investments were to go to her husband. She hadn't divorced him his name isn't on the house title she bought him out. Reid thinks he needed the money to pay the lawyer's fee twelve years ago.

So, still married but had no right to the house. Did the husband know he would get cash? Did he know she'd arranged a medically assisted suicide?

Jules, when you talked to Mrs. Reid, did she mention why Sandy was unpopular in the neighbourhood?

Yeah everyone thinks she unfairly made her husband take the blame for the crash. He loved her and all the neighbors said he never drove after drinking ever.

They think Sandy was responsible for the accident and deaths?

They say Sandy would have driven because she didn't drink as much as Al. He was already passing out at the party they're adamant that he wouldn't have driven. But for some reason no one from the party was called to testify.

Probably because his own wife was there to put him away. The poor guy lost twelve years of his life. Maybe he was innocent and had no recollection. He took the fall, knowing his wife was probably driving and didn't stand up for him. That was a hard pill to swallow.

As for Sandy's death, do you know who called it in? And where was Jarrod? If he was getting the house, he also was at the end of the money trail.

The call came from an anonymous male. Right now the theory is it was u. As for Jarrod I contacted the construction company owner myself and he says Jarrod was at work that afternoon at a site just outside of Norwood.

An alibi and no motive. Sandy's life was to end by the Saturday following her murder. Her death a few days sooner would not likely have made a difference to him. It had to be the husband. Had he known she was about to change the will? Had he been concerned she would cut him out completely?

Then, from directly behind me, Floosy screeched like a banshee, and I nearly hit the roof again.

"Where is the brush? I'm getting bored. BRUUUSSSHHHHH!"

Jules would come running to her little royal pain in the honey after that screech, so I had to type quickly.

Don't forget to erase these messages.

Chapter 26

I scurried out of the office and passed Jules in the hallway. She hurried to find Floosy, to resolve the banshee screeches coming from the imp of a kitten. I headed to the dining room to catch Karl before he left.

Karl was still camped out staring down the chipmunk hole, patiently waiting for some action.

"Karl. Dad! Over here." I batted the glass twice. "Where did you find the wallet?" I called.

Karl lifted his head long enough to respond. "At the south cliff beside the big hole they call a mine."

The open pit mine. I had visited the mine when I was alive. Had my body returned there in death? The mine was the major tourist attraction in this region. It was an open-pit iron ore mine developed in the early 1950s that closed in 1978, leaving a massive hole covering over seventy-five acres of land. It is now filled with water with a depth of about 700 feet. That depth was too much for police divers to recover a dumped body if it was weighted and hit bottom. Scuba divers suffer oxygen toxicity at about one-third of that depth. But in my case, there would be no search, considering no one knew I was dead.

Local legend had it you'd have to go swimming a bit too deep if you wanted to find where the bodies were buried in this town.

Karl lifted his snout from the chipmunk hole, and the chip took that opportunity to charge out like lightning had struck its behind. Karl shot out with equal velocity yet missed and trailed behind the chip, down the driveway in hot pursuit. My distraction had left him too slow out of the gate. Defeated, he trotted back to the terrace with his head held high. "Just a bit of exercise." He winked.

If Karl found my wallet on the edge of the cliff, someone had probably shoved my body over and into the water. It was long gone. I would never to be buried beside Clare, but with what I knew now, it didn't matter. Better not to be found.

Karl spied the chip once more, down the road at the top of a new hole. As he zoomed back down the driveway to hunt the escape artist, Shelley flew past him with six of her family in tow, aiming for me. Seven for a secret, never to be told? Again with that poem for Cat's sake? This was my body. Losing my body to the depths of the mine would spare my daughter from having to face my death. That was a secret that should never be told. I had to keep up the pretense of being a human on the other side of the text messages.

"*Caw, caw!* Boss. We found Sandy's car. It's at the mine beside the cliff covered in brush."

"That's where Karl found my wallet."

Both the wallet and the missing Camaro were at the mine? This answered many questions about my death. But I didn't want the police to discover the evidence.

Shelley hadn't been forthcoming in the past. A pellet in the eye had been her style, but now she was downright chatty.

"I went to find Everett to send him up there to give the area a good sniffing. Everett will be along in a moment with his report, boss."

This time, being referred to as boss reminded me of my guilt and how I had treated Karl. I had replaced my father. Karl stood guard over the second chipmunk hole down the drive. He raised his snout and flashed a smile. He had heard but had forgiven me.

"Can you gather the others for a meeting Shelley? I'll watch for Everett and see what he's found."

"You got it, boss," answered Shelley.

Karl glared at the bird. "Boss!" he harrumphed, squint-eyed at the crow as she flew down the drive-in formation with her cousins. It was as if Shelley had used fowl language (I couldn't help but chuckle to myself over that one).

"Burger time," called Jules. Today, she opened another one of those cans with the cartoon feline on the label. As a human I used to hate those. My recollection of the odour was of spoiled mystery meat on a hot summer day that had been set out to rot in the middle of a swamp.

But today, the can opener called to me. My acute feline olfactory sense picked up the perfume of a perfectly finished roast turkey on a chilly fall day, a Thanksgiving bird swimming in rich golden gravy. I closed my little kitty eyes and sighed at the memory and in anticipation of my dinner.

Floosy's sense of smell drew her to the kitchen. She had never experienced a true Thanksgiving. Flo turned to me with eyes glistening. "I like it here. Getting food for my tummy is easy. This is much better than catching mice that run, scratch, and bite. Too much work. This tastes so much better!"

Yes, Flo was a spoiled and pampered puss undoubtedly suited to the indoors.

Jules glanced down at a text on her phone, jumped up from her chair, and jogged out the front door, my wallet in hand.

"Sorry, kids, no TV tonight. I'm off to a meeting."

We planned to spend the evening together watching a movie. It must have been a compelling text to drag her away from her time off, and our evening.

I sat in front of the dining room doors with a full stomach and watched for my crew. I thought about the Camaro. The car was at the mine. Someone hid it up there. They didn't just dump it over the edge with my body. It was valuable and likely meant to go along with the house under the will to Jarrod. Was Jarrod then aware of its location? Was he protecting it?

At some point, someone would discover it, and the police would find my blood in it, and the jig would be up. A mess in the trunk would reveal how my body had been transported. There'd be prints everywhere. Maybe the perps didn't have time to clean up their mess. Why didn't they just dump it in the mine?

I wandered down to my office just as the familiar ding of a text on my phone sounded.

Dad I'm at work. I got a text from Ray Tickborne his clients want to talk. I'm meeting the Crown at the cells. The renters want protection but will give us the name of the meth cook. Thanks again for ur help.

We were getting closer to a solution. If only I could make a connection between Jules's case and the meth in Sandy's shed. Of course, it was only a circumstantial connection, but if I could figure it out this could help to build the case one step further.

That's great, Jules. I'm glad Ray came through. By the way, when you were talking to Mrs. Reid, did you find out who was supposed to be getting Sandy's Camaro?

Yeah I think Jarrod gets it with the house. It's a sweet ride should I make an offer on it? Are you going to want your Beemer back anytime soon?

No fears. At the rate the investigation's proceeding, I suspect I'll be staying in Tibet for a long time.

If they keep cutting me out of the important cases maybe I'll come join u TTYL

I needed to understand Jarrod better. I Googled his name. Nothing there, of course, but then questioned why there would be anything. Like a wolf cub, he ran wild without money or guidance. He couldn't afford a cell phone and likely didn't understand or use social media. He'd been traveling well below the radar and would continue to do so until the police someday caught him at something.

Jarrod hitched rides to work and occasionally used the broken-down Jeep owned by the contractor for use at the construction site, running for supplies or lunch. Jarrod needed his own vehicle, and if he wasn't involved in the murders, then he would surely hunt down that Camaro as soon as the will was read.

Was Al Cox staying with Jarrod or had the John Howard Society set him up with a place to live? JHS advocates for and assists people to navigate the world when first released from prison. Perhaps Jules could get information through her contacts?

I hated to admit it, but I still felt the husband was the most obvious culprit. Were they bothering to look at him as a suspect? Maybe a nudge through Jules would get this moving.

Jules, where is Al Cox staying? Is he around here? It would be worth finding out. He has more of a motive than I ever did.

I'm sure the investigating officer is on it. I have to be careful I'm supposed to stay off this case but I'll see what I can find out. UGG another coffee with the meathead.

CHAPTER 27

Everett batted at the glass with his very large front right paw. His fur was still patchy, but his eyes were clearer, and his stance was erect. The medicine had the desired effect. When I raised my head, I saw Fran peeking out from a tree at the edge of the forest. She raised a paw to wave as Everett turned his head. Was the wave for me or for Everett?

The big male fox turned and bowed until the tip of his snout touched the ground before me, and he spoke almost in a whisper. I no longer needed to catch another animal's eyes to read their thoughts. At least it was possible so long as they hadn't raised privacy barriers.

Everett's investigation confirmed what I already knew.

"Shelley took me to the vehicle at the mine. I'm always impressed with the grandeur of the site. It's quite the spot. The water is so clear and blue. Lovely to see, particularly on a moonlit night." Again, he turned back to where Fran smiled and waited.

"Karl had already left as I arrived," Everett continued.

"Did you pick up anything or anyone in particular?" I asked.

"Blood primarily. It goes from the trunk of the Camaro to the cliff's edge. I assume the blood was from your human self. With the amount that's spread there, it's easy to conclude that someone removed you from this plane of existence permanently. Such a sad state of affairs."

It would be disastrous if the police discovered the car. Forensic DNA tests were the enemy. The Camaro would not stay hidden unless it had some help over that cliff. As much as it would break any man's heart, the Camaro needed to follow my body into the pit.

"Do you think Walter would help?" I asked. "We need someone able to push the Camaro into the mine and the sooner, the better."

Everett stepped away from me. His snout curled, and his ears lay back as if he had caught an unpleasant stench emanating from my direction.

"Why would he? Has he offered to help investigate Sandy's murderer? I didn't see him at the meeting. Because if he hasn't, you surely don't suggest we *ask* him? You know it wouldn't be right, don't you? Didn't your father teach you this?"

Karl's admonition slammed into my mind. I was not to use animals for personal gain. It was the bee all over again. Walter had no involvement in our investigation. He hadn't raised a paw or claw to help. I switched to willing players.

"Do you think Darling and her older sister (Blossom?) would be strong enough?"

Everett wasn't pleased with that suggestion either.

"No. They would injure themselves trying. And I'm not sure even Walter could even if he offered to assist."

I didn't want to lose Everett's respect. Maybe I should wait for Karl. He had broken the rule with the bee. Maybe he would talk to Walter. For Jules's sake, we couldn't afford to have the police discover the Camaro and my DNA in the trunk.

I changed the topic to something safe. "Were there any other scents?"

"Yes, as a matter of fact. I picked up the lovely perfume Sandy wore, still strong. Rosewater, I believe. And the woodsy scent of her nephew, Jarrod. He was in the vehicle off and on. These scents were relatively old."

"Did you pick up anything new? We're still trying to identify that pair from Sandy's yard," I said.

"I did smell the two scents from Sandy's yard. They were both at the mine, all around the Camaro. They were males. One scent was reminiscent of new cedar and hot tar combined with that same sickly, horrible scent of chemical death that wafted out of the shed. What you call meth. Again, it reminded me of when I first left the den. It was the same scent around the feral colony trailer."

I knew someone removed the burnt-out trailer in the spring of last year.

"Was the chemical death smell recent or old?" I asked.

"It was a recent scent, I'm certain," Everett said.

Everett was confirming my suspicions. A meth lab killed the feral colony but another lab was now stored in Sandy's shed. At least one of the unknown humans was connected to both labs. But the police wouldn't connect the new meth lab to unreported feral colony deaths. And even if they could, who cared about the animals?

"What about the other male who was in Sandy's yard?"

"Same horrible death smells, but very light. He had more of your scent on him. And a specific cheap cologne that I recognized, almost worse than the death scent. It was like old human men, adding a combination of cinnamon, lemon, and vanilla to cover their natural odours. He wore too much of it."

Both of the humans were involved in the feral deaths and my murder. That was a strong connection.

Everett had finished and headed out to hunt. As he started towards the east wooded lot, he turned his head back to me, and the wild and hungry look in his eyes sent a chill up my spine. My tail curled down around my butt, and my fur stood on end as Everett picked up speed and trotted away. He was a gentleman but also a fully grown and hungry male fox.

Fran trotted back from the forest edge as Everett left, providing him some distance for his singular hunt. She looked like she'd already eaten. She didn't even sniff at the cat's bowl.

Maybe it was safe. My last attempt at escape almost ended in being eaten by a juvenile eagle. A new approach was formulating in my mind, and it would hopefully provide speed and security.

"Fran, the Camaro was found. Shelley, Karl, and Everett have seen it and checked for scents. They claim blood trails to the cliff's edge. I need to see it. I need to understand the evidence and see if there is something else that we have all missed. I trust their noses, but I want to use my eyes."

Fran had a slightly worried expression on her snout as she listened.

"I know you're trustworthy, and we have a long history, girlfriend. Do you think it would be safe for me to catch a ride with you to the mine and back? I can't move fast enough on these small legs, and I'm too much of a temptation to just about every other animal I would run into on the way. You wouldn't try and eat me, would you?"

Fran sighed and responded quickly: "You're safe with me, but I can't speak for Everett or any of the others. I don't want to fight Everett, and he's very, very hungry right now. I can try and take you and even protect you, but if we run into Everett or any other serious trouble, you may have to hide and hope I get back to you. Is that acceptable?"

She was my only option. "Let's go. Meet me out back at the porch. I have a hole in the screen there."

We met. As I crawled onto her back I smelled the musky odour of the forest floor. Fran turned and spoke just once before starting her run. "Lord almighty, you smell really good, like a barbequed steak drizzled in butter. I'm glad I finished off that nasty red squirrel you met at Session before coming over today."

It took about twenty minutes. Fran was careful to avoid open roads and fields, and she wound her way up the hills to the edge of the old pit mine - a massive water-filled quarry. There were bushes piled up awkwardly and I could see the metal of the Camaro only partially hidden beneath. My nose and eyes both picked up the trail of blood that ran from the trunk to the very edge of the pit. I looked over the edge to the water and imagined myself down deep, bloating in the water, weighted to the bottom. I choked and coughed and tried to hide tears welling up.

While cats can produce tears when they have problems with their eyes or sinuses, my emotional response was purely human. I still felt like William Hawkins but as I looked over the edge, I finally really understood there was no going back. Jules was going to be hurt. Then I started to "cat". I paced the edge of the mine and howled loudly, vocalizing my sadness. That was a big mistake.

Fran quickly joined me to whisper in my ear: "Hide. I'll be safe. You. Go. Now."

Where? I ran to the bushes and slipped under the front of the car just as a very large coyote arrived at the trunk, snout down sniffing at and following the blood trail.

Fran crouched placing her body between me and the coyote, and let out a deep growl. The coyote had left the blood trail and started to follow my route to the Camaro but stopped in front of Fran, perhaps a little too close.

"Just looking for the cat that was here. I can smell it," said the coyote.

"Gone," said Fran as a long string of drool dripped from the side of her jaw. "Dinner," she qualified.

"Fine," replied the coyote, and he turned and trotted away.

I couldn't believe it. Fran was so brave and stood her ground to protect me. I could not have been more grateful.

"Are you OK? Is it safe to come out? You played that role so authentically!" I said still hiding under the engine.

"Give me a minute. Stay under the engine," snapped Fran. She took a couple of deep breaths and sat staring out at the water for a minute.

"It really is beautiful up here. Everett wants me to come up here tomorrow with him. I think he wants to discuss having pups. His fur is getting better. The mange is almost gone."

Fran continued to enjoy the view before turning back to my hiding spot.

"Ok, Bud. It's safe. Coyotes don't often attack foxes because they know we're good fighters. They're basically cowards and bullies. Coyotes won't take on a fight if they think they might risk getting hurt themselves unless they are starving. They would have smelled your scent, but I gave a performance that told them the kitten meat was no longer available. Except I had to be convincing. I used method acting to get fully into the role. Sorry, it made me a bit hungry for kitten when I was in that moment. But I'm OK now."

I crawled out shaking as much from the confrontation with the coyote, as from Fran's expressive performance. Fran laid down to give me easy access to her back. The trip home felt like it took forever. Fran was watchful for a return of that big coyote, and I sighed my relief when we got to the rip in the screen.

Fran left me without another word. I think the trip was as hard on her as it was on me.

Chapter 28

I was home safe. Just as I had gotten past my nervous, fearful thoughts of large foxes, Flo came up from behind and touched my tail with a paw, which sent me soaring straight up towards the ceiling. I landed on top of the dining table.

"Ha ha! Scaredy-cat knows how to fly." Flo danced around the table leg laughing and snorting until she lost her breath. "Come down. I'm bored. What are you doing?"

I jumped onto the chair and then right onto Flo's head and bit down a few times, hard, shouting my battle cry: *"MEOW!"*

She jumped back and cried out, "What was that for?"

Did she have no idea? "For scaring the crap out of me, you devil-kitten. Don't ever do that again, or I'll tell Jules how much you want to live outdoors . . . with the eagle and coyotes...and foxes."

"All right, all right. Keep your fur on." Floosy paused and peered out into the dark. No moon shone tonight, and the clouds were heavy. It was dark enough that even with enhanced feline night vision, we saw little. Instinct kicked in, and Floosy's fur fluffed a bit while her tail twitched nervously. As long as we stayed indoors, we'd be fine.

I had hoped she would embark on a snipe hunt, but she turned to me and asked, "What's going on with the dead lady case?"

I responded without enthusiasm. "I'm trying to figure out logically who would want Sandy dead. It involves a lot of information you wouldn't understand and would find boring."

"Try me." Flo expressed interest this time. "I'm getting better at hearing you." Ah—so it was her youth, not her impatience limiting communication before.

I didn't hold back this time. "OK. Listen. Sandy had a husband who spent twelve years in jail because of her. That's a motive to cause her harm. He was also likely to inherit a lot of money if she died before she could change her will and give it all away to charity. He's not listed on the house but they're not divorced. But I also need to connect him to the local drug trade since it is involved. Two people connected to a drug kitchen in a trailer two years ago were out back at Sandy's when she and I were killed. They also moved my body to the mine. They're involved. But the husband was in jail two years ago. Someone else had to have set up the drug operation in the trailer and then burned it with the feral colony inside. There was also a house in town running a drug operation that was hidden and had been moved to Sandy's shed. But again, the husband was in jail when the town lab operated."

Flo stared hard, unblinking, through my detailed explanation. She picked up more than I specifically said. "Wow. OK. Stay away from bad-smelling things and places. And wow. The husband was locked up for twelve years? Like an indoor kitty? That's almost a lifetime, though he would be lucky as long as his jail was like ours."

She got the gist, which wasn't bad given her lack of experience. Flo raised her right paw to her forehead and then casually offered a new perspective.

"You gotta think of who's being blamed. The ones that make the poison? They'll blame someone else if they want to make sure they get off scot-free. And they don't want the person they blame to talk or give them up. I'm guessing that's where you come in. They dumped you off a cliff into the water, so they're trying to blame you. But if the cops find your body, who could they line up to blame next?"

I thought Flo was confusing herself, but I let her continue as it was keeping her out of trouble for now.

"I'm not sure what this thing called money is. Anyway, it's something good, so if I were the bad ones, I sure would want to point the claw somewhere, like at someone who would get a bunch of money if Sandy died."

Like the husband.

With that Floosy returned to normal and suddenly jumped on top of me and bit down as she rolled me onto my back. "Payback!" she yelled as she tore off to zoom around the living room before initiating another snipe hunt.

Floosy was good at thinking like the bad guys. (Should I have been surprised?) Flo's idea that Al was the secondary fall guy hadn't occurred to me, because he had a motive. I would keep it in mind, but I still wanted to focus on Al's motives for revenge and money. In the meantime, I expected it would be healthier if I slept in the living room tonight away from the evil spirit that is my sister-kitten.

I got back up, sent a snarl in the general direction of the living room, and then popped myself in front of the window and peered out into the darkness. When I put on my human legal cap I knew Al didn't have a real motive.

The forfeiture rule applied. This principle was adopted from the statement of Lord Mansfield in 1776 Britain: *ex turpi causa non oritur actio*. In modern parlance, it meant that a killer may not profit from his victim's death. If Al Cox was found guilty of murdering Sandy, he would forgo any claim to her estate. He couldn't profit from her death. He was the obvious choice if you tried to follow the money, but he wouldn't ultimately get any if he was charged and convicted.

The annoying sister-kitten had been listening in. "That's not fair if he did all that work," declared Floosy. "Also, what's slavery?" Floosy had done a deep dive into my mental reference to Lord Mansfield. I wasn't even speaking to her or about Mansfield's abolition of slavery, but she had been taking full advantage of her developing skill.

"Oh, never mind," she said. Floosy dove into my brain for the answer herself.

Yes, Floosy had an evil streak. She learned quickly. She was on the side of the criminal. Flo thought he should profit from his criminal activity because he did the work. Yes, I definitely would sleep on the couch tonight with one eye open, in case she perceived some profit in my demise.

If Al killed Sandy his interest in the estate would then go to the next legally defined or named beneficiary - Jarrod. I would bet Jarrod didn't know *ex turpi causa non oritur actio*. Not a chance.

But Jarrod had an alibi. If the killer set up Sandy's husband, there was no reason to set me up as well. Maybe Floosy had it right.

But Jarrod lacked experience and was no more than a pup without the brains or experience to manage a formidable drug operation and two murders.

So, who did?

CHAPTER 29

In the morning light, a calm blue ocean stirred with gentle waves that swelled to kiss the sandy black Cuban shore - my peace. Clare whispered in my furry ear, "You'll have to tell her eventually."

"WAKE UP!" shouted Flo. I leapt straight up, almost to the ceiling again. I landed hard on my tail end. Don't believe those stories about cats always landing on their feet. My butt hurt. I was ready to commit murder myself. "Do *not* do that, you rotten little sister-kitten."

Floosy was unfazed by my fall and anger. She focused on her own interests: "I'm starving. We're gonna die. Where's the food?"

"Go wake Jules. You're the cat here. Just tap her nose or something. Once she's up, she'll feed you. You're not gonna die. Let me go back to sleep."

Flo hissed and spoke through gritted teeth. "She's not in the house and never came home last night. I told you, we're gonna die."

That woke me up. Jules always came home. She would never leave kittens without food or water. This did not bode well.

I ran first to the dining room to check for the Beemer. Nothing. I ran back to my phone in the office. Jules had planned to meet with

Tickborne. There might be a deal and new leads. She should be home and texting me. No text.

A web search of the local paper and the OPP website reported a severe accident on Highway 7 resulting in a multi-car pileup. Several ambulances and a helicopter had removed the many injured. However, there was no report of damage or injury to police vehicles or personnel, thank the Cat. Knowing Jules, she would have volunteered to stay to help secure the area and investigate the mess before the demands of the morning traffic.

Flo leaned in right behind me. She couldn't read, but she could read my thoughts and was always trying to figure out what advantage the phone held.

I bopped my head backward, striking hers, and then turned and said, "She'll be home soon. You won't starve, and we're not gonna die."

But to be sure, I trotted through the kitchen and down the hallway to peek into Jules's bedroom with Floosy in tow. The blinds were shut and the blackout curtains drawn. I almost missed the lump of Jules sleeping deeply. The rumbling sound of a runaway train coming from the lump gave her away.

Jules was home. The Beemer wasn't in the driveway. She must have stopped off for a drink with someone and left the car behind, I thought – not Ewen Keens, I hoped.

Flo's brows clenched, and she crouched to leap onto the mattress. I laid my left paw on her head. Not hard. Come on. It was just enough pressure for her to take me seriously.

"You didn't look carefully, did you, Flo? Do *not* go up onto the bed. Leave her to sleep for a while. That snore means she worked late, and she's exhausted. She'll wake and feed you soon enough."

I was surprised that Flo had not gone into the bedroom. Was she following the rules? I was also relieved that Jules was fine, but there was a lingering shadow of fear hanging over me. What would happen if Jules didn't come home?

Before I fell deeper into that shadow Karl's signal called to me: *thump, thump.* Now what, I thought? I pushed Flo back down the hall. The entire gang had gathered at the usual spot in front of the door. Karl had finally attended a meeting and called it to order by thumping his back left paw hard against the glass.

Floosy moved up and took a front seat, eyes large and sparkling as she searched for her prince, Socks. Darling, Fran, and Everett stood behind Karl while Shelley and her crow cousins were arriving. Shelley bravely pecked at the dregs of the cat food dish, undeterred by either Socks or Karl.

I scanned the group, yawned, and announced, "She's sleeping. She'll be up soon, and everyone will get fed."

"It's not about the mush, Kitten," said Karl.

He'd returned to calling me Kitten rather than my new name. What did I do wrong this time?

"You're the one with all the human experience. What next steps must we take to find Sandy's killer? You called this meeting."

I sighed not really knowing what we should be doing. We'd been busy solving everything except Sandy's murder.

"I'm not sure, but let's go through the facts. I'm open to any suggestions," I said. "Following the money is worthwhile because it's a powerful motivator. The nephew, Jarrod, and the husband, Al, both had a financial interest in Sandy's death. It's unclear whether either would benefit by speeding it up. Sandy had planned to be given a lethal injection by her nurse practitioner on the Saturday immediately following the day of her murder. Both suspects could have waited. A couple of days would have made no difference to either of them, except for some additional funds that only recently came in."

"What are you talking about?" asked Everett. The others shook their heads and shared questioning glances, confused as well.

"You all must have known of Sandy's illness?" I asked.

"No," they responded together, eyes wide and mouths hanging open.

"How sick?" asked Socks.

"Didn't any of you detect sickness in her? I thought you could smell everything." I had read somewhere about cancer-sniffing dogs, so I had assumed feral cats and foxes would have the same ability.

Everett explained his limitations. "I smelled Sandy and your wife together from a distance and knew they shared something, but I kept back because of my skin condition."

Karl nudged forwards past Everett and added, "Being wild animals, we avoid getting too close to live humans, even if they're kind. I think you'd have to get pretty close to smell an internal sickness."

I had become the bearer of bad news, though moot at this point.

"Sandy had been sick for a long time. She and my wife, Clare, went for the same treatment far away." How do you describe cancer to an animal? Skip the details. "After Clare died, Sandy's pain increased. It became too much for her. She wanted it over. Humans can end their lives early, but special, compassionate people do it with dignity and grace. Sandy preferred a dignified death."

The animals murmured their understanding and acceptance of the choice as sound on Sandy's part. I thought they would get it. Clare had explained that many sick animals in the wild hide, lie down in peace, and let go when they feel it's their time.

Karl followed my train of thought and explained, "We animals understand the value of ending unnecessary pain. We respect independence and the right to choose one's path."

"But she didn't choose the death she got, did she?" Everett shifted back and forth, his tail dipping down and between his back legs, visibly upset. "She wasn't prey. This was not predation. A crazed killing?"

He knew the answer, but I had to state it aloud for them all. "By animal standards, it was crazed," I responded. "Sandy wasn't given a choice. The violence of her death would have been a fearful experience. The murderer did not need to, or try to eat her. The death in that manner was unnecessary."

Karl spoke to the group. "Then that's why we'll work together. It's to find who murdered our Sandy. It's not that she's gone—now we understand someone took away her right to choose. We must put crazed killers down."

We took a moment to let it all sink in. Heads dipped, some eyes glistened, and low growls escaped both ferals and foxes.

Karl broke the silence first. "What can we do next? You're in charge."

I turned my head away from the group, sighed, and then turned back and sank down until I was lying flat on my belly. I was at a loss and started summarizing what we knew.

"We found the Camaro that transported my body from Sandy's, and I was likely dumped into the mine. Our target right now is to find the two unknown humans connected to the Camaro. They shared my blood from Sandy's yard and likely killed both of us with the same shovel. They also both smelled of the poison meth connecting them to the feral colony deaths. If we can find these two and identify them by name, it will help us understand what comes next. The foxes and feral cats have the scents, but no one has recognized them yet. So just keep nosing around."

The group was disillusioned. But animals could only do so much with noses, eyes, and ears to steer the police in the right direction. Everett's eyes continued to tear, and Karl still scowled. It wasn't much of a strategy.

I thought we were done, but Karl displayed disappointment for all to see. Was it the strategy or did he just want to take me down a peg?

"Kitten, Everett mentioned your issue with the Camaro and that you wanted Walter to help push it into the mine. I know you are finding it hard to let go of your human self, but do you now understand? It's degrading to expect submission to the interests of another animal. This is worse when the request comes from one who is normally your prey. The proposition is exceptionally insulting. And what do you expect your messenger would suffer once they conveyed such an insulting request to an enormous bear?"

In unison, the group took a single step back, away from me and my failings. I wasn't in charge anymore.

I had planned to raise this matter privately with Karl. I hadn't been trying to get him killed. In retrospect, this was the second time my actions could have placed him at risk with a large, angry Walter. I finally got the message. There wouldn't be a repeat of the bee.

"I'm sorry. I didn't understand before," I said to the group. "Jules and I speak by text, so she thinks my human self is still alive. But if the police find that Camaro, they'll identify my blood, and Jules will find out I'm dead. It would cause her great pain. That's why I wanted to make the Camaro disappear. But I understand now. I was wrong to ask."

Time for me to get realistic. I hung my head.

"I will live with whatever happens with the humans."

Socks stepped up and thoughtfully offered understanding. Floosy had gone down the hallway back to Jules's bedroom and so would miss her paramour's wisdom.

"You're still a kitten," said Socks. "You're still young and haven't come fully into your power. We cats are sensitive. Some cats can control the frequency of their purrs to aid in emotional and physical healing, like Floosy. Another cat power is our ability to tell when a thunderstorm is coming. I can tell you that later today we'll have one doozy of a storm that should wash much, if not all, the blood away. If it's bad enough, it may slide the Camaro into the mine with no help from any of us."

The amazing Socks. I couldn't help but like this cat who showed less concern for my humiliating error and more for my plight. Why hadn't Karl told me the rain was coming? He didn't deserve Socks's attention.

Then Shelley descended to the terrace. Six of her cousins had joined her in the trees to show that they understood the importance of hiding the Camaro – the secret never to be told.

"We birds feel the air pressure as well. It'll be a doozy of a storm for sure. A few trees will be lost to the winds. My family is leaving to take cover. I can barely fly above the treetops without fighting the weight of all the air pressure. If there's flooding, that car will surely slide into the mine."

Before the discussion could continue, Floosy flew down the hall and under the dining table at breakneck speed, smacking loudly against the glass.

"She's awake and coming!" she cried, "SCRAM!"

The entire group disappeared in a flash, and just like that the meeting ended.

<h1 style="text-align:center">CHAPTER 30</h1>

Jules headed to the Keurig coffee maker, not noticing that her two kittens had moved silently to stand at their respective dishes. Flo offered a petite begging *mew,* successfully earning half of the can of turkey and gravy delight delivered with a rub and a smile.

I considered texting Jules about the Camaro but thought it better not to call too much attention to the awkward issue. When Jules and I last texted, no one complained about a missing vehicle. It would have helped my cause if the car remained well hidden. But was Jarrod wondering about the car, or did he know its location? I was missing something.

Jules retreated to the living room with her coffee and cell phone and texted. So, back to the office as fast as my little paws would take me to check for her incoming messages.

I looked into the whereabouts of Al Cox. He has a good alibi went to the east coast as soon as they released him from prison. His train ticket would establish his alibi but the local JHS confirmed he was there to find a job. Cox was a veterinarian and was looking for a job as a clinic assistant until he could requalify for his license.

Did you check?

Of course Father. I spoke with the eastern JHS rep they met in Halifax the same day Sandy was killed. Al was thousands of miles away he only returned to Ontario afterwards because he learned Sandy had died Jarrod likely told him.

Al Cox was not much of a suspect unless he'd worked with a third person.

Did you check Jarrod's alibi?

Give me a break Dad I called his boss. Jarrod worked at the Norwood construction site plus he has no motive. He knew Sandy had already scheduled her euthanasia there was no benefit to hastening her death by a couple of days.

Jules hadn't considered that Sandy intended to change her will on Friday. Jules needed to check on Jarrod's alibi more closely.

Jules. There is a motive. If Jarrod knew Sandy planned to change her will, was he worried he would miss out on his cut? I know you talked to the boss, but he was in Peterborough, right? Did you check with anyone at the actual construction site?

Jules delayed responding. She must have been thinking it through. Or, she was frustrated with my interference. Or maybe she went for a coffee. (Just bored?)

Fine. I'll run into Costco in Peterborough and I'll visit the construction site on the way.

After shutting down the phone in case Jules came by my office, I headed out to the living room only to find Jules and Floosy engaged in a game of chasing the ball (akin to soccer). Flo glanced my way.

"I thought I'd keep her busy while you were on your phone," she said while taking a running smack at the pink rubber ball.

Where had that come from? Flo was not thoughtful or my ally. Suddenly she had acted as a lookout and a distraction on her own initiative. Don't look a gift kitten in the mouth, I told myself. Flo could keep the game going for at least half an hour. I hadn't planned to do more research. Maybe a bit of payback to Flo was in order for her efforts. I trotted back to the phone to send a final text to Jules before returning to the living room to play goal.

Jules, I would prefer it if you called the new kitten Floosy.

I went back to the living room for a rousing game of soccer. Jules was off work for the day and finally left the house, heading to Costco in Peterborough. There was nothing to do for now. But wait. She must have checked her texts in the car before leaving.

Got it. Floozy it is.

NO. Not Floozy. S not Z. She's a kitten, not a cheap tramp. Floosy, OK?

Fine. I forgot to tell u I got a name. Tickborne's clients gave up the meth cook who was threatening them into covering for him it's Bob Hall. We're trying to track him down but he may not be local.

My Cat. Could it be?

The name Robert Hall came from my research of the feral colony deaths. He was the owner of the lot that held the meth trailer. The police wouldn't be aware of the feral colony or the connection be-tween the lots and meth. We animals had made the connection. Bob Hall, the meth cook from the town bust was the owner of the lot that had housed the meth trailer that killed the feral colony. Was Bob Hall one of the two unknown humans scented by Everett? Did Hall plan to use Jarrod like he did the town renters, to set up a new kitchen in Sandy's garage? It made sense. The case was building and maybe my team could genuinely be of help.

I was thinking about picking up another lot as a project and learned that the vacant lot behind Sandy's is owned by someone named Robert Hall. Rumour has it, he may have been running a meth kitchen out of a trailer on that lot a couple of years back. I bet it's the same guy.

Wow great! But rumours aren't proof. If u get more let me know. I'll pass this on to Ewen right away the proximity of the lot to Sandy's leads us somewhere. Thanks for the tip. Someday you're go-ing to have to let me know where u get ur info. I'm off to Triple AAA Construction now. Love u and miss u come home soon.

I rolled my eyes at the thought of Jules lecturing me about what constituted proof of guilt. I was acutely aware that this circumstan-tial case needed a connection between Jarrod and Bob Hall, and we still had not discovered the identity of the unknown third party.

I headed to the dining room and watched Fran as she chased down a black squirrel. A tap of my paw on the window got her atten-tion. She'd already lost the squirrel up a tree and so turned back to join me.

"How's Everett?" I asked.

Fran's eyes sparkled as she spoke: "He's so much better since Jules has been feeding him the meatball medicine. He's getting to be handsome - almost dashing. I just know there will be pups in my future. How did the investigation go? Everett tells me you're getting closer." Fran's ears twitched backwards listening for squirrels or other prey.

"Yes. I think there's a connection between the feral colony's deaths and our murders. Jules uncovered a name that is the same name as the owner of the empty lot behind Sandy's house."

Fran smiled out of one side of her mouth when she asked, "Let me guess. Is it Bob Hall?"

I fell backwards, flat on my back as I twisted my tail awkwardly, blown back from the window by her admission. It took a moment to gather myself as I stared at Fran. She stretched her body to full length while waiting for my reaction. Once I had regained self-control, I marched to the glass and smacked it once hard at her snout. It was her turn to leap backwards.

I peppered Fran with the questions that flew to mind.

"How long have you known that?" I hissed and spat at her as I formulated the questions. "Why in Cat's name, wouldn't you tell me earlier? What else haven't you said that I need to know? Do you know the killer's name? Why were both of us killed? Fran, how could you protect my murderer?" The profusion of spit had started to drool down my chin.

Fran stood her ground, offering that same sly smile out of one side of her snout. "I'm a fox, not a rat. You know who I worked for when I was a human. The cook in this area has always been Bob Hall. You had to find that out for yourself. I live by a code."

With fur fluffed the length of my tail I hissed and spit back at her. "Give me a break, Fran. You're not a human. You're no longer sub-ject to any human code. Your old clients know you're already dead. You can rat all you want, and no one is going to come gunning for you as a fox. Start spilling it. What else do you know? And don't give me any more of this code crap."

As I licked the spittle, Fran waited for a few moments. She

explained, "Like you I'm reincarnated because I haven't fully let go. Maybe no one will gun for a fox, but I still have a certain obligation."

I wasn't to be deterred. "What about your obligation to Sandy? Everett would be dead if it wasn't for her and for me getting Jules to take up the work. Where are your loyalties? Don't you have a greater obligation in this new life?"

Fran stood quietly. She considered the placement of her front paws and then slowly raised her snout.

"Bud. You're tied to this place because of your connection to Jules, right? Can you just stop feeling it? Reincarnation is a powerful expression of our needs. For me, I really liked my old job and my old bosses. They respected me and protected me, and I owe them the same respect and protection."

"Have you considered that the point of being reincarnated is to give you some time to let it all go? It's not an excuse to just keep holding on to your old life. (Was that me saying all of this? Did I mean it?) Besides, Bob Hall was not one of your bosses, was he? You don't have loyalty to him at all, do you!"

"Fine," she said. "I know one other thing that may help. The guy Bob Hall is not the local boss. He works for a more powerful kingpin that runs everything around here. The boys in the city respect that one's style. No one does anything without his permission and without paying a fee. If a person doesn't toe the line, the police will know what they did and how they did it and have witnesses and statements to support a prosecution. This guy has the goody-two-shoes and the crooks equally under his thumb. My clients in the city referred to him by his nickname - the Mayor."

"What's his real name?" I thought this could be the third person we were still looking for.

"I don't have a name," replied Fran. "You want to look for the one person who hides and yet has a reach into both legitimate and illegitimate operations in this area. He takes his percentage, is never caught, and arranges for the arrest of any criminal that doesn't get on board."

We were after the Mayor. We needed a name and a connection to Jarrod and Sandy.

Chapter 31

Darkness had fallen. Floosy had not started her nightly snipe hunt and still lounged on the shawl with her tail curled across my back legs. I pushed it off, got up, and hit the cat box, all the while holding my breath until dizziness set in. The litter needed changing, again. Odd. Jules was ordinarily right on top of these issues. This was the second time, and we were now two days in without a litter box change, My sensitive feline nose suffered.

I took a turn around the house. The TV remote sat on the coffee table. I jumped up and stepped on the remote. It worked. I could have been watching movies all this time. The TV was preset to the national morning news, and I clicked it off again. No sign of Jules. The front windows were open but still covered in screening. Fresh morning air filled the living room. No sign of our Beemer. Why wasn't she home? Did she break down and accept a date with Ewen Keens? Was she out drinking at the Legion?

I returned to the office quietly so as not to wake the sister-kitten and texted Jules.

Where are you? Any luck at Triple AAA?

Who is this? Is that you Bill? Hawk?

Someone had her phone, and they knew me by my first name! Her call display would have shown me as Dad. It had to be the police, and they would triangulate the signal and track me down!

I started to pant and sweat. I released a loud howl before I gathered myself together, deleted the texts, and turned off the phone. I switched the phone back on for a moment to check that the protections I had implemented to stop a trace remained active. I was safe. But they might suspect I was still alive, and would they condemn my daughter for keeping me concealed? My ruse was falling apart.

An ache in the pit of my stomach grew. Something must have happened. Jules hadn't been able to talk. A stranger had her phone. The cat box went uncleaned. Something was seriously wrong with her. My sweet Baby Bear! My worst fears played out in my head. Getting traced didn't matter. I swiped with my paw and turned the phone back on. I had to find out.

With a quick search of the online police bulletin and the local news sites, my fears bore fruit. The local news reported a shooting at a Triple AAA construction site in Norwood. No names were released. A police officer had been shot and was in critical condition at Peterborough Hospital. A second person had been shot and taken into surgery, but they weren't expected to survive.

I started to pant again. My whole body trembled. I couldn't maintain balance on my four legs, and it took all my effort to stop myself from falling over. My mouth hung open, and drool dripped down the left side of my chin. I howled my horror, sounding more like a coyote than a kitten.

Floosy, wide awake now with her penchant for bad timing, clamoured to have her belly filled. She smacked the back of my head and asked, "What's your problem? I thought a coyote got into the house! Where's the food? Where's the water? I'm gonna die. Do something, Buddy." Then she moaned dramatically to emphasize the point.

Enough! I stopped howling and bopped the top of Flo's head with my paw. Not so hard as to cause damage. Just a blow with enough power to get her full attention.

"Jules is missing. There's a news report. She might be injured. She might be in the hospital or even dead. I can't listen to your bellyaching right now, so just stop." I panted hard, barely able to catch my breath. My heart raced double quick.

Floosy rubbed her head, and then squinting angrily, she searched my mind for information. I resumed my position in front of the phone and kept my eyes down on the screen. It was all I could do to keep my shaking paws on and my drool off the keyboard. Jules shouldn't have been at risk out here. This was not the city. Country living was supposed to mean fresh air, home cooking, and no street gangs. What had happened? Was she OK? How could I find out? What would I do without her?

Flo got up, laid her head on my back, and started to purr. It was a strange sensation. I felt my muscles relax and my heart rate slowed. I stopped shaking. We were together in silence until emotionally exhausted, I fell asleep. Not Cuba. Just fire and screaming and . . .

Flo swatted me on the head again to wake me, and as I opened my eyes, she whispered, "Get up." I could hear someone walking around. Immediate relief. Ears perked up and back legs coiled to spring, I prepared for a breakneck dash to Jules in the kitchen. But using a strong paw across my shoulders, Flo laid me down flat, with all four of my paws sprawled out in every direction. I couldn't move. I hadn't known her strength.

She leaned in toward me and whispered again, "No. Not her. Someone else. Someone bad. Can you smell that?"

I stopped squirming and listened to the welcome of the familiar whirr of the can opener and sniffed. Turkey mush was mixed with... Old Spice? It still made my stomach growl. Or was that Flo's stomach? She squatted on top of me holding me down. Why wasn't Flo running for the turkey mush?

I eased back, dragged myself out from under her, and edged my way on paw tips down the hall for a view of the kitchen. A man stood at the counter, digging mush out of a can and onto a plate. He didn't know about the two ramekins but had already filled the water bowl.

"It's OK. He works with Jules. It's Ewen Keens. The guy who wants to be her boyfriend," I said. He wore civvies and had arrived in a black-and-white vehicle that was painted up like an old squad car. Is this what he normally drove? Or was he undercover full-time now? If only I could ask him what had happened to Jules.

I came out first, mewing, and went straight for a drink. Flo followed cautiously, found the officer's boot, and mewed, rubbed, and rolled over to attract a scratch behind the ears or on the belly. But Ewen Keens nudged Flo with his foot to remove her from his boot and then kicked the bowl enough to splash my face.

"Meow," we chorused.

"You hungry? You little rats sure are small. Don't worry. We coppers take care of our own one way or another." He said that with a chuckle. "Jules won't be home." He continued to hold the can of mush. "Sarge sent me with the key to feed you. And I have to keep up the image of the good little copper, don't I?"

We stood glaring at each other for eons. What a tease. Finally, he reached down and with his index finger against his thumb, Ewen flicked my ear again and started laughing.

"MEOW!" I yelled at him. It hurt the same as it did the first time the jerk did it. Was he here to torment us? What did he find so funny? Where did he get off calling a couple of cute kittens, rats? Where was *Jules*?

The officer's pocket rang, and he withdrew his phone. "Keens here . . . Yep. I'm here now. I fed and watered the cats for her. Smells like a crappy zoo in here. What a pig. She's never gonna get a husband if she can't clean a house."

I caught Flo's eye. "It is not Jules. It's likely another cop calling. At least we can listen in on the conversation. See what you think. Something is wrong here," I said. Flo had settled down in front of the mush but stopped eating to concentrate on Officer Keens and his side of the discussion.

"I know. We've never lost one yet. Though I'm betting Jules will beat herself up if she survives and the perp dies."

Jules wasn't dead. Thank the Cat.

"No. She put in some overtime out of uniform at Triple AAA to confirm the nephew's alibi on that murder case. She was supposed to leave it alone . . . No, her dad's not a suspect anymore. If you ask me, Sarge made a mistake on that one. They should still go after him. He's a retired defence lawyer, eh? They're all on the take. But Sarge says the guys in forensics found his DNA on the shovel underneath the blood of the female victim. It matched a large dent. I don't understand what all that means, but Sarge says he's no longer a suspect because someone hit him first. How can they know that? Jeez."

It's called forensic science, numbskull, I thought.

"Yeah. How'd he get up and walk away if they hit him that hard with the back of a shovel? I don't trust it. I still think he did it all, and I'll bet she's in on it and hiding him. They should kick her off the force."

Ewen wanted my daughter fired. He pulled out a dining room chair from the table and flopped down oozing grease and sweat that was sure to have a trace on the upholstery. His left leg bounced nervously as his heel tapped the floor.

"No, she hasn't been told anything. When she wakes up, someone will have to tell her the old man is dead, even if they haven't found a body. I say kick her off the force, and she'll run back to Daddy, and then we'll get both of them."

Off the hook for Sandy's death, but now Jules would wonder if I am alive. Who had she been talking to on the phone all this time? Why did he want her fired? She must have recently let him down hard. What did he try to pull on her? I wondered as my claws stretched out.

Keens's right leg now bounced like a jackhammer, making the whole house shake and rattle with the vibration as it undulated through the floor. Floosy and I sat still in the kitchen, listening.

"Yeah, the nephew's alibi didn't hold up. The owner had no clue what was going on in his own company. One labourer at Triple AAA told her Jarrod Bailey and his supervisor had buggered off together in the company Jeep the day of the murder. Neither of them were at work. The supervisor turned out to be Bobby."

Bobby? Bob Hall? Ewen calls him Bobby? Hall must have a long arrest record to gain such familiarity with the police.

"Jules called it in when she accidentally ran into Bob ... Ya, she followed procedure. I arrived first, so I could help ... Yeah, I got him. He's dead. He's not going to make it to trial . . . SIU? Yeah, I'll be right back as soon as I take care of her rats."

It was normal for the Special Investigations Unit to get involved whenever an officer fired their gun, was injured, injured another, or even caused death.

Keens hung up and stood. Flo shook her head at me. "Bad dude," she whispered. "Watch out for him. He's gonna try something." I trusted her judgment on this issue.

My mind was spinning.

The police no longer wanted me even as a person of interest. He'd initially told Jules that I was innocent. But on the phone, he'd claimed I was the murderer.

Keens turned back to us. "Hey, little rat dudes. I'm outta here. I may head out to the hospital to pay your mom a little visit. Or go for a drive up to the old mine."

Why would he go up to the old mine? We followed him keeping our distance. Flo hissed as he walked back into the kitchen and kicked over the water dish. The dish slid back and missed me by a centimetre. I was numb and didn't even move when the water flew over my paws. Flo took off to hide under a chair back in the dining room.

Keens walked to the spilled water dish, spread the puddles around with a dirty boot, and tried to connect that boot with my body. He laughed. Awake, I now moved too quickly for his boot to find its mark. He targeted Flo under the chair and tried to grab her but managed only to flick her ear as she scampered down the hall. Keens finally walked towards the front door, muttering.

"You little rats are on your own. Don't expect me back to feed you. Jules should have learned. If you live around here, you do what you're told, and keep your nose out of other people's cases."

My whole body began to shake again and it was hard to think straight. I headed to the dining room only to discover Socks, Everett, and Karl. They raced about sniffing all around the old black and white squad car that Ewen was driving. Karl examined the driver's door and handle. They both disappeared as Keens walked around to the driver's door. The motor roared to a start, and Keens reversed down the drive as both Everett and Karl raced towards the terrace.

"It's him. It's *him*! The third person in Sandy's backyard. The one we've been hunting!" shouted Everett.

Shocked and confused, I couldn't breathe. Could such a meathead actually be behind it all? He was the investigating officer responsible for collecting evidence in Sandy's case. Of course, his scent was there. He would be all over the scene.

It made me dizzy to watch thirteen of Shelley's family fly circles around the old used cop car, all the way down the drive until it turned onto the road. I counted numbly. Thirteen, including Shell. It's the devil himself.

Karl shouted, "Everett and I picked up that death stink all over him. The stink that killed the feral colony. The same stink from Sandy's garage."

Everett also stepped up. "That horrible stink of death was all over the Camaro too. I recognize it from the feral colony deaths. He drove a black-and-white vehicle a couple of years back when they burned the trailer. I remember. I smelled him then!"

There was a connection between Jarrod and Hall and between Hall and Ewen Keens.

Then it all started to fall into place. Keens knew about the mine. Did he only know about the Camaro? Did he know about my dead body?

Keens had kept Jules from the investigation at every step. He wasn't a detective but was already in plain clothes when Jarrod showed up at Sandy's and when Jules first arrived on the scene. Off work but there first. How had he known a murder had occurred? Because he had already been at the location.

If Ewen was supposed to be an experienced senior officer, how did he make such a rookie mistake as handling the murder weapon? He'd picked up the shovel before it was bagged and tagged, smudging and corrupting the earlier prints. Was he giving his prints an alibi for being on the weapon? He had tainted the evidence intentionally.

He acted like a bumpkin, but he was one smart, dirty cop. He was the killer who had been running the drug trade, playing on both teams at the same time.

Ewen Keens was the Mayor.

CHAPTER 32

I had to know. We had to follow Ewen to the mine. Whatever he intended to do, I was confident it would not be in my daughter's interests.

Could I trust Everett for a ride? Fran wasn't around, but she told me not to trust that he could keep his hunger under control around kittens. Flo was hiding somewhere in the house. I wasn't worried that she'd follow. She had not found my hidden exit from the house.

I hollered to Socks to meet me out back behind the porch before I turned to Everett.

"Keens is going to the mine. I have to follow him. To be honest, I don't think you could handle being that close to me. Can you please go look for Fran and just let her know where we are and what we've discovered about Keens?"

He may have been a hungry large fox but he was a class act and immediately left. He would not put me at risk intentionally.

I ran through the house to the back and threw myself out the hole in the screen, flying through the air to land on Socks.

"Do you mind? Can I ride on your back to the mine? It'll take too long if I have to walk there on these stubby little legs."

Socks didn't comment but started to trot while I found my purchase. Karl joined us and we ran through the feral territory in leaps and bounds. Socks knew every shortcut through the woods and yards. We shot across the highway and an open field, Karl taking point until we got to the mountain of gravel that surrounded the mine. There was a worn path through the gravel and stone on one side of the mine. As tired as I knew they were, both ferals heaved themselves and me straight up the side of the hill to the location of the Camaro.

Once there, we got up onto the roof of the Camaro and waited.

"Where is he? Is there a plan?" asked Karl.

"He must be hiking it," I responded. I hoped he had not gone to the hospital first. And I assumed driving would cause him to be delayed. He would have to take the long route, through town, along the highway to a sideroad, up to the mine, but on the opposite side of the pit. So Keens would have to hike it over to our side. But I was thinking like a tourist.

Socks listened to my thoughts and disavowed my assessment. "There's an old mine road. It's just past us on this side. He could drive it. It's likely how they got the Camaro up here."

We waited about 15 minutes before we saw him coming. Socks was right. But the lights and sounds were not his car on the old mine road, but those of an ATV.

"Looks like he intends to push the car over the cliff with that noisy thing," said Karl.

That made sense. His bloody fingerprints were all over the vehicle. Jarrod would have wanted to keep the Camaro and just clean it up. But now that the gig was up, there was no time. Keens was not going to let Jarrod's inheritance stand in the way of his business interests or his continued freedom.

'What's the plan?" asked Socks as we watched the ATV come closer and closer.

I wanted to get my claws on him and scratch his eyes out.

"Not you, Buddy. You're too small. Let Socks and I try to scare him off," said Karl.

As the ATV pulled close, I had second thoughts. There was no way that Karl and Socks could stand up to a powerfully large, psychopathic human male. They would both end up tossed hard against the rocks or strangled or beaten to a pulp. But I could see both had teeth bared and claws extended, ready to jump him.

Keens got off his quad and started chuckling at the sight of us.

"Little rat! What are you doing so far from home and with these two sorry-looking stragglers. Are you all looking for a ride into the drink?" Keens snorted when he laughed.

If he was going to push the vehicle forward, he'd have to get it out of gear first, but as he reached for the driver's side door handle, Socks leapt. The enormous cat aimed for Keens's shoulder, all claws ex-tended as he bit down on the back of his neck. Then Karl's jaw clamped down on Keens's hand, immediately drawing blood (not mine for a change). The human jumped and started running back-wards, shaking his head and arm to dislodge the grips of these two wild ferals until he lost his footing. Just before he found the edge of the pit, Socks and Karl let go falling to the ground, leaving Keens to drop 10 feet down, splashing into the water.

I flew off the roof of the Camaro and ran to the edge and looked down.

"Keens is swimming. He's pointed to a spot that's only a few yards away, to those natural steps in the rock. He'll be coming back. Are you two OK?" I turned to look at where Karl and Socks had landed.

"All good," said Socks. "Just dandy," said Karl. They both started to hack and spit out the remains of the blood they had drawn.

"I don't think we're going to be able to go another round with that guy. He knows what to expect now and will be prepared. Look at him. He's all red and is that slather coming out of his mouth or just water? Oh, yes, he is one angry dude," said Socks.

"This could be the end, Kitten," said Karl. "Stay back and hide.

Fran will come and find you and take you home, but whatever happens, stay out of the way."

Karl's fur stood straight out. He started to howl as Keens walked closer towards us.

I had fallen into a trance listening to the melodic war song emanating out of my feral father. I was mesmerized by the sounds and had failed to hide. Fran arrived behind me and whispered: "Get on my back, Buddy. Now. Don't be a distraction for Everett."

Shelley's family now sat in readiness on top of the Camaro. Everett was ready to offer backup and moved behind the two feral cats. But just as I finally got well under the Camaro, I noticed a large male coyote also arrived. Karl continued his war song leading the group. Fran confronted the coyote.

"Leave now. This is not your business. We will protect the cats," as she gestured with her paw to Everett who stood tall behind Karl and Socks.

"Easy, babe. I'm here to help the kitten. He was the Protector at Session and stood up for my mate. I've been watching and this human is causing him some trouble, so I'm here to help."

That was a shocker. But I thought we could use the help. Ewen was a powerful human.

But then, Walter arrived. There was an audible sigh of relief from the whole animal group.

The bear walked forward and roared his judgment: "You are guilty of the crime of the crazed killing of the human, Sandy, beloved of the animals. You are sentenced to death."

Ewen Keens, eyes wide, heard the roar but didn't understand its meaning. Still, he turned and threw himself down the slope of the hill but was not fast enough to escape the wings and beaks of Shelley's crew or the justice of Walter. We heard one scream from the bushes at the bottom of the hill. It was done.

One down.

Chapter 33

I was home safe, but I didn't know Jules's status and couldn't use my phone without giving myself away. My paws were tied. Afraid to do anything, I waited by the phone while Flo once more lay purring on my back, trying to settle me down. My shaking had finally stopped. I had to warn Jules about Jarrod and Bob Hall. The risk was worth it even if I got caught. Maybe whoever was on the other side of the phone could at least tell me what had happened to Jules.

I swiped the phone open, hit the text box, and tapped hoping to get someone official.

Can someone tell me what's happening with Jules? I'm worried.

Dad I'm betting u have seen the news. Sarge gave me my phone back he said u texted. I'm OK I'm being released from the hospital. I'll be off for a bit I caught a bullet in my leg but no serious damage.

My body slumped to the floor, and I breathed deeply and carefully to get control of my emotions. I had to think fast if I wanted to keep her out of trouble.

Honey. Thank the Cat. I was terrified. Are you in pain?

Cat? What happened to God? LOL I'm OK just need Tylenol and a big band-aid. I'm ready to come home but can't walk very well I expect to be home for a while. Can u come back now from Tibet and take care of me? I need my daddy!

It almost broke me to deny that request. I had to remind myself that her daddy, Bill Hawkins, was no more. Floosy kept purring and leaned hard against my body.

Ah, my sweet Baby Bear. I can't yet. I'm too far away. But I'm there in spirit. You have the kittens to take care of you. They'll keep you company.

Not the same.

Her disappointment leached through the phone. My heart broke. This had to end badly. There was no way out of Tibet.

I have information for you, and it's good for you to know, but you're not going to like it. I've been working on a case and have a source who is a major drug dealer in the city. He's a client, so I can't tell you who it is. You can't use him to prove anything that he tells me. But he's highly credible, and it will help you in your case. Find another way to back it up.

I know I know solicitor/client blah blah blah. What is it?

Officer Ewen Keens is dirty and runs the drug trade in our area. He also is in charge of most other criminal activity. He goes by the nickname the Mayor. He has Bob Hall cooking and Jarrod com-

pletes the threesome. Think about it, Jules. Keens grew up in the area. You told me yourself, he was connected to everyone, everywhere. As a cop, he's in the best position to play all sides to his personal benefit.

WHAT???

Seriously. He was the first on the scene at Sandy's but was in plain clothes. Had he already been there? He certainly took charge right away. He was sufficiently experienced to know you don't crawl around in a garage without permission. You don't manhandle a murder weapon right in front of the forensic team without your blue rubber gloves.

You're on to something Dad. He was already at Triple AAA when I got there. Do you think he's involved in my case or in Sandy's murder? I had texted him that Bob Hall was a suspect before I left for the construction site he was already there when I called for backup. Do u think he was waiting for me?

Remember Jules, Tickborne implicated Bob Hall as the guy running the meth kitchen, but Keens is the franchise owner. He controls all aspects of the trade, including distribution and security. Hall worked for Keens. And now, when fingers could be pointed in his direction, what did Keens do? He shot Hall dead when he was your key suspect or witness.

Hall's not dead yet. We thought he would be but he got out of surgery just now. Doc says he might pull through.

Great! But you get my point. You didn't shoot him. I'm betting they shot you before Hall went down, right? The extra gunshots that took down Hall were after you were lying on the ground, right? So, it wasn't your shots that hit Hall. And you thought it was Hall shooting you, right? You didn't expect it could be someone else.

U r right I can see it but I can't prove it yet. Are you sure your privileged client won't help me?

What about ballistics? SIU should do an analysis. Make sure they get a subpoena to confiscate all of Keens's weapons, work, and personal stuff. Check his personal vehicle. I'm betting he shot you and Hall both and hid the gun. He'll come up with some story like you were shot by Hall's gun or some stranger who ran away into the forest.

Also, Hall is important to your case, not Sandy's murder, so you can control who protects him in the hospital, right? Can you get someone who didn't go to school with Keens up there to watch over Hall while he recovers? Maybe it's time to chat face-to-face with Jarrod since he and Hall appear to have been a team, together when they left work in the jeep. And he showed up at the house in the jeep alone. Where'd he drop off Hall?

How do u know that?

Honey, I still have a few contacts. Also, your boss is about to tell you I'm no longer a person of interest or a suspect because they found my blood on the shovel underneath Sandy's blood. The shovel hit me first, and I would've been out cold when they killed Sandy.

Why didn't u tell me that in the first place? U could have been home all this time.

I had my excuse already worked out.

I didn't want to worry you. The fact is, I don't remember any of it. The doctors told me I have retrograde amnesia. I don't recall the injury or events right before I was struck. I don't know what happened, but I found myself in a hospital.

Well u can come home now u couldn't have been handling the shovel when Sandy died. U r no longer a person of interest.

Honey. I'm not coming home. I'm travelling. I am actually going to Tibet. For real. I needed some time after your mother died and some distance from everything. I'm too far away now to get back to you, and to be honest, I'm not ready.

I don't like it but OK. I'll text u again later. I have to go. The doctor is here. I think they're going to sign me out.

Flo followed me to the dining room and sprawled on the floor in front of the window. I snuggled up into her fur and leaned in. We were waiting for Jules to return. It had been a long, windy, rainy day and a long and violent night. Flo snored. I dozed off on a Cuban beach with Clare asleep beside me.

CHAPTER 34

Another intruder? Flo and I flew to the front door as another police officer shut it with his big fat boot. I was ready to run and hide but stopped. He carried my sweet Jules in his arms as she leaned against his shoulder, eyes half shut. He placed her gently on the couch in the living room.

"I'll be back in a minute with your walker. Just lie there and don't do anything stupid," he said as he turned to go back out.

Flo and I ran into the living room and jumped onto Jules, snuggling into her arms and purring together as loudly as we could. Jules's eyes were open, and she giggled. Thank the Cat.

The police officer returned with a metal walker with a built-in seat and dropped it off beside the couch. He ducked into the kitchen, saw the mess, and wiped the still wet floor with a paper towel. He then put down some more water and opened a fresh can of food.

"Use the two white ramekins on the counter," called Jules. He split the can between the two small bowls and then returned to the living room to relax in the armchair. Flo and I were not in a rush to eat.

"Oh, sorry. Did you want a drink of anything?" he said to Jules. I liked this cop's priorities.

"No. But I'm dying to get the blow-by-blow. What happened? I assume you've charged both Hall and Jarrod Bailey. Will Bob Hall survive? And what's going on with Ewen?" Jules asked.

"Hall's fine. He was released into custody before you left the hospital. We didn't waste time following your tip. We got the two of them into separate rooms and let them know the other was spilling his guts. They both started talking."

Jules brought herself up straight and let her feet drop to the floor. Flo and I had to scramble to stay on board and maintain the purr.

"But Jules, did Sarge talk to you about your father? I'm sorry, but we think he might be dead. No one has recovered his body, but the forensic evidence suggests the blow to his head was severe and probably killed him. We suspect the murderer dumped his body in the open mine. We found the Camaro, and even with the rain, we had evidence of his blood remaining in the trunk. And we got a confession."

"I know. Sarge called me. He's not dead. Where'd you get a confession?" Jules asked. Her arms tensed as she stopped petting us. Flo and I lay there, ears up, attentive to the conversation. Jules frowned now.

"Hall said your dad died," the officer continued. "Hall initially refused to talk to anyone but Officer Keens. I told him that wasn't possible and that Keens would be charged as well. Hall then claimed Jarrod struck both your dad and the Cox lady. Hall said he was there just to set up the meth cookery. Jarrod wanted your dad to disappear so we would blame *him* for Mrs. Cox's death, but he wanted his aunt to be found so nothing would delay his inheritance. He told us where to find the Camaro and how it had transported your dad to the mine. He said he was confident your dad was dead because there was too much blood."

"He was mistaken," Jules said.

The officer hadn't finished. "We told Hall the Crown's office would charge him with planning the murder and running the meth operation. Jarrod was not that bright. He could never have organized all of that. Again, Hall insisted on talking to Keens. We explained that ballistics had implicated Officer Keens in both shootings at AAA. We had planned to charge Keens with attempted murder for shooting you and Bob Hall. We had not picked up the Camaro and had not found Keens. Suddenly, Hall's story changed. It was Keens who did both murders."

This was fascinating, like listening to an e-book told by a cat lover with a deep, warm voice. I liked him a lot.

"Ewen Keens had been running the drug kitchens and distribution business in this area for years. Bob says his nickname was the Mayor. All Hall did was cook for him. Jarrod was a dumb kid who could provide them with a new private space to cook. With Keens' connections growing up and working as a cop, they could operate without interference. No one survived long enough to give evidence against him.

"We still got Hall on the town meth operation with the renter witnesses. The deal to go easy on the renters is solid."

Jules sighed and closed her eyes for a moment, taking deep breaths as the officer continued the story.

"Hall's prints were all over the driver's side of the Camaro. He says they tied a boat anchor to your dad's leg and Keens dumped him into the water at the mine. I can't see how he could have gotten out of that. But if you're sure, do you think he could testify?"

I suddenly got that sinking feeling in my stomach again. Would Jules doubt me? How could I come clean at this point?

Jules responded quickly, "I spoke with him before I left the hospital. I don't know how he did it, and neither does he. He had amnesia. Hall may think Keens tied a good knot to anchor my dad, but it didn't hold. Someone found him and got him safely to the hospital. When Dad got out he began travelling. He told me he was going to

Tibet. But he can't testify to anything—He's no use to us without his memory."

The nice officer took over the armchair. Is he married? He could be perfect for Jules. I learned his name was Ian McKenzie. I'd be watching for him in the future.

Floosy hopped down off our shared lap. She walked over to Ian and stretched her front paws and claws up his leg until he reached down and lifted her onto a warm place in his lap. Ian shifted in his seat and leaned towards Jules as Flo's purr grew at a different frequency. Yes, Ian deserved the purr as well. His thumb traced a line across Flo's forehead as she closed her eyes.

"OK. I hope your dad is well and you see him soon." He stood up to help lift Jules's bad leg onto the couch. Flo and I shifted again to maintain the purr.

"When we interviewed Jarrod Bailey he denied everything, as expected," Ian said. "He started by insisting your dad killed his aunt, and he struck him with the shovel in self-defence. I asked how your dad's blood got underneath Sandy's on the shovel. He continued to deny it. What a dumb cluck. We asked why he hadn't reported the missing Camaro. He answered he believed the Camaro was still at his aunt's house, and if it wasn't still there, your dad stole it. Oh, and he denied any knowledge of the meth paraphernalia in the shed. Just deny, deny, deny."

"You told him what Hall said?" asked Jules.

"Yep. We started by telling him Hall would testify that it was Jarrod Bailey who had killed both his aunt and your dad, and together they took the Camaro to dump your dad's body. You should have seen his face. Bright red, eyes bulging, his jaw hanging down to his waist. He then claimed Keens and Hall were the true murderers and he was just victimized."

Flo quietly snored from Ian's lap. She had purred herself to sleep.

"Then we finally told him that Keens would be charged which

took him out of the picture. He dropped his head down onto the table, silent for a couple of minutes. We let him think. I got him a glass of water. When he finally lifted his head, he spilled his guts.

"Keens had threatened to kill him and Hall both if they didn't cooperate when he took it upon himself to kill Mrs. Cox and assault your dad. Keens couldn't afford to have anyone ask why he had been inside the shed. It was nothing to him to drop them both. They left the boxes in the shed until things blew over, and they could set up shop again at the Cox residence."

Jules thought about that and asked, "Why did they bring the meth kitchen into the shed for storage? Why not leave it in the woods for a few days until Sandy was gone?"

"Keens wouldn't risk some neighbour walking around in the woods and finding it all. Jarrod's aunt was sick enough. She wasn't going into the shed anyway, so that seemed to be the best storage. The sudden murderers attracting our fine police force to search for evidence changed the plans."

The police had statements that would send the other two to prison for a long time. At the end, Officer McKenzie added, "We found the Camaro where Hall said to look, but we also found Ewen Keens' ATV beside the Camaro and his body in the bushes below the site. He had non-lethal small bite marks on his arm and neck, and his eyes were pecked out. But he actually died from the effects of vicious mauling, likely by an enormous bear.

The human predator met his match. The Mayor was no more. Walter had done his job.

CHAPTER 35

For weeks, Jules sat at home as her leg mended unusually quickly once Floosy found the correct purring frequency to promote healing. Jules had been traumatized. She found it hard to return to work as a cop. Deep down, I thought she had better options. Why couldn't she just sell real estate? Why did she have to return to work at a job where people shot at her?

Jules returned to work eventually. As soon as she left, I scrambled impatiently down the hall and back to the office, already on the phone when Jules drove down the driveway.

Through these experiences, Floosy had grown some and become bolder, if that were possible. We had a charmed life. Without Jules, she knew we wouldn't last long locked in the house. Flo still feared getting stuck inside and starving. Yes, she had talked herself into believing we were *all gonna die* if we didn't become more independent like real feral cats.

While I played blackjack, she asked if I'd ever tried a live mouse.

"No!" I replied. "Not gonna happen. I'd rather starve to death."

Flo felt we needed an escape route in the future just in case something happened to Jules again. What would happen the next time someone shot Jules dead? Of course, I wouldn't listen and I wasn't about to tell her about my hole in the screen porch. But Flo was a natural survivor, born feral, and her true nature came out.

After a run at the online casino, I fell asleep on top of the phone. Cuba, the sun, the sea, and the sand, with Dream-Clare on the sand beside me. I was in my happy place. I no longer thought of her as the real Clare. She had already gone beyond. But Dream-Clare, still lovely, lay on the beach beside me.

"She found the phone. It's a good thing you fell asleep on it. She didn't pick it up right away because she didn't want to wake you," said Dream-Clare.

What was she talking about? I rolled over onto my back and looked up at her.

"Who found the phone?" I asked but didn't get an answer.

"You have to tell her," Dream-Clare said as she placed both hands on my shoulders and pushed hard. "And while you're at it, wake up fast and go save Floosy."

I woke immediately, still lying on top of the phone. In my confusion, I looked around the room for Clare. She must have been wrong because Jules had already left for work. But there was no sign of Flo anywhere. She would normally be asleep on Clare's shawl or be swatting me awake out of boredom. Snipe hunts were no longer an attraction. (All the snipe had gone north for the season.)

Flo's baby powder scent took me to my small hole in the screen porch. She had pulled it apart a bit more with the growing strength in her kitten claws, making a hole large enough to fit her growing body through to escape.

Flo had left a scent trail that led into the front yard. I kept low at the edge of the lawn and then the underbrush of the hedge. I sniffed and surveyed and finally spied her out in a clearing in the grass. Just as I was about to call out, my fur stood on end, and I ducked away from the swoosh of the wings of an enormous eagle. That bird missed me and flew back up to the trees. It zeroed in on Flo. I yelled, "TAKE COVER!" But a chipmunk hole had Flo's full attention.

Caw, caw, caw, caw!

En masse, the crows swooped and fluttered, diving repeatedly at the eagle as a group, cawing for more help from the cousins in other territories. Shelley's group took turns striking the eagle with beaks and wings.

Floosy would have been an eagle snack had it not been for Shelley and her cousins's brilliant and swift response. They hadn't harmed the eagle but had caused a sufficient distraction for Floosy to escape and join me under the bush. The crows then worked at driving the eagle away completely.

Caw, caw, caw, caw!

Multiple cries declared their success with final cawed warnings to the eagle never to come back. Shelley's family gathered together in the trees, watching out for and ready to protect Flo and me.

Flo and I stayed crouched down, afraid to move. Neither Karl nor Socks were available for backup, and Fran was nowhere to be found. I spied the Beemer, parked across the street. Jules hadn't gone to work yet and must have stopped to chat with Al Cox.

I could see her. Jules witnessed it all. She ran down the drive to our bush and scooped us up before charging into the house. And as she did so, she screamed repeatedly at Shelley and her cousins to leave. They weren't moving. Hadn't Jules seen the eagle?

I would have to apologize to the crows later. I told Shelley and the family to leave quickly. When I turned to look at Jules, she watched me closely, frowning. I was being oddly helpful again. But she couldn't honestly think I made thirteen crows suddenly leave the yard, could she? This wasn't like the slipper incident.

It shook me a bit, but this time, it was Floosy who trembled and mewed, quietly crying at the frightful experience. I couldn't purr for her. Jules had dropped us beside our bed and headed back out to discover and fix Flo's screen hole. When she returned, still in a huff, she found Flo in bed and me standing guard over the phone.

Jules crossed her arms and glowered down in my direction. She was holding her own phone and sneering at the one beside my small body.

"There's the phone. Where are you, Dad?" she called out angrily. "Are you in this house, or are you in Tibet?" She thought Bill Hawkins had hidden somewhere in the house. She should be smarter than that.

Frowning, Jules reached down to retrieve my lifeline. Would she turn it off or hide it? Or would she smash it to pieces? I couldn't let that happen and leapt onto her hand, hissing and biting and scratching. Clare yelled in my head, "Tell her!"

Shocked, Jules jumped back and drew her bleeding hand away from me and the phone. I reached out, swiped it on and tapped out a quick message.

STOP. It's me. Dad.

A *ding* came from her phone. She lowered her eyes to her hand holding the phone, and retrieved the text. She looked from the phone to me, grimaced, and then replied straightaway.

Who are u? not my father. How are u calling me? Where are u?

When she pushed Send, the *ding* sounded on my phone. Jules could see the screen as my little paws raced across the keyboard. She saw me type.

I'm using my phone. I'm in the office in our house. I hate to get all Darth Vader on you, but I am your father, Jules. I'm the handsome kitten, Buddy Hawk, typing madly at your feet.

She stood staring and started to waver and sway before she fell. She passed right out.

"I think she fainted," called Flo from the other side of the room where she'd snuck off earlier after witnessing Jules's anger. Flo had stopped trembling.

Jules' eyes fluttered, and as she raised herself up on her elbows, she began to crab scuttle backwards out of the room and into the hall before gaining her feet and raising her phone again.

U r not real how are u doing this?

No one in the world knew my pet name for my darling girl except Jules. She wavered again as she stood up at the door to the office. Before she could pass out, my left paw hit the keypad.

Please take deep breaths. I want you to know you will always be my sweet Baby Bear.

That did it. Jules's knees buckled again. She slowly sank to the floor, staring at me with shock and awe. She stretched out an index finger towards me. I extended my paw to meet the tip of her fingernail before turning back to the keyboard. She recoiled at the touch. I thought to try a bit of humour to introduce reality.

I know. It's impossible. Look at me. I'm a darned cat. And a runt at that! I never believed in whacko stupidity. I never listened to maniacs talking about ghosts, reincarnation, and voodoo priests. It was all a sham, I thought. Frauds, all of them, right? But it turns out that maybe reincarnation is legit for some people. At least the ones who won't let go or have something to finish, so I'm told.

She had been watching me type and then read every word a second time on her phone.

"Who told you? What didn't you finish? Sorry, but I'm finding this very challenging," Jules said. She was not typing anymore, but just looking at me.

My heart ached for her, but Clare had been right. It was time. Flo approached and sat beside me, waiting for Jules' reaction. "No more jokes," said Clare in my ear. Flo had somehow heard Clare in my mind and added a mental nudge for encouragement. I'd have to talk to Flo about this new ability she had manifested, but later.

Honey. I died. I don't think I've accepted it. Not really. I can talk with all the animals and have met one old friend. They explained it all to me. If I had known how or why I got into this mess, I could resolve it and join your mother. Baby Bear, I died in Sandy's yard. I didn't survive. They dumped me in the mine. The body is too deep ever to be recovered. I'll never be buried with Clare. But I couldn't tell you or leave you. You still need me. I know that. I ...

I stopped typing. Jules had started to cry quiet tears. Our hearts were breaking. Nothing I could say would help right now. Flo approached Jules without a mew, crawled onto her lap, and started to knead. Her purr was like a jet engine flying low but at a frequency that made a human sigh. Flo had a gift, and she understood how to use it.

"Is this one reincarnated too?" Jules snorted back the last of the tears, looking first down at Flo and then directly at me. I responded with the phone.

No. Floosy's just another darned feral cat you stuck me with.

I smiled my best kitten smile.

"You never liked cats. Isn't that justice?" Jules giggled as if she were a kitten herself and petted Flo who continued her healing purr to calm Jules down and relieve her growing anxiety.

The team still hadn't been told about the outcome of our efforts. They were afraid of Jules now and wouldn't come near. It was time. I raised this with Jules.

Would you like to meet my friends? I have some now, you know. Their actions were critical in gathering the evidence to resolve both the drug and murder cases.

"You have friends?" Jules couldn't take her eyes off me as I started towards the hall to the dining room. Flo followed. Jules picked up the phone and brought it along (smart girl is my Jules).

I stopped at the dining room door and turned to thump the glass with my hind leg, longer and stronger now than when I first arrived in the house. Karl had done this effectively, and I figured someone would pick up the sound and pass the word. Karl, Socks, Charlotte, Fran, and Everett arrived cautiously. Everett was quite healthy and handsome in a fox sort of way. And did Fran have a bit of a baby bump? Darling and her sister came next but stayed back, leery of the human. Shelley and nine cousins stayed back a bit, nervous of Jules having felt my daughter's wrath.

Jules placed the phone down conveniently beside me. All wild animal eyes were on the device. They had heard about this glorious method of animal-to-human communication and were enthralled, their eyes following back and forth between Jules and my paws. I typed, and Jules responded verbally as I translated everything telepathically to the team.

I introduced each by their proper name and explained their various strengths and special skills. I added that Socks did, in fact, sing and had been an operatic tenor in a prior life. Socks had not yet sung for me. Flo sighed, her eyes wide as she stared at him. Jules recognized that look.

Jules turned to me and asked, "Has Socks been fixed?"

Flo could hear me repeating the question in my own mind and responded herself. "He's not broken," meowed Flo. "There's nothing to fix."

I texted, "Yes he has." Jules smiled. Flo had questions for me so I blocked her. "I'll tell you later," I said.

Walter arrived, and I introduced him formally as the local judge and executioner in the animal court. I didn't want to let her know that he was responsible for Keen's execution. It had been his job as far as the animals were concerned. But humans would hunt him down if they thought he was a killer. The concept of an animal court intrigued Jules. She agreed he could stay, but "in the back, please." He made her as nervous as he made the rest of us.

When I got to Fran, Jules perked up. She'd known her in life. "So, you're back too, and as a fox. That suits." Jules smiled wide, like a sly fox.

Fran also listened to me repeat Jules's comment and responded. "Yes, it does." Fran smiled back, also like the sly fox she was. I didn't need to translate her answer.

I made it clear to Jules that the heroics of the Shelley's family had saved Flo and me from the eagle. Jules had not seen the eagle. She only saw crows taking wing in a mad cacophony. She apologized formally to Shelley. I was proud.

I explained to Jules on behalf of the team that while the police did their job, our efforts identified Bob Hall's connection to the trailer and the Camaro. The animal investigators had been my contacts all along. It was the animals who caused Jules to check Jarrod's alibi. Our team never stopped hunting the person who carried the smell of death and Old Spice. Jules admitted she was impressed. She said it was like having your own squad.

The team was also told of our success in both Sandy's case, and in the deaths of the feral colony. Walter rumbled with displeasure at a missed opportunity to deal with the other crazed humans.

Karl stepped up and asked whether the remaining killers or at least the feral colony killer (Hall) would be "put down." Walter roared approval for the proposition, offering to take on the role of executioner himself if the humans weren't up to it.

I explained, "I'm sorry, but the human court in Canada does not order murderers to be put down. They are locked in cages in large buildings so they can't get out and hurt anyone."

"Sad. It sounds like being an indoor kitty?" Floosy piped up. Even though her frustration with indoor life had been enough for her to tear that screen, the eagle incident had thoroughly frightened her. She had accepted she wouldn't survive as an outdoor cat. Her attraction to Socks was the other reason why she snuck out but I'd ruin that soon enough.

Karl had kept Queen Charlotte up to date. She, too, arrived, carrying herself with the grace of royalty even as she waddled, pregnant to the front of the group. In her wake was Daryl, my barn brother, a large and powerful tom with darker brindle fur like his father. Daryl was mute like Karl and hung back. He was not very social and was used to gentle farm animals, instead of the wild ones lined up in front of the dining room doors. But he was there to offer support for his mother. I hoped in the future to get to know him better.

"My feet hurt, and my back is killing me," the queen declared when I congratulated her. She wasn't happy at all. Jules should get her fixed, I thought. In her case, it would be a blessing.

Charlotte asked, "What happened to Al Cox? I expected the killer to be the husband. Isn't it universally understood that you can't trust a husband?"

I tapped out the message to Jules. She laughed and said Al Cox inherited it all as the surviving husband and sole living relation. Sandy hadn't changed the will. Jarrod was implicated in Sandy's death as a co-conspirator and so could not benefit from his crime. In the end, Al got the Camaro, the house, and all the money. As a veterinarian, he would also achieve Sandy's other wish. He intended to start a wildlife center and rehabilitation program in the empty lot, once owned by Bob Hall. Al moved right across the street into his old house, so we had an animal doctor close by.

Our animal community agreed that both Jules and Al Cox had the souls of animals, and Al's plans for that lot would finally put the feral colony deaths to rest. Justice could mean something more than protecting predatory rights. Even Walter declared he wanted in from the start on our next caper.

I'd learned two important things so far from this new life. First, a large group of crows is called a murder. I now understood. They could take down and drive out almost any predator - human or animal. They were a powerful group when they worked together. Second, life as a cat was good, full of fun, friendship, and love. And there would be so many more crimes that would need to be solved.

I listened as Socks began to sing. It was truly magnificent.

About the Author

I hope you enjoyed this bit of fun. It was long in planning.

My fiction writing only began a month after retirement from a thirty-three-year career in law, starting out in criminal law and ending in the field of worker's compensation law in Toronto. I have written extensively in my field, including a manual and an ongoing legal periodical published by Carwell Canada and Creighton Publishing.

In this next chapter of my life, I am chasing that lifelong dream of writing fiction, starting with Buddy's story.

www.ingramcontent.com/pod-product-compliance
Lightning Source LLC
Chambersburg PA
CBHW032004050726
47590CB00006B/2044

Weeks later at the seminar, Eric and I connected. I heard him and others discuss the successes and challenges associated with advocating for dying with dignity rights. There were breakout sessions and universal talks. A woman brought the audience to tears as she described being alongside her lifelong partner as his dementia progressed to the point where he no longer recognized her. She handed him the drug cocktail that ended his life.

Professionals spoke about the difficulty of adopting and implementing medical assistance in dying ("MAID") laws in the jurisdictions where they practiced. In some countries where the procedure had been legalized, physicians continued to face internal challenges finding colleagues to provide the necessary patient evaluation and medication administration. I was surprised to hear that many palliative care physicians across the globe opposed MAID, believing it violated their Hippocratic Oath.

On the second morning of the conference as I sat eating breakfast at a table with a few other attendees—a Norwegian, a Scot, and an Australian—I was struck by the fact that assistance in dying was a controversial issue that transcended national borders, cultural boundaries, and legal, medical, religious, and moral lines. By the final day of the symposium, I realized the story of my father's struggle to end his life voluntarily, and my assistance and support of him along the way, had to be shared widely. Not only did I feel the duty to adhere to my dad's wish to share his message of finding peace and resolution before dying, but I also felt a call to action for greater education and advocacy of the process of assistance in dying. The act of writing forced me to confront aspects of the profound experience that I had been either unable, or unwilling, to deal with while living through it.

I never thought I would write a book of this type, let alone a memoir. But my father's words echoed in my head: "Tell the story. You are in charge of the story, Danny." My dad's quest and the remarkable experiences it evoked were too important to let fade into oblivion.

The term "Wingman" stems from the military, specifically from the cockpit of a fighter jet. Though there are hundreds of dedicated people who make a military mission possible, a fighter pilot's wingman is the only person who accompanies the lead pilot from takeoff to touchdown, providing key support and back up over unfamiliar and sometimes hostile territory.

My father had many family members, friends, and medical professionals who provided emotional, physical, and medical assistance on his mission to a dignified death, but I alone served as his wingman. I was with my father day and night as he prepared for the end. He allowed me to assist him during the most exposed point of his life: his death. I shared in my father's transition, up close and personal, with all the intimacies, vulnerabilities, and distresses that accompany such a passage.

When my dad took his last breath, he was in the arms of my sister, my brother-in-law, and myself. I was immensely proud to have brought my father safely to that moment. I knew how important my role was to mission success and accepted the position with honor and a heightened sense of privilege. I can think of no greater gift than the one my father bestowed upon me: to be his wingman on his journey to death.

My father's odyssey was not smooth. Unusual and ludicrous obstacles kept showing up in the final week of his life. Only when I put all the experiences together in this book did I come to the realization that his passage was not meant to be easy. His death, like his life, was unconventional.

By sharing his experience, I hope others who are facing this agonizing decision can find solace. And for all of us, may my father's story illustrate how to leave this world peacefully—with love, grace, and dignity.

Daniel Zimberoff

ONE

MY FATHER'S HUNCHED body lurched forward, his hands trembling as they let go of the metal walker and dropped to his side. He straightened as best he could and reached awkwardly toward the aircraft's doorframe for support. I tenderly gripped his shoulder to provide further assistance.

"Pop, take your time. There's no rush," I reassured him as he slowly and shakily stepped onto the United Airlines 787 bound for Frankfurt. "I've got you."

"Can I help you to your seats?" asked a kindly flight attendant.

"No," my dad bellowed as he reached for one of the plane's seatbacks to help steady himself before continuing to shuffle forward.

I turned to the flight attendant and smiled as best I could. "Thank you so much. I think we have this."

She returned my smile and gently patted my eighty-six-year-old father on the shoulder as he passed her. "You let me know if you need anything, dear."

"Thank you," he muttered in a conciliatory tone while continuing looking straight ahead.

My father plodded forward as we made our way to his business class seat. I carried his backpack, remaining vigilant for any trip hazards that may lie ahead. As he trudged along, my mind wandered to a distant time.

I was probably thirteen years old and my father somewhere around forty. He and I were playing tennis at the Newport Beach Tennis Club in Southern California. I was a decent athlete, but Dad schooled me that day, as he often did on the tennis court. I remembered believing at that point in my life that my father was bulletproof—a physical and mental warrior.

Now, I looked down to see an unrecognizable old man straining to walk a few feet toward his airline seat. Once acute, laser-focused eyes were watery and blurred. What had been a muscular body tottered feebly. The right hand, strengthened like a vice after fifty years gripping a tennis racquet, could scarcely grasp the seatbacks. Close-cropped white hair lingered at the fringes of a freckled, mostly bald scalp. Legs, formerly sinewy in firm athletic stance, now barely supported a hobbled frame racked with tremors from a despicable disease. This strange figure shuffled forward with my hand holding steady on his shoulder. *Was this really my dad?*

How did he get here? How did my father go from an invincible hero to frail, irritable man flying halfway across the globe to end his life?

It's probably best to start at the beginning.

TWO

DAVID MORRIS ZIMBEROFF, my Pop, was born in 1937 in Chicago as the third of what would become seven offspring of a pianist and dancer. His father, my grandfather, Manuel "Zim" Zimberoff, had immigrated at the age of three with his parents and four siblings to America from Russia thirty years earlier to escape the pogroms of the Czarists era. Like many immigrants in the early twentieth century, the family arrived at Ellis Island with no more than what they carried in their pockets and on their backs. The young family identified culturally as Jewish but did not attend synagogue nor keep a kosher home.

Zim was not a concert pianist, as that would have required significant study and discipline. Instead, he played live piano at movie theaters and accompanied small orchestras for variety shows. Think Vaudeville acts. The story told for two generations around the family table is that during the run of one such show, a shy dancer named Selma became enamored with Zim. His tall frame, dark complexion and mischievous smile, coupled with quick wit and confidence some would rightly call arrogance, made him seem like a good catch for any young woman seeking a husband. The steady paycheck didn't hurt.

The dancer was not as confident as the pianist. Rather than walk up and introduce herself, each day of rehearsal she would move her warm-up mat closer and closer to the piano until one day Selma was practically on top of him. Zim had no choice but to notice and before long, the pianist and dancer began a courtship. They shared commonality of being first generation Jewish immigrants to America. Within a few months Selma Stenn and Manuel Zimberoff were married, with their first child, Sylvia, following close behind. Zim's talent kept food on the table and a reasonable life for his family during and after the Depression.

The Zimberoff household was filled with force and turmoil, ambiguity and confusion. At times, my grandfather could be loving and doting, bouncing his children on his lap while singing a show tune. Hours later, he would denigrate their mother in front of them for spending an extra dollar on food at the grocery store.

Zim's tyranny was countered by Selma's overly protective mania. Her affection was suffocating. The two opposing forces merged to create a toxic family environment. Sure, every American family has at least some component of craziness, but my father's childhood contained a striking fill of hurt and *meshugganah*.

In contrast with Zim's mercurial moods, Selma ran the Zimberoff household like a Swiss factory. The seven children had their own set of index cards outlining specific chores to be completed daily, weekly, and monthly. Each day at five thirty in the morning, Selma, "Nana" to her twenty-two grandchildren and "Doll" to Zim, thumbtacked a schedule to the kitchen door assigning additional tasks. Zim was often away on business trips, and during those instances, my father, the eldest male sibling, acted as the surrogate father for the Zimberoff clan.

As often is the case in life, the ying danced with the yang. For every abusive or neurotic event, an equally emotional loving moment befell. My father's formative years included a constant clash between syrup and vinegar, leaving an indelible taste of antinomy that persisted long into adulthood.

At 1811 W. 47th Street, the Zimberoff three-bedroom, two-bath apartment was in a rough neighborhood on the City's southwest side. When the family moved into the building in the early 1940s, they were greeted with taunts of "dirty Jews." Neighbors threw dead rats into the backyard of their apartment. The Zimberoffs never fought back, confident in knowing they were a good family and realizing the neighbors were simply too ignorant to change.

The seven children shared a single bathroom, two bedrooms, and rotated into a double set of bunkbeds on an enclosed porch. During the winters, the porch got so cold, the children could see their breath and slept under a pile of blankets while wearing football helmets to stay warm.

The children were allotted five minutes for bathing each morning, hot water being an indulgence. Mealtimes were as much engineering feat as culinary act, with each child assigned a different job in the assembly-line production. Lunches were prepared in the morning and packed neatly in brown paper bags that were reused the following day. Selma, decades ahead of her time regarding proper nutrition, prioritized eating fresh vegetables and fruits, which resulted in staggering amounts of rinds, skins, and other produce detritus. The landlord limited garbage removal in the apartment building to a small debris bin emptied weekly. Nana solved the refuse problem with ingenuity and precision. In the evenings, two children were tasked with wrapping the produce discards from the day with old newspapers. Each package was neatly packed and bundled with twine. The next morning, the seven children took their packages with them on the city bus or streetcar and left the refuse under their seats when they exited. To the casual observer, the packages looked like forgotten gifts or small bundles of books. Nana's plan may have aggravated a few bus drivers, but she resourcefully subverted the landlord's stingy waste rules.

During his childhood, my father's family spent entire summer months at the Indiana Dunes, an hour east of Chicago. There are dozens of home movies and hundreds of photos showing an idyllic environment of sun, sand, lake, bonfires, lazy days and nights. The celluloid images reflect a sublime childhood among a loving, nurturing family. The photos do not lie; they simply omit the fury that coexisted with the tranquility.

Nana's father, Eli, known as "Edda," the son of a rabbi, was an atheist—one of several quirks of an extraordinary man. He and his son Arthur lived together in a home where they ran a part-time medical clinic in addition to their physician jobs working for the City's health department. As my father's family could not afford to move to a more affluent neighborhood, my grandmother insisted that my father and his siblings attend school in a district several miles away where Edda and Arthur lived. In addition to better schools, the people in the neighborhood were mostly of Eastern European descent and more tolerant of Jews.

The Zimberoff children took buses or trollies the long distance to the school, where they ate lunch every school day with their uncle and grandfather. Nana wanted her children to benefit from the positive influences of both Arthur and Edda. Her plan worked, especially for my father.

Through his teens, my father was a skinny kid with a mop of thick, jet-black hair slicked back in the style of the times. He hung out with friends and loved spending time with his grandfather. Edda did not own a car or have a driver's license. On weekends, the two walked across the South Side, the lakefront, Lincoln Park, and throughout the entire city for hours at a time.

Both men had inquisitive minds and loved to ponder lofty philosophical questions about the mysteries of life and what motivated people. Though he was the son of a rabbi, Edda viewed religion as a contagion of a curious mind. This deeply held ideology helped shape my father's own atheist beliefs. A voracious reader, Edda favored scholarly publications and biographies over religious texts. Pop's love for biographies, especially statesmen and political figures, likely also derived from his grandfather's weighty influence.

My father often said Edda was the most important person in his life, a surrogate who filled the void induced by his father, so much so that my dad insisted I be named after him. My mother pushed for a more traditional name. My parents compromised by using my middle name, Eli, as tribute to my great-grandfather.

THREE

MY FATHER'S FORMATIVE years were far from calm; he often referred to that time of his life as "nutso." His mother was manic, fluctuating between overly protective and shrewdly manipulative. She showered her children with gratuitous praise one moment and severely disciplined them for minor deviations from her strict schedule the next. Pop's father was equally unpredictable: adoring one minute and threatening the next. Zim's moods shifted with the prevailing winds.

Pop survived his childhood with emotional scars that tormented him for the entirety of his life. The experience left him with a rapacious need to control, compensating for the powerlessness he possessed over his own life as a child and young adult. On the flip side, he also developed exceptionally strong bonds and loving relationships with his siblings, each of whom uniquely dealt with the aftermaths of Zim's and Selma's imprints.

Fearing he would injure himself, Nana did not allow my father to play youth sports. Pop had to find alternative ways to spend his free time. He was drawn to the literal black-and-white world of photography. As a high school freshman in an affluent north Chicago suburb where the family had moved when he was in junior high school, my father turned his photography hobby into an entrepreneurial business. Pop photographed school teams, student clubs and organizations, and many private functions. He sold the prints to schools, individual students, and on occasion local newspapers. Pop saved enough money, along with financial help from his parents, to attend the University of Chicago. He knew from Edda the importance of education in finding life-long success and fulfilment.

Though Zim could be undermining of his children and did not go to college himself, he acceded to Nana's strong influence ensuring their children received college educations. Each of my aunts and uncle graduated from college, with several attaining graduate or doctoral degrees.

Before heading to college himself, Pop bought a TWA ticket and flew to Europe where he spent the summer backpacking and youth hosteling. He financed the trip with savings from his photography business. My grandmother disliked the idea, thinking it was too dangerous, but Zim reluctantly agreed, and the decision was made. If he did not have the support of both his parents, my dad told me he would have gone anyway. He needed to create some physical distance between himself and his parents before starting college a few miles from home.

The trip ignited a life-long wanderlust within my father, especially for international locales. His love for tasting exotic cuisines, interacting and photographing everyday foreigners, and exploring offbeat destinations persisted for the next six decades, spilling over to my sisters and me. After close to three months traveling and meeting scores of other teenaged backpackers, Pop was ready to return home and commence his college years.

Though intelligent, with a thirst for knowledge and a love of reading, my father was not academically gifted. He used to say he got through college through hard work, persistence, and a lot of help from his friends. Throughout his college years he continued his photography business, which helped not only financially, but socially, too. Freshman year he joined a fraternity and was voted Freshy King by his peers.

Also during freshman year, he met an intelligent and confident young coed from Indianapolis who would become my mother. Dorothea Cayton, Dot or Dotti to her friends, was charismatic, warm, and articulate. She stood five-foot-six inches tall with a slender figure. Her light brown hair fell off her shoulders revealing soft features and a scattered smile. She had grown up in a conventional, working-class Presbyterian family. Her father, Ernest, sorted mail on train cars for the postal service while her homemaker mother, Virginia, taught at the Sunday school of their local church. She had a younger sister named Sally.

Dot was the proverbial "good girl" growing up: obedient, got good grades, and regularly attending church on Sundays. She had a secret side she hid from her parents. During her late teens, after claiming to sleep over at a friend's house she'd take clandestine overnight trips with friends across the border to

Wisconsin where the drinking age was just sixteen. Dot was careful never to get caught. With her strong academic performance, she had no difficulty getting into the University of Chicago, where she excelled academically.

Away from her parents for the first time, Dot fully embraced college life. She loved cocktails at late-night parties, staying up to the wee hours of the morning drinking, debating politics and social issues, and smoking cigarettes, something she never did at home.

My parents were an unlikely couple: he, emotional, intuitive, and impulsive from a Chicago Jewish immigrant family; she, calm, reasoned, and conservative with a wild streak from an Indianapolis staid Presbyterian family. Despite their on-again-off-again relationship throughout their college years, they always returned to one another.

Both my parents obtained business undergraduate degrees. Right after graduation, my mom ended up pregnant. At the time, in 1959, abortions were not only highly controversial and dangerous, but they were also illegal. My parents had no reasonable choice but to get married and allow the pregnancy to proceed.

My father had not yet met my mother's parents or sister. Shortly after discovering the pregnancy, Pop borrowed a car from his best friend and he and my mother drove three hours south to Indianapolis. They arrived early evening and as they drove down my grandparents' street, my father could see several neighbors peeking from behind living room curtains. Pop used to say that the nosey, conservative neighbors were curious to see what "Jew boy from the big city" was dating Ernest and Virginia's eldest daughter.

By all accounts, my mother's parents were cordial and inviting. They welcomed my father, a dark-complected, Jewish young man from Chicago, into their home as their soon to be son-in-law. If they felt otherwise, they never expressed it out loud.

This attitude may have been progressive for a conservative Presbyterian couple in 1950s Mid-America, but that's who my grandparents were. My grandmother would go on to volunteer as the leader of an inner-city African American Girls Scout troop. They were accepting people who avoided conflict at almost any cost.

The opposite held true on my father's side of the family. When Zim and Selma found out about my mother, they were not pleased. Though nonobservant Jews who could hardly find their way to a synagogue, Zim and Selma wanted their son to marry a "nice Jewish girl." My grandparents were not openly hostile to my mother, choosing instead to treat her with indifference.

At the age of twenty-two, my father and mother married in a simple civil ceremony. To save money, the wedding and reception were held at my father's oldest sibling, Sylvia, and her husband Bob's Chicago apartment. Less than thirty people attended, including relatives, siblings, and several friends. Zim and Selma boycotted the nuptials.

The pain from my grandparents spurning the wedding ran deep for both my parents. After a month, in an effort at reconciliation, Zim bought my parents a car as a belated wedding present. My parents initially rejected the gift but quickly realized the practicality a car had on a young family and reconsidered. Though saddened by their initial rejection, my mom did not hold a grudge and always treated her in-laws with respect. It took some time, but my grandparents finally warmed to my mom, the mother of their soon-to-be third grandchild.

After my oldest sister Aleen was born, my parents moved into a small apartment in Lincoln Park, a budding neighborhood on the north side of Chicago. Mom continued to stay home with Aleen while my father went on to law school at DePaul University and worked part-time in his photography business. Pop credited Edda as being the primary reason he went to law school. Pop hated the sight of blood and could never be a doctor. He chose the legal profession for its intellectual challenge and opportunity to help others; traits gleaned directly from Edda.

Two years later, right after Pop graduated from DePaul Law, my sister, Wendy, was born. I followed three years after that. Partly to maintain a relationship with his grandchildren and partly to prove his indispensability in the family, Zim provided financial assistance to my parents as they grew their young family while my father started his legal career.

During this period, as variety shows died out and movies had their own soundtracks, Zim needed to find new work. He, along with three of Selma's brothers, formed an ambulance-chasing scheme. One of the brothers befriended a police officer who tipped him off whenever a pedestrian was struck by a car. Either Zim or one of the two brothers would visit the victim in the hospital and refer them to a third brother, a personal injury attorney, who signed them on as a client in an ensuing lawsuit. Zim and the two brothers received kickbacks from the third brother for the referrals. The enterprise expanded to vehicular accidents of all types and became quite lucrative over subsequent years.

A year after I was born, Zim invited Pop to join as a second attorney in the racket. Pop declined, not wanting to become embroiled in what he perceived as an unethical and potentially illegal operation. Not surprisingly, the rejection irked Zim.

A few years after Pop turned down the offer, money from the personal injury venture started to dwindle. Their police contact retired from the force and competition emerged. Zim began exploring other options. After a decade working the hospital wards, Zim had retained numerous hospital contacts throughout Chicago whom he had paid off with portions of his referral fees.

One of these contacts introduced Zim to a small company specializing in photographing newborns at hospitals and selling photo packages to new parents. Zim liked the idea so much he quit the ambulance chasing scheme altogether and bought the business. He leveraged his hospital administrative contacts to gain access to the delivery rooms of hospitals across the city. Within a few years, Nursery-Identi-Photo was in just about every hospital in the city.

While my dad was getting his start in the legal world, my mother delayed her professional career to be a stay-at-home mom. But she was far from a Betty Crocker homemaker; she was a "women's libber," member of the 70s- and 80s-women's movement. As a young child, I remember her attending several women's rights marches. Decades later, regrettably, my mom reached the proverbial business glass ceiling, as sexism remained rampant in large corporations during that era. She helped pave the way for others but did not benefit from women's employment gains of subsequent generations.

Pop was progressive for his generation. As a husband and father, I am sure he felt societal pressure to succeed in business. He had a big ego, but when it came to my mother, he did not protest when she decided to start her career as a Certified Financial Analyst with a large insurance company after I began kindergarten. From that point forward, my sisters and I were latchkey kids who were provided with ample independence during after-school hours.

I relished the freedom and autonomy. We were living in Highland Park, an upscale north shore Chicago suburb. It was a time when kids rode Schwinn bikes around town freely, drank water from garden hoses, and played sandlot baseball, basketball, and football until dinner or dark, whichever came first. I think back to those days thankful to have experienced an innocent period of life that no longer exists, especially when I compare it to the austere childhood my father endured.

FOUR

POP SPENT SEVERAL years grinding out work as a young associate at a small firm practicing bankruptcy and business law while doing accounting on the side. The work was rote and uninspiring; he looked for a change. His entrepreneurial spirit tugged at him. Around this time, Zim invited my father to join him at Nursery-Identi-Photo, extending an olive branch and signaling he would groom Pop to take over the business sometime in the future.

Pop viewed the offer as an opportunity to heal the relationship with his father and accepted. My father had enjoyed running his photography business for years and knew the commitment required of a business owner. He did not have a financial stake in Zim's company but dedicated his full energy to the endeavor.

It didn't take long for the collaboration to sour. Zim undermined my father at almost every turn. After three years of doing most of the work, including establishing outlets in neighboring states while Zim "managed" the business a few hours a week from his plush corner office while *schtupping* his secretary, Pop had enough. He told his father he wanted out.

Angered by the rejection, Zim threatened to sell the business, keep all the profits, and leave my dad with nothing for his hard work. Though reeling from yet another vengeful action by his father, Pop could not find it in himself to detach from him. Instead, my dad agreed to assist with the transaction without compensation. He negotiated a profitable sale to a third party. He also kept Zim's infidelity with his secretary confidential.

My grandfather never had to work another day of his life. For all his good fortune, Zim repaid my father with scorn and indictment, going so far as to accuse my dad of stealing from him. The allegation struck deep, reopening childhood wounds. Though his father's conduct severely damaged their relationship—always the dutiful son—Pop continued to assist his parents in various ways over the coming decades. My dad was simply wired that way.

Whenever a legal or financial issue popped up for my grandparents and other family members, Pop stepped in irrespective of whether they wanted his help. I recall overhearing countless conversations over the years with my father providing counsel to his sisters, sister-in-law, or parents in both personal and business affairs. "Let me handle it for you. This is what we're going to do," he'd say.

Over time, my mom reluctantly accepted my dad's steadfast

allegiance to his father. There were times she lashed out at Zim, like the time she forbid him from visiting our house or seeing his grandchildren when he accused my dad of stealing from him. But after a few weeks or months, she would relent. My mother understood the importance of the grandparent-grandchild relationship.

I do not remember ever hearing my mother complain about Zim or my father's family; Mom did not have a vengeful bone in her body. We endearingly referred to our mother as a bull, partly due to her stubbornness, partly due to her patience, and partly because she never got sick. These traits were likely offshoots of her Scots-English roots, which sometimes pushed up against my father's controlling nature. My dad never backed down and rarely took advice from anyone—except from his wife. This inclination to spurn others' opinions sometimes came back around to bite him in the arse.

FIVE

IT WAS 2022 and my dad had been sick for some time. I had flown down to Chicago from Toronto to help my father move out of his condo into an assisted-living facility. Never in a million years did I imagine I would be doing such a thing. Infallible, indefatigable, indestructible Pop moving into a nursing home! His physical and mental conditions had deteriorated to the point where he felt he needed access to twenty-four-hour care. My sisters and I disagreed, but there was no changing our father's mind.

After Ubering from the airport to his condo, he and I immediately went to work. I started packing numerous knick-knacks and personal items scattered about his living room. As my fingers touched several of the items, childhood memories awakened. A bronze tea set bought at a Marrakesh bazaar.

Fifteen-century clay pots gathered from an Israeli archaeological dig. A chipped stone edifice from an ancient Crete fort.

When I was just four years old, my parents boxed and stored all their possessions, packed two duffle bags, pulled my two older sisters out of school (I wasn't yet in kindergarten), and whisked us off on an adventure to Europe with the intention of moving there. Later in life when talking about the endeavor, my parents said they felt they needed a change. My mother was not yet working, and my dad had just helped my grandfather sell the family business. They wanted to do something exciting with their young children while they still had the chance. They knew in a few more years, when we kids got older and settled into school, we would not have another opportunity to do something so bold. When they heard about my parents' plan, my dad's siblings remarked, "That's just Davey, being Davey."

We landed in Luxembourg where my parents bought a 1968 Volkswagen camper. The five of us spent the next three months traveling the Continent and beyond. I slept on the floor of the camper, my sisters shared a bed in the pop-up roof, and my parents slept on a mattress in the fold-out rear. We ate meals in cheap restaurants or simply bought bread and cheese at markets and endured cold showers in primitive camp sites. Regrettably, Pop contracted Hepatitis in Turkey and almost died from dehydration and kidney failure. We were forced to terminate the expedition prematurely as my father was rushed home for medical care in Chicago. But for Pop's medical emergency, it's likely we would have settled in one of the European countries we encountered. Instead, we returned home to embark on future international travels over subsequent years.

During these times, my parents were living their dream of travel and wanted to instill its value in their children. The more exotic destination, the better the exposure and learning opportunity. It is said that travel is the best education. If so, I would have a PhD. My dad often said that seeing how most of the world lived gave perspective on how lucky we were to have been born in America. For my sisters and me, the trips constituted exciting adventures in foreign lands. These were halcyon days when complete strangers opened their doors to a young American family. I have albums filled with photos of our family smiling widely on a train in the Swiss Alps, eating croissants next to the Eiffel Tower, fishing with a family on Santorini, and visiting a dozen other countries throughout Europe and the Middle East.

My mother and father were selfless in bringing us children along on these family trips. I say "trips" because they were more trek than vacation. There wasn't an ancient relic within two hundred miles of our itinerary that my mother didn't drag us to. I distinctly remember complaining as a pre-teen and teenager, "No, Mom, not again! No more Roman ruins. You've seen one two-thousand-year-old cobblestone, you've seen them all." She ignored my protests, and thankfully so. Mostly due to my mother's insistence that we view classic artwork and artifacts, I have a lifelong appreciation of art and history.

After allowing the flood of emotions and memories to flow, I got back to work packing my father's belongings. Pop was the antithesis of a hoarder. In fact, he strongly subscribed to a theory I once heard from a former Navy squadronmate of mine. "Zimby," Troll remarked one afternoon while I helped him move, "You can either have a house filled with stuff or a life filled with memories. I choose the memories." As did my father.

Other than the travel mementos and a few pieces of art, my father's prized possessions consisted of thousands of digital photos and several writings stored on his computer to go along with his treasured trove of memories. Eighty-five years of my father's well-traveled life fit into fewer than a dozen moving boxes.

SIX

AS A YOUNG child, I idolized my father. At well under six feet
tall with a receding hairline and slightly bowed legs, Pop was far
from a physically imposing figure, but he talked, walked, and acted
as if he were six feet three inches tall. Pop did not play golf or
pickup basketball like some of my friend's fathers. He did not work
out in a gym. His game was tennis, and he played it with passion.

On a tennis court, a friend once described my dad's play as that
of a bulldog: relentless in tracking and returning the ball. He never
overpowered his opponents; his tenacity simply wore them down.

The tennis court acted as a microcosm of my father's life. He
was not blessed with many innate gifts but overcame any shortfall
through sheer force of will. He was a self-made man who forged
an exceptional life for himself and his family. Since he was not

allowed to play organized athletics as a child, he made sure I had the opportunity to pursue whatever sport I wanted.

Hockey was my game. Pop had learned to skate in college. As a tyke when I said I wanted to play hockey, he taught me how. One of my favorite photos from my youth captured me at five years old in full hockey gear, standing like a penguin with a mouthguard covering half my face. Pop coached several of my youth hockey teams and we shared a passion for the Chicago Blackhawks hockey team.

At age seven, I went to an overnight camp in Wisconsin called "Bucky's Boys Camp" where I learned archery and canoeing and ate s'mores until my belly ached. When I returned, my father started calling me "Bucky" and the nickname stuck.

———

I did not necessarily believe my father was perfect, but he was as close to flawless as a dad could be in a young boy's mind. As I grew into adolescence, I still viewed my father with high reverence. I loved my mother equally but with two older sisters and no male sibling, I looked to my father not only as a parental figure, but also as a male role model.

When I was nine years old, I played goalie on my youth hockey team. During the middle of the season, I became gun-shy when players wound up for a slapshot. At one practice, Pop, my coach at the time, saw me flinch, leaning backward on my heels. He immediately blew his whistle, shouted for all the players to line up thirty feet in front of me, and directed that they take slapshots aiming for my head. He knew my face mask and pads would protect me from injury. Initially, I continued to flinch. But after the fifth, seventh, or tenth shot, as I started to get my confidence back, I began leaning forward. By the time the drill ended, I was aggressively moving out of the crease, cutting down the shooter's scoring window.

That was Pop: direct, pragmatic, aggressive. He could have tried to teach the lesson by talking to me, attempting to convince me not to be afraid. He could have waited until I overcame my fear. But Pop knew shooting pucks at my head would be the quickest, most effective method to allow me to work through the issue on my own. Other than blowing the whistle and directing the drill, he did not say a word. At the time, I did not question my dad's tactic.

One of Pop's favorite sayings was, "Do your homework." If you do not know your stuff, learn it. Even if you think you know, go the extra mile to better prepare yourself. He applied this simple yet powerful adage to most aspects of his life and instilled it in me. In elementary school, he administered the lesson literally.

My father thought I was not sufficiently challenged academically and scheduled a meeting with my fourth-grade teacher to request she assign me more homework. When he noticed no increase in my workload, he made an appointment with the school principal and repeated his request. I didn't find out about either meeting until I was a young adult when he relayed the story to me. Initially, I laughed it off. But the anecdote stuck with me, as did the hockey drill.

As a child and young adult, I accepted my father's severity as his way of pushing me to be my best. Looking back as an adult, I realized his conduct caused a level of resentment that I had hidden deep within myself that would take years to reveal itself.

SEVEN

AROUND 1970, MY PARENTS wanted a major change. They had tired of the frigid winters and Chicago North Shore suburban routine. As they had done five years earlier when heading to Europe, they quit their jobs, traded our VW camper for a Winnebago RV, and once again, uprooted our lives in search new experiences for themselves and their children.

Though my aunt Donna, uncle Marc, and grandparents had relocated to LA, my father was not set on moving there. Pop loved the mountains, and my mom, the sea. Without a specific plan in place, we said goodbye to family and friends, piled into the Winnebago, and headed out on I-90 in search of new opportunities somewhere out west. We made the trek in the early summer before Aleen was set to start high school, Wendy middle school, and me, fourth grade. I'm not sure about my sisters, but at eight years old, I was still young enough to take the move in stride.

After three weeks of traveling through the plains and mountain states, we arrived in California. Driving south along Coastal Highway 1 somewhere south of Los Angeles, I distinctly recall the sea air flooding the camper and my lungs, bringing with it a feeling of excitement and rejuvenation.

We turned off the Coast Highway into a small beach community named Corona del Mar (Crown of the Sea) to grab lunch. We parked the RV on a bluff above the ocean, grabbed sandwiches at a sub shop and ate them at a picnic table overlooking the beach during an idyllic Southern California day. We watched bright sun from a clear sky reflect off the topaz blue waters of the Pacific Ocean while surfers pirouetted on and off head-high waves and sailboats glided along the ocean aided by a warm breeze. Having spent our entire lives in the flat Midwest, each of us felt the same sensation that afternoon. We had found our new home.

Over the next few days, Mom did research and found that the West Coast headquarters of a large insurance company was in nearby Newport Beach. She made some calls and got an interview. Since we were living in the Winnebago in a coastal campground, her only option was to shower in a beach parking lot bathroom before her interview. True to her skills and personality, Mom got the job. That afternoon, my parents visited a real estate office and two weeks later, with proceeds from selling our Highland Park home, they bought a house on a hill overlooking the ocean.

Though born landlocked in central Pennsylvania and raised in the Midwest, the ocean called out to my mother. Even though my father preferred the mountains, my mother wanted to live near the beach, so Pop acquiesced. His parents were an hour away, close enough to see on occasion, but not too close to become a burden. Pop viewed proximity to his parents as an opportunity to reconcile and improve the relationship with his father. Mom getting a good job in Newport Beach sealed the deal. Relocating to a swanky town a mile from the beach made the Chicago-to-California move a much easier transition for all of us.

Moving vans arrived by the end of the summer, just in time for school to start and our new California lives to begin. The first thing I wanted to do after moving into our new home was buy a surfboard.

At that time, there were very few Jewish families in Corona del Mar, which for us, wasn't a concern. My family appreciated being Jewish from historical and cultural perspectives, embracing the ethos and ethics of Judaism, but did not attend synagogue nor study Torah regularly. We were, after all, two generations of non-practicing Jews. My mother grew up in an observant Christian family but abandoned her religion when she married my father, choosing instead a progressive agnostic lifestyle. In Highland Park, we were members of a temple, but I do not remember attending services regularly or attending religious school. Growing up, I characterized our family as being Jew-*ish*.

After settling into our new home, with my sisters and me in school, Mom started her new job. Pop began looking for work. His license to practice law in Illinois did not transfer to

California. While continuing his job search, he studied for the California bar exam. He failed on his first attempt. Determined to pass, my father took a professional prep study course and passed on his second attempt, six months later. However, with an economic downturn in full force from the 1973 oil embargo persisting, local firms were not hiring.

Other than his parents and two siblings whom we visited occasionally, my father did not know anyone in California and had no leads. He spent months traversing the Southern California freeway system cold calling prospective employers, putting thousands of miles on the used Chevy Impala he bought after trading in the RV. Mom commuted to her nearby office on a ten-speed bicycle with her briefcase and heeled shoes stowed in a handlebar basket.

Since he could not find a job, consistent with his entrepreneurial streak, Pop hung out his own shingle as a sole practitioner focusing on business and real estate law. Without professional contacts, he had difficulty amassing a solid client base. My dad used to tell me he made more money in the first two years in California in a bi-monthly poker game than he did as a lawyer. I think he was serious.

It took a few years, but Pop succeeded in growing his solo practice. He focused primarily on commercial and residential real estate closings, spearheaded investment syndications, and negotiated business purchase and sale agreements. Based on his solid "midwestern values," legal acumen, and hard work, his client book flourished. Pop's tenacity won out—as it always did.

My father leveraged the success of his real estate practice into a profitable real estate development business. He cherry-picked some of the best deals he helped put together by joint venturing with clients. This is where Pop made his real money—in the deals, not the lawyering. His timing could not have been better, as the Southern California real estate market was just starting to take off.

As his business grew, he took on a series of business partners. Pop may have been an excellent lawyer and deal maker, but he was not good at choosing partners. Perhaps his need for control rubbed partners the wrong way. Maybe after his abortive experience partnering with his father, he had a hard time trusting partners. Whatever the reason, except for one longstanding real estate joint venture, the partnerships never worked out.

For Pop, practicing law and conducting business was never solely about the money. He had an affinity for helping people, especially those who were less fortunate and particularly if they were foreign born. He loved to interact with and assist people of diverse cultures and ethnicities. As a teenager in California, I remember several times when lower income clients, many of them immigrants, stopped by our house to say hello and drop off a bushel of dates or marinated lamb instead of paying my father in cash.

"Bucky," Pop told me, "find something you like, and the money will follow."

My father's relationship with his parents was complicated as they were complex people. Predictably, their wide behavioral swings lessened with age. During the last few years of his life, Zim began to express his failings and regrets in letters to my father. Initially, he tried to justify the pain he had caused by defining his actions as differing perspectives of morals and judgments. As life's end neared, my grandfather let his ego retreat and allowed a more honest assessment emerge:

"Dear David, in the last few days, I have gone through 87 years of living life. Not being aware of other people's feelings and not caring. My selfishness—the misery—the hate—discomfort, I have caused—knowingly, and not knowingly. I think of forgiveness. Truly, I am ashamed and sorry. I ask forgiveness.

I am unhappy about our relationship—you are my oldest son. I've always trusted you. I always appreciated what you have done for me and the family. I am guilty of not expressing it. I have lied and cheated, sometimes to even a score, because of greed, sometimes pride.

Please by my (who's my dearest) again. I love you.

-Dad"

In obscure comments he made to me over the years, I believe my dad conditionally forgave his father, but more likely out of pity than respect. He absolved my grandfather, yet simultaneously, acknowledged the harm could never be undone. Notwithstanding the rocky relationship that existed between them, Pop remained loyal and devoted until the end. Zim passed away at the age of ninety, unresolved with his oldest son. Nana lived to be one hundred and two. Pop visited his mother in the nursing home regularly, often bringing her a pastrami sandwich on rye from Zucky's, her favorite Santa Monica deli.

EIGHT

POP'S PRIMARY DRIVING force in life was to help others. Family members. Friends. Total strangers. I observed countless instances of this mentoring. When I was young, I visibly cringed whenever my dad confronted a stranger asking them deeply personal questions about who they were and what they wanted to do with their life. The look on their faces said it all. "Who is this person and why are they asking me what I want to do with my life when I don't even know?" Sometimes, they would play along and engage in substantive discourse. After five or ten minutes, when my father was done grilling them, they usually left smiling. Some shook my father's hand. Others hugged him. Most felt more enlightened about themselves.

In this game—I call it a game because my father found great

satisfaction and fun—Pop never provided answers to the questions he posed. The essence was the inquiry, of asking the question, even if the answer was not immediately evident. He clung to a quote from author Elie Wiesel as his philosophical touchstone: "The wise man knows there are no answers, only questions."

I often wondered how a man who got up in so many person's faces, challenged strangers to tackle their innermost fears, and openly attacked others' vulnerabilities, got away with it without being punched in the nose, sworn at, or, at a minimum, rudely rebuffed. As my friend Chris so poignantly pointed out when viewing a photo of my dad, it was Pop's eyes. His brown eyes sparkled with a blend of mischief and caring. His motivations and actions emanated from a place of love and empathy, even if they were sometimes self-serving. Most strangers intuitively picked up his benevolent motive and allowed him liberal leeway.

Pop was like a bee going from flower to flower, pollinating the world with self-reflection, introspection, and soul-searching. He strove to make the world a better place, one enlightened person at a time. He possessed a true gift of nurturing human interaction through raw communication. Enigmatically, he lacked the ability to challenge himself in the same manner he demanded of others.

When my sisters and I became adults and bought our own houses, Pop loved to plod in our gardens whenever he visited. A stop at the local nursery to fill a cart full of annuals, perennials, and biennials was required on almost every first day of the visits. If we were lucky, he might add a fruit tree to the mix.

Pop would then take our respective children into the garden teaching them about everything associated with soil, insects, and nature. I loved to look out the window and see my children, their hands muddied in dirt, crouched down on their haunches looking up at their grandfather as he extolled the wonders of pollination, flowering buds, bees, photosynthesis, or other nature lesson for the day.

Though my father was a weekend horticulturalist who tended healthy gardens throughout his life, there was one aspect of his gardening I questioned. He would prune the heck out of bushes, hedges, and even small trees. On many occasions the aftermath of his shearing looked like a Marine recruit after indoctrination— few leaves, bare branches.

I challenged my father asking him if he thought he may have gone too far.

"No, it will grow back healthier than before."

"Hmm, if you say so," I responded while thinking to myself, *If it survives the trauma.*

I never understood Pop's brute method until much later. Just as Pop shocked a plant or tree into near fatal existence believing it would grow healthier unencumbered by excess leaves or branches, he did the same to humans thinking it served to weed out their extraneous excuses. Pop trusted nature in its evolutionary drive. Survival of the fittest.

Would he apply the same standard to himself when it mattered most?

NINE

SOMETIME AROUND 2013, Pop noticed he could not hit a tennis ball with his usual skill. He also felt occasional tingling in his hands. At first, he attributed the complaints to aging. When the condition persisted, he spoke with his doctor. After several rounds of testing, he received the news that forever changed his life: he had Parkinson's Disease.

I was stunned when Pop shared the news with me. For most of my life, my dad was a rock: healthy, active, unstoppable. He never had surgery of any type or spent a day in the hospital other than his bout with Hepatitis in Turkey on our first trip to Europe. His worst ailment was tennis elbow. Hearing him tell me he had a debilitating disease took me aback.

I knew nothing about Parkinson's other than Michael J. Fox

had it and it affected one's nervous system. As he was prone to do when conveying important news, Pop included the analytical and factual perspective, meeting the challenge directly without denial. Pop learned that Parkinson's is a brain disorder that causes uncontrollable movements of the body, such as shaking, stiffness, and difficulty with balance and coordination. In speaking with his doctor, he found the disease also adversely affects cognition and emotional stability. Symptoms begin gradually and worsen over time. As the disease progresses, people have difficulty walking and talking. They may also experience disabling mental and behavioral changes.

Pop used a basic analogy when describing Parkinson's: "Think of the nerve bundles from the brain to various parts of the body as highways. Healthy individuals have well maintained roads, whereas a person with Parkinson's has roadways full of potholes that crisscross around themselves and sometimes shut down completely, leaving the messages from the brain scrambled.

"If you know one person with Parkinson's, you know one person."

What he meant was the disease affected each person differently. One patient can exhibit tremors, difficulty with sleeping, stomach bloating, but not restless leg syndrome, memory loss, or excessive sweating. Another has difficulty defecating but not swallowing. The combination of symptoms is nearly endless. There is, however, one common thread with each patient: a downward trajectory. Symptoms never get better, only worsen, leading to eventual mental and physical debilitation. Being diagnosed with Parkinson's is like receiving a death sentence, but with an indefinite stay of execution.

Pop was in the earliest stages of the disease; his symptoms were minimal. Over the next few years his life continued unaltered.

TEN

MY FATHER'S OPEN hand crashed against my cheek, causing me to lose my balance and fall to my knees. I was dazed, not expecting a physical onslaught. My father yelled, "I don't understand the words, 'I can't.' Don't ever tell me you can't do something. Ever!" There was an intensity in my father's voice I had never heard before.

I was twelve or thirteen. My dad had me weed weekly a side yard of our home that was filled with gravel. There was no fabric mat underneath the pebbles, so weeds grew wild. I hated that job for obvious reasons. I would have rather cut grass with tweezers. Pop would get on me constantly whenever he saw a handful of weeds pop up.

On that afternoon, I complained that his expectations were

too high, that I couldn't get all the weeds. I don't know if he was having a bad day, or what, but suddenly, without warning, he had struck me.

Arched over and dazed, looking down at the ground, I saw my tears splashing on the rocks and slowly straightened. "I'm sorry, Dad," I muttered as I meekly turned toward him. He glared at me and walked away. I got back on my hands and knees and resumed weeding, sniffling until I was done. I learned that day never to say, "I can't," around my father.

A few years later when I was a sophomore in high school, I came home late on a Saturday night after hanging out with friends. Ordinarily, my parents were in bed before eleven, but on this night, my dad was waiting for me in the kitchen. He asked if I had been drinking. I admitted I'd had a couple of beers. Without speaking, his eyes narrowed and he slapped me across the face, knocking me back against the kitchen counter. He said something I don't remember, turned off the light, and went off to bed leaving me dazed alone in the darkness.

These two events in my teen years proved transformative in the relationship with my father. The first time he struck me I had pushed it aside, rationalizing that I probably had deserved it; plus, he had never hit me before. The second instance jarred not just my jaw, but my equilibrium as well. The weeding incident had created a fissure; the second strike caused a wider chasm. The combined occurrences led me to not only question who my father was, but what he stood for. I also felt a degree of intimidation by him. The doubt and fear caused me to withdraw internally to protect myself from his judgmental, controlling nature. For many years I was not nearly as open and carefree around my dad.

My father never struck me again. Years later when I reflected on those two episodes, I was sure my dad had suffered much worse from his father, and his father from his father before him. Thankfully, any cycle of abuse slowed with my father and ceased completely with me.

My parents, especially Pop, emphasized the importance of working. He knew that kids with jobs were introduced to financial responsibility at a young age, breeding confidence, independence, and self-esteem. I embraced these principles right away with my first job as a weekly paperboy at eight years old in Chicago. I progressed to a daily route at twelve after we moved to California. While other kids had parents drive them along their route whenever it rained, neither my dad nor mom ever did. I don't know if that was because I was too proud to ask or afraid of their response if I did.

At fourteen, I got a job at a gas station pumping gas where I learned to drive a stick-shift on a beater '73 Datsun pickup truck. The day I turned sixteen, the owner of the liquor store next to the gas station offered me a job. I went on to stock inventory, deliver alcohol, and work the cash register for the next three years—all of which helped catapult my popularity in high school as friends relied on me to supply them with alcohol on the down-low. I also worked construction as a laborer during summers.

Pop was a strict taskmaster, often saddling me with odd jobs around the house to further build my character and work ethic.

Whenever I complained that none of my friends had similar chores, he would snarl, "I don't care about other kids, I only care about YOU." This was my dad's steadfast response throughout my childhood if I used my friends as leverage to try to gain a concession or avoid having to do something. He would say it with spite, as if he resented me for even thinking the thought. I figured his reaction stemmed from his own childhood when he was forced to perform so many household chores without the privilege to complain.

Looking back at my life, I realized our home contained a constant but unstated undercurrent of expectation. Though never expressed out loud, there was a strong message sent by both Mom and Dad for my sisters and me to play by the rules, be good people, contribute to society, and most importantly, become professionals of some type.

I adopted these tenets without question but challenged my parents' expectations in a few areas. The first occurred when I was fifteen years old. As much as I loved hockey and had no delusions of playing in the NHL, I longed to play collegiate hockey. At the time, especially for a California player, the best route to a Division One hockey team was through the Canadian junior program. My sophomore year, I had an opportunity to play in a junior hockey league in Canada, which meant I would move to Ontario or British Columbia, board with a family, and play hockey while attending Canadian high school during the school year.

Both my parents immediately shut down the dream. Pop claimed that Mom thought I was too young to leave home, but I knew the real reason was that he did not want hockey to overshadow more professional career aspirations. Ironically, he had nothing to fear. Unbeknownst to my father at the time, my long-term career goal was to be a lawyer like him. Over the years, I'd observed him counsel and assist clients while building a successful law practice. Even at a young age, I felt I could do more for society and have a fuller life as an attorney than as a pro athlete.

Along with hockey, flying had always been one of my early passions. My parents told me when I was three years old, I would run along the sidewalk flapping my arms like a bird. Every time a plane flew overhead, I looked skyward. Between the ages of eight and thirteen, I probably assembled two hundred model airplanes. I was enthralled with planes and always dreamed of becoming a pilot.

In high school, I achieved that dream. Sophomore year, with the savings from my various jobs, I started taking flying lessons. My parents did not push back, as they applauded my independence and initiative—even if flying a plane may have scared the bejesus out of them. On my seventeenth birthday, the earliest eligible date, I passed the FAA's flying exam and obtained my private pilot's certificate. It was the greatest day of my young life.

The very next day I rented a tiny, single-engine, two-seat Cessna 150 and flew my best friend Tom to Catalina Island off the coast of Southern California for hamburgers and fries. They say a Cessna 150 is so small you strap it on like a jacket. Once buckled in, pilot and passenger sit crammed together, shoulders and knees touching. On that day, as a freshly certified teenaged pilot, the compact Cessna felt like a multi-million-dollar Lear jet.

My first flight with a passenger other than my instructor was twenty-six miles each way, three thousand feet above the Pacific Ocean. Tom and I landed on the small island strip, had lunch, then successfully returned. After I stepped out of the plane back at my home airfield, I felt ten-feet tall.

The following week I took my mother for a flight in the same airplane. Mom and I took off from a postage-sized runway at a small airfield near her office for a short flight to Santa Monica for lunch. Initially, I could see she was trying to hide her nervousness as we lined up for takeoff. When I pushed the throttle full forward, her jaw tightened. Minutes later as we flew along the coastline at roughly a thousand feet, I saw her face relax noticeably as she looked down at the familiar beaches passing beneath us. We could see dogs running along the sand, kids throwing a frisbee, and surfers paddling among the waves.

After a quick twenty minutes, I started our descent toward the airport. At a mile from the runway, the tower directed me to make a three-hundred-sixty-degree turn for spacing. I acknowledged and immediately banked the plane hard to the right. At five hundred feet above the ground it felt as if I could reach out and touch the houses and cars immediately below. I smiled confidently as I finished the turn and completed the approach culminating in a smooth landing on the long runway. We disembarked and had lunch at a small restaurant located on the field. The return flight was uneventful.

At dinner that night while I was away at a friend's, my mother told my father she had been terrified when I banked the plane on the approach. She thought we were falling from the sky and were about to crash. In her typical fashion, Mom had kept a poker face and did not say a word to me for fear of discouraging me from my dream of flying. I didn't hear about her anxiety until years later when we laughed about it. Pop took it all in stride. I caught him a few times bragging to his friends about my flying exploits, proud that his son was doing something he never would have been allowed to do in his youth.

ELEVEN

OVER THE YEARS, I came to realize while my father had a conflicted connection to Judaism, he constantly sought insights into his place in the world. He shared with me that he had engaged in psychotherapy as a young father back in Chicago to address the emotional residue stemming from his childhood and tense relationship with his parents. Pop was in and out of traditional therapy for several years and eventually quit, believing he had gotten all he could out of the sessions. The conflict with his father continued, as did his difficulty maintaining business partners and persistent urges to control others. Pop had enduring issues to work on.

When our family moved to California, he was introduced to an assortment of more progressive psychological and spiritual self-help methods, programs, and seminars aimed at finding greater self-awareness, emotional health, and a deeper understanding of himself.

One such approach he came across was The Landmark Forum, an organization offering "methodologies and approaches enabling pathways to introspection and fulfillment." From a layperson's perspective, the program provided a different way of looking at life, from a clean slate void of judgment and clouded perspective.

Pop elected to attend a three-day workshop followed by several weekly evening classes. Upon graduation, he had a lighter, more integrated sense of self. My father did not pressure anyone to take part, but felt the information and experiences gleaned from the trainings would be highly beneficial for all of us.

After seeing his enthusiastic response, positive changes in his behavior and a softening of his hard edge, my mother and sisters decided to attend the program. During these early years in California, the entire family embraced a spirit of self-improvement and awareness working toward transformation to a more aware and purposeful way of living. At age ten or eleven, I was too young to participate. There was a separate training for teenagers called "Lifespring" which I attended. It was my first introduction to structured interpersonal self-improvement. Following Lifespring, I continued my inner journey in my late teens and early adulthood with years of reading spiritual, new age, and religious books to widen my life, personal, and spiritual perspectives. Through this gained insight, I realized my default was a kinder, gentler disposition over the hardness modeled by my father.

Around the time Pop completed the Forum classes he read

Johnathan Livingston Seagull, a widely popular book written by Richard Bach. This allegorical tale of a young seagull's successful search for self-identity, true independence, and distinguishing yourself from the flock—all traits my father enthusiastically embraced—fascinated my father. Its message struck a chord so emphatically that he adopted the nickname, "Zgull," which was used by friends, acquaintances, and business associates for the remainder of his life.

For all the transformational work my family did, challenges remained. My parents always spoke about direct communication and "tapping into your feelings." However, familial emotional issues run deep, and this approach occasionally resulted in cracks. I suppose all families have dysfunction on some level; ours was especially splintering.

Coming from our mixed-up family dynamics, after Wendy finished her second university degree and was living on her own, she set boundaries with our father to offset his controlling ways. She would sometimes refuse to speak with him and chose to call him by his name, "David," as a way to differentiate and take charge of her adult life. As the years passed, and after she married Joe and welcomed their daughter Emma, a very special bond grew between Emma and her grandfather (albeit long-distance). The two shared weekly Facetime or Zoom calls where Pop sent her articles or books and they'd discuss empowering subjects from accomplished women scientists to books on human anatomy, encouraging her desire to become a doctor.

Throughout this time, as difficult as it was hearing Wendy call him "David" in lieu of "Dad;" and as painful as it was to be out of contact with her for months at a time, he did not give in to his ego and walk away from his daughter. Pop was far from blameless in the events that caused the rupture with Wendy. He tried the best he could to love and support her. Though Wendy often shut the door, he kept opening it: day after day; month after month; year after year.

Despite the therapy and transformational work my father pursued over the years, he continued to struggle internally. In 1988, at the age of fifty-one, he sought yet another process to identify the root of his issues. A friend of his from Chicago had just completed a training called the Mankind Project's intensive New Warrior weekend and told my dad it had turned his life around. Pop was intrigued and wanted to know more.

My dad discovered that the program was created as a retreat for men and incorporated native American rituals and meditations, Jungian psychological protocols, and physical challenges. The retreat expanded to include follow-on workshops and seminars designed to foster personal growth and community, with emphasis on promoting the emotionally mature male role model. Pop was drawn to the rawness and directness of the intensive training segments. He thrived in that kind of environment of direct communication without BS.

The Warriors provided my father with tools to dig deep inside and perform self-directed work rather than by a psychiatrist in a sedate office. The process enabled him to progress toward healing childhood wounds using demanding, confrontational, honest methodologies that were quite comfortable for him.

Pop was a fighter, a hardworking and charismatic, practical and outward-looking, successful man who also had an inextinguishable need to control—or at least significantly influence—others. Though he identified underlying causes for much of his adverse behavior, primarily his flawed parental upbringing, the Warrior work also served to reinforce his aggressive, hard-edged communication style. The intensity of the work energized him like never before.

New Warrior graduates receive animal monikers. Not surprisingly, my father chose "Zgull" as his. He advanced in the program and became a trainer for a dozen or more weekends over the next decade. Early on the pathway, he suggested I attend a weekend training.

Having personally observed the renewed energy and insights Pop received from his Warrior work, and having a disposition myself toward inner growth processes, I took his advice and signed up for my own Warrior weekend. It was 1990, I was twenty-six and about to ship out for the Gulf War. At that time in my life, I was single and loving life as a naval aviator yet wanted to see if I could achieve more in life—emotionally and spiritually. When I told Pop I had signed up, he celebrated my decision and arranged to be on staff for my weekend.

The training involved intensive physical, emotional, and spiritual individual and group exercises. One of the most demanding segments was "The Carpet." Men were called up individually to stand in the middle of a large carpet surrounded by staff and other initiates. The initiate was then led through a concentrated inward trek facing his greatest challenge. Most often, the process led the initiate to identify a wound suffered early in life from a flawed relationship with one or both parents. The process culminated in a face-to-face confrontation with a trained staff member who played the role of the parent.

Actual family members did not typically participate in the trainings. My weekend was an exception with Pop on staff. His personal participation that weekend led to truly remarkable and powerful experiences for us both.

As my name was called to the carpet, I tentatively stepped forward. My mouth was dry; I could feel my heart pounding in my chest. The leader of the process asked my father to come forward and stand directly in front of me. My pulse quickened.

My father, now standing a few feet from me, asked if there was anything I wanted to say. I stared at my dad, who stood silent and motionless. My fingers tingled. Tears welled up in my eyes. As I stared unblinkingly into his eyes, a cauldron of fire erupted inside my gut. In that moment, twenty years of unexpressed hurt and anger burst forth. The slap, the rejection of my hockey dreams, the pressure to be perfect, the demand to succeed and always do the right thing—all contributed to the rage boiling within. I began sweating. My hands tightened into fists as unfiltered words spewed from my mouth.

"You asshole! You fucking bastard!" I yelled. "You always try to control me! Control others! Fuck you!"

As the fury and verbal assault on my father continued, detachment washed over me. I transcended my physical body and felt like I was floating above the ground. After a spew of words and emotion that went on for many minutes, I returned to my physical body and began weeping. Between sobs, my venomous attack continued.

"You're a fucking bastard. I was just a kid. Why did you treat me like an adult when I was ten? Fuck you!"

Throughout the entire episode, Pop followed protocol and stood in front of me, silent, accepting my rage with his own tear-filled eyes. I shouted that he only loved conditionally; that he was judgmental and condescending; that he demanded perfection but was far from perfect himself. My voice was hoarse. I paused and bent down on one knee. After several deep breaths, I lacked the energy to keep yelling; instead, I spoke softly and directly.

In the ensuing minutes I told my father for the first time in my life that he could be a real asshole. As I heard my own words, I was struck with the realization that my childhood belief that my dad was perfect no longer served me, and that I'd known somewhere in my subconscious that he was imperfect; he was man who controlled and judged others. He judged me. I had touched those feelings as a teenager after he had struck me with his hand but then stuffed them away. In the grueling moments on the carpet, the feelings resurfaced. The perception of my father shifted before me from youthful idolatry, to adolescent intimidation, to adult reality.

I began weeping once more. Pop leaned down and gently placed a hand on my shoulder.

On the carpet, my father and I forged a bond which enabled us to create a more genuine and fully transparent relationship—man to man, Warrior to Warrior—not simply father to son.

Following the exercise, I earned my Warrior name, "Screaming Eagle," given to me for my love of flight and for finding my voice that evening.

Afterwards, we often spoke about the shared experience as it had changed our lives forever. From time to time when I would call him on his judgmental bullshit or he would push back on my avoidance inclination, we would address the issue head-on by simply saying, "Let's have a Warrior conversation."

Sure, we had occasional differences of opinion and certainly made decisions from time to time where we disagreed, but we never lost the union we created as Warriors. The closeness we built that weekend would serve us both well in his final journey years later.

TWELVE

IN 1991, I MARRIED my first wife. We met while I was in the Navy stationed in San Diego. About this time, my parents purchased a vacation condo in Cabo san Lucas, Mexico. It became their home away from home and a destination for an annual gathering of our family. Years later, after retiring, my mother spent most of her time there while my dad flew down for months at a time. As much as he tried, Pop found it difficult to adapt to the slow-paced Mexican culture. His directness contrasted markedly with the Latin avoidance. "Mañana, Señor, mañana," did not sit well with him. Unlike my mom who could spend all day roaming the sanguine beaches and relishing in the relaxed seaside environment, Pop needed more of a challenge.

It took years, but Pop eventually shed the fast-paced

treadmill of American life and accepted the easygoing tropical lifestyle. He spent many a morning fishing on the beach at the foot of their condo. Cabo san Lucas is a world-class offshore fishing destination, but boats made my father seasick, so in typical Zgull fashion, Pop bucked the trend. Rather than participate in fishing miles out at sea, he refined techniques to become an accomplished shore fisherman—no easy feat among the large waves of the Sea of Cortez.

Pop would wake at daybreak, amble down to the beach, and in his bathing suit and collared work shirt, throw his line into the surf. When I close my eyes, I can still see the image of him—bowed legs with bare feet in the surf line—casting cut bait across the waves with the sun reflecting off the ocean surface. Whenever the line tightened and spun from a bite, my dad would grab the spinner and fervently reel in the fish with the elation of a young boy. His childlike enthusiasm for fishing never waned.

Pop did not drink much, a single vermouth cocktail or lone beer on rare occasions. While in Mexico, with the steady holiday vibe, his attitude changed. The first time I visited my parents at their condo, I was enjoying a spectacular sunset view on the lanai when I heard the blender whirring from the kitchen. I peeked my head inside to see my dad smirking with a bottle of tequila raised in his hand. "Want a margarita, Señor?" he asked me. I just about fell over.

Other than family and cooking, my mother favored time at the ocean above all else, which is strange coming from a woman born in Pittsburgh and raised smack, dab in the middle of

America's heartland, Indianapolis. Every weekend in California, or most every day in Mexico, she could be found taking long, meandering walks barefoot on the sand. Back when I lived at home, I often joined her before organized sports and girls grabbed my attention. Some of the fondest memories of my mother include the many walks and talks we took along the six-mile stretch of Scotchman's Cove or five-mile expanse near Cabo San Lucas.

I vividly recall the day I told my parents I wanted to join the military. I was a freshman in college. My family was celebrating Thanksgiving in Fort Lauderdale where Aleen was working as a journalist after college. Wendy was talking to our father during this time and flew in from college in Chicago, me from Boston, and Mom and Pop from California. We were walking, where else?, but along the beach. Out of left field, I nervously announced that I was joining the Marines. I would attend boot camp the following two summers and then be commissioned a second lieutenant upon graduation from college. My parents stopped dead in their tracks. My mother's mouth agape. Pop stared at me. My heart pounded. No one spoke for several seconds.

There was virtually no military history in my family. Going back generations, I was unaware of a single relative who had joined the military, other than my uncle Marc who was drafted during Vietnam and served two years stateside as an administrative typist. It's not as if my ancestral roots were imbedded in pacifism or extreme liberalism—my mother's family could be linked to the Daughters of the American Revolution—we simply were not military folk.

After the long pause, Mom and Pop realized I was not joking and asked me why. Aviation was in my blood. I had been flying since the age of sixteen. Recently, a sense of patriotism had seeped into my blood. I explained that I wanted to fly jets and the Marines were the toughest branch of the services. My parents knew I had a passion for flight but had no idea I wanted to pursue flying in the military.

That day began a multi-year journey for the three of us: my parents acclimating to the fact their Jewish son was joining the military, me getting through two officer boot camps, flight school, and eventual life as a fighter pilot (along the way shifting from the Marines to the Navy).

Initially, my mother stuttered when friends or acquaintances asked what I was up to. She tripped over her words explaining I was in the Navy. Pop, a firm believer in bold, decisive life choices, took my decision in stride. Mom eventually relaxed and not only openly acknowledged what I was doing but embraced my career choice; though she never got used to me flying on and off aircraft carriers or going to war—what mother could? On the day I flew home in an F-14 Tomcat from the Gulf War, Mom stood in the family section at Naval Air Station Miramar wearing a T-shirt emblazoned with the American flag and a Yankee-doodle hat while carrying a red-white-and blue welcome home sign. From that day forward, she was my Yankee-Doodle Mom.

The year after I married, my parents separated after thirty-three years of marriage. Neither Mom nor Dad shared the specifics of their falling out, but I believe my father's occasional coarse treatment of my mother finally caught up to him. Despite all his work on self-transformation, Pop remained unable to exorcise the influence of his father's overbearing and derogatory treatment of his mother. My mother could only take so much; she deserved much better.

Mom retreated to their Mexican vacation condo while Dad rented an apartment in Aspen, Colorado. The transcendental community offered business seminars and varied intellectual events that attracted my father. He also found comfort in the Rocky Mountains. They leased their Southern California home. Neither initiated legal proceedings, choosing instead to take a time-out from their multi-decade relationship.

While apart, my father looked inward. He realized he needed to change, not just for my mother but for himself. Pop did not want to be alone. He loved my mom. They had been together since freshman year in college as teenagers. They had become parents at age twenty-two.

Pop could have given in to the prevailing winds. Divorce rates in California were sky high, especially for empty nester couples. He could have remained static succumbing to the demons inside. Instead, Pop opted to fight for his wife. He strived harder to work on his emotional failings.

After almost two years, he discovered a softer, more loving side that he wanted to share with his life partner. He penned this letter to my mom:

Dear Dotti:

What do you mean to me? What does the sky mean to the earth? What does the ocean mean to fish? How have you affected my life? What blessings and insight have you brought to me? How can I possibly answer these questions? They are too vast and complex for me to even comprehend, let alone explain.

We met many moons ago when we were but buds on our trees of life...not knowing or ever believing or anticipating where the branches would grow and lead us. Fortunately for us, the tree was healthy, its roots anchored deeply in fertile soil and grew in a field of sunshine, love, loyalty and commitment. Yes, we were buffered by storms, hurricanes and tornadoes, but that initial spark of energy that ignited when I first saw you has grown and kept us together all these years...yet sometimes bending, sometimes groaning but always firmly binding and holding us together as a unity.

Your impact on me is immense. You made me realize the impact of my words and conduct on others. I thought being aggressive, controlling and manipulative was strength and smart. What you modeled for me was gentleness and kindness. You also taught me to hang pictures exactly straight and square and drive over every possible road, gully, and hill to find and see each antique, mound and landscape. Sharing meals with you was like playing the lottery...I never knew what spice, sauce or flavor was concealed and hidden in the food.

Yes, you were always there for me. I knew that when I yelled "Dot", you would appear and be there, almost like magic...sometimes with a smile, sometimes with disappointment, sometimes with irritation...but always there...even when I tripped and fell into our pool fully dressed, I remember yelling..."Doottttt" as I hit the water. Yes, I could always count on you...you never failed. You filled the hole in my chest and made me a full and complete person. You transplanted your love and spirit into that vacuum and now I forever carry your spirit and love within me.

My love for you springs from the smallest molecule and atom in my body and encompasses me totally...we are really one...together and always.

When my mom received the letter, she believed my father had changed. She agreed to a reconciliation, but Pop's actions needed to be more than mere words. He made sure they were. In 1995, they moved back together into their California residence. Instead of bringing all his old, angry, controlling baggage with him, Pop's new devotion to my mom filled their home with a refreshing tenderness.

THIRTEEN

After getting back together, Mom and Dad shared a lighter, loving relationship. Seeing my father hold my mother's hand and hearing him compliment her, and mean it, was touching. Before their split and reunion, I could not recall a time when they showed public tenderness with one another. I had known they loved each other, but they didn't display affection. Together again, they felt free to do so.

Tragically, their renaissance was cut short. It was 1997, my first wife and I were living in Seattle, now with our two-year-old son, Levi. I received a call from Pop, his voice unsteady.

"Mom has cancer," his words stammering between sobs. "Fucking cancer . . . ." My mother had been diagnosed with pancreatic cancer, a dreadful disease. I couldn't breathe; the weight of his words pushed down on my chest. I finally caught my breath and asked to know more but he broke down and could not continue.

I soon found out that pancreatic cancer is slow to grow and metastasize. By the time it reaches the stage of detection, its fatality rate is staggeringly high, at over ninety-two percent. The average time from detection to death: a mere four months.

After receiving her diagnosis, my parents knew they had no time to waste. They spent hours on their dial-up modem researching the best cancer doctors and treatment centers in the country. When it came to health, Mom and Pop spared no expense. They flew to consult with specialists at the renowned MD Anderson Cancer Center in Houston and Mayo Clinic in Minneapolis, but neither facility could offer appropriate treatment or hope. Ironically, they found a fit at the UCLA Jonsson Cancer Center, a mere fifty miles from their home. A specialist at the center was acclaimed for his work with pancreatic cancer patients. My mother started outpatient treatments which allowed her to sleep in her own bed at home.

With monumental odds stacked against her, my mom declined the recommended chemotherapy protocol because of the pain, weakness, and nausea it would generate. For her, undergoing the suffering was not worth the few additional weeks of life the chemical poison may have provided. Mom chose a shorter, yet higher, quality of life. She allowed the terminal disease to follow its natural course while seeking palliative treatments.

Mom continued to attend numerous medical appointments and took handfuls of medications, painkillers, and supplements.

Thankfully, she was able to remain out of the hospital, obtaining all medical treatment through outpatient services, and near the end, via hospice.

I never heard her complain, not once. My mother accepted cancer's fate with forbearance. She demonstrated extraordinary grace and serenity. Her one regret—not being around to see how the lives of her grandchildren would play out—is one I share to this day. They would have respected and adored her.

Upon accepting my mom's fate, my father retreated into sadness and resignation. My mother's cancer took a degree of optimism from him. Like an unbeaten prize fighter who suffers a knockout punch, Pop lost, at least temporarily, his brashness. Cancer was one devastating opponent he could not dominate or control. He would face a similar foe soon enough.

The first time I remember seeing my father cry was shortly after my mom's diagnosis. I flew down to California one weekend to be with her and my dad. I lay asleep in my old bedroom at the back of the Corona del Mar house where sports trophies, model planes, and an old baseball glove sat on the same dusty shelves. I awoke suddenly to the sense of someone in my bedroom. Opening my eyes, I saw my father standing above me, staring blankly ahead. With subtle rays of dawn broaching the darkness, I could barely make out the silver glistening of tears sliding down his cheeks.

Shuffling the sleep from my brain, I reached out for my dad. Without saying a word, he climbed into bed next to me and began weeping. A slow moan oozed from his belly like sludge from a primordial spring. I hugged him as best I could as the moans devolved to irrepressible sobs. I, too, started crying, though not nearly as deeply as Pop. His sobbing came from a guttural place deep within his soul, mine from an awkward fear of not knowing what was to come. We cried together.

I probably had seen my dad tear up prior to that moment, but I had never witnessed him in such a vulnerable state. As his adult son lying next to him, I felt helpless—powerless to ease my father's suffering, or my mother's, or my own. Tears continued down both our cheeks.

I would have a similar feeling nineteen years later when my father broke down telling me he couldn't live any longer, that his suffering and debilitation were too great to bear.

FOURTEEN

IT WAS FIVE FORTY-ONE in the morning on April 20, 1997. The day and minute were imprinted upon my soul like an indelible black timestamp. The sun had not yet started to rise. Stillness filled the air outside my parents' home, the same Corona del Mar house where my father had crawled into my childhood bed four months earlier.

My mother lay alone in her and my father's bed. He had moved to the guest room to allow her more comfort. I watched her chest slowly rise and fall under a hand-sewn comforter. Soft light from a bedside lamp brushed against her ashen skin, imbuing a sense of warmth to an expressionless face. Her breath was shallow, rhythmic, matching the movements of her belly. In and up . . . out and down. Pause. In and up . . . out and down.

Pause. Just a few minutes earlier both were stronger, longer.

Two hours earlier my father and sisters had left the room to retire to their beds. The four of us were taking turns the past few nights sitting vigil by my mother's bed at night. During the day, we came and went individually or collectively. Mom remained in a semi-comatose state; eyes closed with virtually no communication under the care of hospice. Doses of morphine controlled her pain. We sensed this might be the night.

As my mother's breath continued to shallow, it also became more labored. A slight wheeze accompanied the hiss of the air entering and exiting her lungs. I continued to stare at my mother, the woman who breathed life into me, as the breath of life was leaving her.

I jumped up and ran to the guest room.

"Dad," I exclaimed, "this is it. Mom's going."

My father sat up from the mattress, his face wrenched with agony as he struggled to speak between sobs. "I can't. You be there for her, Bucky."

"Are you sure?"

He nodded. I hugged him with all my might.

"Okay," I said as tears started to fall onto my cheeks. "I have to go tell Aleen and Wendy."

A similar scene played out. Neither Aleen nor Wendy could bear to see our mother die. They wanted the last memory of her to be alive.

I dashed back to my parent's bedroom alone. Thankfully, my mother was still breathing, though shallowly. I took her hand in mine. "It's okay to go home, Mom," I whispered. "Dad, Aleen, Wendy, and I will be fine." After a minute, I said it again and let go of her hand, subtly giving her permission to leave.

I did not want to hover, and instead, sat back in my chair. I stared at her face, unsure which breath would be her last. An eerily silence filled the room, interrupted by the faint hissing and wheezing fitfully emanating from her mouth. Hiss and wheeze, up and down . . . then, without any perceptible change in her face or body . . . nothing. Silence. My mother simply stopped breathing.

I offered a blessing of peace and serenity to her and said aloud one final time that I loved her. Tears streamed down my cheeks. I was numb, paralyzed in the chair until my father and sisters entered some minutes later.

Mom was my true anchor, as dependable as the rising sun. I had a strong and connected relationship with my father, based heavily on explicit communication and shared interests. The link with my mother was different. We were bonded by birth, our relationship evolving naturally over the years. We shared intimacies in an effortless, seamless manner. She never wavered in her unconditional love for me.

The character and clarity my mom exhibited from her diagnosis to her painful death taught me not to fear death. Being with her in the moment as she took her last breath—witnessing her serene transition from life to death—was a truly remarkable and beautiful experience. Little did I know at the time how this experience would prepare me for the future that lay ahead with my dad.

———

When my mother died, I was a thirty-four-year-old husband and dad trying to navigate marriage, a civilian career, and fatherhood for the first time. Following flying, law had been my second passion, and at the time of my mother's death, I was an associate attorney in a Seattle litigation firm working long hours. Within a year of losing my mom, my daughter, Ariel, was born. There is no good time to lose a parent, but during that hectic phase of my life, it was especially trying.

As hard as saying goodbye to my mom was for me, her death devastated my father. For the entirety of my father's adulthood, from age eighteen to sixty-one, he had my mother as a partner. Most every adult experience and memory were inextricably linked to his wife. After forty-three years of waking up next to her, the bed was now empty beside him.

After my mother's death, Pop sold their California home and moved back to Chicago to be near his sisters, his daughters, and many childhood friends. He lived in a tower apartment on the Gold Coast just off Lake Michigan in the same building as his sisters Sylvia and Sandra.

Pop resurrected many of his childhood and college relationships that had been dormant for the thirty-odd years he lived in California. He started a small lending business to keep busy and to help people in financial distress. Amidst all, a void remained. He felt too young to live out his remaining life alone in some sort of homage to Mom. Neither he, Wendy, Aleen, nor I believed our mother would have wanted that. After she became ill, I believe she told my father to go on with his life with someone else after she was gone.

Over the next decade, Pop tried to fill the pain by dating a number of women, then had a short-lived marriage of four months, and another multi-year relationship. At the age of seventy-one, Pop finally found a second life partner. Leslie lived nearby, was Jewish, divorced with adult children and grandchildren. Pop agreed to a first date, and they clicked immediately. Leslie possessed an intellect and curiosity that challenged my dad's viewpoints.

My father and Leslie did not live together but spent much time enjoying all that Chicago offered. They would go out to the theater or attend political and intellectual events throughout the city. The couple loved staying at home debating current events and sharing a couch reading or playing Scrabble, Leslie with a glass of wine and Pop with a Pepsi. One of their favorite annual activities was attending a Christmas sermon in a south side Chicago Baptist Church. They also traveled extensively abroad, including unconventional destinations like Albania, Uzbekistan, and Tunisia.

While Aleen, Wendy, and I knew Leslie could never replace our mother, she brought renewed excitement and companionship that eased our father's pain. My sisters and I got to know Leslie quite well, as she attended family events and traveled with our father whenever he came out to see us. I also saw her whenever I visited Pop in Chicago. We thought she would be with my father for the remainder of their lives.

FIFTEEN

AROUND 2019, MY FATHER'S physical condition began to worsen, resulting in him having to give up playing tennis entirely—an inflection point in his life. By that point, Parkinson's had progressed well past the initial physical clumsiness and difficulty sleeping. He shared with us about his declining condition, including dizziness, expanded muscle tremors and instability, and mood shifts. He was seeing two specialists: a neurologist and a Parkinson's expert, in addition to his primary care physician and cardiologist.

Pop did not fear death but was terrified of the process of dying. He had shared with me and my sisters many times over the years that when his time was up, he would be ready to go. He did not want to linger or suffer in any way. He also did not wish to become a burden on his children.

When the family gathered at Aleen's Michigan vacation home during Thanksgiving that year, Pop announced he was contemplating voluntary assisted dying. By then, he had been living with Parkinson's for six years and experiencing its compounding effects. He was slowly but inevitably losing control of his life. "I can't beat Mr. Parkinson's," he said.

It was so much like Pop, wanting to confront his challenges and control his situation. In Warriors we learned that when a pack of lions hunts, it places the eldest lions in the middle with the younger predators at the sides. The elders roar and scare the prey to the sides, where agile hunters await. "Run toward the roar," he used to say.

Having sat alongside my mother twenty years before as she passed away in her own bed overlooking the Pacific Ocean, I innately understood my father's desire to end life peacefully. Consequently, his decision did not come as a shock to me. He referred to the MAID process as his insurance policy: hopefully never needed, but if so, accessible.

Aleen and Wendy also accepted his decision, as we believe it is a personal decision that each individual has the right to choose a dignified death. Given Wendy's spiritual beliefs in God and Judaism, she had concerns of what may become of his soul. She made inquiry with her rabbi and was told that it is universally accepted that God gave us free will. Some clergy believe that when a person is suffering to such an extent that their body is losing its faculties—when the person's mind/cognition is being taken from them—the soul is being suffocated. And if the person chooses, he could exercise his free will to end the suffering by electing to die with dignity, grace, and peace and release his soul from the bondage of the physical body, consistent with God's intent. She relayed this perspective to our father, Aleen, and me.

——— ———

After announcing his desire to voluntarily end his life at some point in the future, my dad described the broad process. He had "done his homework." At the time, there were only three countries that allowed medical assistance in dying for nonresidents whose deaths were not foreseeably imminent: Switzerland, Ukraine, and Colombia. Voluntary assisted dying in the US was in its infancy with only a few states allowing the procedure along with numerous restrictions.

My father said he had chosen Switzerland over Ukraine and Colombia because it was the only country that allowed a citizen or non-citizen who suffered from an incurable disease, was plagued with unbearable suffering, or disabling multiple pathologies associated with old age, to be eligible for MAID. The one caveat was that the lethal drug had to be self-administered. While conducting research, he came across an article in a British online newspaper about Pegasos, a Swiss organization that provided this service. He contacted the reporter for more information and discovered Pegasos only communicated by electronic mail; there were no websites, phone numbers, or names to contact. All communication had to be conducted by the candidate themself. Pop obtained an email address from the journal reporter and had been in contact with Pegasos's director for several weeks before sharing his news with us.

After his initial announcement, Pop began referring to the process as "heading east." For a while, Pop also called the procedure his "party." As his mortality loomed, he ceased using those euphemisms.

SIXTEEN

MY MOTHER WAS the product of a conservative Presbyterian, white bread Midwestern family with Scots-English lineage while my father came from a liberal eclectic Jewish family with Russian roots. Pop's critiquing was offset by Mom's acceptance; his brashness by her modesty; his false security by her assuredness. Where am I going here? I am the product of both my parents. I learned the value of integrity, accountability, trustworthiness, and work ethic from my dad. I was introduced to the importance of intimacy, sacredness, intelligence, and unconditional love from my mom. Importantly, I also gleaned a love of the beach from my mother. And whether by genes or choice, I adopted my mother's grace over my father's ferocity.

During my adolescence, I shed my religious and ethnic history altogether, choosing instead to blend into the Southern California surfer lifestyle. I simply was not comfortable enough in my own skin to broadcast my religion as a minority. For a long time, my sisters clung to their Jewishness much tighter than I did.

Somewhere in my late teens, I shunned institutional religion altogether, believing traditional religions pushed blind faith over self-determination and independence. I now realize this to be a gross generalization, but that was the summary conclusion I reached as a young adult.

Over the years, my general attitudes regarding religion softened from hostile and antagonistic to warily accepting, but my core belief remained intact: I do not believe in a singular god as described in Judeo-Christian or Islamic traditions. That said, I respect the beliefs of others and do not criticize their faith.

Instead of religious dogma, I believe in the synthesis of the Universe as a cosmic energy force spiritually connecting all living matter. Upon birth on this planet, we are provided with an opportunity to learn and help the entire species and Universe evolve. I came to this conclusion after many years of introspection, reading multiple books on new age mysticism and spiritualism, attendance and follow-on work involving seminars and spiritual retreats.

When I had my own kids, I decided to raise them Jewish, even though I did not believe in a singular, all powerful God. With the perspective of time and maturity, I came full circle embracing the principles and cultural identity of being Jewish while retaining my belief in self-determination and independence over strict adherence to a deity and conscious afterlife.

Pop did not share my beliefs. Agnostic, Pop cared more about the here and now on this planet than a possible transcendental afterworld somewhere out there. He believed that the memory of those who died remained in the living, helping to stitch together the fabric of humanity.

Pop would discuss God, the afterlife, and faith with you, but he did not elaborate on his perspective on what happened after death. He did not spend much time thinking or worrying about things out of his control. His belief mirrored one of the insights gleaned from Confucius, "If you cannot understand life, how can you understand death?"

Consistent with my spiritual beliefs, I am a strong believer in the power a person's emotional attitude has upon their mental and physical well-being. This notion encompasses the physical and metaphysical aspects of life. I believe physical ailments are primarily caused by emotional and mental unwellness.

I was first introduced to this concept in my late thirties through the writings of Louise Hay and others. I adopted the philosophy, and it has rung true for me. Each time I experience physical pain or illness, I am often able to tie the malady to emotional distress.

If Pop disagreed with my spiritual ideology, he vehemently rejected my beliefs linking physical health to emotional wellbeing. "Bucky, physical ailment is simply Mother Nature's imperfection," he would tell me.

My father's position was not surprising because if he had agreed with me, he would have had to admit a disconnection existed somewhere inside himself—that Parkinson's was related to his mental and emotional states. Pop adamantly rejected this notion. For me, it was crystal clear. Parkinson's is characterized by the lack of physical and mental control of one's body. That's what made this disease so devastating for my father.

I believe Pop carried what some might call "a hole in his soul"—something he himself had described that way in his letter to my mom. As much as he tried to fill it by assisting others, he failed to address the core issue in himself: his need to control every aspect of his life. He lacked control as a child and desperately tried to compensate as an adult by attempting to control others through interrogations of strangers, friends, and family—and the imposition of his thoughts, suggestions and judgments upon others. Pop boasted about transparency, about doing his "work." He completed a great deal of introspective and transformative processing over the years—the contemplative walks with Edda, psychotherapy, the Forum and Warriors trainings, among others— and was a better person for it. Despite the gains he made in softening his harsh behavior and attitudes following the temporary split with my mother, Pop's overbearing treatment of others remained. As he battled Parkinson's, he constantly fell prey to his need to control the lives of those around him.

The stranglehold from Parkinson's two decades following my mother's passing simultaneously aggravated his emotional turmoil and provided a final opportunity for Pop to fully embrace his lessons. In the time he had left on the planet, I hoped, but was not optimistic, he would find the catalyst to heal himself and find genuine peace.

———

Around a year after he stopped playing tennis, my father heard about a fitness club not far from his condo that offered bi-weekly boxing classes for persons with Parkinson's. According to experts, physical exercise is one of the best antidotes to slowing the progression of Parkinson's. Pop met the owner, Jim Kroeger, who had been diagnosed with Parkinson's right about the same time as my father. Jim owned three neighborhood health clubs. He became aware of Rock Steady Boxing, a program designed specifically for Parkinson's patients. He believed by offering the boxing program he could help not only himself but others who suffered from the disease.

Even though Pop had never exercised at a gym in his life, he joined Jim's program on the spot. After many months without tennis, he'd finally found a physical outlet.

My dad spent time with Jim in and out of the club. The two men became close as they shared a mutual fight against Parkinson's. It helped that Pop was a sucker for a small business owner and saw an opportunity to mentor Jim as well as attend his classes. They were a natural fit.

During one of my visits to Chicago, I went with Pop to one of his boxing sessions. Pop out-jabbed, out-punched, out-lunged, and out-ran his classmates, regardless of their ages or disease progressions. My father was most proud of the twenty or more push-ups he could muster at the end of class. Pop enjoyed the class so much, and benefitted from the physical exertion's positive impact on Parkinson's progression, that he installed a large heavy punching bag and a smaller speed ball, along with a stationary bicycle, in the bedroom of his condo.

In 2019, I met in a chance meeting in a San Diego bar the woman who would become my second wife. Salima was

Canadian, an urban planner by education who was working in the real estate industry as a developer. We got along naturally, and I sensed an undeniable potential for more. Our relationship blossomed to the degree that I decided to move in part-time with Salima, planning to split my time between San Diego and Toronto. But when the US–Canadian border shut down due to COVID in the spring of 2020, I relocated permanently to Toronto.

The fact Salima is Muslim, and I am Jew-ish, never became an issue. She and I viewed the dichotomy as an opportunity for shared learning and growth. In 2021, Salima gave birth to our baby girl, Ellie Amir Zimberoff. Before she was born, my father referred to her as Baby Joy. Pop was spot on. Ellie brought immediate, immeasurable joy not only to Salima and me but to all our family members during an especially trying period.

In mid-2021, Pop created an Excel spreadsheet that he sent to his medical team and family members listing his many ailments. I distinctly remember a family Zoom call where he shared the list, supplemented by a detailed oral description of each condition. Pop suffered from sleep deprivation and difficulty in basic daily activities such as eating, walking, standing, defecating, and showering (he installed stability bars in his shower/tub). He experienced body tremors, stiffness, pain, difficulty in swallowing, abdominal cramps, numbness in fingers and toes, loss of taste and smell, lack of energy, slurred speech, and cognitive decline, among other afflictions. Due to an inability to focus, he had given up reading, a lifelong pleasure.

Perhaps in his troubled mind, my father believed that if he could communicate precisely how he felt and what he was experiencing, those closest to him could ease his suffering. Tragically, neither I, nor anyone else, could spare my father from his distress—only he had the ability to do so. Yet his dogged intransigence blocked him from doing so. At times, it was as if Pop wore the torment and suffering of Parkinson's as a badge of honor. This attitude was completely out of character for my self-assured father. Witnessing the mental and emotional decay as Parkinson's tightened its grip had me doubting everything I previously believed about my father. It would only get worse

Dr. Eli "Edda" Stenn circa 1950 in Chicago.

Manuel "Zim" Zimberoff at the Uptown Theater in Chicago Pre-Depression era.

My Pop as a high school senior in 1956 in Chicago.

Wendy, Mom, Dad, Aleen and me in Greece in 1972.

Mom and Pop cooking dinner on Pismo Beach on our trip "out west" in 1973.

My family following brunch in Laguna Beach, CA in 1982.

Pop and his mother, sisters Donna, Sylvia, Lilah, Sandra, Helia, and brother Marc.

Pop and Yankee Doodle Mom at NAS Miramar in 1991.

Mom and Pop in Cabo san Lucas in 1996.

Aleen, Pop, Wendy and me at Aleen & Brent's Michigan home in 2017.

Pop the pruner about to decimate one of Aleen's bushes in 2017.

Pop tussling with Ellie the day before departing for Switzerland.

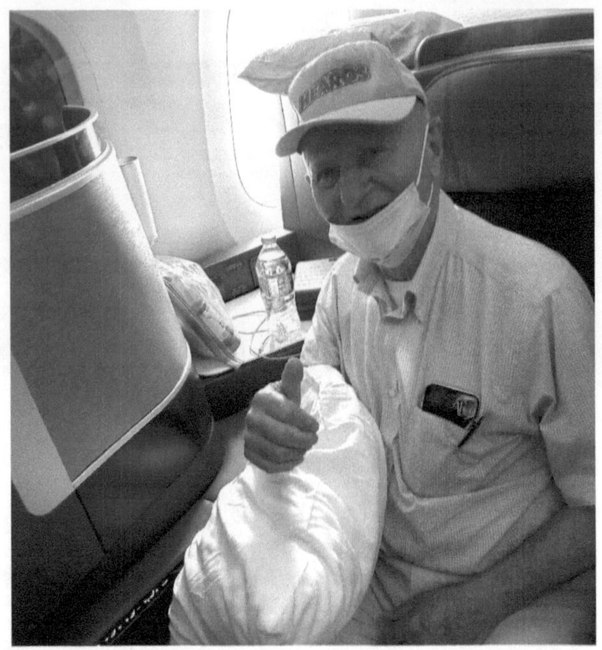

Pop on the transatlantic flight to Frankfurt before he met Tory.

Me, Pop, Brent and Aleen moments before he passed in our arms.

SEVENTEEN

I WINCED WHEN I first saw my father use a walker. I did not recognize the man behind the apparatus "elderly" people used. As I watched my father shuffle from the couch, grab his walker, and trundle out his apartment, it was as if I was watching a movie of some aged actor portraying my dad. It was the spring of 2022, and it marked the radical decline of my father—physically, mentally, and emotionally.

Please keep in mind that for the totality of my life, my dad was a rock. He may not have been muscular or uber fit, but he was consistently healthy. Most of my friends' fathers complained of bad knees, or bad backs, or bad hips, or all the above. Many underwent various joint replacements but not my dad. Pop was an Iron Man. Not only did he never have serious joint or bone ailments, the man also never had surgery of any type. Pre-Parkinson's, his worst ailment was tennis elbow.

Pop was a terror on the tennis court, sometimes playing two matches in a day as a sixty-something year-old wearing down his opponents. His grip was like that of a pro wrestler. Into his eighties, he would ask a male bank teller, or food server, or concierge to take his hand and squeeze as hard as they could. Nine out of ten times they could not make him shrink. "Wow, you've got quite the grip!", they often said genuinely surprised.

Now I observed my father clutch onto the walker like an old man. Initially, he was reluctant to use it, determined to maintain his mobility and independence. However, he soon figured out how best to use the device. On a later visit we were taking a stroll down the sidewalk near his apartment when he began power walking like one of the middle-aged women in Lululemon we saw dashing along Lake Shore Drive. I had to increase my pace just to keep up. I teased him that we should paint racing stripes on the walker. He chuckled at the notion, proud that he maintained the dexterity and stamina to walk briskly despite the litany of his other symptoms. He may not have been able to play tennis, but damn if he didn't scoot around the neighborhood like a sprint walker.

It was no coincidence that my father's quality of life deteriorated during and immediately following the COVID lockdowns. Pop couldn't meet and interact with people at the park, bank, grocery, or drug store. Additionally, COVID suspended Jim's boxing classes. When the classes resumed, Pop failed to attend. COVID and Parkinson's robbed my father of his energy and zeal. Though he continued riding the stationary bike, I never saw him hit his boxing bags post-2021.

Dad's sleeping patterns were disrupted throughout the night by a combination of restless leg syndrome and night sweats (both common effects of Parkinson's). He scheduled an appointment with the University of Chicago Hospital's sleep disorder clinic which involved staying overnight for observation. A week later, Pop received a written evaluation which confirmed the disorder with a note to confer with his primary care physician. After speaking with his doctor, the physician prescribed medication that could help alleviate some of the discomfort but not eliminate either condition. As with the other ailments, Pop was forced to live with the worsening trajectory of Parkinson's onslaught.

Notwithstanding his difficulty with physical activities, Pop remained fiercely independent in all his daily activities except for driving. Due primarily to his decreased night vision and occasional cognitive lapses, Pop decided to stop driving and sell his car. He already had been using Uber part-time and easily shifted to complete reliance on the ride-sharing service.

During this period, Pop continued to live alone, spending fewer evenings overnight with Leslie. His interrupted sleep proved too disruptive for them both. Another casualty of COVID and his worsening condition was international travel. Globetrotting had been one of his and Leslie's primary shared interests. Travel opportunities evaporated, replaced by COVID-isolated neighborhood walks and shuttering in-home. The inability to travel, physical decay, and diminished mental state put undue pressure on his thirteen-year relationship with Leslie.

Pop's overall quality of life deteriorated during and immediately following the COVID lockdowns. Zgull lived for one-on-one human interaction. His favorite activity, bar none, involved discussing politics, a play or book recently seen or read, a business venture, or just about any other non-trivial subject with a family member, friend, or stranger. COVID robbed him of these connections. For my father, the physical distancing took immeasurable and profound tolls on his mental state. Sure, he had Leslie and Aleen living close by, but they could not satisfy his thirst for widespread human interaction. COVID and Parkinson's did a one-two punch to knock down my dad.

In mid-summer 2022, I flew down to be with Pop several times for a few days. During these trips I left Salima and our toddler Ellie back home in Toronto. I was also able to see my two adult children from my first marriage, Levi and Ariel, who were then living in Chicago. One visit in May functioned as a turning point in my father's Parkinson's battle.

Leslie had lobbied hard for my father to sell his condo and move into a senior living facility. She thought he would benefit from the security and assistance of having full-time healthcare professionals co-located in his residence.

Pop feared that if he fell and broke a hip or other bone, he would be forced to endure surgery. He was convinced if he were placed under general anesthesia, he would never awaken and would be doomed to remain in a coma until he faded away. That belief terrorized Pop and was a factor in many decisions made in the last months of his life, including his decision to enter a senior facility.

I was disappointed when Pop announced his decision. My sisters and I argued against the move. We understood our father's white-knuckle grip on independence and urged him to stay in his condo, hiring necessary at-home professionals to assist him. At the end, love overcame sensibility; he placed a deposit on the facility the same day he first toured it with Leslie. I thought it was premature and impulsive, but when Pop made a decision, that was it. There was no use in trying to change his mind.

Pop is the only person I have ever known whose confidence was unassailable. He was always right, and when not, thought about it for a day, and after an evening of reflection, came back the next morning with additional arguments proving to you that he was still right. Additionally, my father was ailing, and I wanted to do everything I could to support him and ease his suffering. Lastly, the facility had twenty-four-hour care which alleviated some of the stresses we all were feeling, especially his fear of falling.

We were at Brookdale, the assisted-living facility, having finished moving his furniture and boxes into his apartment. Leslie, who'd lobbied hard for my father to move, was noticeably absent. After the movers left, and my father lay down for a nap, I called Aleen and Wendy.

"There is no way Dad is going to stay here. No fucking way," I asserted. "Sure, it's a nice enough facility physically, but the staff is obsequious and constantly smile like Barbie dolls. All the residents are old and in wheelchairs. He's going to be miserable."

My sisters sounded surprised as Leslie had given such rave

reviews about the place and Pop was also enthusiastic. I told them that I did not want to be negative but just did not see our father surviving in such an unctuous environment.

I wish I had been wrong, but my intuition proved prescient. A few days after the move, Pop started complaining. He complained about his bathroom plumbing. About mold in his kitchen. About carpeting being too high and a trip hazard. About staff ignoring him. About the food. About the loss of independence. Mostly, Pop complained constantly about how the other residents seemed to be in various stages of dementia, unable to engage in any lively discussion. At dinner, they would ask him the same questions repeatedly. Pop was being robbed of the greatest passion in his life: the ability to meaningfully interact with people.

My dad also grumbled of perceived loss of independence. I say "perceived," because practically speaking, living in the senior facility did not detract from his autonomy. He had his own apartment with a full kitchen. He could come and go as he pleased. There were social groups he could join, or he could be left alone and retire to the privacy of his apartment.

I tried to have a Warrior conversation about his attitude.

"Pop, I think you are being too hard on the facility. I think maybe your judgment is a little off."

"Bucky, you just don't understand."

My heart sank as I realized that Pop was just not the man he used to be. I no longer felt judged by my father, I simply felt sorry for him.

EIGHTEEN

"ALEEN, WENDY, AND I grappled constantly with how to relate to our "Parkinson's dad." We witnessed his personality shifts increase in frequency. My sisters and I came up with a way of dealing with his mood swings caused by the disease by describing him as David One, David Two, or David Three.

David One is the person I had known for fifty-seven of my fifty-eight years. Fiercely independent, he clung to the notion that he was in control of his life. If he could not control the events around him, he surely would control their impact upon him. David One could be forceful but was mostly civil and respectful. He was ardently consistent, unwavering, and unapologetic.

One of the cruelties of Parkinson's, like some other brain pathologies, is its insidious impact upon the patient's mind and emotions. Parkinson's is known to alter the brain's pathways, leading to emotional imbalance, mood swings, cognitive discord, and even hallucinations. My sisters and I witnessed each of these maladies during the last months of our father's life.

David Two was a direct descendant of Parkinson's. I first met David Two about a year before my dad died. My sisters and I described him as David One suffering from emotional and cognitive lapses. He exhibited zero patience, cut us off routinely, never accepted being contradicted, and often acted unreasonably. He demonstrated a hair trigger with little remorse.

I observed David Two confront several vendors, including a bank manager and multiple senior living facility employees. In each exchange, my father was rude and overly aggressive. By the end of each conversation, he calmed. Afterwards, when I called him out on his behavior, he replied that he needed to get the person to tears or close to crying to effect change. Sadly, this was the Parkinson's talking.

David Three was the most difficult incarnation of Pop's transition, a real-life Mr. Hyde. Fortunately, he only came out a few times during the last year of Pop's life. Unfortunately, when David Three did present, he was openly hostile and verbally abusive. When Pop raised his voice, narrowed his brows, leaned forward, and spit out expletives, one easily could have felt physically violated. I'm convinced when in this state, my father was channeling Zim. I hoped he would not worsen and become violent as his Parkinson's progressed.

NINETEEN

"DANNY, PLEASE COME." My father was crying on the phone repeatedly saying he needed to see me. It was shortly after he had moved into Brookdale.

I asked what was wrong, but he just kept telling me to come. I asked about Leslie, but he didn't reply. By this point, Pop's and Leslie's relationship had deteriorated severely. Even though he was in the assisted-living facility with full-time professional care, the strain of his condition and his uncharacteristic victim attitude apparently weighed heavily on her. She continued to withdraw. Neither she nor my father was in a good place.

Salima was sympathetic as always and urged me to go be with my dad. I booked a flight for the next day. After landing at Midway Airport, I took the "L" train and walked the final half mile to Brookdale. As I turned the corner and headed down his street, I reflected on how far my father had deteriorated in a relatively short period. I never thought of my dad as old until the past few years. Prior to his eightieth birthday, I saw an energetic, healthy, vibrant man. After he turned eighty, he seemed to age virtually overnight. One day he was my lively, animated dad, and the next day he had become a little more hunched over, a bit slower physically and mentally. His hair thinner and whiter. Eyes more glazed over. He went to bed earlier and slept later. We hardly ever talked sports or current events. Our walks became shorter. Then Parkinson's hit hard.

I entered the building and made my way to the elevator. At this point in my life, I'd never been a caregiver of the elderly. I love—absolutely adore—caring for infants and young children. With three kids of my own, I certainly am not put off by changing diapers. Baby poop, no problem. Puke, even infant projectile vomiting, not an issue. Hand me a cloth and bottle of Lysol and I'm good to go.

I also am a decent medic. Not a serious paramedic. Cuts, scratches, splinters, the sight of blood doesn't faze me. I'll jump in with Bactine and a Band-Aid and kiss and make it all better.

Just do not ask me to bathe an elderly person. Or help them eat. Or dress them. And I hate to admit this publicly, I really do, but I despise the odor that accompanies the elderly. The smell literally turns my stomach. I know, I'm going to hell for thinking this, but truthfully, that's how I felt.

I never thought much about my aversion nor did any introspective work to uncover the roots of my discomfort. I never had to address the issue with my mom, as she died at sixty-one and

I wasn't tasked with caring for her during the short time she was ill. Perhaps being around frail elderly people triggered an inner fear of aging? Or mortality? Maybe I projected my anxiety over losing control of my own body, of my own life? Whatever the reason, I steadfastly avoided physically assisting the elderly until Parkinson's took over my Pop.

When the elevator stopped on the twenty-eighth floor, I walked down the hall to my father's apartment and took a deep breath, unsure which David would greet me on the other side of the door. Would my father be crying? Asleep? Pacing restlessly with his walker? Agitated and angry?

With a feeling of unease, I opened the unlocked door and looked around. "Pop," I called out. "You there?"

I heard a faint response from the bathroom. I turned the corner from the hallway and could see my dad in the bathroom, hunched over the bathtub clothed only in his tighty-whities, barber's clippers gripped in his right hand. His scalp was partially shaven in strips with clumps of hair clinging down his back. His head hung low; he had not raised it to meet my eyes. I struggled to recognize the alien figure who sat before me.

"Pop, what are you doing?" I asked tenderly.

"My scalp is so itchy. It's aggravating me! Help me shave my head."

So much for a genial greeting.

"Okay," I responded, and took the shear from his hand. I slowly began to shave the remaining hair from his scalp. As I gently glided the shaver from hairline to hairline, I thought back on my first day in Marine Corp bootcamp when I got scalped. I was a nineteen-year-old kid starting an exhilarating journey.

Pop was an eighty-five-year-old man nearing the end of his. The irony was not lost on me.

As I continued to shave his head, I felt my aversion to assisting the elderly begin to fade like a waning rash. I wanted to ease my father's pain. If shaving his scalp helped alleviate some discomfort, I was all in.

It was my Pop, and he needed me.

After finishing, I took a step back and checked to make sure I had gotten it all. I saw a tired, listless, bleary-eyed old man. His skin was pallid, shoulders slumped. I hugged him. He tried to hug me back but could not raise his arms above his waist. I reassured him it was okay, that everything would be all right. In the moment I was unsure of my own words but wanted—needed—to comfort us both. I told him I loved him. I helped him get dressed and got him to bed.

During those two days we didn't do much. We filled the time with naps and stories of the past. Mostly, Pop needed me close by. I slept on the couch in his office and either ordered meals from the cafeteria or cobbled something together in his kitchen. I asked if he wanted to see Leslie and he declined. I did not call her, as by then, our communications had all but ceased.

During one of his naps, I met with the facility's executive director to resolve some of the issues identified by Pop early in his stay. She was attentive during our meeting and took notes, but I sensed nothing significant would be done to address his concerns, many of which she'd probably heard repeatedly from other residents.

During one of our down times, Pop told me he despised living at Brookdale. He hated being around the other residents.

They reminded him of what would lie ahead. He wanted out.

In hindsight, I believe his decision to move into the facility sped his decline. Pop never lived with regrets. He refused to relive the past. If he could hit rewind, however, I am certain he would have chosen to remain in his condo and receive in-home care for as long as possible; but he never admitted it.

My father continued to act like a victim. Though he often would say he did not want to be a *kvetcher*, that's exactly how he was acting. On occasion, he had the self-awareness to understand what he was doing and chastised himself for complaining but could not stop. He blamed his conduct on Parkinson's. I blamed it on his stubbornness in not letting go.

When I say, "letting go," I do not mean giving up. I mean releasing the fantasy he had control over his health at that point. Pop tried to fight Parkinson's in a boxing ring. He fought on its home court, relentlessly battling against the odds instead of accepting where his body and mind were in any given moment and focusing on his strengths that remained. He continued to reject any type of mental or physical therapy. Pop had been a lone street fighter all his life relying on brute force and sheer determination. He was not going to change now. The harder he fought Parkinson's, the less he succeeded, and the stronger the disease took hold.

After my return to Toronto, Pop called me daily, sometimes multiple times during the day and evening, relaying his latest infirmity and complaint. He did the same with Aleen. I do not know how often he spoke with Leslie, if at all. I believe he reached out so often because he had an unquenchable need to share what he was enduring, as if expressing his constant anguish could ease his suffering.

"No one understands what I am going through!" became his mantra.

Over my life I have observed other people with debilitating conditions. Many were severely hunched over, barely able to walk, straddled with walkers or confined to wheelchairs. My uncle Bob, Aunt Sylvia's husband, had Parkinson's, was in much worse condition, was older, yet managed a decent quality of life with a strong will to live. When I compared Bob and the others to Pop, I tried not to judge him but wondered why my father was not trying harder to cope. Where was the bulldog relentlessly chasing down the tennis ball?

On the one hand, I wanted to fully support my dad, act as a sounding board during his calls and help him in every way I could. On the other hand, I wanted to kick him in the ass, tell him to buck up—be a Warrior, run to the roar and maximize the time remaining with his loved ones. Honestly, I resented many of his phone calls. They reminded me how powerless we both were to change his circumstances. He sounded weak and needy, the anathema of the man I had known my entire life.

I felt terrible when resentment crept into my thoughts, causing me more anxiety and guilt. I battled to push these feelings aside in favor of being the understanding, dutiful son. The constant seesaw of conflicting feelings sapped my energy. I could only imagine what my father was experiencing.

While struggling with my emotions, I had several conversations with Pop where I suggested he accept the fact he had Parkinson's and instead of trying to fight *against* it, learn to live *with* it. He rejected my viewpoint. "You don't understand. Nobody understands." He was right. At the end of these calls, I felt powerless to ease either my or my father's suffering.

TWENTY

LESS THAN TWO MONTHS after moving into Brookdale, my father abruptly announced in a random phone call that he "can't go on living like this." He needed to "head east." He said he would contact Pegasos to schedule the procedure for the soonest available date.

The proclamation did not come as a complete shock, as Pop's mental and physical condition continued to deteriorate. But I was still surprised by the finality of his declaration. Knowing that sometime in the future my dad planned to voluntarily end his life was one thing, but to hear he wanted to get it done now was quite another. In a moment, Pop's death went from something to face sometime in the future to an imminent event.

I remember thinking it was too soon. At his core, Pop was a

fighter. He had boxing bags in his bedroom to prove it. He could do twenty pushups. Pop had his mind, his intellect. He had grandchildren who benefitted from his wisdom and love. I did not want him to die. But for him, continuing to live with Parkinson's was torture. It was time.

My upset lingered. For two straight mornings after hearing his news, I awoke agitated. I sat in bed and thought that if Pop could just let go of trying to control the disease and get on with living as best he could, his decline would plateau. Uncle Bob was fighting while I perceived my dad was giving up.

Where was my Warrior Pop? Where was the man who grilled countless people, challenging them to reach inside, probe inward, and move past the blockage? In my mind, this was the time for my father to do what he had demanded of others his entire adult life: drop all facades, dig deep, and ask himself the difficult question he so often asked others, "What don't you want me to know?" I desperately wanted him to ask himself the same question so that he could find peace before he died. Instead, I heard how tired he was, or how he could not concentrate, or sleep, and a host of other complaints about his condition. I felt my dad was giving up on his life and the lives of those who loved him.

My sisters and I were unaware of the details and protocols used by Pegasos. Due to heightened international scrutiny and aggressive backlash by people who protested MAID organizations, Pegasos kept a very low profile. We knew he had submitted a five-thousand-dollar deposit along with an extensive application a few years previously with an open-ended date to proceed.

Pop told us Pegasos needed eight weeks' advance notice once he decided to move forward. He also told us he would be required to have a psychological evaluation after arriving in Switzerland. Other than that limited information, that's all we knew.

Within a week, Pop heard back from Pegasos and reserved a date: July 18, 2022. Less than two months away. Aleen began making airplane reservations for the three of us, as she and I planned to accompany our father to Switzerland. Wendy had to stay home but flew to Chicago right away to ensure she saw him in-person before he headed east. She was able to lend emotional support and assist Pop as his Parkinson's symptoms continued to intensify.

When Pop told Leslie of the date, she vehemently reiterated her opposition. Leslie remained adamant in her belief that MAID constituted suicide and was forbidden by God. She fervently rejected my father's intention and told him so in no uncertain terms.

Leslie's opinion carried the day. Less than a week after he had heard back from Pegasos with a firm date, Pop told us that upon conferring with Leslie, he had changed his mind. He canceled his trip east. Switzerland was off the table, perhaps permanently. He stated he was committed to allowing his doctors to treat the disease and let it progress naturally.

Pop's action seemed like a repeat of his decision to sell his condo and move into the assisted-living facility—impulsive and heavily influenced by Leslie. To me, the cancellation seemed to be made in desperation to gain favor with Leslie to save their relationship. Her possessing so much power over my father pissed me off.

In my entire life, I had never witnessed Pop bend to anyone's will, not even my mother. I thought it so ironic that a man who could never relinquish control suddenly did so regarding the most important decision of his life.

A few weeks later, I flew to Chicago and accompanied Pop for a three-hour evaluation encompassing physical, occupational, and speech therapies at Northwestern University Hospital's Shirley Ryan Ability Lab, a renowned provider of comprehensive physical medicine and rehabilitation care. Though I still resented the sway Leslie had over my father, I was encouraged that Pop was re-focusing on treatment. Perhaps he would resume his boxing classes with Jim, too. If Pop was recommitted to living, however difficult his life might become, I would remain staunchly by his side.

There was a noticeable change in Pop's attitude. During our calls, he concentrated more on the positivity in his life. He seemed to be sleeping better and described having more energy to stay awake and take walks. These were monumental shifts in his mental state and behavior. I felt encouraged.

Pop's new outlook jumpstarted our efforts to find live-in professional assistance who would come to his apartment at the assisted-living facility. Wendy and Aleen resumed phone calls to get people in front of our father for his input and final say.

Leslie's attitude also shifted. She told my father, sisters, and me that she would be more present for my dad. She agreed to take him to medical appointments and generally would be more available to help him.

During this time, I reflected on the similarities between my Parkinson's dad and toddler daughter. My father's decline and my daughter's growth coincided like two fabric strands joining in the tapestry of life.

In the summer of 2022, Ellie was almost eighteen months old. She had just started walking and was quite unsteady on her feet. I held her hand as she teetered and tottered around the house keeping my hands close to her body whenever she climbed stairs.

I did the same for my father. Though he mostly used a walker, I helped support him much in the same way I did Ellie in getting up or down, or to the bathroom, or making him meals.

Dressing was also similar. For the most part, my father could put on his pants and shirts, extending his legs into the pantlegs and arms into the sleeves, just as Ellie did. But he had difficulty buttoning his shirt, working zippers, or fastening buckles. I helped him with these tasks in the same loving manner as I did Ellie.

Pop would recoil with a gruff "I got it!" when strangers offered to help him open a door or assist with an item at the grocery store, yet my father did not protest my assistance. His need for total independence often trampled common decency, except with me.

I recall several times thinking how idiosyncratic it felt experiencing first-hand these two bookends of my life. Witnessing these actions brought home the "circle of life" playing out before my very eyes. The difference was my daughter was improving, while Pop continued to decline.

TWENTY-ONE

THOUGH BUOYED BY Pop's resurgence, after just two weeks following our visit to Shirly Ryan, I noticed a void in the tone of his voice during our phone calls. When speaking of having more energy, his voice fell flat, bereft of conviction—almost as if he were trying to convince me, or more importantly, himself, that he was doing better.

Pop vacillated numerous times between wanting to live and die, between feeling good and miserable, and between having faith in his doctors and claiming they did not understand what he was enduring. A "lack of understanding" by others remained his constant complaint. One day Pop would sound positive and tell me how he had gone outside for a walk. The very next day, he could barely get out of bed, could not sleep, and almost fell.

He would call me at all hours of the day and night. His mood shifts continued from miserable to positive . . . often within the same day. I lost count of how many times he called me crying, "I can't live like this, Danny," all the while refusing to see a mental health professional.

I did my best to respond to my father's varied requests, many of which bordered on the absurd. I did this as his loving son, not wanting to let him down, especially during his time of need. Even though I wanted to stay strong and be positive for him, I wrestled with sadness and guilt, anger and resentment.

When he instructed me to do something—unless it was something straightforward that I agreed with—I would delay doing it. Most often, he would forget about the request or take the opposite position by the next phone call. One morning, he might tell me to draft a lawsuit against Brookdale due to supposed lack of maintenance of the shared laundry room. The next day, he would have forgotten all about this complaint. During these tirades, I found listening, nodding, and doing nothing to be the sanest course of action.

At this point, to maintain my own sanity, I needed to shift internally. I had to take more control over my life by not allowing Pop to dictate my daily conduct and feelings. For the first time in my life, I found myself saying no to my father.

I felt awful. I empathized with his struggles. I loved him unconditionally. I knew in my head and heart that he had little control over what was occurring. Yet, emotionally, I was a wreck. Our conversations mostly involved his disease and its debilitating impact upon him, his issues with Leslie, and Brookdale.

I dearly missed our phone calls discussing current-day events, politics, sports, family, and the stock market. I missed walking with my father along Lake Michigan or through Lincoln Park. I missed joining him for a Blackhawk game and buying him a Budweiser. I missed flipping through family photo albums and hearing stories of great aunts, uncles, cousins, and Mom. I missed looking at his hundreds of photos from across the globe while he told me stories about the strangers whose photographic portraits he had taken.

Most of all, I missed my ol' Pop.

My father also began to repeat himself. I heard the same story about leasing his condo a half-dozen times. He exhibited a noticeably short temper, rising to emotional outbursts with little provocation. He often criticized my sisters and me when assisting with administrative tasks like coordinating issues with Brookdale, managing financial matters, or simply buying a comforter for his bed.

Nights were the most difficult time for Pop, as he often only slept a few sporadic hours. The medication prescribed by the sleep clinic only served to mitigate, not eliminate, his discomfort. He would get out of bed at four or five o'clock and obsess over some issue and then fire off an inflammatory email. He would then go back to sleep for a few hours. By the time he woke up, he often had forgotten what had set him off just hours before.

Once I identified the pattern and shared my thoughts with him, he mostly stopped. From then on when an issue aggravated him, he would write in the subject line of an early morning email, "I am sane, this is not Parkinson's talking, please read."

Sadly, many of these emails were still comprised of gripes regarding Brookdale or about his ongoing physical, emotional, and mental problems that could not be solved.

During this period, Aleen and I were Pop's primary family contacts, speaking with him daily. Wendy fully engaged and committed to helping manage his situation, retained boundaries and still called him David. Leslie faded in and out of Pop's life depending on how she felt on any particular day. One week she would accompany him to doctors' appointments and have dinner with him, and the following week, she'd fail to answer his calls. On top of everything else he was going through, the ambiguity surrounding their relationship drove him crazy.

The more Leslie pulled away, the harder my father tried to push them together. Watching my father chase after her in desperation and loneliness was heartbreaking and frustrating. Pop's desire to maintain their relationship was all-consuming, bordering on obsessive. His neediness was completely uncharacteristic of the man I had known all my life—the antithesis of Zgull. He kept clinging to Leslie like a shipwreck survivor clung to a life-preserver, but the more he flailed about trying to bring her closer, the further she drifted away.

The difficulty of witnessing the erosion of my dad's relationship with Leslie paled compared to the front-row seat I had on the roller-coaster of his everyday life. The optimism over my father's decision to cancel his trip to Switzerland and cope with Parkinson's through a renewed regime of medical appointments and physical and occupational therapies began to fade.

My father's mental, physical, and emotional conditions continued to break down during the summer of 2022. My sisters and I had little doubt our father had become clinically depressed. Pop did not disagree but would not consent to treatment.

"I'm eighty-five, Bucky. What else am I going to learn?"

My sisters and I urged him to see a geriatric mental health professional that Wendy had found to help him navigate the combined distresses of depression and declining health. He refused. Finally, in a passing moment of rare capitulation, we were able to convince him to see a psychiatrist to treat his depression. He only saw the doctor for one session and never went back, refusing to take the prescribed medication because he felt it caused confusion in his already Parkinson's-afflicted brain.

One Saturday afternoon during this period I received a call from Pop saying he could not take it any longer. His words stuttered and his voice cracked. I could hear amplified noise in the background.

"Pop, where are you? It doesn't sound like your apartment."

"I'm at Weiss Memorial," he said plainly.

"Is that a hospital?" I replied.

"Yes."

"What happened, are you okay?"

"My blood pressure is over two hundred and I was dizzy."

"Is Leslie with you?" I asked.

"I didn't want to bother her."

Bother her, I thought incredulously. Leslie lived three blocks away.

"How did you get there then?"

"I took an Uber."

"You took an Uber? What about the staff at Brookdale?"

"I didn't tell them. They're worthless."

I stood dumbfounded. I told him to sit tight and wait for Aleen to get there.

By the time I got in touch with my sister and called Pop back, he had already walked out of the hospital before the doctors could complete their tests. He said the doctors were not helping him and he had called an Uber to take him back to Brookdale.

At this time, Pop had a team of physicians, coordinated by his primary care doctor to ensure his treatments did not fall through the cracks. Aleen and I generally had been in touch with the lead physician, as our father had signed a consent form that allowed us access to his medical records and for the doctor to communicate freely with us. After this incident, we both became more involved in his treatment.

Throughout all these episodes, Aleen and I relied on each other for emotional support. We commiserated. We shared anecdotes of our father's latest cuckoo behavior. We tried to find some levity to balance the trying circumstances. Initially, I vented to Aleen, needing an outlet for the frustration, pain, and confusion I was feeling from Pop's actions. We spoke every day, as there almost always was something our dad had done, was doing, or was about to do that prompted at least some level of concern.

We would speak while at the gym, while driving, eating, and walking. It didn't matter what we were doing, we would always pick up for one another. "What's he done now?" was a more common greeting than, "Hiya" or, "Good morning."

Pop's calls often sucked time and energy away from my ability to be an attentive husband and father while at home. Additionally, each time I flew to Chicago, I left Ellie with Salima who had to be a single parent while working full-time. Salima never complained; instead, she told me many times to stay longer or go more often. Having her support allowed me to be there for my father without worrying about how my family was doing in my absence. Her compassion and understanding acted as an anchor, allowing me to commit unbridled emotional energy to my father. In the same way my father knew my mom always had his back, I knew Salima had mine.

TWENTY-TWO

MY FATHER'S MANIC episodes worsened throughout that summer. More frequent. More conflicted. More David Two with lapses into David Three. My sisters and I were becoming increasingly distraught. Then on August 29th, Pop announced to each of us in separate phone calls that he had decided to contact Pegasos to establish a new date as soon as possible.

"Danny. I can't go on like this any longer. I can't."

Though Pop had requested and received a date earlier in the year, and then changed his mind shortly thereafter, this time felt different. There was a clarity in his voice I had not previously heard. This time it was for real. A sickening feeling swept over me.

Pegasos had told my father they required six to eight weeks

of lead time to coordinate details. It was a small organization run by an individual who relied upon multiple volunteers. In addition to coordinating schedules, the director also had to submit preliminary paperwork to the local and federal governments for approval before moving forward.

When Pop first applied for the program years before, he had submitted a detailed, multi-page form describing his general background, medical and mental health history, and explanation for why he desired to proceed with MAID. As Pop explained to me, now that he'd informed the director he wanted to proceed, the organization still needed two months to complete details on their end.

In a heartfelt email to the director, my father pleaded for them to expedite their protocols. After a week of back-and-forth correspondence between my father and Pegasos, the director agreed to accelerate the process. This was the first time I was included in email communication with Pegasos. I now had a direct line with the director. Up to that point I had been virtually in the dark involving the organization, reliant on my father to share details.

The director sent an email with the date: September 19, 2022. My father was scheduled to die in just over a week!

I was torn. While I wanted my dad to continue fighting to live despite all his manic calls, his moodiness, his forgetfulness, his endless list of demands and complaints—as difficult as I knew it was for him—I wanted, needed, him to remain part of my life and my children's lives. At the same time, I was relieved that his battles and suffering, along with the anguish to him and the rest of us caused by Parkinson's, would soon be over. Though ambiguity persisted, once the date was set, I no longer found myself resentful of my father.

I cried, a lot, alone, in my office that day.

September 19, 2022.

A looming date. The closest comparison I can come up with is a cesarean birth. But in that instance, the scheduled date marks a celebratory time ushering in a new life. Joy, excitement, bliss. Death lies on the opposite end of the spectrum.

When my mother died, we knew the end was near, but it could have come in another day, another week, another month.

With my father, September 19, 2022, marked a date in my calendar—a date menaced with finality. I had just over a week to manage details of closing my father's personal and business affairs, rearrange my and my family's scheduling, and coordinate travel. Aleen and her husband Brent were on an extended vacation to Italy when Pop made his announcement. Once the date was confirmed, she arranged for them to fly from Italy to Switzerland to join me and our father.

When Pop called Wendy to inform her of his urgent need to get to Switzerland as soon as possible, he told her he wanted to say goodbye to her and Emma in-person, since they would not be accompanying him to Switzerland. Wendy immediately booked flights, and they arrived in Chicago on Tuesday, September 13th. With Joe needing to stay home, he used Facetime to privately say his goodbyes.

With the timing of his impending death, it would mean Pop would not be alive for Emma's upcoming Bat Mitzvah. With such an important milestone in her life that they both had intended for him to participate in, Wendy arranged for her family's rabbi to facilitate a Bat Mitzvah ceremony by Facetime. Emma, Grandpa, and Wendy sat together in his Brookdale apartment, with the rabbi and Joe on Facetime. Emma chanted Hebrew prayers as Pop held her hands, tears of joy streaming down his cheeks. It was a beautiful, spiritual experience that helped ease the pain for them all and provided a level of comfort and peace with his impending transition toward the unknown.

* * *

For eight straight days and evenings, I was constantly on the phone and computer. I spoke to my father and Aleen five or ten times per day and night. Thankfully, Salima was an absolute angel, supporting me in every aspect. She listened to me vent as I faced administrative and bureaucratic hurdles, rubbed my shoulders and neck when I started to get emotional, and ensured Ellie received the attention demanded by a toddler.

When my mother was dying, a dear friend offered the advice to treasure the time remaining with her; I would have ample time to grieve after her passing. Such sage counsel. I tried to do the same with my father, leaving the tears and grief, as much as possible, for a later time.

Arranging for international travel, in business class during what remained of the summer tourist season, was tricky, to say the least. I couldn't get a direct flight, so the best I could do was for us to fly throughout the night from O'Hare to Frankfurt, Germany, and then catch a commuter flight the next morning to EuroAirport in Switzerland, a short drive from the town where

Pegasos was located. I grabbed the last business class seat for Pop and secured the last seat on the plane, in coach, for myself.

Our plan was set. Salima, Ellie, and I would spend the day and evening on Friday, the 16th, with my dad, giving them an opportunity for a last goodbye. We would all then leave his apartment for the airport the next day, Salima and Ellie heading to Toronto and Pop and I for Europe, for his fated day on the 19th.

As I clicked on the online confirmation for a one-way ticket for my father, a jolt passed down my spine. This was it. He was leaving and not coming back.

TWENTY-THREE

ON THE MORNING of September 16th, Salima, Ellie, and I landed at Midway Airport and headed straight for Brookdale. We checked into one of the guest suites made available for family members and freshened up before heading upstairs to see my dad. Levi would join us later that morning, and Ariel later that evening for dinner.

We took the elevator to the twenty-eighth floor. The door was unlocked, and we walked in. Ellie, in a cute purple jumper with curly hair bouncing, strolled into the living room and stopped in her unsteady tracks when she saw Pop seated at his desk. Ordinarily, whenever my daughter met someone she either did not know or had not seen in a while, she would smile nervously or look away. But with my father, she had a different routine.

Ever since she was a newborn, Ellie and my father had an immediate connection. They established a custom where they would stare at one another for several moments in silence, surveying each other's faces and eyes from a distance. They did so that morning.

Pop finally broke the silence, "Hey, where's your nose?" Ellie laughed, pointed to her button nose, and gleefully ran to him. He patted her on the head.

Following Ellie, I walked over and hugged my dad warmly—a Warrior greeting.

"Hiya, Pop." I started to snivel but wiped away the forming tears with the back of my hand.

"Hi, Bucky." He hugged me back. Salima walked over and hugged my dad.

Levi showed up a bit later and the four of us chatted casually while Ellie played on the floor. My father wanted to review with me several investment and estate files. He and I sat at the kitchen table while Salima and Levi entertained Ellie in the living room. After an hour, I asked if Pop wanted to take a short walk, but he was too tired. We had reservations for dinner at six thirty, so my dad laid down to take a nap.

When he awoke, he found the energy to play with Ellie. I do not remember my father horsing around with any child—me, my sisters, my cousins, my kids—none of us. But there he was, on his hands and knees on the carpeted floor of his senior living apartment, tussling with Ellie. I smiled broadly and took videos to capture the precious moments.

When it was time to leave for dinner, Pop said he was too exhausted to join us. We agreed to bring him back something to eat. We met Ariel at a nearby Italian restaurant and after dinner the five of us returned to my father's apartment. Ariel had homework to get to and after a short while, said her final goodbye to her grandfather. She had spent the better part of the day with him the weekend before.

Pop's relationship with Ari was like the tide: sometimes high, sometimes low, always shifting. My father was a direct communicator with little interest in small talk and mediocrity. Ari was finding her path and not always open to the kind of serious, confrontational conversation offered by her grandfather. Eventually, they found a middle ground and saw one another on a semi-regular basis.

As I watched Ari hug her grandfather for the last time, I started crying. My biggest regret about my mother's death was knowing she would never have a relationship with her grandchildren. Levi was not quite two years old when she died and Ari had not yet been born. At least Ariel and Levi had time with Pop; Ellie barely any. Soon, all three would be without their grandfather.

Ariel wiped tears from her eyes as she left the living room. I hugged her in the doorway, not wanting to let go. A whimper escaped from her chest. Finally, she pulled away and headed for the elevator. "I'll see you in a few days," I said.

Like his younger sister, during the last few years Levi had been adrift searching for purpose and direction. Pop could be hard on Levi. Initially, he was judgmental and critical. As much as he fought against it, I think Levi appreciated the tough love my father exhibited. Pop's parenting was very different from my style of flexible, positive reinforcement. At times I wished I possessed the fortitude to exhibit the same forcefulness toward my children as my father did.

As his health continued to decline, my father started letting go of his harsh judgments. Over the past year, his relationship with Levi had grown exceptionally close. They maintained a regular Sunday evening date when Levi, a burgeoning chef, cooked dinner for them at Pop's apartment.

Pop was also quite close with his two other grandchildren, Aleen's son Adam, in his early thirties living in New York with his fiancé, Rachel, and Wendy's teenaged daughter, Emma. He would see them at least annually, and sometimes more frequently. He stayed in close contact through telephone and Zoom calls, mentoring each in his inimitable style.

Pop treated his role as grandparent for each of his grandchildren as vital, no doubt sublimating the profound impact his grandfather, Edda, had upon him.

As the evening wound down, Levi headed back to his apartment while Salima, Ellie, and I headed downstairs—but not before hugging my father goodnight.

The next morning, Ellie, more dependable than an alarm clock, woke up with her usual six-thirty-reveille of pre-toddler gibberish. I got her dressed and took her for a walk to grab a tea and a few croissants at a local coffee shop while Salima dozed.

After our walk, Ellie and I ventured to my father's apartment. Pop was awake. He picked up where he had left off the night before, rolling on the floor with his youngest granddaughter. Again, I smiled as I observed Ellie climb over Pop's back. *Who is this man?* Pop was not a "get on your hands and knees and play" type of dad. Conversely, this was a man who my cousins used to call "Uncle No-No" because, like his mother, he often curtailed kids rough-housing or play for fear of hurting themselves or breaking something. I was unaware of just how much my dad had mellowed until this visit with Ellie. His smiles and her squeals were an elixir to my frazzled psyche.

I offered Pop a croissant, which Ellie quickly glommed onto. Pop got a kick out of Ellie's signing the words for "more," "please," and "thank you." He playfully mimicked her with his own hands, eliciting giggles from her.

This journey was not without its hurdles. The first complication arose when I checked my email on my phone. United Airlines informed me that my reservation had been canceled. Not the flight, but my reservation. *What?* I frantically called the 800 number and was placed into "please hold" purgatory. Then, after speaking with a reservation agent for almost ten minutes and hearing him click away furiously on his keypad, he informed me that he needed to talk to his supervisor. My heart rate jumped—my dad and I were scheduled to leave for the airport in less than three hours.

After more excruciating minutes ticked by, the agent told me my reservation was intact. He could not give me a reason why it had been temporarily canceled. At least we were back on track.

Pop always pushed the envelope when traveling. He did not arrive at an airport early like most people. He was not the type to sit around an airport lounge or coffee shop waiting for his flight to board. No, my dad was "that guy" who arrived at the gate just before they closed the door. I was the exact opposite that day and built in ample time to ensure a less stressful travel experience for us both. While Pop played with Ellie, I called and reserved a taxi. I made sure to request a min-van, allowing ample space for Pop's walker.

Neither Salima nor Levi had made it to the apartment yet. I gave Ellie a toy to play on the floor in the living room, while Pop and I moved to his kitchen table to review a few last-minute estate items.

The previous week, I'd reached out to my father's estate attorney to introduce myself and let him know of my dad's plans. I wanted to ensure that Pop's estate affairs were in order. The attorney was aware of the general plan, but like all of us, was caught unaware by the accelerated timeline.

During the call, the subject of estate taxes came up and we quickly determined that my dad's estate would likely exceed the exempted threshold for Illinois state inheritance tax. The attorney mentioned that my dad could provide gifts up to a set threshold per person to reduce the overall tax liability. The only catch was the money had to leave the account before his death.

After hanging up the phone, I called Aleen. We agreed to wire several payments out of my father's bank account to ourselves, our spouses, and adult children to be repaid to the estate right after my father's death. We didn't think we were violating any laws, simply employing a loophole to save on taxes. I let Pop know about the plan.

As we waited for Salima and Levi to arrive, Pop asked about the status of the gift payments. Upon hearing my explanation, his expression changed.

Oh shit! I thought. *Here it comes.*

"Danny, you're better than that," he began in a tone I'd not heard since I was thirteen years old. "You could go to jail. The state could hold up the estate transfer for months in audits."

He continued. "Violating a law is violating a law. It undermines one of the primary foundations of cohesive society—the rule of law," I wasn't ready for a lecture and sat silent. He continued, "Laws do not deviate, do not compromise."

I finally replied, "Says who? If eighty percent, or even a slight majority of society—the same people for whom the law is designed to protect—violate a law, doesn't that make it morally justified to break it? If the rule or law is disregarded by so many, why does it get unassailable protection?"

"Because it has been adopted by the very system that is designed to uphold it. The system is undermined every time someone breaks the law." My father turned the tables and hit back with the legal argument he knew I strongly believed.

I wanted to return serve and defend my actions but could tell by his slouched shoulders and weary eyes that he was tired and lacked the energy to continue.

"Want to lie down for a few minutes before we continue packing?" I offered.

"Yes."

After he ambled to the bedroom to lay down, I sat on a chair and reflected on our conversation as Ellie lie asleep, curled on the floor. Here was a man mere hours from leaving this planet yet still concerned about "the rule of law." Pop was uncompromising in his moral and ethical code until the very end.

After his rest, I told him he was right and that we would not bend the law. The "gifts" would remain as is and not flow back to the estate. He nodded.

Salima and Levi finally made their way to the apartment. The five of us spent the remaining time together without purpose or plan other than to just be together. The mood hovered between relaxed and anxious. As the hour drew closer to our departure, we engaged in several hugs and a few tears. None from my father, as he showed staunch resoluteness and a keen focus on his routine: taking his many pills, dressing, and finishing packing. It was apparent to me that in his mind, he already had begun his journey east.

I helped my father pack his last items, fitting two days of clothing, toiletries, and a large Ziplock bag filled with dozens of pills into a backpack. I confirmed for the third time that I had our passports.

Salima and Ellie said their final goodbyes, my daughter oblivious to the fact she would never see her grandfather again. The gravity of the situation sucked the air from the room. I labored to take in a few deep breaths as I walked them down to a waiting Uber and kissed them both goodbye. Salima gave me a loving hug and reassured me I would be okay, that I would be there for my dad.

Back in my father's apartment, Pop and I went over our bags a final time. My phone rang. It was the cab company. The driver was lost.

After several minutes of back and forth with a language

barrier wafting between us, we determined the driver inexplicably had the wrong address. He was over twenty minutes away from our scheduled pick-up time. First the airline reservation SNAFU, now this. I took a deep breath. *It'll be okay,* I tried to reassure myself.

Our taxi finally arrived almost forty-five minutes late. Fortunately, I had padded the schedule, so we were still okay on time. Levi decided to accompany us to the airport. Three generations of Zimberoff men climbed into the minivan for the drive to O'Hare.

TWENTY-FOUR

AFTER PULLING UP to the terminal, Levi took the walker and helped his grandfather as I grabbed Pop's and my backpacks and my roller case from the taxi driver. It felt strange carrying such minimal baggage on a transatlantic flight. As soon as he had his walker, Pop shot off into the crowded terminal. Levi hurried after him while I paid for the taxi and followed with our luggage.

We stopped at a United kiosk to print my boarding pass since I could not check in online due to the confusion about my reservation. I also checked my case to free up my hands to assist Pop on the flights. Levi and my father said their final goodbyes. My son, who usually shows little emotion, teared up as he hugged his grandfather for the last time. For the third instance in the past twelve hours, I watched a child of mine say their final farewell to their grandfather. Tears streamed down my cheeks before I had a chance to wipe them away.

I thanked Levi for joining us, gave him a robust hug and headed toward security with Pop leading the way. I could barely keep up with my power walking father. I was taken aback by his determination. Here was a man on a journey to his death and if you did not know any better, you would think he was headed on a much-anticipated holiday.

We had ninety minutes to get through security, grab something to eat, and make our way to the gate. Ample time, or so I thought.

As soon as we entered the security entrance, my optimism plummeted. Even with TSA Precheck, the line wound around several bends and aisles. Pop had stubbornly refused the wheelchair I'd reserved, which would have allowed us to skip the line. As I looked at the length of the queue, I had no doubt we would make the flight but was concerned I might not have sufficient time to grab a bite to eat. Neither of us had eaten anything all day other than a croissant back in his apartment hours before. We were both hungry and lunch on the plane wouldn't be served for quite a while.

As we painstakingly made our way through the turn reversals, a female TSA officer saw my father and his walker. "Why are you in line, young man?" she asked Pop in a sweet Southern drawl. The woman turned to me and inquired if I was with him. When I nodded, she lifted the partition. "You two gentlemen come with me." Our uniformed angel escorted us around a couple hundred passengers to the front of the scanning line.

Everything with my father was slow. Taking off his jacket

took time. Collapsing the walker took time. Shuffling through the scanner took an eternity. My father and I knew the routine, we were just painstakingly slow.

We finally got through security, and I gathered our backpacks and Pop's walker. As soon as I placed Pop's backpack on his walker, it was as if the starter's pistol had fired. Pop was off again bypassing and darting around distracted passengers in the packed terminal.

Ten minutes later, as we approached our gate at the very end of the B terminal, I failed to see the expected throng of passengers huddled for an international flight. Instead, we arrived at an empty Gate B-18. No passengers. No agents. No one. I checked a nearby monitor and saw that our flight was departing from Terminal C, Gate 16.

"Shit!" I said as I looked at my boarding pass. I had neglected to note the gate change. I'd never made such a boneheaded mistake in my life.

"What's wrong?" Pop asked.

"We're in the wrong place. We need to be at Terminal C. I'm going to call United and get us a wheelchair." Forty-five minutes to boarding and we had not eaten or had a pre-flight bathroom break.

I glanced around for a courtesy phone. Not seeing one, I looked for a gate agent but the nearby gates were also empty. I turned back to my dad, but he was gone. Vanished. I looked side-to-side across the terminal. No Pop.

Okay, I thought to myself. *He could not have gone far. It's only been a minute.*

I scanned down the terminal but could not see any sign of Pop or his walker. I started back toward Terminal C, keeping my head swiveling as I walked.

After five minutes without seeing my father, I started getting nervous. I backtracked a couple of gates and still did not see him among the mass of passengers rushing past. I tried calling his phone. No answer.

How the hell could I have lost my eighty-five-year-old father with a walker?!

I continued searching when I finally glimpsed Pop's signature tennis cap through a gap in the crowd. He was at the United Airlines Customer Service desk. I quickly approached.

"Pop, why did you take off?"

He ignored me as he continued speaking animatedly with an agent about upgrading my seat to business class. I was destined to fly for ten-and-a-half hours in the cattle section with the other coach passengers, a trivial inconvenience in exchange for accompanying Pop on this crucial crossing. My father pleaded that he was an eighty-five-year-old man with a walker who needed his son close by. The agent stated there simply were no available seats. The entire flight was oversold.

I thanked the agent and led my father toward the C concourse. We had no time to call for a wheelchair. Thirty-five minutes to boarding. For once, I appreciated Pop's power walking. Suddenly, he halted. "I need to use the restroom."

I moaned inside.

I accompanied Pop to the men's room and waited anxiously as he relieved himself. The process seemed to take forever. He finally finished and we continued toward the gate. As we arrived, we could see passengers standing and gathering their luggage. Just over twenty minutes until boarding.

My father insisted on getting something to eat. Again, I

worried about time but agreed; my stomach rumbled too. Immediately across from C-16 stood the entrance to the United Club. We ducked in. I showed the receptionist my father's business class boarding pass and asked if I could escort him down the elevator to where the food and beverages were set up. She declined, saying I was not authorized to use the club. My father responded with the "eighty-five-year-old man" schtick. He was more successful this time. The receptionist reluctantly agreed to allow me to pass, but not before telling us she was breaking the rules and repeating that I was not authorized to eat anything myself.

I thanked her and escorted Pop down the elevator and got him situated at a table near the buffet. I grabbed a plate, quickly piled it with food, put it on the table, and told him I'd be back in ten minutes.

He thanked me and dug in.

I headed upstairs and did my own power walking toward the Panera Bread I had spied a few gates away. After grabbing a take-away sandwich, I headed back to the lounge. A large cluster of passengers was queued in the gate area. Our flight was midway through boarding.

As I entered the foyer to the club lounge, I noticed the previous receptionist had been replaced by another woman who had a line of three guests in front of her. I bypassed the line and headed straight toward the escalator stating that I was simply going to get my elderly father who I had dropped off ten minutes before.

"Sir, let me check you in," the receptionist snarked from behind the counter.

"I don't need to be checked in," I responded while stopping

just before the escalator. "I only want to go downstairs and escort my father who is eighty-five and has a walker."

"You can't do that, Sir," she blared imperiously, and stood defiantly.

"Listen," I said in a more agitated tone, "Our flight is boarding, and I just need to grab my father!" I stepped onto the escalator. Three days of heightened stress began to boil over. I felt like screaming at her, "My father is dying in two days and I need to be here for him!"

"Sir, Sir!" she shouted as she rushed around the counter toward me.

"We'll be back in two minutes," I cried as I descended the escalator. Tears were filling my eyes. "I am under a lot of stress right now and just need to get my father."

"Sir, I am calling CPD!" she hollered and turned toward the counter.

Neurons fired and synapses bridged in my brain. In an instant I realized that once the police arrived, my father and I would miss our flight. I would be perceived as a trespasser until proven innocent. It would take some time to sort out the mess. I knew I had no other choice than to comply.

I turned and started walking up the down escalator. My head drooped as I ascended.

"Sir, I will call an escort for your father as I cannot leave my desk." *Great*, I thought, *that will only take fifteen minutes.* When I got to the top of the escalator I looked down to the lower floor and could make out the feet of my father sitting in his chair. He literally was a hundred feet from me.

After five minutes of pacing back and forth, I saw a gentleman with a United nametag rush into the lounge. He acknowledged me as he walked quickly past. "I'll get your father now." He stepped onto the escalator.

A couple minutes later the elevator door opened and the man and my father walked out. The gentleman was apologizing profusely to my dad. I walked over, took Pop's arm in mine, and escorted him with his walker out of the lounge. As we were leaving, the receptionist sarcastically told us to "have a nice flight." It took every ounce of self-control for me not to flip her off.

As Pop and I turned the corner out of the lounge, I instructed him to follow me closely as I politely—and not-so-politely—asked people to step aside as we made our way forward. Once we edged our way to the front, an agent saw my father's walker and welcomed us with open arms. I sighed audibly as we entered the jetway.

TWENTY-FIVE

WHEN POP AND I stepped onto the Boeing 787, the mood instantly transformed from mayhem to tranquility. The flight attendants assigned to my father's cabin could not have been more pleasant and helpful. Though we were in the middle of the boarding rush for all passengers, they ensured we had the space and time needed to get him settled comfortably.

Pop finally made it down the aisle to his seat. He sat down, exhausted, as I tried to comfort him. I leaned down, took off his shoes and helped him stretch out his legs into the footrest. As I kneeled to assist him, I thought back to the previous twenty-four hours of helping him in and out of vehicles, in and out of chairs, to the bathroom. A sense of grace washed over me. My prior reluctance to assist the elderly had been replaced with feelings of tenderness and service. By helping my father with these menial tasks, I was offering my love, which he accepted willingly.

One of the flight attendants had given us a second blanket, which I used with the first to tuck around my father's legs and torso. I confirmed he had his water bottle and that his medications were within reach. I set up his headphones and we cycled the reclinable seat twice to remind him how to do it. My father was a seasoned traveler, but never in this compromised condition. Once I confirmed Pop was comfortable and had everything he needed, I started to take my seat.

"Danny, I need to go to the bathroom. Grab my sweatpants."

Really? I thought.

"Sure, Pop, let me help you there," I said, trying my best to hide my frustration. I grabbed his backpack from the overhead and pulled out a pair of sweatpants. I then proceeded to undo everything I had just done and helped him to his feet. We shuffled to the lavatory. Once the door opened, he paused then proceeded without me. I had come a long way helping him but was not ready to assist him in the bathroom, especially one with such tight quarters.

"I'll be right outside," I said as he shut the door.

I waited in the aisle facing the rear of the plane. A passenger in the business class cabin caught my eye in a furtive glance. I self-consciously wondered what she was thinking. *Is that old man going on vacation with his son? He doesn't look good and can barely walk.* I chose to block out the negative thoughts swirling in my mind. A smile then crossed my face as a memory came to mind. I was four years old. We were in Turkey when my father gripped me by the back of my shirt to stop me from falling into the toilet hole in the floor of a crude bathroom. It was one of my earliest memories of my dad and me.

Minutes later Pop emerged from the lavatory holding his jeans just as the purser announced the crew was shutting the door and that everyone should be seated. We shuffled back to his seat and I repeated the routine getting him settled. After returning his jeans to his backpack and kissing him on the forehead, I headed for my seat, but not before giving the flight attendant my seat number with instructions to contact me if either she or my father needed me.

Once the aircraft leveled off at cruising altitude, I got up to check on Pop. He was partially reclined but awake. His legs were restless. I spent the next ten minutes massaging and manipulating his feet and legs. Pop felt better and wanted to sleep. I helped him arrange the blankets and pillows and fully reclined the seat. One final sip of water and another kiss on the forehead and I was headed back to coach.

I had been in my seat for about an hour and just started nodding off when a flight attendant came by to say my father was asking for me. When I reached him, he said he needed to go to the bathroom. We repeated the routine from earlier. When he finished, I checked my phone. He needed to take his meds.

I took out the quart-sized plastic resealable bag from his backpack. It took considerable time for him to complete his med protocol. I had to identify and dispense the proper medications and supplements. For this round, there were only seven pills to take. Pop had difficulty swallowing which prolonged the process. I stood by patiently wanting to assist, but helpless to ease the process. When he finished, I could tell he was uncomfortable. I offered a shoulder and neck massage, which Pop willingly accepted. I was starting to enjoy these tender acts.

Over the next seven hours of the flight, I checked on my dad pretty much every hour to help him go to the bathroom, take his meds, take a lap around business class, or simply *kibbitz* with a hand on his shoulder. A couple of times when I checked on him, he was, thankfully, asleep. During one visit, I made my way to the galley to grab a bottle of water. A flight attendant was relaxing on a jump-seat reading a magazine. She asked where my father and I were going.

I told her we were on our way to Switzerland for a medical procedure. We talked more and she shared that she recently had lost her father to cancer. At that point, I nearly broke down. I had not shared my father's plan with anyone outside of close family. When the flight attendant mentioned cancer, something triggered inside, and I revealed what my father was really planning on doing the next day.

The flight attendant responded compassionately. Tears welled up in my eyes, but I held them back. I needed to continue being strong and not break down. Not yet. After a few more minutes of talking, I thanked her for listening and headed back to check on Pop before returning to my seat.

Just prior to descent, I gave Pop a final leg massage. He was fidgeting but assured me he would be fine. I told him I would see him after landing. By the time I made it back to my seat, over nine hours into the flight, I had only slept for about an hour. My biggest fear was the same as my father's: falling. I would never forgive myself if during this transit I allowed my father to fall and derail his plan. I did not realize until that moment that I was on heightened alertness. Subconsciously, I had shifted into care provider mode with surplus adrenaline. Ever since the United Club incident, something had kicked in. I felt an innate call to protect my father. This subliminal mindset allowed me to function with minimal sleep. My military background helped, as I was accustomed to going extended periods with no rest.

After the crew prepared the cabin for landing, the plane touched down gracefully at Frankfurt Airport. *Must have been an Air Force pilot*, I thought. Navy pilots land with a 'thud.' I helped my father put on his shoes, grabbed our luggage and prepared to deplane. As we reached the exit, a flight attendant whom I had not previously noticed, took my father's hand in both of hers and thanked him. She was middle-aged with slightly graying dark hair and a glowing warm face. She took a full minute to state how grateful she was for meeting and speaking with him. She wished him well with tears welling in her kind eyes. He smiled and thanked her.

I helped my father out of the plane to the jetway where his walker was waiting.

"Pop, what was that all about?"

"Tory and I had a good connection," he replied. She shared with me about her ex-husband's adultery and how it affected her. We had a good talk at my seat while others slept."

"Of course, you did, Pop," I replied. *The Mayor up until the end*, I thought. My sisters and I called our father "The Mayor of Cabo" when he lived in Mexico. Consistent with his personality, he would go out of his way to talk to everyone about everything. The moniker was shortened to "The Mayor," as his predilection for speaking to strangers extended beyond Cabo, to any city in any country across the globe. Apparently, this penchant also reached the friendly skies at thirty-nine thousand feet.

TWENTY-SIX

UNLIKE O'HARE, when we debarked the 787 in Frankfurt, I insisted that my father utilize the wheelchair I'd reserved. After the long flight, Pop relented rather easily. As we emerged from the jetway, a young man in a wrinkle-free suit was waiting for us with a wheelchair. My dad plopped in.

We did not head out immediately, as the gentleman notified us in perfect English that we needed to wait a few minutes for him to obtain clearance to escort us to the regional terminal of the airport. I told him we only had fifty-five minutes before our next flight, and he reassured me there was ample time.

As we sat waiting, the United aircrew walked by. Tory stopped in front of my dad, bent down, and again took his hands in hers. Tears trickled down her cheeks as she repeated how special he was and how fortunate she was to have met him. Initially, on the plane a few minutes earlier, I was surprised at the affect and sincerity this person had shown my father. Now, watching her cry and cradle my father's hands in hers, I was stunned by this touching but completely unexpected moment between my father and a woman who'd been a stranger to him only hours ago.

Tory finally let go of my father's hands and tearfully said goodbye, but not before hugging him first. As she rejoined her colleagues, I turned to my dad.

"Okay, Pop, I know you can have an impact on a person, but I have never seen anything like that."

"I know, Bucky," he replied, "she needed to be heard."

"Pop, she held your hands, hugged you, cried."

"What can I say? We connected." My dad displayed a Cheshire smile from ear to ear.

Replaying the scene in my mind, I realized that the flight attendant I had told the real purpose of our trip must have informed Tory of what was really going on. I did not have the heart to tell Pop she probably was so affected by him because she knew he was going to die the next day. If this connection made my father gleeful at the end of his life, there was no reason to spoil his joy.

At that moment, our escort interrupted to tell us it was time to leave. He guided us through several locked doors and discrete elevators using his key card before arriving at border control. The attendant bypassed the long line of people by taking us to a side section that only had one other passenger waiting with an escort. Within two minutes, a passport control officer had stamped our passports. We then walked another ten minutes to the regional terminal, arriving at our gate fifteen minutes prior to boarding. We had just enough time for a bathroom break before being escorted down a final elevator to the tarmac and a waiting minibus.

My father and I were the only passengers on the bus, having received preferential treatment due to his physical condition. It was still pitch dark when we drove away from the terminal. I helped Pop change from sweatpants back into jeans as the bus pulled up to the Lufthansa regional jet parked on the tarmac. We were then escorted onto the jet with only aircrew onboard. Pop immediately began schmoozing with an attractive female flight attendant. *Guess he got a second wind*, I thought as I smiled to myself.

As the flight attendant began prepping the cabin, I took advantage of the downtime by helping Pop take his early morning meds, an arduous process lasting almost fifteen minutes and involving over a dozen pills. The sun was just rising over the airfield when a coach bus carrying the remaining passengers arrived. They stepped onboard as the crew finished preparing the cabin for taxi and takeoff.

The flight from Frankfurt was short and uneventful—just what you want in air travel. The quick hop was much easier than the overnight transatlantic crossing we had just completed. Having already cleared customs and border control in Germany, I grabbed my roller case from the baggage carousel, and we walked outside to snag a taxi.

I gave the cab driver the name of our hotel and we were off. The now familiar sights of Europe came into focus: streetside cafes, bakeries, butcher shops with plucked chickens hanging in the windows. The windows of the taxi were down, allowing crisp morning air to enter the van. The dawning day was lovely, yet the circumstances of our visit sullied it. I felt like a thief stealing the day's sanguinity.

Without pretext or warning Pop blurted out, "Maybe I should get a hooker tonight."

I almost choked.

"I've never had a hooker. It's my last night."

My father's unexpected levity instantly shifted my mood. "Sure, Pop, let's get you a hooker."

We both belly laughed.

"And blow," I added between guffaws.

"Blow?" my dad asked.

"Cocaine. You know, hookers and blow."

Our laughing felt marvelous. The randomness of his comment was the perfect antidote following the grueling red-eye flight and melancholy mood. We still had several miles to go before reaching the hotel. Pop closed his eyes. A minute later, leaning against my shoulder, he fell asleep.

The taxi stopped abruptly at our hotel, waking my father. I grabbed our bags and the walker, and Pop and I made our way to the front desk. The ornate lobby was empty. The early morning sun was just starting to stream into the vestibule. The hotel was well arranged with sloping baroque and neoclassical grandiosity, hints of old-world elegance. A view of the Rhine River, sunshine glimmering off its surface, prominently shown through café windows adjacent to the lobby, bringing warmth to the ambiance as well as my aching body. Thoroughly exhausted after flying all night, I just wanted to head to our room and go to sleep.

As I signed for the room, I already was imagining my head falling effortlessly onto a pillow. Over the past three days, I had slept a total of perhaps four or five hours.

"Your room will be available in six hours," the receptionist said. My head dropped. *Six hours!*

Pop walked up to the counter. "Sir, may I please speak with you?" he said politely.

The hotelier, surely well accustomed to such protestations, walked toward my father, meeting him on neutral ground at the end of the desktop.

"I will do my best but cannot guarantee a room before three o'clock."

"Sir, can you see me? I am an eighty-five-year-old man who has been flying for the past eighteen hours. I am sick and need to sleep. What can you do for me?"

I was surprised by my dad's tact. He was forceful, yet not condescending or rude. David One.

"Let me check again," the receptionist said and started typing away on his computer.

After a minute of lively keyboarding, he announced that a small room was available where we could rest until our suite was ready. He offered us a discount.

"We'll take it," Pop stated. "Thank you."

Following the bell hop, we walked through the lobby to the elevator, passing several impressive works of art. Pop commented on the beauty of the hotel. We were originally scheduled to stay at a hotel much closer to Pegasos, but I switched us to this one based on the director's recommendation.

The bellhop unlocked the door, revealing a single bed. I sighed heavily. I tipped the bellhop and dropped our backpacks onto the small desk chair.

After the door closed, Pop turned to me and chastised me for selecting the hotel. "This is not a celebration. You should not have spent so much money on this hotel!"

My dad's words stung. "What do you mean? Pop, we're not celebrating; Aleen and I are trying to accommodate you as best we can."

"You should not have changed hotels!" he barked back.

What I wanted to reply was, "Are you fucking kidding me?! It is the last night of your life, and you are complaining that the hotel we are staying in is *too nice!*"

What I said was, "Pop, Pegasos recommended this hotel. The other one does not have a restaurant, and the lobby was not open this early in the morning." After further back and forth my father acquiesced, finally accepting that he would stay in a charming hotel, in comfort, for the last night of his life. I helped him undress and pulled back the covers. Pop plopped onto the bed. He fell asleep before I could finish washing my face in the bathroom sink.

I was bushed. The desk chair looked cramped and pointy. The thought of sleeping on a plush chair or couch in the hotel library drooling on myself in full view of staff and guests similarly was not an option. Instead, as tired as I was, I decided to walk around town and perhaps get breakfast. Tucked securely in bed, I wasn't worried about my dad and left him to sleep soundly.

I walked out of the hotel to a warm, sun-filled morning. Ordinarily, I am a major vacation planner. I research the best places to stay, eat, and walk. But this wasn't a vacation. For this trip, I had done none of that, and instead, relied on the director of Pegasos for information about the hotel and town.

It was a national holiday, and all shops and cafes were closed. I took full advantage of the serenity and emptiness of the streets to contemplate what was about to occur. I had been so busy the past week planning, coordinating, and traveling, that I failed to check in with my emotions. I sat down on a park bench and closed my eyes. A strong feeling of foreboding began to rise from my chest. I was anxious and fought to follow the advice about grieving—to push it aside until after my father was gone. For now, I needed to remain focused on the mission. I opened my eyes, stood up, and, once more, forcefully attempted to push my feelings aside.

I was marginally successful. Over the next hour, I mostly distracted the inner turmoil by aimlessly walking the streets of Basel, a small city known for its museums, art, and cultural scene—none of which I saw over the next two days. I made it back to the hotel just before noon.

I checked on Pop, who was still sleeping soundly, and headed to the hotel restaurant for brunch. I had not eaten anything since the United flight seemingly days before. Indulging on pastries, fresh fruit, and two lattes felt decadent. Here I was, eating so well on the eve of my father's death. It felt awkward, but not awkward enough to stop me from partaking. My hunger functioned as a familiar anchor during unnerving times; at least that's how I rationalized gorging so wantonly that morning.

With a full belly and drooping eyes, I checked on my father. He was still asleep. I headed toward the mezzanine lounge down the hall from our room. It was empty so I dropped onto one of the overstuffed chairs. I drifted off to sleep, not caring if I drooled for the entire hotel to see.

An hour or so later, the sharp alarm of my iPhone pierced my deep sleep leaving me discombobulated. I hadn't a clue where I was. It took me a few moments to recalibrate. I wiped my mouth (I had drooled) and headed down the hall.

Pop was still asleep. I sat in the desk chair and checked my phone. That afternoon, we were scheduled to meet with the anesthesiologist who would provide the drug that would end my father's life. About an hour before our scheduled meeting, the director of Pegasos called to let us know they had to postpone the procedure one day to accommodate another patient under exigent circumstances. My father's death sentence had been commuted twenty-four hours.

Even though I was thrilled to spend another day and night with my father, I had been preparing myself to say one last goodbye in less than twenty-four hours. Apparently, this change was part of a grander plan.

When Pop woke up, I informed him of the delay.

"There are no accidents, Pop. We now get a full day tomorrow to enjoy Switzerland," I said enthusiastically.

"I'm hungry," Pop responded with a poker face. I could not tell if he was disappointed or relieved. I couldn't imagine being in his shoes—after everything he had been through to be prepared to leave this world only to be told, "No, not today, mañana."

After lunch in the hotel's restaurant, Pop devoured, I nibbled, the front desk advised us that our room was ready. We gathered our items and accompanied the receptionist to the new room, which he unlocked with much fanfare. It was a large, beautiful space with lavish drapes, a small office area, several chairs, and a splendid view of the Rhine a hundred meters below. Aleen had ordered a bouquet of yellow daffodils (my father's favorite color) which filled a vase on the windowsill overlooking the river. "Is the room to your liking?" the man asked anticipatorily.

I looked at the queen-sized bed. "I think I requested twin beds."

"I'm sorry, sir, but that is what the room has."

My father and I had shared many hotel rooms over the years for hockey tournaments, but never a bed. I was too tired to argue, so I just nodded and tipped him.

"Let us know if we can be of any further service," he said and left.

I helped Pop unpack the few clothes from his backpack into a wardrobe. The bare hangars and empty shelves stood out somberly.

TWENTY-SEVEN

ABOUT HALF AN HOUR after my father and I had relocated to our regular hotel room, the front desk called to say that Dr. Marx was in the lobby. I walked down to greet the physician while Pop stayed in the room.

I found a middle-aged man with glasses and a bushy mustache waiting for me. Dressed in khakis and a casual fleece shirt, he looked more like a favorite uncle than a doctor who facilitated MAID. His handshake was hearty. He spoke English fluently.

We walked up two flights of stairs to our room where the physician introduced himself to my father. Within minutes, I could tell my father liked him. Doctor Marx was well-versed in these matters as evidenced by his excellent bedside manner. They discussed my father's European travels and a smattering of international politics. Doctor Marx gave the impression he had all afternoon to be with my father.

After about twenty minutes of getting to know one another, Dr. Marx got down to business. He explained the procedure in detail.

He would direct the process, but Pop would be in control of the timeline and the actual administration of the drug. With Pop's consent, Dr. Marx would establish an intravenous line through a vein in the back of my father's hand. It would be connected to an intravenous line regulator. The physician pulled out a sample of the plastic apparatus for Pop to touch and familiarize himself with.

I was struck by Pop's calmness as I watched him twist the regulator on and off. He handled the device that would kill him in less than forty-eight hours with the placidity of a curious child.

Pop listened further as the doctor explained that Switzerland's MAID laws were extremely strict. No one except my father would be permitted to activate the device. Though supporting and assisting someone in dying was legal, direct administration of the drug had to be done by the patient himself. Any proof of direct participation by another person, such as DNA evidence, could result in criminal prosecution for manslaughter or even homicide.

My father questioned Dr. Marx about the drug that would be used. The physician said it was sodium pentobarbital, a fast-acting barbiturate typically used as a sedative in medical procedures. It was the "sleeping drug" that "puts the patient to sleep almost immediately—no pain or even memory."

He explained the dosage he would give my father would be

much higher than that provided during a routine medical procedure.

"My colleagues and I ordinarily give our euthanasia patients an amount sufficient to anesthetize four elephants."

Without missing a beat, my father quipped, "Doc, you see this?" pointing to his own trunk-ish nose. "Maybe you should up the dosage."

Dr. Marx laughed, "I've got you covered, David." He continued, "Upon your activating the regulator, you'll go to sleep in a few seconds, then your heart will stop within two to three minutes."

"I understand," Pop said calmly.

The physician gave my father a few forms to review and sign. After the paperwork was completed, Dr. Marx inquired if my father had any last questions. "No, but I want you to understand why I'm doing this."

"Go ahead, Mr. Zimberoff."

"I've lost all control of my fingers. I don't see well. Everything is out of focus. I can't read anymore. My eyes are heavy. Who am I if I cannot communicate, if I am not able to be me?"

The physician nodded.

"We all have choices in life," Pop continued. "We can be proactive or reactive. I choose to be proactive. Instead of letting Mother Nature—in her own confusing, slow way—dictate my end, I choose to do it myself. For me, it is the most natural decision in the world. I can take care of myself until I cannot . . . and then I am gone."

"Thank you for sharing your thoughts. I fully comprehend." With an air of understanding, the two men shook hands and bid farewell. I thanked the doctor and walked him to the door.

After he was gone, my father and I shared our impressions. Pop appreciated the physician's personality and professionalism. I agreed.

"I'm tired," he said. "I think I'll lie down."

While Pop napped, I opened my laptop and tried to catch up on work emails but was distracted. After hearing about the procedure from Dr. Marx for close to an hour, I was filled with adrenaline. I had to go for a run.

Scores of people were casually enjoying the holiday afternoon. As I ran along the water, I had a strange sensation of wanting to blurt out to everyone I saw, "My father is dying the day after tomorrow! And I'm ushering him to his death!"

I imagined the passersby—couples hand-in-hand, families with dogs, elderly gentlemen or women meandering—innocently going about their lives without a care in the world while I would be accompanying my father's dead body home in two days. I felt like the entire world around me was operating at its usual pace as I was racing against a ticking clock.

One moment I accepted my father's death as imminent, then the very next instant I anguished in doubt as to my role in escorting him to the unknown. I thought I had been at peace with Pop's choice to proceed, and my role as his wingman, but now as I ran along the Rhine, I was unsure. I'd ensured my father's safe arrival in Switzerland to this small town where I then stood, and in less than thirty-six hours, would be literally taking him by the hand as he took his last breath. I had lived with conflict since my dad first made the decision to move forward with assisted dying. Now that his death was mere hours away, everything welled up—a conflation of thoughts and emotions twisting and binding. I did not doubt the decision was correct from an intellectual perspective, but emotionally, as hard as I tried not to, I had begun grieving his loss. The desire to be the loyal, military, unwavering son clashed with the impending sadness of a son losing his father. I ran faster.

Finishing my run seeped in sweat, I gave myself permission to feel whatever I was feeling in the moment, knowing in my heart my father had chosen the correct path to end his suffering. Most importantly, I acknowledged to myself that it was my father's decision to make and I needed to respect it. I walked the final quarter mile back to the hotel, showered, and woke Pop. He wanted to head downstairs for a bite to eat.

While my dad and I were in the lobby café, Aleen and Brent arrived and sat down with us. They had driven a rental car directly from Zurich Airport and were anxious to see Pop. They were happily surprised to hear that the procedure had been delayed and were grateful for the opportunity to spend an extra day together. I wanted to pull Aleen aside and tell her about Pop's outburst regarding the hotel room, and share the difficulties regarding our travels, but thought better of it. Aleen and Brent were staying at a hotel two blocks away. After our brief greeting and catch-up, we made dinner plans to meet back at the hotel restaurant. Just seeing my sister and brother-in-law, and hugging them both, brought an immediate sense of relief. Being with them, with family, felt like pulling on my favorite sweatshirt on a brisk autumn day. I hoped the feeling would last.

TWENTY-EIGHT

BACK HOME AFTER the September 19th date was set, Pop had started his final goodbyes. He preferred face-to-face contact and met with several friends and family members in person before we left Chicago. Now, in the Basel hotel room, he called the people for whom a personal meeting had not been practical at the time.

Pop was steadfast and grounded during these conversations. I believe each of the people he spoke with knew of his situation, but several were caught off guard by the abruptness of his decision to end his life so quickly. They were surprised to be receiving a long-distance call from Switzerland so close to his death. They all thought they had more time with Zgull.

Following the calls, it was time for dinner with Aleen and

Brent. We made our way down to the hotel restaurant where I'd made a reservation since Pop didn't want to venture out. For the first time since we left his apartment twenty-four hours previously, Pop was not power walking with his walker. Instead, he shuffled along slowly.

As soon as we were seated, Pop let us know he was too exhausted to eat and wanted to go back upstairs. I was disappointed, as I thought the four of us could spend an upbeat dinner together. Aleen graciously escorted him upstairs. Once she returned, the three of us ate a subdued meal where I shared some of the details about the demanding trip. Afterwards, I walked Brent and Aleen to their hotel. With the holiday lingering, the streets remained empty. We said our goodbyes in the lobby and planned to have breakfast together the next morning.

I decided to check in with Wendy, as it would be early afternoon in Seattle. My sister picked up and asked how I was doing. Not wanting to burden her with a lot of detail, I simply said I was okay. She knew me well enough not to probe. I explained the delay and gave a brief overview of the medical procedure that would take place as described earlier that day by Dr. Marx. I thought she might want me to do or say something in the final moments of his life. Wendy thanked me for thinking of her and said she would let me know if she thought of something. We ended the call by saying we loved one another and agreed to talk the next day.

I entered the hotel lobby prepared to walk upstairs when I saw Pop seated at a table in the café. I walked over to him and noticed a half-eaten plate of food in front of him.

"Hey there, I thought you were too tired to eat?"

"That was hours ago." He cut off a piece of schnitzel.

Pop kept cancelling dinners at the last moment, first in Chicago, then here in Switzerland. I sat down and ordered hot tea. On the second-to-last night of Pop's life, he had eaten dinner alone. I sensed something else was going on but didn't pursue it.

After finishing his food, we went upstairs. We sat down, he at the desk chair and me on the side of the bed. "Danny," he said. "I want you to understand something." He leaned forward, speaking deliberately. "I love life. I know that I have much to look forward to, to be with you and your sisters and your children. But this is just too hard." Pop looked down at the hands trembling on his knees, as if they belonged to someone else's body. He gestured to the large bag of pills spread on the table. "It's not a life of joy."

He paused while reaching for a cocktail napkin that lay on the table. His right hand shook as he grasped a pen beside the napkin. He tried to hold the napkin steady with his left hand. The pen quivered in his fingers as he jotted in wavy words: I LOVE LIFE.

"All said, I do love life," he declared with tears in his eyes.

"I know, Pop."

I walked to him and hugged him.

"I'd like to take a bath."

I hesitated. I'd never done this before. I felt a pang of resistance in my gut. How was I supposed to get him in and out of the deep, clawfoot tub?

I helped my father strip to his underwear. I chuckled as I looked down and saw him in his tighty-whities and V-neck white undershirt, the identical style of sleepwear I had seen him wear since I was a tot. Except for skinny ties, my dad did not alter his wardrobe choices to coincide with the times. He wore the same collared shirts and pants until holes emerged. Ostensibly, he never discovered boxers or boxer briefs.

We plodded to the bathroom together. Over the past three days, I had become quite adept at helping my father walk. I stood immediately behind him, bracing his left forearm and hand with my left hand while placing my right hand on his right shoulder for lateral support, allowing him to choose the pace and direction.

I started the water in the bath and helped him undress completely. This was only the second time I had seen him completely naked as an adult. My father exhibited no modesty, and at this point, I took it in stride.

I had to find a graceful way for him to enter the tub. The sides were slippery and there were no mobility handlebars. After two failed attempts of me bearhugging him while trying not to throw out my back, with buckets of water sloshing over the side, I finally got him settled into the tub. He sat back and let the warm water soak his aching body.

I wet a washcloth and slowly massaged his arms, shoulders, and legs. My initial unease in caring for my naked father gave way to a feeling of compassion. With each pass of the cloth, I tried to ease the stress and restlessness from his body. I was bathing my eighty-five-year-old father in the same manner as I bathed my eighteen-month-old daughter.

He sighed audibly with relief.

By the time we finished the bath, it was close to eleven o'clock. We were both beat. He dried off and I helped him put his underwear back on. It was time for his medications. I took from the desk a two-page excel spreadsheet with each of the seventeen medications and supplements identified by name, dosage, and frequency. I filled a glass with water and helped him distribute the pills from the various containers. He then took one at a time. It was nearly midnight by the time he finished.

We then made our way to the bed. Getting onto the mattress posed another challenge. Unlike earlier that morning in the temporary room when he had more energy, at this time of the night Pop could barely muster the strength to move. He refused my suggestion to first sit down with his feet on the floor, fall backward, and then turn on his side. Instead, he tumbled forward onto the bed on his arms and knees with his body splayed awkwardly on the mattress. I hopped onto the bed myself to shimmy my father onto his back and then properly position him on the mattress. After several grunts and grouses, we made it. I'm sure Ellie would have giggled if she were there to see us struggle.

It only took a few minutes before Pop started moving restlessly.

"Do you need a leg massage?" I asked.

"Yes."

After massaging his legs, he tried to sleep again. He continued to toss and turn but finally fell asleep around one o'clock in the morning. I drifted off quickly. What felt like only minutes later, he woke me to help him to the toilet. After he was done, we walked around the room to relieve his restless leg syndrome. Then back in bed. Pop fell back to sleep around three a.m. I followed him a few minutes later.

TWENTY-NINE

A RUSTLING IN the sheets awakened me. Pop was beginning to wake up. I opened my eyes to see the early morning sunlight filling the gaps in the drapes. I sat up and stretched, content to have gotten a few hours of sleep. I realized this would be the last full day with my dad. I sighed, took a deep calming breath, *Don't go there . . . stay in the moment*, and climbed out of bed.

I showered quickly, dressed, then helped Pop get ready to meet Brent and Aleen in the lobby. We planned to take a morning stroll along the town's streets to a nearby restaurant the concierge had recommended.

It was a glorious day with bright sunshine, cloudless sky, and crispness in the early autumn air. My father led the way, power walking with his walker. He navigated the curbs and trolley tracks easily. I stayed close, just in case.

"There," he pointed to a restaurant with outdoor tables.

"But Pop, the concierge recommended a place a block further."

He remained undeterred and crossed the street. I looked at Aleen, rolled my eyes, and followed his lead.

An elderly couple sat at one of the half-dozen tables located along the front of the restaurant overlooking a bustling square. Electric trolleys, their horns blowing and chimes ringing, carried locals and tourists alike. The holiday had come and gone, and today, the morning rush was in full swing.

A female server appeared and sat us at one of the empty tables, plopping menus in front of us and leaving before we could give her our beverage orders. After a long wait, she re-appeared. Pop liked to play a game with servers in restaurants. Either he would close his eyes and place his finger somewhere on the menu and ask the server if the dish he blindly chose was good, or ask her what she recommended. He did the latter with our server, but she did not seem to understand. Perhaps it was the language barrier. She continued to ask my father what he wanted to eat. He kept on asking her what she recommended.

As the server became increasingly frustrated, Aleen mercifully intervened and told my dad the waitress did not comprehend what he was doing. My sister suggested he order a waffle. The server appeared relieved to be done with this annoying customer. She quickly took our remaining orders and vanished.

Though the view and fresh air offered by the outdoor seating were pleasant, the continuous horns and chimes from the trolley cars proved too loud. The noise made it difficult for my father to hear our conversation. Eventually, we signaled to our server that we wanted to move inside.

She wasn't thrilled but steered us to a table alongside a panoramic window overlooking the square. We were able to hear one another much better. Though slow, Pop was able to use his utensils moderately well to cut the waffle, smiling and almost chortling between bites. He didn't seem to have trouble swallowing, thanks to the copious amount of syrup he poured over the waffle. Seeing him relish his meal with such zeal brought a warmth throughout my body.

Between bites, both Aleen and I asked our father various questions about our family history. We recorded the exchanges on our phones. At one point, he reflected upon us children.

"Each of you has found your own path . . . of tranquility, acceptance, love for each other. And I've been the beneficiary of that. On my last trip on earth, I thank you for that." Aleen and I smiled. We both reflexively reached for our father and squeezed a hand.

Following breakfast, the four of us took in the sights of the quaint town. After a few blocks my father was getting tired. I accompanied him back to the hotel while Aleen and Brent headed off to do some window shopping.

When Pop and I got back to our room, he headed straight for bed. I barely removed his shoes and helped him into bed before he fell asleep. We had an appointment with the director of Pegasos and the psychiatrist who would conduct a competency exam later that afternoon. Seeing that Pop was fast asleep and safely in bed, I decided to decompress by going for another run.

Aleen and Brent arrived at our room a few minutes before the scheduled appointment. None of us doubted Pop would pass the competency test, but I had one concern I wanted to discuss with him before he met with the doctor.

"Pop, I want to make sure when you talk to the psychiatrist that you don't convey ambiguity over your choice."

"I understand," he replied.

"It's one thing to appreciate and love life, and completely another situation to be conflicted and have reservations about moving forward with dying," I added.

"Dan," he almost never addressed me by my given name. "I get it." He peered directly at me. "Look at me. Look at my eyes. Do I look ambivalent?"

I shook my head.

"Don't worry. I will be very clear with him."

The front desk called announcing the arrival of Dr. Ponser, the psychiatrist, and Eric, Pegasos's executive director. I met them in the lobby. Dr. Ponser looked like a university professor. He wore glasses, a casual plaid shirt, a corduroy jacket with elbow pads, and khaki pants. Eric emanated a unique presence and aura. With unkempt hair, round glasses, and long flowing cotton shirt looking more like a mystic's shawl, he resembled a shaman I once met. His warm smile and gracious embrace exuded loving energy. His soft voice breathed benevolence. I liked Eric the instant he said hello.

I accompanied the gentlemen to the hotel room. Aleen had

arranged chairs in a circle. My father sat directly across from Dr. Ponser and Eric, with myself, Aleen, and Brent beside my dad. The six of us engaged in friendly small talk. Dr. Ponser did not speak English well. Eric translated much of our conversation.

Dr. Ponser explained his legal role in determining my father's competency. Eric intervened several times assisting the psychiatrist find the proper terms in English. With his thick Swiss accent, initially I found it almost comical that a doctor charged with determining my father's competency could barely communicate with his patient. I had to suppress the urge to break out laughing. I looked over at Aleen and could tell she was thinking the same thing and had difficulty controlling her own mirth.

My father, conversely, sat upright, intensely staring into the doctor's face.

As the evaluation continued, I realized that Dr. Ponser, like Dr. Marx before him, was extending himself and taking a significant legal risk in fulfilling this role. There really was no professional benefit to him, as he was not gaining a long-term client and could not discuss his work with colleagues. To the contrary, any misstep could lead to the loss of his license in a best-case scenario, and criminal prosecution at worst. When this thought sunk in, I no longer had the urge to laugh. Instead, a wave of appreciation and gratitude washed over me.

After approximately half an hour of questioning and note-taking, the evaluation was over. Both Dr. Ponser and Eric asked my father if he had any questions.

"No. My body is broken, but I still have a strong core and can do twenty pushups." He stood unaided from his chair. "Look, I'll show you."

Over our protests, Pop proceeded to knock out not twenty, but twenty-five pushups on the hotel room floor. He had a message he desperately needed to share.

"I do pushups to show people so they understand why I am making this decision. My disease is not in my muscles, but in my brain. It is to show others that I am not running from but running to."

I helped my father stand up and he returned to his chair on his own. He continued, "To me it is a teaching piece. Because it is so rare in our society for someone to make this choice. I know what will happen if I don't make this choice. I'm helping Mother Nature complete her task." He paused. "I didn't select this disease. For the first few years, I didn't even know I was sick. Once I found out it was Parkinson's, I knew that eventually I was going to be a cripple, a burden on society consuming medical resources. My children would look at me and cry."

"Pop…" I began, but he stopped me.

"Let me finish. I've had a wonderful life. I've done everything I wanted to do. Now I'm ready to say goodbye on my own terms in this simple, dignified manner with your help. It is not courage, it is logic."

Dr. Ponser and Eric nodded in agreement. I held back my tears of admiration. In that moment, I had never felt so proud of my father.

The two gentlemen conversed in Swiss-German. Eric then stated that they had all the information they needed and that my father had passed the assessment. Dr. Ponser would draft his report later that afternoon.

With the evaluation completed, we agreed to meet at Pegasos's office at nine o'clock the next morning. Eric provided driving directions and his mobile number in the event we got lost. He also warned us not to be put off by the façade of the building as it was in the middle of an industrial zone.

"We did our best to make the facility comfortable. Once out of the parking lot and inside, you will feel better," he assured us.

We said our goodbyes, and I politely showed the gentlemen to the door. I did not want to think any more about the next day.

THIRTY

I HAD MADE dinner reservations for seven thirty at a nearby restaurant recommended by the concierge. It would be our last supper with our father. Just before we were scheduled to leave the hotel, he told me he was too tired to go out. Yet another dinner cancellation.

"Are you sure, Pop? We could change the reservation to the hotel restaurant."

"No, you go on. I'm not hungry anyway. I'll be fine."

No point trying to change his mind. I knew that all too well.

Before leaving, I accompanied Pop to the bathroom and then helped fluff a few pillows on the bed for him. I made sure he was as comfortable as possible, kissed him on the forehead, told him I would not be gone long and would bring back some food.

As I walked the two blocks to the restaurant to join Aleen and Brent, my sadness lingered. As with many families, meals in our family were the main event around which all celebrations were centered. On birthdays, we ate together. On holidays, we ate together. Thanksgiving was our annual family reunion. Many of my fondest memories took place at the dinner table eating what my mom lovingly cooked. Regrettably, the last meal with my father involved a cranky server and loud trolleys.

When Aleen and Brent saw me walk into the restaurant alone, I could read the disappointment on their faces.

"Where's Dad?" my sister asked. I explained and she just nodded.

During dinner, we each shared our thoughts and feelings about the meeting with Eric and the psychiatrist. I also shared with them what Dr. Marx had explained about the procedure the day before. By this point, any reservation or ambiguity was gone. Aleen and I had come full circle, from accepting the concept of a voluntary assisted death to wanting our father to battle back, to surrender and acceptance. Though certainly sad, Aleen and I were committed as ever to supporting Pop. Neither of us thought he would change his mind at the last minute. We were as prepared as possible for what lay ahead in the morning.

Following dinner, I left Aleen and Brent at the restaurant. With some roast chicken and a berry tart in a takeout bag, I walked back to the hotel. On the way, I did something I rarely do. Under the clear, starry night sky, I looked upwards to the heavens and prayed to the cosmos for the strength and courage to be fully present the next day for my father.

When I got back to the hotel, it was nine o'clock. Pop was awake. His shoulders slumped, his hands hung low, and his eyes blurred. I offered him the food from the restaurant. He ignored the chicken and dove right into the dessert.

I asked him if he wanted to get ready for bed. He declined saying he still had a few more phone calls to make. He didn't seem to mind that I was there since he kept the phone on speaker.

Pop first called his surviving sisters, then his brother. His sisters, Sylvia, Helia, and Donna were calm, loving, and supportive. The calls did not last long, as he had been in touch with them frequently over the past few months. The conversations did, however, manifest a sense of finality.

The call with Uncle Marc went differently. When my father first announced his decision, my uncle made it clear he vehemently disagreed with my father's intention to end his life. Marc is a physician focused on naturopathy and holistic medicine. He believes ailments can be overcome through positive attitude and holistic treatment, similar to my philosophy. My father had refused to consider Marc's suggestions for natural supplements or cannabis to ease his discomfort and sleep disorder.

My uncle called me a few days before we planned to leave for Switzerland to commiserate and share his objections with me. I had not spoken to or seen my uncle for several years. I suppose he hoped that I could dissuade my father from following his intended course of action. I listened, then I told my uncle that my father's decision was final and that he knew better than most that once my father made up his mind, there was no changing it. Marc said he remained hopeful.

On this final call, Marc pleaded with my father not to go forward with dying. "Don't do it," he begged my dad. "I need you," he cried openly, his voice cracking.

I became upset hearing Marc try to talk my father out of moving forward. He hadn't seen my father in months. If he had, he would have seen how his brother was suffering, and how miserable his life had become. I felt Marc's pleading was selfish and detached from my father's welfare.

Unlike me, Pop handled his brother's protests with patience and grace in a manner I had rarely seen him display. He listened and then comforted his younger brother, telling him he would be okay and that they had had a marvelous relationship built over many decades. Pop focused on the positives and reiterated that he loved him. At the end of the conversation, Uncle Marc was still crying, but Pop remained calm and steadfast. Sadness replaced the anger I had been feeling toward my uncle just minutes before. I knew in my heart my uncle was acting out of grief, fear, and love. After all, he was a sibling about to lose his old brother.

Right after the conversation with Marc, Wendy called. I sensed it might be a difficult call and left the room to give them both privacy. I wandered to the mezzanine lounge and aimlessly browsed several books. After about fifteen minutes, I returned to find my father in tears. He was sitting at the side of the bed heaving. I feared the worst.

"She called me 'Dad,'" Pop sobbed. A smile broke across his

tear-strewn face. "She hasn't called me 'Dad' in forty years." The sobs released four decades of sorrow, pain, and torment.

I walked over and hugged him, crying myself.

"She called me 'Dad,'" he repeated.

We continued to embrace for several minutes. The weeping finally subsided. As I stepped back, I saw something in my dad's face I had not seen in years, perhaps ever: serenity. Wendy had just given our father the wonderful gift of closure—allowing him to die with reconciliation and peace.

Pop sat on the bed for several more minutes without saying or doing anything, his face glowed in the soft light of the room.

Wiping his tears, he broke the silence, "I have one more call to make." I had a queasy feeling this was coming. "I need to talk to Leslie."

I flinched. Pop had not spoken with Leslie since before he had set the final date for Switzerland. As far as she knew, he was still in Chicago. Before he left, he texted her daughter-in-law a cryptic goodbye but received no response.

While I respected her position concerning my father's decision, I remained disappointed in her behavior. Leslie had completely checked out. Her absence had caused my father additional pain. I heard it firsthand in his words and saw it in his actions. Witnessing his tumultuous odyssey toward death, was hard enough, but for him to proceed without the support of his partner of the past thirteen years was heartbreaking.

At this eleventh hour, I had hoped my father would let her go and free himself of the anguish he felt about her.

"Pop. . ."

"Bucky, I need to do this."

"Okay, take the time you need." I left the room and softly closed the door. I had no interest in hearing Leslie's voice or what, if anything, she had to say to my father.

I went back to the mezzanine and paced around the room fuming. After several minutes, I realized how much negative energy I was manifesting. Just an hour earlier I had prayed to the Universe asking for the strength to be there for my dad. I sat down and took several breaths, calming my body and easing my mind. I knew at the core Leslie was a good person who loved my father. I began to let go of the anger and negative energy, refocusing my attention toward loving and supporting my dad.

When I returned to the room, Pop was sitting on one of the bedside chairs. He turned to me and calmly said, "I can now die in peace." I smiled at him, and he smiled back. He then broke down. I held him closely as the tears returned for us both.

"She and I are good. Wendy called me 'Dad'," he added between sobs. "Bucky, I'm crying not from sadness but from joy. Like listening to the symphony, and the weeping violins of Mendelssohn. It touches my soul. I can leave in peace knowing Leslie and Wendy are okay . . . will be okay after I'm gone. I can just relax and go wherever I am going now."

I held his hands in mine. Several minutes elapsed before either of us spoke.

"You know, Danny, I had a great run." Pop then looked directly into my eyes. "You must tell people, Bucky. You have to write about all this. People need to know it's an opportunity to find peace. It will help Wendy, Leslie, Marc, and anyone who needs to understand what a true gift it is. Every person should be able to accept a peaceful passing on."

"Sure, Pop, I will." At the time I had no idea what his words would propel.

It was close to midnight. I finally got him into bed and adjusted the pillows and sheets to make him more comfortable. I wanted to ask him what he was thinking and how he was feeling the last night of his life. After the calls with Wendy and Leslie, I knew he did not have the energy to respond. He had shared so many intimacies in the past forty-eight hours, especially the last hour; I did not want to belabor the point. It almost felt trite asking him such a clichéd question so close to the end. I let it go.

As I settled into my side of the bed, my father took my hand in his—such a simple gesture, but so powerful. As he closed his fingers around mine, loving energy flowed through my hand, up my arm, and into my heart. I squeezed back gently.

Before he could ease into sleep, my father began tossing and turning; his restless leg syndrome in full force.

"Pop, did you take your Parkinson's medicine?" With all the emotion at the end of the evening overflowing, I had completely forgotten about his medications.

"No."

"Let's do that."

I helped him get out of bed and walk to the desk at the other end of the room.

As usual, Pop labored with swallowing the medication. He tried several times before finally getting the pills down. I knew from prior discussions with his doctors that it would take at least half an hour for the drugs to begin taking effect.

"Pop, let me help you back in bed and I'll massage your legs."

After rubbing his legs for maybe fifteen minutes, he tried

sleeping again. It only lasted ten minutes. After a period of further thrashing, Pop declared he wanted to take a shower.

We ambled to the bathroom, each step laboriously slow. Once in the bathroom, in the same way I helped Ellie at bath time, I helped him take off his underwear and shirt. I stripped, as well, to avoid getting my boxers wet. Though there would have been a time not long before that I would have felt uncomfortable being naked in front of my father, any modesty or awkwardness had left the building days before. In this moment, I was willing to do whatever my father needed me to do.

I opened the door to the separate shower stall and then supported him as he turned to put his hand on the wall. I remained hyper-vigilant to support him and make sure he didn't slip or fall. I turned on the shower, checked the temperature, and handed him the wand in his free hand. He stood motionless, seeming to enjoy the sensation of the water flowing over his head and body. Steam from the hot water filled the bathroom.

After quite some time, my dad proclaimed he was done. We dried off, got dressed, and shuffled back to the bed.

Between the hot shower and meds, he fell asleep quickly. I was hopeful it would last.

I had just started to doze off when I heard a noise from the other end of the room. I opened my eyes to see my father standing in front of the closet where the refrigerator and room safe were located. He was mumbling. I walked over to see what he was doing. He was repeatedly touching the keyboard for the safe.

"Pop, what do you need?"

"I can get this," he stuttered.

"Let me help."

"I can get it. I need water."

I could tell by his demeanor and slurred annunciation that Pop was confused. He had mistaken the room safe for the courtesy refrigerator.

"Let me help."

I opened the fridge door, took out a bottle of water, unscrewed the cap, and gave it to him. He drank slowly, still having difficulty swallowing. After a couple more minutes, I led him back to bed.

Even in his dazed state, he resisted assistance and fell back sideways, half-on and half-off the bed. I had to wrestle his legs and body into the proper position.

As I climbed back to bed myself, I looked at the clock. 3:38. *Maybe we'll get a few hours of sleep now.*

It felt like I had just closed my eyes when I heard the sound of water running. I opened my eyes to see my father standing at the other end of the hotel room in front of the draperies. *What is he doing?* I thought, still in a sleepy haze. It took me a moment to figure out Pop was urinating on the carpeting. I jumped out of bed and rushed over to him.

Pop was clueless as to what he was doing.

"I need to take a shower," he said.

"You're right," I responded.

I guided him to the bathroom and stripped off his stained underwear. I turned on the shower and helped him as before. When he was done, I dried him, put on clean underwear, and got him back to bed. I grabbed two towels from the bathroom, wet them, and tried my best to clean up the mess from the carpeting. Mercifully, Pop fell asleep quickly. It was five a.m. when I climbed back to bed, my mind spinning. In a few hours, my dad would be gone.

THIRTY-ONE

THE PHONE ALARM rang in my ears. I slowly rubbed the sleep from my eyes and reached for my phone.

Tuesday, September 20 – 07:00.

I got out of bed and opened the drapes, careful to avoid the urine-stained carpet. Streaks of the rising sun burst over the Rhine. Thin high clouds were slowly transforming from navy blue to purplish orange. For others, this was the beginning of a spectacular Tuesday in the northwest corner of Switzerland. For my father and me, it was anything but.

I walked around the bed to my dad and touched his shoulder.

"Morning, Pop."

He opened his eyes and looked dazed. His mouth and hands were trembling.

"Help me to the bathroom."

I got him up and took him to the bathroom. He finished and splashed water on his face and washed his hands.

"We need to get dressed. Aleen and Brent will be here in about an hour," I said softly.

He followed me to the wardrobe where I selected his shirt and jeans. Like everything that morning, it would be the last time I'd be able to assist him. Something as ordinary as helping him dress took on beloved significance. The military's emphasis on uniforms and clothing influenced me so I took my time, wanting to honor my father as he put on the last fabrics of his life.

When we finished, I showered quickly while Pop gathered his personal effects and a few special items and placed them in his backpack. We repeated the medication routine; thankfully, he only took a half-dozen pills. After he was done, we both walked over to the window overlooking the Rhine. We stood silently, lost in our thoughts looking out over the lovely vista. The same conflicted feeling as the night before came over me. I wanted to ask my father how it felt knowing this was the last day of his life, yet I also respected his privacy—for his thoughts to be his, alone, for these last few hours.

Watching the water of the river move slowly below us, Pop broke the silence.

"Such a gift," he said. "Wendy and Leslie . . . at peace."

I nodded.

He repeated his instruction for me to be sure to tell his story.

"Yes, Pop. I will." I looked at my phone. "We better grab our stuff and head down."

Pop and I made our way to the lobby and were checking out

of the hotel when Aleen and Brent arrived. It was a strangely routine, yet awkward moment. Brent grabbed our bags while I put Pop's walker in the trunk of their car. Aleen went with Pop as he walked slowly to the car, then helped him into the front seat. The four of us looked like tourists about to set off on a scenic drive through the Swiss Alps. But we were not tourists. Our destination was not a striking peak, antiquated castle, or art museum. We were headed to Pegasos's studio, driving straight toward my father's last breath.

Brent drove while Aleen assisted him with directions via Google Maps. My father sat in the passenger seat just a few feet from me. I wanted to reach out and touch him—caress his shoulders. But I did not. To this day, I'm not sure what held me back.

As the rental car bumped along potholed streets, I tried to put myself in his shoes. If there was a chance to live, and as long as my children were alive, I doubted I could voluntarily end my life no matter my physical state. Yet at the same time, I did not begrudge my father. I had seen his suffering with my eyes, heard his complaints with my ears, and felt his pain in my heart.

Pop sat stoically while Google navigator announced each upcoming turn. As my father watched the cars and mile markers pass by, I wondered if he was measuring the milestones of his life. Knowing my father, probably not. Pop never looked back, only forward—even if forward in this instance was capped by mere minutes.

In the silence I was not nearly as calm as my father appeared. A sense of dread started to fill my stomach. I knew what to expect in the coming hour from a procedural aspect but had no idea how I would react emotionally. Throughout the trip, I had struggled to keep my grief in check. I often pushed down my feelings to maintain a "strong soldier" persona for my sister and father. A pretty ridiculous stance, as neither expected bravado from me. With all the internal work I had done over the years getting in touch with my authentic self I knew better, but this forgery enabled me to remain focused on completing the mission.

I continued to wonder what my father was thinking. Did he have regrets? Doubts? Was he scared? What would he miss most? Now that death was literally right around the corner, did he still not fear it?

As we neared the offramp to the industrial part of the city, I glanced at Aleen's phone and saw we were just six minutes away. In moments, I would be holding my father's hand and helping to usher him out of this world into whatever lay ahead. My fingers tingled.

Brent continued to drive through a series of nondescript commercial roads ending in front of a large orange tower. Eric had mentioned the tower in his directions the day before. We knew we were close. My heartrate increased. We continued down an alleyway toward a small parking lot lined with asymmetrical commercial and industrial buildings. Dark smoke wafted from a chimney rising from one of the structures. We entered a parking lot in front of a building with a large number "14" on its façade, another clue left by Eric. After driving in a wide circle in the lot, Brent spotted an empty parking space in front. As we pulled into the stall, Eric emerged from a door. He opened his arms and smiled widely as he stepped toward us.

I got out of the car and offered to help Pop set up his walker.

He refused and shakily did it himself. I walked over and greeted Eric with a long hug. Though he had been a relative stranger until the day before, this morning he felt like a trusted friend. My eyes welled up. *Hold it together.*

Eric led the way with my father close behind. Aleen, Brent, and I followed as we entered the entrance to the building that housed Pegasos. Dr. Marx stood in the vestibule and welcomed us. He opened a door that led directly into a large room. There was a plastic conference table, chairs, worn couches, and a kitchenette. Scattered around the room was an array of photographic gear and a lot of other random stuff. A ten-foot-by-eight-foot photograph of a seascape hung from the back wall. I thought it all odd for the venue where my dad would be leaving this planet.

Eric invited us to sit at the conference table. He explained that the room doubled as a photography studio and let us know the actual procedure would be done in a more comfortable adjoining room. Eric offered us Swiss pastries, dried fruits and nuts, and a variety of beverages laid out on the table. He then excused himself to join Dr. Marx at an adjacent desk to complete final paperwork.

Pop dove right into the snacks. I grabbed a pastry, as we had skipped breakfast. I ate more out of nervousness than any actual hunger. Aleen and Brent poured themselves coffee.

Aleen, Brent, Pop, and I sat nibbling and drinking as we waited for Eric and Dr. Marx to complete their work. Aleen took out her phone to record additional thoughts from our father, like what we had done the morning before at breakfast. Pop elucidated one of his last life lessons.

"Wendy helped me find my softness. That's been my struggle my entire life. To give up the harshness of my father and to become gentle like Wendy. That's been my work. I still go off occasionally and say things that hurt people. I'm very sorry for that. Wendy became my model, my mentor."

Pop spoke softly, almost inaudibly. His words trailed off. Aleen stopped recording. I couldn't sit any longer. I stood up to walk around the room. I heard Pop ask for the braid and feathers.

Before we left Chicago, my father had me pack three eagle feathers and a braid of sweetgrass from his apartment. Each feather represented one of his children. Braided sweetgrass is the symbol of kindness in body, mind, and spirit. Rebecca, a spiritual person and close friend of my parents who lived seasonally in the same Cabo san Lucas condo complex, had given him the sweetgrass when he was struggling with anger over some past, long forgotten incident.

I took the objects out of his backpack and placed them in front of him. He picked up the braid and stroked it.

With a crisp shutting of his laptop, Eric announced they were done. He pulled several sheets of paper from a nearby printer and handed them to Pop to review and sign. I walked back to the table and stood behind my father. He struggled to pick up a pen in his right hand and in typical Pop fashion, placed his left hand over both eyes and asked, "Where do I sign?" I had seen this stunt from my father before. He was joking even now, moments away from his death.

Pop removed his hand from his eyes, reviewed the pages quickly, and scrawled a short, shaky line as his signature. Eric took the pages from my father and he and Dr. Marx signed on their respective spaces. Eric then walked over to a copy machine and made several copies of the documents.

With the documentation completed and signed, Dr. Marx politely announced that we could move into the other room whenever my father was ready. Aleen, Brent, and I looked to my dad. He immediately stood. My jaw tightened as I helped him to his walker. Aleen picked up the braid and feathers. The grip I'd kept on my emotions started to slip.

We entered the adjacent room as a group. It was much smaller, about a third the size of the studio space, but far less cluttered. On one side sat an adjustable hospital bed with an end table and lamp. An empty IV stand stood at the other side of the bed, along with a simple metal table with what looked like medical equipment lying on top. Stacks of boxes and other stored art and photography materials filled the opposite side of the room. There was a small bathroom at the far end.

As I scanned the space, I was struck by the contrast to my mother's death twenty-odd years earlier. Mom died in her own bed overlooking the magnificent Pacific Ocean with all the comforts and familiar trappings of her home nearby. Just outside the sliding glass doors of her bedroom—almost within reach—lay her blooming rose garden.

My father was about to leave this earth in a stark, impersonal, and unfamiliar office park of a foreign land. Just outside the studio lay a paved parking lot and belching smokestack. The juxtaposition between my mother's passing and impending father's death tore at me. Mom died in her bed; Dad was about to die in an art studio doubling as a medical suite tucked in an industrial warehouse. Dignified death? Questionable. I desperately wished he could experience the same tranquil setting that my mother experienced when she passed along, but that was not to be.

I looked back at my dad. Aleen and Brent were helping ease him onto the bed. Brent, a physician of over forty years, was well accustomed to working around medical equipment. With Pop situated on the bed, my heart pounded in my chest and ears like the steady beats of a bass drum. I lost all sense of time.

Dr. Marx worked with calmness and respect. Putting on latex gloves, he handed my father a glass of water and asked if he was comfortable.

"Anything else I can get for you?"

"No, thank you," Pop said. He turned to me. "Where are the feathers?"

Aleen gently placed the feathers and braid across our father's chest. He patted them gently.

"Okay, let's go," Pop announced summarily.

Tears began flowing down my cheeks. This time, I could do nothing to stop them.

"Wait, Helia's music," my father blurted out.

As we were planning the expedition to Switzerland, Pop had told Aleen and me that he wanted to hear his sister, Helia, playing his favorite violin concerto as he passed into the unknown. Aleen contacted Helia, who recorded Jules Massenet's Meditation from Thais and emailed the audio file to Aleen. My sister now took out her phone and began playing the melodic composition. The sweet tones of Helia's violin filled the ascetic room.

I stood to the right of Pop, rubbing his shoulder. Aleen, across from me, bent forward and looked directly into our father's eyes.

Brent stood at the head of the bed with his hand on Pop's other shoulder. Dr. Marx began preparing the IV drip and needle. Eric had faded into the background. The distinctive acrid smell of antiseptic hit my nose as the physician wiped the back of my father's hand with a small swab.

I watched as Dr. Marx inserted the IV needle into the back of my father's hand and secured it with medical tape. Sniffles from Aleen and me intruded upon the beloved sounds of Helia's violin. Tears streamed down both our cheeks. Brent began to choke up.

As the saline dripped into my father's veins, Dr. Marx checked the regulator attached to the tubing and announced that it was a good line. He softly advised my father to take his time and let us know when to proceed. He then stepped back and allowed Aleen, Brent, and me unfettered intimacy.

I tried my best but could not stop crying. I continued to tell my father how much I loved him. Aleen was doing the same.

"I'm ready," our father said simply.

Pop's assuredness took me by surprise. I began sobbing uncontrollably.

Dr. Marx emptied the IV bag with a syringe. He then injected the poison directly into the intravenous tube.

"David, you may twist the regulator whenever you are ready."

I looked down and saw my father immediately begin to thumb the dial. I choked and quickly looked into his eyes.

"I love you, Pop. I love you, Pop." I kept repeating the phrase. I tried to say something else but those were the only words that escaped my mouth. I could hear Aleen and Brent saying something, but all my senses were focused on my father.

"My hand is cold," Pop said softly.

"It is the medication entering your veins," Dr. Marx replied.

At that point, I had only seconds remaining with my dad. He looked directly into my eyes. I told him I loved him a final time and gripped his shoulder tightly. Pop took a breath and then his chin dropped, his mouth opened, and his eyes closed. He looked like he had just fallen asleep.

He was gone.

Aleen and I continued to weep and hold him for several more moments. She withdrew but I held on. I could not let go of my father. At some point I stepped back while continuing to gaze at Pop. I blessed his soul and sent white light and positive energy to accompany it wherever it was going. Earlier on, Eric and Dr. Marx had withdrawn completely. I now sensed Dr. Marx as he stepped forward and checked my father's pulse. He scratched a note on a clipboard and told us to take all the time we needed.

The stillness was overwhelming in its calmness.

Aleen and Brent moved to the adjoining room, but I remained. I wanted to ensure I continued the positive energy sent to my dad's soul. Flooded with emotion, I had no idea how long I stood there. After the tears finally stopped, I composed myself and joined the others in the main studio.

I walked over to my sister and embraced her. Brent joined us. Within our circle, shoulder-to-shoulder, arm-in-arm, I felt great relief.

"He's at peace," I said.

"He's at peace," Aleen affirmed.

After giving us a moment, Eric walked over to tell us he had notified the authorities. It could take anywhere between thirty minutes and several hours for the officials to arrive to investigate and record Pop's passing.

Thankfully a male police officer and two female coroner personnel arrived within forty-five minutes of Eric's call.

The officer spoke to Eric and Dr. Marx for several minutes and then entered the adjoining room where my father's body lay. The two coroner attendants followed. Aleen, Brent, and I stayed out of their way. I was surprised at the length of time they took to confirm no foul play was involved. The officer sat down and reviewed the documentation Eric had provided to him.

When the coroner personnel finally left, I went in to check on my father's body. It was completely covered in a sheet. When I pulled it partially down, I could see they had removed all of Pop's clothing and folded it neatly on a chair. I assumed they did that because they were required to examine his entire body thoroughly.

The officer finished his paperwork and handed me a form to sign. The document was written in Swiss-German. I had no idea what I was signing but Eric's nod assured me it was routine. I also provided a copy of my father's passport to the officer as required.

The officer grabbed the last strudel from the table, said goodbye to Eric and Dr. Marx, and left the studio with a polite nod to me. My sadness lingered. Grief was but a breath away, but my mission wasn't completed. Not yet.

THIRTY-TWO

WITH THE PAPERWORK completed and death signed off by the authorities as non-suspicious, we were done. It felt strangely anti-climactic. After such a hectic week-and-a-half and the preceding six-month emotional rollercoaster, I felt lost. What was next on the list? What did I need to do?

Pop planned to be buried next to my mom at the Zion Gardens cemetery in Chicago. It's where Edda and several other relatives were interned. He had purchased the plot years before and provided me with the cemetery's contact information before we left for Switzerland.

I had planned on bringing my father's body back with me on my flight to Chicago. As career military, I was accustomed to bodies of fallen soldiers, sailors, airmen, and Marines being escorted home with care and respect by a uniformed comrade. As Pop's wingman, I wanted to fulfill this final role.

Regrettably, Eric said that my father's body would not be ready for transport for four to seven days, depending on how long the local authorities and US Embassy took to process the necessary documentation and approvals. Once the paperwork was approved by the US Embassy in Zurich, his body would be released for transport home. In the interim, a local funeral home would embalm my father's body. Eric gave me the contact information for the business.

This was distressing news. I did not want to leave my father's body alone in the care of strangers in a foreign land.

I had not previously discussed the details of the repatriation of my father's body, naively assuming it would not be an issue. Likewise, I hadn't spoken with the airlines about the logistics of transporting a deceased relative. It all came as an unanticipated complication to an already complex operation.

Eric suggested I contact the Chicago funeral home we'd chosen to handle the interment, who would then coordinate with the local Swiss funeral home. I already had reached out to the Chicago folks chosen by my father on the Friday before we left. Now that I knew the process, I would call them to initiate the coordination.

As I sat on a plastic chair in the studio, I felt terrible having to leave my father but knew there was no reasonable alternative. I couldn't hang around for what might be another week for his body to be released. I walked back into the room where my father lay and apologized to him that I could not accompany him home. "I love you, Pop. I'm sorry I can't stay with you."

With nothing else left to do in Switzerland, I called United to re-book my flight home. They did not have any available flights, but Swiss Air had a business class seat on its 9:10 p.m. direct flight from Zurich to Toronto. I booked it and called Salima.

Aleen and Brent were returning to Sicily to resume their vacation early the next morning from the same airport. They had reserved a room at an airport hotel, so we did not need to rush to get to the airport. Eric suggested that we grab lunch at the local village, less than a mile away. Several quaint shops and restaurants were situated in the town center.

We gathered our belongings and started to say our goodbyes to Eric and Dr. Marx. How do you say goodbye to two gentlemen who take such professional risks to help so many in the most desperate and trying times of life? How do you say goodbye to two virtual strangers who only minutes before had assisted in helping your father die peacefully and with dignity? There were no more words left to say other than a sincere, "Thank you." I shook their hands and hugged them both.

Aleen, Brent, and I walked out of the facility as changed people. One cannot experience such a momentous life event and not be transformed. Like being alongside my mother when she took her last breath, I was honored and privileged to have held my father when he left this world. From my mother I learned not to fear death; from my father, I'd learned to face dying head-on.

―――――

Brent found a parking spot near a municipal garden adjacent to the village's main street. As I exited the car, I paused to take in the scenery. The late morning dew was lifting from an array of plants and flowers. Birds filled the trees and sang sweetly. Dad would have loved this garden with so many bushes and trees to prune. I wondered out loud if my father's soul was circling the park. "Pop, are you here? I love you! Safe journey."

After a light lunch, we browsed through several stores and shops. I bought Ellie a German picture book, then headed back to the car for our hour-long drive to Zurich. The three of us talked some but mostly sat in silence. In some perverse way, I felt like a criminal leaving the scene of a crime. Why did I feel that way?

This isn't right, I thought. I should have felt content celebrating Pop's decision, knowing that I helped him die peacefully with grace and dignity, not like I just committed a crime.

Our actions were not illegal, nor immoral, nor wrong. On the contrary, we acted out of compassion and love in accordance with dad's wishes and Swiss law. Perhaps I felt like a criminal because so much of the MAID process is shrouded in a veil of secrecy. Perhaps it was because there was so much societal opposition to it. Whatever the reason, I felt a twinge of guilt.

As we approached the outlines of Zurich, the disquiet slowly subsided and I spent the remainder of the drive replaying in my mind the events of the past few hours, days, and weeks.

Upon arriving at the airport hotel, I was able to fit in a quick workout and felt relatively relaxed before my long flight home. I showered and changed clothes in Aleen and Brent's hotel room and prepared to say goodbye.

Aleen walked me to the door. We stood facing one another, sharing an unspoken moment. It was one of the most bittersweet farewells of my life. The heaviness of my father's death lingered. My sister, brother-in-law, and I forged a unique bond in our shared grief. Not many family members have the privilege of ushering a loved one to the unknown so intimately and lovingly.

I smiled and kissed my sister on her cheek. "I'll see you when I see you," I said, using one of our father's standard parting phrases. She laughed and dabbed at her eyes. Brent stepped over and we hugged. I turned and headed toward the elevator.

Since the hotel was on airport property, I only had a short walk to the terminal. When checking in with the airline agent, a wave of sadness swept over me. I checked my roller case and backpack and had my father's backpack as my carry-on. The backpack still contained several of my father's personal items, including his wallet and the tennis ballcap. We had left the remainder of his clothes at the hotel and had donated his walker to Pegasos for use by other patients. I grabbed his cap from the backpack, placed it on my head for the journey home, and somberly made my way through security to the gate.

When I boarded the flight, another pang of guilt shot through my gut as I thought of my father's body alone in some Swiss funeral home. The feeling that I had abandoned him continued to gnaw at me. Should I have waited until he was released and ready to return to Chicago? I knew Salima and Ellie were waiting for me. I missed them. I had to get home. Pop would understand.

The flight was only half full. No one occupied the seats next to or behind me. A woman sat across the business class aisle. After the plane took off, I had an urge to introduce myself and tell the stranger what had happened earlier that day. Instead, I closed my eyes and kept replaying the images of what had occurred back at Pegasos. I blessed my father's soul once again.

A few hours into the flight, I broke down and began weeping. I turned toward the bulkhead and buried my face in a blanket. After a few minutes, I calmed down. About an hour later, I broke down again. I recovered, asked the flight attendant for a glass of water, then tried to sleep.

No luck.

With about two hours remaining in the flight, I opened my shade to see day had replaced night. I looked down from thirty-eight thousand feet and could see a large expanse of whiteness below. Checking the inflight map, I saw we were over Newfoundland. Almost home.

Looking down upon the earth from such an altitude, I reflected further upon my father's journey. Pop had battled his entire life fighting for control. Of his family. Of his career. Of nearly every aspect of life. Ironically, he was plagued with a disease that would eventually take away all control of his body and mind. In choosing to die on his own terms, my father exercised the ultimate act of control. I replayed a video on my phone taken at breakfast, two days earlier. Pop, with the same tennis cap sitting atop his head, sat in front of me and said:

"I don't want to let Mother Nature dictate to me. I'm challenging her. How presumptuous of me. Who am I not to allow her to do her thing? But when I see friends—what they've gone through in their dying days—I'm just preventing that. The burden on individuals and society. Consuming medical attention that young people are entitled to.

"There is no way of stopping this disease. It's nature. The way we live and die; the way trees live and die; the way an animal lives and dies. It's not a choice. Who the hell wants to die? I don't. I've had so much fun in my life! The places I've gone to, the things I've done. I love it. But I can't enjoy it now. I no longer want to be a burden on my children.

"I'm not happy I'm doing it. It's contrary to my belief about life, which is so precious, so unique, so wonderful. I don't want to do this. I don't want to leave this wonderful world—leave the ones I love. But I don't want to end up like people I've watched. It's brutal. That's where I'm headed. And I have a choice not to do it. I have a choice to be remembered as being alive and not looked at with pity."

I'll always think of you Pop as alive and full of life, I thought. *You were your own person— Zgull, a true Warrior.* I reached for his cap from the seatback pouch in front of me and held it.

I recalled my father breaking out laughing several times while in Switzerland—in the taxi, at breakfast, joking with Dr. Marx. At the time, I was surprised to see him so jovial. I now understood. When my father moved forward with his death, he seized control. In his final days, he liberated himself from all constraints, from all pain, from all self-judgment and perceived judgment from others.

Did Pop have a choice? Absolutely. He could have continued to live on Parkinson's terms. Instead, he took control over his life by choosing death to end the suffering for himself and for those whom he loved. I felt immensely proud of him. A sense of gratitude and respect for my dad filled my soul. As the Airbus began its initial descent into Toronto airspace, I was invigorated. I was still running on fumes but having fully accepted my father's plight and decision, I finally felt at peace.

After landing, I put Pop's cap and backpack back on. It felt good to have them attached to my body, almost as if my father was right there with me. Channeling Pop, I power walked toward customs and border control. As soon as I cleared customs with my luggage and entered the international terminal's welcoming area, I saw Salima holding our daughter in her arms. Ellie was holding a "Welcome home, Daddy!" sign. I rushed to my wife and daughter and hugged them with all my might.

THIRTY-THREE

THE MORNING AFTER I arrived home, I called the Chicago funeral home. When I had contacted them from Switzerland, I spoke to an assistant. This day, I was transferred to the owner/director, who expressed his sincere condolences.

"Daniel, I met your father two months ago," the director began. "We sat and talked in my office for almost an hour. He was an amazing man. Sincere, direct, focused. It was obvious to me he cared most about family. He talked at length about you and your sisters."

This came as a surprise. I didn't know Pop had been there.

The director emphasized that he personally would take care of all the arrangements. One of his assistants already was in contact with the Swiss funeral home. We discussed further details and documentation that would be required before the Swiss government would release the body for repatriation. Coordination needed to occur between the Swiss funeral home, Swiss government, US Embassy, Chicago funeral home, Chicago cemetery, and United Airlines. None of this could have been conducted beforehand, because the entire process relied upon the receipt of the official death certificate to move forward.

When I left Pegasos, I thought Eric's paperwork submission with the police signoff was sufficient to order a death certificate. After speaking with the funeral home director and corresponding multiple times via email with the Swiss funeral home and US Embassy in Zurich, I discovered because my father was a US Citizen, only US authorities could issue what was known as a Consular Report of Death Abroad, the equivalent of an American death certificate. The embassy official assigned to my father's case was exceptionally courteous and efficient but told me they were dependent on the Swiss government to provide the necessary documentation, and that it likely would take four to six business days before my father's body would be released.

In the interim, I continued to stay in touch with both the Chicago and Swiss funeral homes. The Swiss funeral home informed me they would arrange transport for my dad's body to Chicago. The Chicago director explained he would handle all details once the body arrived at O'Hare. The director and I began the burial arrangements in advance of the actual date of repatriation.

Four days after I arrived home, I received an email from the US Embassy that Pop's body would be coming home in two days. I forwarded the correspondence to the funeral director, who replied that he already had been informed and that the wheels were in motion. We agreed on an interment date of September 28, 2022.

I flew to Chicago for my dad's burial. Pop had instructed my sisters and me not to conduct a funeral. He expressly stated no rabbi and no formal ceremony. Pop was always about the here and now—not the past. Neither Aleen nor Wendy attended the burial. Aleen was still in Sicily with Brent. Wendy did not feel comfortable with funerals of any type. My sisters and I would plan a celebration of life event later in the year.

The burial was a simple affair. We had not invited friends or relatives, as that would be done later for the life celebration. Levi attended because he wanted to pay his last respects in person. A cousin, Joel, Aunt Sandra's son, and his wife, Cessy, also attended. They had asked specifically about the burial. Joel was quite close to my father.

Like the morning my father died the week before, birds were chirping and the sun shone brightly from a perfect blue sky. A light breeze brought with it a nip in the air, a harbinger of the approaching winter.

Before the ritual began, I walked over to the modest wooden casket and placed my hand on it. I apologized to Pop again for leaving him alone in Switzerland. I looked up to the sky and told my dad I was back with him. I had not prepared formal remarks but did manage to say a few words. The funeral home director provided a Jewish blessing, the mourner's

Kaddish, as Pop was lowered into the ground.

In accordance with Jewish tradition, I poured a shovelful of earth onto the coffin. I handed the shovel to Levi, who did the same, and then Joel. After Joel finished the ritual, we said our last goodbyes to Zgull's body and reunited a few steps away. I thanked Joel and Cessy and hugged them goodbye. I also thanked the funeral director for all that he had done for our family the past two weeks.

With Levi by my side, I looked back a final time at the gravesite. Workers had already begun to fill in the grave and were leveling the dirt. Joel, Cessy, and the director were gone. After twenty-four years apart, Mom and Pop were finally reunited.

Afterward, Levi and I met Ari for lunch at Greektown, one of my parents' favorite restaurant spots in Chicago. We shared a reflective meal together. Like Wendy, Ari did not feel comfortable attending the interment and would join the family at the celebration of life.

Because of the nearing holiday season with people expected to fly in from out of town, and since the three of us were still recovering from the tumult and emotional turmoil of the past few months, we delayed Pop's celebration of life until the following spring. Aleen reserved a banquet room at a University of Chicago conference center overlooking the Chicago River. We thought our father would appreciate the venue at his and our mom's alma mater. Pop was finally getting his party—as the man of the hour—even if he wouldn't be attending.

It was an uncharacteristically cold March afternoon. About eighty guests attended, including three of my best friends who knew my father. Salima, Ellie, Levi, and Ariel were there, along with several of my cousins and the surviving aunts. Uncle Marc did not attend.

The night before the celebration I sat in the hotel bar with my good friends Chris and Jerry. I intimated that I felt a tremendous responsibility to my father to eulogize him properly. I did not want to let him down by failing to accurately portray the distinctive person he was. Ordinarily, in public speaking, I strive to speak extemporaneously from an outline. But for this event, I had been preparing my eulogy for weeks and decided to read it word for word at the celebration:

"Pop modeled love through action, not simply words," I said.

"His love took the form of indefatigable respect, staunch dedication, and tireless commitment. Like the wind, he always kept showing up," I continued.

"Talking with Pop was like talking to a mirror: reflective—everything open and fair game. No hiding of warts or wrinkles. Reality untouched, unedited, and sometimes—when needed—directly in my face," I said.

Afterward, I regretted the choice to read my eulogy verbatim, believing my tribute was too staid. Pop would have encouraged me to trust my gut and speak from my heart in true Warrior spirit. But like my father, I can't look back.

In addition to my tribute, Aleen, Wendy, Emma, Leslie, and Jim Kroeger, his boxing partner and friend, also eulogized my father. At the reception that followed, several people walked up to the mic and shared personal anecdotes about Pop. People laughed and cried. Everyone's words paid tribute to Pop's uncompromising nature.

When the reception wound down and people started to leave, I stood alone looking at an enlarged photo of my father taken years before. There was Pop, smiling widely, razor stubble on his suntanned face, sports sunglasses perched on the brim of the tennis cap covering his head. The photo looked to have been taken years ago near a beach in some far-off land, maybe Turkey or Tunisia, perhaps Bali. What stood out were his sparkling, mischievous brown eyes—the ones Chris had commented upon. He looked content, not a care in the world. This is how I wanted to remember my father.

As I stood gazing at the image of Pop, I felt a tug on my leg and looked down to see Ellie pulling on my pants. I bent down to her and pointed to the photo.

"Ellie, that's Grandpa."

My daughter walked to the photo and stood still staring at Pop's face from a few feet away. "Where's your nose?" I could hear him say. As if on cue she placed a finger on her nose, giggled, and then ran down the hall to find her mom.

I smiled with tears forming in my eyes knowing how much Pop would have enjoyed the moment.

EPILOGUE

[JONATHAN] RECOVERED TO level flight and was quiet for a time before he spoke. "Very well," he said, "who are you?""

"We're from your Flock, Jonathan. We are your brothers." The words were strong and calm. "We've come to take you higher, to take you home."

'Home, I have none. Flock, I have none. I am an Outcast. And we fly now at the peak of the Great Mountain Wind. Beyond a few hundred feet, I can lift this old body no higher."

"But you can, Jonathan. For you have learned. One school is finished, and the time has come for another to begin."

As it had shined across him all his life, so understanding lighted that moment for Jonathan Seagull. They were right. He could fly higher, and it was time to go home.

He gave one last long look across the sky, across that magnificent silver land where he had learned so much.

'I'm ready,' he said at last.

And Jonathan Livingston Seagull rose with the two Starbright gulls to disappear into a perfect dark sky.

Jonathan Livingston Seagull
By Richard Bach

Do any of us truly die, as in a permanent, eternal end? I do not think so. I believe both my parents', and all deceased people's souls, continue to live on in another form, in another plane, perhaps in another version of this physical existence we call life. Whenever I see a lone seagull flying in the air, I know my father is with me, inviting me as his wingman to fly higher and faster than the rest of the flock.

A month after we buried my father, his sister, my Aunt Donna, sent me and my sisters a video of a conversation she had with Pop two weeks before he "headed east." Here is an excerpt:

Aunt Donna: *Is there anything you would do differently in life?*

Pop: *To learn earlier in life what I learned later about human nature, about love and forgiveness and acceptance.… I thought being a jerk: aggressive and sarcastic made me stronger. To show how strong I was. It really was a weakness—me trying to overcome my insecurity.…*

Like wine and cheese, it takes time.

At eighty-five-and-a-half, I'm still learning. I'm learning for myself, for my children, and for those who love me. My ego is not that important. I have learned acceptance in a way I never thought possible.

Aunt Donna: *Do you have any regrets?*

Pop: *One of my few regrets is that Dotti was not the beneficiary of who I am today. She deserved better.... I leave with a huge bundle of acceptance and gratitude. I got to see the growth of the family. Dotti died twenty-five years ago and did not.*

I leave with pride. I leave with smiles, not sadness. I am helping Mother Nature. I am sparing society, myself, and my family the indignity of the last days of one's life which are usually not very pleasant.

I have a choice and am making that choice.

My father shared his truth as a Warrior—a man who inquired and learned until the very end. A man who finally, after eighty-five-and-a-half years—accepted himself.

Sometime after Pop died, I read an email he had sent to a relative midway through his Parkinson's struggle in which he said: *Underneath it all, I think there is anxiety. There are questions. I'm really by myself. There's nobody with me who understands what I am going through. So I'm lonely. That makes me scared.*

Reading that, I finally understood the significance of his "Nobody understands me" mantra. I wish I had known at the time that Pop's need to continually convey his ailments and suffering was driven by fear. Even after all the Warrior work we did together—and the transparent relationship we maintained—he and I were unable to peel back this layer. Had I reached this conclusion on my own, perhaps I would have felt less resentment, suffered less myself, and would have been able to offer more comfort for my father in the last weeks of his life.

I once asked Pop what he wanted his legacy to be. He shrugged off my question, not wanting to comment on a future he would not experience. However, I think he would agree that his legacy was to urge everyone—family, friend, stranger—to live life on their own terms. For better or worse, Pop truly believed he answered to no one but himself. That's the way he lived his life. He was part wounded child, part husband and father, part Warrior, part counselor, and part rescuer who faced challenges head-on and helped others do the same. In the end, he placed his love for his children and the dignity of life before all else. Zgull lived and died on his terms.

I LOVE LIFE

ACKNOWLEDGEMENTS

AS I HIGHLIGHT several times throughout the book, I could not have made it through the assistance in dying journey with my father without the guidance, support, and love of my big sisters. I would not have been able to remain as sane as I did throughout all the *meshuggahah* surrounding the last few months of my father's life without my siblings. We supported each other from Pop's initial announcement of his intention on die voluntarily through his last breath. His death brought us closer together. I am so very thankful for them both.

I may have been my father's wingman, but Aleen, Wendy, and Salima were my wingwomen. Their unwavering emotional assistance lifted me during times when I doubted myself or the path Pop had decided upon. The entire odyssey was unchartered ground for us all. Their clear thinking and resolute commitment to what was best for Pop shone like a beacon and never extinguished.

Aleen and Wendy's trust in me to escort our father to Switzerland and to complete the financial and business transactions following his death emboldened me to persevere through trying times. Their love and support continued in association with getting this book published. I remain forever indebted to them.

My adult children, Levi and Ari, also deserve credit for providing emotional support along the way. I think it is rare when a parent can be fully transparent with a child and show vulnerability. I did so on several occasions during the last year of my father's life and felt no reservations in doing so. Levi and Ari were always there to listen and offer their love. I know they greatly miss their grandfather as much as I miss my father.

My brother-in-law Brent has been a true brother to me for many years. We have shared legendary times on the golf course, as well as many wonderful memories at various family events. Brent was an integral piece of the Switzerland story and acted as a son to Pop. He and I are more than brothers-in-law, we are kindred brothers.

I am forever thankful for the laudable care, personal service, and exemplary professionalism Eric, Dr. Marx, and Dr. Weber exhibited throughout the entire process. These are not their real names, but they know who they are. I've stayed in touch with Eric. He shared with me that Pegasos is building a dedicated, comfortable retreat center in the pastoral foothills to conduct future procedures far from its current urban setting.

I thank my development editor, Paul Dinas, for his expert

input, without which, the initial manuscript would not have made it onto the page. He demonstrated extreme patience to the project as I struggled to turn my raw, fragmented writings into a cogent story.

I owe an immense debt of gratitude to Elizabeth Crook from No Filter Editing for her exemplary expertise, unwavering dedication, and meticulous attention to detail in polishing the convoluted manuscript to help bring it home. Her insightful feedback and gut instincts struck the perfect chords. Her belief in me and my father's story from our initial meeting onward acted as a driving force, motivating me to persevere and refine my vision of the project. Thank you for your invaluable guidance and for championing my work with such passion.

I also wish to thank my mom, Dorothea Zimberoff. Though she has been gone from this planet for a quarter of a century, her memory, energy, and impact endure. She was a vital part of the story, and arguably, the most important piece. But for my mother, my sisters and I would not have existed, and my father would not have had a reason to push so hard to improve himself. My mother encapsulated all that is good in each of us. During many times in my life, including some of the experiences described in this book, I would think to myself, *What advice would Mom give?* She remains a lasting inspiration in my life. I often tell my children about her and remind them that she lives on within them.

Finally, to the man to whom this book is dedicated, I thank my father. Zgull overcame a neurotic childhood to forge a prosperous life resolute to the end. We may not have always seen eye to eye, and we butted heads early in my life, but he was always there for me—my wingman as I grew from a child, to an adolescent, to a Warrior man. I am beyond grateful to have been able to return the favor at the end of his life. His battle with Parkinson's provided a profound lesson for us both: he learned to let go of control while I learned to accept my dad for the man he was. Whenever I feel pressure to compromise my ideals, I think of my father. I hear his words of support and advice: "Danny, you are better than that." Thank you, Pop, for your steadfast commitment to keeping me true to my ideals. I will always love you!

If you feel so moved and would like to broaden
exposure of *Wingman* to other readers,
please consider writing a quick review
on Amazon or Goodreads

READING GROUP TALKING POINTS:

1. THE MEANING OF A "GOOD DEATH"

After reading the memoir, how would you define a good or dignified death?
Did your definition shift as Daniel and his father's journey unfolded?

2. THE EMOTIONAL BURDEN OF DECISION-MAKING

Who carries the heavier emotional weight in this story — the parent choosing to die, or the child asked to support and participate in it?
Is one burden more understandable? Harder?

3. IDENTITY, ILLNESS, AND PERSONALITY CHANGE

How did Parkinson's Disease alter David's character, dignity, and relationships?
How does witnessing personality disruption affect one's grieving process?

4. THE ETHICS AND EMOTION OF MAID

Was it courageous or selfish — or neither — for David to
choose an assisted death?
How do we hold compassion for both autonomy and
abandonment fears?

5. LEGACY AND STORYTELLING

David's final instruction — "Tell my story" — becomes the
book's catalyst.
What responsibility does someone have when entrusted with a
loved one's narrative?
Can any story ever be told completely or only interpreted?

6. LOVE AS SURRENDER RATHER THAN RESCUE

Daniel confronts a key question many caregivers face: Is love
defined by trying to keep someone alive, or by letting them go
peacefully?
What emotional or philosophical stance did you take by the end?

7. INTERGENERATIONAL WOUNDS

How did David's childhood and early life ripple outward into
Daniel's personality, values, and conflicts?
Do we inherit emotional patterns, or do we invent them?

8. SCHEDULED DEATH VS. NATURAL DEATH

How did knowing the exact date of David's death change the
tension, pacing, tone, or emotional experience of the narrative?
Would you want to know?

9. SOCIETAL INFLUENCES SURROUNDING MAID

When driving to the airport, Daniel feels "like a criminal leaving the scene of a crime." Can you empathize with his feeling?

What societal judgments allow for such feelings under these circumstances?

About the Author

Daniel Zimberoff is a Top Gun graduate, combat veteran, and former trial attorney turned author and advocate. After his father's decision to pursue an assisted death, Daniel became a voice to help establish the right for those with terminal illness or intolerable suffering to choose a dignified death. A dual citizen of the United States and Canada, Daniel lives in Toronto with his wife Salima and their daughter. When not writing or advocating, he can be found at a local ice rink playing beer league hockey. Compelled by his father's last wish, this memoir marks his debut work of narrative nonfiction. His previously published works include *Avoiding Homeowner Wars: A Comprehensive Guide to Successful HOA Governance,* and *The Last Top Gun, a Story of the Last Generation of Navy Fighter Jocks.*

Substack: Daniel Zimberoff @zimby; LinkedIn: Daniel Zimberoff; Instagram: @zimbydan; www.danzimberoff.com

www.ingramcontent.com/pod-product-compliance
Lightning Source LLC
Chambersburg PA
CBHW032004050726
47590CB00006B/2037